"A TERRIFIC THRILLER ABOUT THE ULTIMATE MEDICAL DISASTER. AND THE CHILLING THING IS YOU REALLY BELIEVE IT COULD HAPPEN."
—David Viscott, M.D., author of *The Making of a Psychiatrist*

"CHILLINGLY AUTHENTIC. GUARANTEED TO SCARE THE LIVING DAYLIGHTS OUT OF YOU!"
—*Hartford Courant*

"SUPERIOR! . . . AS DISASTER BOOKS GO IT IS ONE OF THE BEST."
—*Columbus Dispatch*

"THIS IS A THRILLER THAT FRIGHTENS AS WELL AS THRILLS. IT WILL LEAVE THE READER TAKING TETRACYCLINE FOUR TIMES A DAY AND AVOIDING ANYTHING WITH FUR OR FLEAS!"
—*Houston Chronicle*

THE
Black Death

by
Gwyneth Cravens

and

John S. Marr

BALLANTINE BOOKS • NEW YORK

Library of Congress Catalog Card Number: 76-26905

ISBN 0-345-27155-6

This edition published by arrangement with E. P. Dutton, a Division of Sequoia-Elsevier Publishing Company, Inc.

Manufactured in the United States of America

First Ballantine Books Edition: March 1978

for Lucy

"THAT PESTILENCE deprived of human inhabitants villages and cities, and castles and towns, so that there was scarcely found a man to dwell therein; the pestilence was so contagious that whosoever touched the sick or dead was immediately infected and died; and the penitent and the confessor were carried together to the grave. . . . I am waiting for death till it come . . . so I have reduced these things to writing; and lest the writing should perish with the writer, and the work together with the workman, I leave parchment for continuing the work, if haply any man survive, and any of the race of Adam escape this pestilence."

—John Clyn, Friar Minor of the
Convent of Kilkenny, 1349

AUTHOR'S NOTE

The Black Death is a work of fiction rooted in fact.

The third great pandemic of bubonic plague did in fact begin spreading throughout the world at the start of this century. In the western United States there have been fourteen separate small epidemics of the disease, and in the last five years the number of cases has sharply increased. Medical experts fear that since more and more people are now venturing into previously inaccessible wilderness areas where plague thrives in the rodent population, it is only a matter of time before someone contracts bubonic plague, returns to a large, crowded city and subsequently develops pneumonic plague. The pneumonic form is not readily identifiable, and the case will probably go unrecognized and unisolated. Because pneumonic plague is the most infectious disease known, the potential for a major, uncontrollable urban epidemic is, unfortunately, no longer in the realm of fiction.

Other themes in the novel are also based on actual events and disclosures. To name a few:

• In 1974 an aerospace corporation demonstrated to the Army a working model of the Rotocraft Monocopter for possible use as a photo reconnaissance vehicle and chemical sprayer.

• In 1975 the Senate Select Committee on Intelligence heard testimony from two former directors of the Central Intelligence Agency and from several other officials of the CIA and the Department of Defense. They revealed that scientists working at laboratories in

Fort Detrick, Maryland, run jointly by the Army and the CIA, developed and stockpiled a variety of biological weapons; invented sophisticated delivery devices for biological agents—some of which were deployed unsuccessfully in attempts on Fidel Castro's life; and dispersed a "simulated poison" in the New York City subway system "to test the city's vulnerability to germ warfare." These activities have been woven into the plot of this book.

• The secret war conducted against Cuba in the 1960s by the CIA, with assistance from the Mafia, has been the subject of Congressional hearings, of investigative reporting by respected journalists such as Taylor Branch, and of the published recollections of former employees of the CIA.

• Recent Army documents on biological warfare are the source of several of General Phillip Sheffield's speeches in the novel.

• The speech of Irving Kaprow is derived from a 1976 preliminary report of the New York City Mayor's Task Force for Emergency Preparedness.

• The conduit described on page 286 does exist; construction has not yet been completed.

Gwyneth Cravens, John S. Marr

New York City
September, 1976

ACKNOWLEDGMENTS

We would like to thank Henry Beard (U.S.A. ret.), for his enormous help in the preparation of this book. We are also grateful for the assistance and encouragement provided by David Obst, Taylor Branch, Pascal James Imperato, First Deputy Commissioner of Health of the City of New York, by the staff of the Bureau of Preventable Diseases, New York City Department of Health, and by Margie Walker, Elaine Cariello, Henry Korman, Tony Hiss, Dr. Susan Zolla Pazner, and John Marks.

Gwyneth Cravens, John S. Marr

New York City
September, 1976

1

"WELCOME TO New York City! Can I help you with your backpack?" the man crooned. "You look like you had a rough trip. You need some help, I can tell."

The girl shook her head and tried to push past him, but the crowds in the lobby of the Port Authority Bus Terminal blocked her way on all sides.

"Come on, darlin', I'm a psychologist of human emotional nature," the man continued. "I can tell you runnin' away from home. I won't report you, don't worry. I bet you from Minnesota, yeah. You look like a Minnesota honey, you do." He pressed his long, dark face close to hers. He smelled of cologne and pomade, and he wore a shimmering green suit and a matching broad-brimmed hat. "Would you like Flash to give you some money? Dinner? A place to stay? Flash can help you . . . I've helped many a stray to find her way, yes I have—"

The girl, who had a round, freckled face and shoulder-length brown hair, shifted the straps of the heavy backpack and frantically looked around. She was pale and perspiring. Suddenly a cough exploded in her chest, and then another. She could not stop coughing. The man drew back and brushed his spattered lapels. "You little bitch!" he exclaimed. "What you tryin' to do to me!"

She found an opening in the crowd, made her way to an exit, and ran down the stairs, the backpack bumping against her neck. She jumped into a waiting taxi and fell back against the seat, coughing.

"Eighty-third and Fifth Avenue," she shouted hoarsely through the partition.

As the taxi pulled out of the shadow of the terminal, a stab of late afternoon sunlight made her wince. What a disgusting welcome home, she thought. It had been her first big trip on her own. She had been eager to return early in order to spend a few days in the apartment alone before her parents returned from Europe: Jim might be back from the Cape. But now she did not want to do anything but fall into bed. She felt small and sick and isolated.

The city, where she had spent most of her life, looked rotten and alien. Garbage, packed in lacerated black plastic bags and overflowing from cans, erupted on the street corners, filling the air with a warm stench. The sidewalks seemed populated by evil, menacing creatures—rapists, muggers, pimps. The taxi driver himself might assault her, and she was glad he was separated from her by the partition of scratched plexiglass.

She began to feel better when they entered Central Park. She blew her nose, scratched her arms, and leaned her cheek against the cool glass of the window.

Now that the day was ended, everyone was abandoning the park. People carried transistor radios, blankets, hampers, and babies as they trudged back to the subway and to their steamy apartments. Masters summoned dogs, mothers shouted to their children, children cried for their toys. Long shadows fell across the meadows and broad pathways.

Yes, she had a cold coming on: her head throbbed, her neck ached, her throat was scratchy, and she had the usual warm, bone-prickling sensations. A crappy thing to happen when she might be seeing Jim for the first time in three months! What if he was back? Excitement rippled up from her stomach.

As the taxi pulled up in front of the apartment building where she lived, her skin tightened painfully. Somebody new, a man she didn't recognize, was helping her out of the taxi. The memory of the man in the bus terminal was still raw, and now she shrank from this other dark-skinned man who wanted to carry her backpack.

But he was friendly and insistent, if unintelligible, and he wore a gray uniform like the other porters and doormen she knew. Stifling a cough, she surrendered the backpack and followed him inside to the elevator.

The apartment was dark and airless. She dropped the backpack in the foyer, locked all the locks on the front door, and went down the long hallway to her bedroom. It was gloomy and close, too, and, after her bare, sunny, whitewashed room of the summer, it seemed childish and cloying. The canopied four-poster, the stuffed furry animals on the bed, the pink ruffled curtains, and the Brearley pennant definitely would have to go. Then she would fill the windows with plants and paint the walls white.

She opened the curtains and raised the window. A cool breeze entered the room. She leaned out. The Metropolitan Museum looked like an immense gray ocean liner that had run aground among the dusty, drooping plane trees. On the steps, some musicians in odd costumes—medieval perhaps—were playing strange-looking instruments. Fifes, lutes—what were they? Was the tune "Greensleeves"? One man wearing a peaked cap and striped tights cavorted on the steps and sang.

Then the song was over, the fountains in front of the museum were turned off, and the light drained rapidly from the sky, leaving it a clear, deep violet.

She was glad to be back.

She sat down on her bed and picked up the telephone. She dialed and listened to the ringing for a long time. Then she hung up and, coughing, returned to the foyer. From her backpack she took a stack of letters tied with a red ribbon, then went back to her bedroom, and hid the letters under the mattress. She took off her clothes and examined herself in the mirror over her dresser. Her tan made her legs look good, but there was still too much baby fat around her middle, and her breasts could be bigger. Although Jim had said he didn't mind at all.

She fell back across the bed and into sleep, wishing for the thousandth time that she would lose her virginity soon.

2

THE MUSICIANS returned to the steps of the Museum on Sunday morning, and vendors of jewelry, etchings, baskets, belts, and quilts spread out cloths on the sidewalk nearby and arranged their wares.

Crimson bunting draped on the facade of the museum announced an exhibit of paintings from the Middle Ages. The bright colors and the lighthearted mood of the gathering gave the impression of a medieval bazaar. The notes of the flute rang out, and a slender woman stepped forward and began to sing,

> Woman should gather roses ere
> Time's ceaseless foot o'ertaketh her,
> For if too long she make delay,
> Her chance of love may pass away,
> And well it is she seek it while
> Health, strength, and youth around her smile.

Fragments of the song floated into the room where the girl lay sleeping and awakened her. It took a moment for her to come to herself, to place herself in the empty apartment. She recalled her long journey, the bus terminal, the horrible man. She brought her hand to her throat. It was very sore. Her head was heavy, her bones ached, her lower abdomen felt tender on both sides. Her forehead and underarms and back were hot and sticky. She was thirsty.

She got up and a hot bolt shot up the back of her neck, shattering her head. Dazed, she sank down into the bed. She waited, and then tried again to get up. Once she was on her feet, she didn't know why she was up. Her hands were light, floating. She went into her parents' bedroom. A slit of yellow came through the drawn curtains. The faint aroma of her mother's perfume hung in the air. The carpeting was thick and fleecy, the chairs overstuffed, the bed piled high with cushions. The girl had always loved to curl up here, but now the room was too warm, too dark, and there was not enough air. Her mother was four thousand miles away.

The girl lay down on the bed and cried. Her sobs turned into deep coughs that tore upward from the bottom of her lungs and sucked in her breastbone as they burst from her mouth. From across the street came the sounds of laughter and applause. She reached for the telephone by the bed and dialed Jim's number again. How long before he came back with his parents from the Cape? Of course—it was Labor Day weekend; maybe he wouldn't be back until Tuesday! She cried some more, listening to his phone ring. Still holding the receiver, she fell back among the pillows and was pulled swiftly into a long, strenuous dream. She was being suffocated under a piece of plate glass. As she ran out of air, her mouth kept forming the words *Help, Help Me Please!* and from far above the glass, her mother looked down, her face fixed in a gracious, distracted smile.

At the end of the afternoon, the girl awoke with an explosion of vigor. She had to get up! Why had she been sleeping all day? She wanted to walk in the park! Her hair was a mess—she'd have to wash it right away! The phone was beeping—why was the receiver off the hook? She hung it up, and then decided to call her best friend, Missy—maybe she could go visit her! If she did not move around she would jump out of her skin. She started to dial Missy's number and then couldn't remember it. Well, it would be in her mother's little telephone book.

She hurried into the study, and stopped in front of her mother's writing table. Where her legs joined her body, the girl had a throbbing sensation like nothing she had ever felt before. She began to shiver. She forgot why she had come into the study. She ran out again. A motor at the base of her skull was pumping loudly and telling her to keep moving, to run, to scream.

"Ahhhhhhhhh!" she cried. "Owwwwwwwww! Jesus God!" That didn't help at all. "Hey, I'm really sick," she said, the sound of her voice surprising her. "I must have the flu!" Now she was in the dining room, staring at her warped reflection in the long, dusty surface of the table. She dug her fingernails into the veneer and clawed at it. "Mama!" she shouted. "I want my Mama!" Now she was in the icy white kitchen, now she was in the murky living room, its furniture shrouded in dropcloths. Now she was all over the place. Everywhere she looked, a black-walled tunnel opened up. Night clung to the edges of her vision. Bright figures, too radiant to look at directly, jumped at her from the corners of the rooms.

Within her, something surged and flowed, at ease with itself, at war with her.

Her teeth chattering, she ran to her mother's closet and pulled out a long, heavy coat. At the top of her thighs were two burning coals shooting flames in all directions. She kept wiping her mouth. She was going to go for a run, tell the people, tell anybody, what was wrong, find her mother.

The elevator took forever to arrive, forever to descend. As it ticked downward, she slid to the floor, banging her head against the side of the elevator as the numbers flashed above the door.

When at last she reached the lobby, she jumped to

7

her feet and began running and shrieking. The cool mirrors reflected her chalky face, her streaming hair, her flailing hands.

The porter, who had helped her with her backpack the night before, jumped back in alarm. Some freak from the street had gotten inside, he thought. A junkie, *una loca*. "Hey, you!" he shouted. "Hey!"

But she leaped past him and crashed into the glass doors.

The girl hovered weightlessly in a green and glassy room. Was she under the sea? Objects, heads floated past. Muffled noises, footsteps, voices. "She's hot as hell, get her temp rectally. Probably has pneumonia. Septic too."

Suddenly there were blinding lights. Hands tugged away her clothing.

"On a hot day like this a cashmere coat? My *land!*"

"I'll do an EKG now. Note those needletracks on the lower forearm. Let's try to get some sputum for Gram stain and an AFB. Better get some blood for barbiturates and heroin too."

In the tiles on the low ceiling were thousands of sparkling pinpricks. Something in her danced toward them. Her chest, her throat, her nose, her head were filling with liquid. It was wrong to cry out, she remembered that.

"Look, she's coming around. What's your name, honey?"

She replied with a deep, wet cough. The room was filled with her coughing; its mist settled over her face. She was trembling with the cold.

"Honey, just tell us your *name*."

She coughed again and again, and with each cough the room contracted a little more until it was a watery, throbbing lens surrounded by blackness. Green plastic prongs were inserted into her nostrils, and oxygen made its way into her lungs. Things were jabbed sharply into her left forearm, then her right. The pain in her groin spoke. Had she done something terribly wrong?

She was being wheeled along again. She felt like nothing, like air, like ripples in water. Now she was in a tiny box of a room. The oxygen made the sea around her clear. On a pole above her head was an inverted plastic bottle. Silver drops ticked out of it and slid down a plastic tube into her vein. Her mother was very far away, the girl couldn't remember where. Only black faces in this small, jiggling room.

"God, it's hot. Even with them fans working—"

"And this elevator be *slow* enough—"

"Si el viene, el doctor—"

"I says to her, '*I* ain't workin' no extra shift on Labor Day! Just because they fire half the staff don't mean you gonna push *me* around!' "

Another place, green walls again, red light slanting in from the wide sky.

"Get Dr. Lipsky in here quick."

She dozed, entering a sharp-edged dream burnished by fever. Hands touched her throat, her chest. A finger lifted her eyelids. She was rolled on one side and a cool disk pushed against her back. Her rib cage was tapped, triggering a cascade of coughs. Needles pierced her arms. Gauze was applied to her wet mouth. Her legs were opened: slick rubber fingers found her vagina.

At last she was left alone, in a purple-tiled room with yellow walls, a row of windows with brown paper shades, and a glass-and-mesh partition. Plastic tubes ran into her nostrils and wrists. Some very small part of her knew where she was. She was with doctors, she was being taken care of, she was supposed to lie very still and not cry out. How could she explain the pain in her abdomen? She had become a baby again, sequestered, floating, fed by a silver cord. She fell into a deep sleep.

A few blocks to the north, in the basement of a tenement in Spanish Harlem, Domingo Ortiz awoke from a sweaty nightmare about the girl in the lobby. Pink foam had bubbled out of her mouth. He had done what he could. Called an ambulance. What else could he do? Why had he come to this terrible country? He felt miserable. God wants to punish me, he thought. I should have stayed in Cienfuegos and taken care of my poor sick grandmother. *"Madre!"* he whispered, sitting up and crossing himself.

3

THE NURSE finished taking the girl's pulse and paused to look at her for a moment. She lay motionless except for the rise and fall of her chest. Nothing happening with that little lady, the nurse thought. She's practically not even here.

Every day, the city hospitals received men and women who were absent like this, whose pasts were gone and whose outer lives were diminished almost to nothing. These were the unidentified, of the tribe of Doe, and they remained John Doe or Jane Doe until someone turned up to label them otherwise, or until they themselves again became present and could speak. Some never came back: Potter's Field, out on an island off the coast of the Bronx, was full of Does.

Although the girl was absent to her name and to the people around her, she was very much present to herself, to the intricate city of molecules, proteins, cells, tissues, organs, and systems that she had worked continuously to build and maintain from the instant of her conception. Like every other human being, she had been present and self-aware, as a fertilized egg within the womb, to sift chemicals from her mother's bloodstream and use them to weave a delicate network for the storage and release of energy. Like every other human, she knew how to control, distribute, recycle, repair, and eliminate chemicals, and how to combine them into increasingly complex structures, and how to envelop all these constructions and their millions of processes in a single image. And, above all, she had been present to her own profound accomplishment: From energy originating in the heart of a star, she had made a body and an awareness to enclose it and care for it.

All of this knowledge had been hers, deeply and thoroughly hers, before she had ever seen the light of day or heard her mother's voice, before she had been given a name.

Now, under attack, she had withdrawn almost all her energies from outer expression and turned them instead to the task of maintaining and defending her body.

The invading organism also possessed an elaborate and ancient knowledge. The girl—intricate and mortal —and the organism—primitive and immortal—shared a common ancestor; now something in each of them, a memory buried for a billion years, had set off powerful forces of recognition in the other.

The organism that had slid in under the girl's first line of defense, her skin, was deeply familiar with the curves and courses, the latticework, and the continual traffic within her body. It knew that with very little effort it would eventually be carried to the place that suited it best. The organism had not been under the girl's skin more than a few seconds when white blood cells, monitoring the subcutaneous plains for invaders, touched it, engulfed some of its cells, recognized them as alien, and killed them. Other of the invading cells were surrounded and carried by other white blood cells into the lymph system and through its fine, hair-like tubes to the regional lymph nodes in the armpits and groin. There, the interior awareness of the girl read the information on the organism's cell walls and sent an alarm to all systems; the ancient and terrible enemy was here, and must at all costs be destroyed. More cellular memories, millions of years old, were awakened.

For its part, the invader knew that after decades in the dank burrows of rats, after centuries of absence and retreat in the dusty Asian steppes, after thousands of miles of travel and hundreds of way stations, it had arrived in a splendid and fertile kingdom. It knew how to wait, and after so long, a few more hours would not matter. In the abundant fields of tissue and the rich streams of blood, it feasted, letting its poisonous wastes drift where they would.

Almost all of the girl's attention was turned toward seeking out and destroying the invader. At the second line of defense, the lymph nodes, white blood cells flooded over the alien cells, trying to surround and immobilize them. The bone marrow, the spleen, and the liver made extra white blood cells; the lymph nodes swelled and became inflamed. The invader multiplied its cells more rapidly than the white cells could kill them. Riding on white blood cells, the surviving alien cells made their way into the small veins around the nymph nodes and through the lymphatic system into the tiny blood vessels of the lungs. The body, trying to seal off the alien, clogged the capillaries. But the organism slipped out anyway, surrounding the tiny air sacs of the lungs.

At last it had broken into the air sacs. These pockets, womblike, warm, and lush with sugars and oxygen, were exactly what the invader needed to begin colonization. It began to increase itself: every cell split in two, and those two split into four, and those four . . .

Destroy, destroy, commanded the girl's inner awareness. The poisons were beginning to short-circuit her defense mechanisms.

Most of the spectrum of her attention was now taken up by this absorbing new event. But part of her awareness concentrated, as always, on getting energy. Energy dripped into her veins from a plastic tube; it rode in on each breath; and a fraction came from the dim reddish light passing through her closed eyelids and from the muffled sounds of the corridor vibrating in her ears.

Humming to herself, the nurse peered through the glass partition at the girl and then stepped across the corridor to the nurses' station. From a rack, she selected an aluminum clipboard labeled DOE, JANE #4 MICU, opened it to a form headed "Nurses' Notes," and wrote: "3:00 a.m. IV running well in rt. arm. No evidence of swelling. Nasal O_2 at 5L per minute. B/P 104/70—P110 R32 T101° F. Pt.'s color good. Resting fairly comfortable at this time. I. Daniels, R.N."

The nurse, a big, heavy-boned woman, clapped the chart shut, poured herself a cup of coffee, adjusted her wig, and went into the darkened solarium, where the other nurses, aides, and doctors from the Medical Intensive Care Unit were gathered for a coffee break.

Daniels dropped her bulk into a rocking chair. She quickly lit a cigarette and threw the match on the polished floor. "We got one open bed left," she told the intern, an owl-faced man named Lipsky.

"*I* could certainly use it," Bergman said. He was a fourth-year student from New York Medical College, assigned to the Medical Department of Metropolitan Hospital to assist and to observe. Tonight was his first all-nighter—from 8:00 a.m. on Sunday to 5:00 p.m. on Monday—and he did not like it. Two more hours until dawn, fourteen hours until he could finally crawl home. A shitty way to spend Labor Day weekend, if anybody asked him. Nobody did.

Dr. Lipsky, one year out of medical school, looked wearily over at the complainer. Wait till the fucker has to do this every other night for three months. Lipsky himself was in for two straight nights and days, working his own shift and covering for a colleague who had wanted to take the long weekend off; he had started on Sunday morning and would not go home until

Tuesday afternoon. Now this little son-of-a-bitch was whining at losing one night's sleep.

"Worst we can get tonight is one more admission," Daniels went on, looking past Bergman as if he weren't there. "Mr. Coe is stable, Mrs. Baretto is sleepin' and her vital signs are stable. Annie act up a bit so I give her that p.r.n. dose of Demerol." She was pleased. It would be a light night. "That Jane Doe. She's a sick one. She going to be okay?"

"I think she will." Lipsky stretched out in his chair. "Her X-ray isn't too bad. Her blood gases aren't great, but we'll be doing them again at five to see if they've improved. Her white count is high—thirty-five thousand, most of them stabs. I guess you could say that's good, too, since she's pouring out cells. Worse if it was thirty-five hundred."

"So young," Daniels said. "Pretty, too."

"Frankly, I don't know what's going on with her. There are some scratches on her arms that the ER people said were needle tracks, but I'm not convinced. And besides, her blood was negative for barbiturates and opiates."

"This could have been her first trip on something," Bergman said.

"Possibly. But the problem is her pneumonia. It's pretty bad. Could be due to aspiration, but that doesn't seem right to me." Lipsky stared out the solarium window at the random lights along the East River, trying to sort out patterns. "If she'd aspirated her vomit, the pneumonia would be in the upper lobes and on one side, but this is bilateral, so I'd say she has pus somewhere inside. Maybe her heart—but there are no murmurs. Her pelvis is clean, her legs aren't swollen. Teeth are good, so are the gums. She was a healthy kid. God knows what the source of the bacteria is. The gentamicin and Keflin should work on almost any bug inside."

Bergman cleared his throat and took up where Lipsky had left off, talking to Daniels in severe tones, as if he were a real doctor. "It's a Gram-negative pneumonia. Maybe an *E. coli* or some other coliform. Could even be GC."

"Not GC," Lipsky said, irritably. "The bacteria in the stained sputum specimen was not a diplococcus, it was coccobacillary—looked like a bunch of pink Good and Plenty candies. It's not gonorrhea, that's for sure. She's a virgin, man. I did the pelvic on her. She wouldn't get sepsis and pneumonia unless she'd done a lot of balling. We get junkies who are hookers in here, and their uteruses are swollen like balloons."

"Miranda!" Daniels bellowed down the corridor. "Miranda, you through in there yet?"

A small voice with a Spanish accent came from inside the closet adjacent to the solarium. "Be there in a minute. I change Baretto's bed. She's gone and wet herself again. You save some coffee for me, okay?"

"How long have you worked at Met?" Bergman asked Daniels, hoping to get on her good side.

"Hmmmmm." She cocked her head in the direction of this medical student, this dumb mother who didn't know shit from Shinola. "Since before you was born. I been here since the place opened. Yeah. Been here since fifty-three, I guess. Right. It was fifty-three that Billie come in here and died."

There was a silence. She rocked and smiled to herself. "Yeah, Billie."

Was that Daniels's secret? Lipsky wondered. Was that why she had never married? A lover she had failed to nurse back to health, perhaps? "Miss Daniels," he said gently, "who was, uh, Billie?"

"Why, Billie Holiday, of course. She died right here at Met, from complications. She had seven hundred and fifty in fifty-dollar bills strapped to her poor old leg. They come right here and arrested her for drugs. A police guard at her door. That's what the newspapers said was wrong with her. Drugs. But it wasn't. Oh, she was on drugs all right. But she had pneumonia. She come in all dehydrated and sick as hell, coughing and delirious. Just like that Jane Doe we got in there. Died the next morning."

Daniels leaned back and smoked, the broad planes of her face reflecting the faint light from the corridor. "I seen a lot of things here you wouldn't believe," she said to nobody in particular.

Mrs. Miranda, a diminutive woman with an elaborate, curly chignon, appeared in the doorway. "They all sleeping, all the IVs okay."

"Good," Daniels said. "Sit down, woman, we're telling Dr. Lipsky and the boy here what goes on in this crazy place."

"Dios mío, many things. Mostly bad, I think. Much suffering."

"Not always," Lipsky said. "Miss Daniels, were you working in the ER when the beast with two backs came in?"

Daniels chuckled. "Yes, honey, I was. Never forget it. There was an intern there, forget his name. We hear the ambulance coming, and he says to me, 'Miss Daniels, that better be a surgical case, 'cause I'm tired and I don't want any more stroked-out gorks tonight.' So. They wheel the stretcher in and the body's covered with a sheet. I see it's a big, fat person, but then I look at the head of the stretcher and there's this young, thin-lookin' woman's face. I look down to the end of the stretcher, and there her feet are, sticking out. 'Great God a'mighty,' I says to myself, 'cause her feet are all turned around. That does somethin' to me right here—" She thumped her stomach. "But I take a deep breath and tell the doctor that it looks like a surgical. It has to be. Probably an ortho problem. So he's feelin' better—he won't have to do anything, he can just pass the patient right on to surgical. But we're both of us wonderin' and *wonderin',* so we go into the room to watch when they take off the sheet. And when they do—*wow!"* She laughed.

"Come on, what happened?" Bergman asked.

"Shit, honey, that wasn't jus' one person. It was

two! There was the woman, and she had a *guy* on top of her. Turned out the woman had one of those experimental IUDs, with the little plastic line hanging down—so you could tell if it slips out of place? Well. Those two was makin' love and that plastic string got snagged on the guy's foreskin. Yeah, jus' hooked onto the skin, and he couldn't get his thing out! They had to circumcise the guy right there in the ER."

A cough came from one of the rooms and Miranda slipped out.

"Well, it ended okay." Daniels looked at her watch. "Four and a half more hours, then home."

"You didn't tell the 'Stronger than Dirt' story," Lipsky said.

"That was something," Daniels said.

"Let's hear it," Bergman said.

Miranda returned. "I just check on that Jane Doe, Dr. Lipsky. She no look too good. She no is breathing so good."

Lipsky got to his feet. If the girl was cyanotic, that would mean a tracheotomy. Not tonight, he hoped.

When he bent over the slight, crumpled form of the girl, he was relieved to see that her nailbeds and lips were not blue. But her breathing had become more labored; the congestion in the throat and lungs had increased. "Her one-a.m. blood gases were pretty good," he said to Miranda. "Let's see what they look like now."

He picked up her hand. It splayed softly over his like a delicate sea-creature, and he thought for a moment of his baby daughter. Miranda gave him a syringe, and he slipped its needle into the pulsing artery at the girl's wrist.

"I remember the 'Stronger than Dirt' TV commercial," Bergman was saying to Daniels, his voice coming flat and clear through the partition. "A white knight on a horse bombing through the suburbs with a lance, right? Advertising detergent?"

Was I ever as callow as that? Lipsky shook his head

and drew the dark red blood up into the syringe. The girl stirred as he pulled out the needle. He pushed its point through a cork and laid the syringe in a basin containing ice cubes.

"Right," came Daniels's voice. "Late one night this guy in pajamas comes screamin' out of nowhere. He's runnin' down the corridor to beat the band and carryin' one of them window poles, holdin' it out in front of him and yellin' 'Stronger than Dirt! Stronger than Dirt!' See, he'd been transferred over here from psychiatric because he had diabetes or somethin' like that."

"And?" Lipsky stepped back into the corridor, basin and syringe in hand, ready to go up to the Blood Gas Lab on the eleventh floor.

"And he runs into the solarium and smashes right through these windows here," Daniels replied. "Seven floors down. They found him down there on the concrete with the window pole still in his hand."

"He live?" Bergman asked.

"Nope. The white knight died."

"Bergman," Lipsky said. "Keep an eye on the Jane Doe while I take this up to the Blood Gas Lab. She's getting worse."

4

THE DIRTY windows of the Medical Intensive Care Unit scattered the incoming dawn light, filling the room with a hazy red glow.

"Another hot day," Bergman said, imagining himself asprawl on a white sandy beach.

"Scalpel," Lipsky said.

19

The girl's rib cage heaved up and collapsed, heaved up and collapsed. She was working hard. Her defense systems were much more powerful and complicated than the weaponry of the invader. All it could do, in its million-headed single-mindedness, was release a few thousand molecules of various poisons. They triggered the arsenal of her body, which grew increasingly panicky in its attempts to free itself of the enemy. The organism had only to exhaust and outlast her.

She was already using a great deal of strength just to keep breathing. The air sacs of her lungs were brimming with the organism and the moist residue of her battle. Destroy, destroy, her body said, and tissues harboring the enemy were sloughed off and coughed up. Burn it out, burn it out, her body said, and her fever increased. Block it, seal it off, ordered the body, and capillaries began shutting down. The flow of blood through arteries now slowed, and her blood pressure dropped. She was starving for oxygen, and the tips of her fingers were turning blue.

Lipsky sank the scalpel neatly into the skin just below her Adam's apple. Tiny spurts of blood appeared. Bergman clamped off the blood vessels with small metal pincers. Lipsky spread apart the skin and muscle overlaying the trachea and then carefully punctured it with the scalpel. A pink spume shot into the air. It rose high into the room, in a fountain of shimmering droplets.

The droplets painted delicate arcs across the white jackets of the two men; they made a pink cloud on the girl's bedsheet; they floated over the bed, wafted this way and that by the motions of the men stirring currents in the air.

Lipsky inserted an L-shaped plastic tube into the hole made by the scalpel. The intrusion sent the girl into a long coughing fit.

In each tiny globe of moisture, the organism swam. It sensed the warmth and pulsations of the men, and it flowed into their breath, into the moist linings of their nostrils and throats, and prepared for the next stage of its journey.

The wall fan in the MICU whirred back and forth. A monitor on the wall above the girl's bed amplified her heartbeat and made it visible as a wavy line with spikes at regular intervals. The record was made permanent on graph paper that spewed from a machine. Lipsky studied the graphs and looked at the girl. He held her X-rays up to the light.

What the hell was wrong with her?

He still didn't know. The blood and sputum cultures wouldn't be ready for lab analysis for a few more hours. As he stared at her white, slack skin, her purplish eye sockets, her wet and tangled mass of hair, the tranlucent tubes trailing over her chest, her face, her arms, he grew angry. From the outside, what could you ever tell? At moments like this he remembered what one of his teachers had said: "I don't want to know about interest-cases—they always mean grief for somebody. When I was an interne, I knew everything. Now, after twenty years, working day and night, I'm uncertain about everything. I make an effort, I use everything I've got, but I never forget that I'm working in the dark. So don't ever come and gleefully tell me about 'interesting' cases you've seen. I don't want to hear from it."

This case was interesting, all right. She had been subjected to almost every test possible: blood, urine, sputum analyses and cultures, X-rays, a complete physical examination. . . . She had been given the best medication he could think of. She had pneumonia, but what caused it? And she kept getting worse.

There was one more test. "Bergman," he yelled. "Get in here. We're going to do a thoracentesis."

"Wonderful—I've never done one!" Bergman came in, refreshed from a nap in the doctors' room.

They cranked the girl's bed up so that she was almost sitting. Bergman leaned her forward and parted the hospital gown, which was wet from perspiration, to expose her back. "Look at *that!*" he exclaimed. Here and there, under the smooth expanse of skin, were red and blue blossoms. "Super weird!"

"My God, it's a hemorrhagic rash," Lipsky said. "She probably has a DIC syndrome. We'd better draw more bloods after we do the thoracentesis."

Lipsky found a spot just above a rib and injected Novocain. He waited a minute for the area to go numb and then slowly inserted a large needle through the skin, through the muscle, and into the hollow cavity containing the lungs. A yellowish-red fluid rose into the syringe. "It's on her lungs all right." He withdrew the needle and handed the syringe to Bergman. "Put this on some slides for Gram stain and the rest for culture. We have to see if it's the same as the stuff in her sputum—the Gram-negative. If it is, then whatever this thing is, it's outside her lungs, inside, and she's coughing it up like crazy."

The invader occupied more and more cells, and the girl's immune responses became increasingly frantic: all the occupied cells had to be sloughed off. The lungs and the pleural cavity filled, choking and suffocating her. Within the unconscious girl a deep dream began.

All the universe contracted to the dimensions of her body, and all awareness—except for a particle—was now contained within the faint field of energy that extended a few inches outward from her skin. That particle of awareness glowed at the base of her brain. It watched itself. Imperceptible to the men and women who busied themselves around the girl's bed, the particle observed them, as from the top of a high tower. It dreamed their actions for them, dreamed the room, dreamed the rusty smear of the girl's mouth into a half-smile. It noted that the others were made uneasy by the tearing, gasping struggle to breathe that they were witnessing.

For the girl, wholly present with the particle of awareness, the inside was the same as the outside. She did not know or care where she began and where she left off. Time passed. Light shifted in the corners of the room as the sun moved toward the west. The shape of the room and the passing seconds were the same.

At each moment the girl was content and complete: at each moment she had achieved herself. The man and the women at work over her did not see this. They had expectations for her. They did not see that she was complete just as she was. The men, the women, the chemicals, the machines—they could give her nothing. She did not want anything. Over time, she had made a body and watched over it, sensed it, used it to carry her through the world, to do what needed to be done, to see, to hear. To live. That was enough.

The same self-aware nexus of energy that had told her to build herself from an egg into a baby, to drop into the birth canal, and to make her way out into the world of light and sound and breath now began telling her to unhook her awareness from the cells, the tissues, the organs, and the systems she had made while moving through time.

She obeyed.

She gave up everything. She discarded and discarded until she was almost nothing in a vast, empty room.

She stopped breathing.

A buzzer sounded. There were running footsteps. A black rubber bag was attached to the L-shaped plastic tube in the girl's trachea and rhythmically squeezed. In and out, in and out, it whispered. A green machine with dials and rubber tubes was wheeled next to her bed and attached to a wall socket marked OXYGEN. The black bag was taken away and the tube quickly connected to the machine.

Lipsky opened the girl's eyes. He noticed that they were blue-gray. She looked puzzled and amused to him, even though he knew she was unconscious.

"Code 99!" a woman's voice announced over the public address system. Throughout the corridors of the hospital the voice echoed. "Code 99, Medical Intensive Care Unit! Code 99, Medical Intensive Care Unit!"

Lipsky watched the march of the spiked line across the monitor screen as he adjusted the dials on the green machine. The pattern skipped and faltered.

The room began to fill with men and women in white who had heard the Code 99 announcement. They came to help in whatever way they could.

Lipsky raised a shiny gloved fist and struck the girl's breastbone.

He looked up at the monitor. No change in the pattern. He struck her breastbone again.

A tube was inserted in a vein in her arm and attached to a plastic bag set to drip a chemical similar to her own adrenalin. It made her heart race, its beat increasing the ripples on the screen.

Another machine was wheeled up to the bed and six people crowded around, adjusting wires, tubes, and dials. Lipsky placed two metal paddles on the girl's chest. When he pressed a button, all six people backed away from the bed in synchrony.

The paddles sent an electrical shock through the girl's body. Her muscles contracted violently: as her spine arched and her legs stiffened, her form lurched up from the bed.

Lipsky realized he had been holding his breath. He exhaled and inhaled deeply.

The line on the monitor flattened.

There were more fist blows to her breastbone, more shocks to her heart. Lipsky and the others worked hard, doing what they believed needed to be done.

After ten minutes of intense effort, the pattern on the monitor remained the same—a horizontal line.

"Let's call it off," Lipsky said. "She's dead and that's it." He gently pressed her eyes closed and left the room, a discarded glass vial crunching under his shoe.

The others filed out, talking and passing the chart around. A nurse switched off the machines.

Suddenly the corridors filled with squeals of sirens. An aged orderly who had come into the ward to clean up walked around the girl's bed, broom in hand, and went to the window.

Below, on the FDR Drive, a big motorcade was passing by. There were dozens of motorcycle police leading the way toward midtown, their sirens constant. They were followed by six long black limousines, one with flags, and more police escorts.

"Now who be them folks?" muttered the orderly. "Make a joyful noise unto the Lord, and enter into his courts with thanksgiving." He turned from the window and slowly began sweeping. The floor was littered with stained wads of gauze, empty needle containers, a bedsheet, folds of inked graph paper, crumpled cellophane, cardboard syringe packages, pieces of IV tubing, sterile plastic wrappings, and shattered vials.

One by one, the eight million million cells in the girl's body ceased to live. It would take time for the entire city to learn that it had been vanquished. Meanwhile, the victor scavenged in the ruins, and waited.

5

"THERE'S NO crisis in New York," the woman said to the man passing by her park bench. "There are no problems. God just wants us to say thank you." She wore a dusty raincoat, and across the lower half of her face was tied a red bandanna. She had arranged her shopping bags, filled with bread crusts, coat hangers, and shoes, around her knees and was ready to begin her day's work. "I am God's spokesperson and I am going to tell you God's plan even though you want to marry me."

It was morning in Central Park. The man stopped a few paces past the woman's park bench and waited for a traffic light on the Park Drive to change. "What is God's plan?" he asked the woman, studying her with interest. He had a soft, clear voice, wavy blond hair, and sharp blue eyes behind wire-rimmed glasses. His blue seersucker suit was rumpled, his briefcase was battered, and he looked as if he had not slept the night before. "I promise you I won't marry you."

The woman scowled at him. She saw blue rays shooting out of the top of his head and could read his mind. That was how she knew he was an ally of Jerry Lewis's. "The Jerry Lewis Labor Day Muscular Dystrophy Telethon is part of God's plan to poison the cripples and don't think I don't know it, sonny!"

"How do you know that?"

"Just look on any twenty-dollar bill!" she shouted. "On the back of the twenty there is one hairy Martian spy standing in the shrubs next to the Capitol, and he has the face of God, and he is telling us, and this is God talking, young man, he is telling us 'God through George Washington established the country of the United States of America and made Washington the capital because you must go among the people and Wash them by the Ton that they may know New York is the center of all things in the land of those who deny my divine existence controlled by the President's spy conspiracy to knock off all free people in the streets to stop God from poisoning the air.' Ask the hairy Martian spy. Ask him, if you dare! Ask him, is God an *idiot* or a *maniac?*"

"Thank you," the man said. "I'll look him up next time I'm in D.C." The light changed and he crossed the street, looking back to see if she would follow him. But she had redirected her attention to an audience of scavenging pigeons. "Blood on the cathedral floor!" she told them.

TB, the man thought to himself. Her sidewalk-colored skin and reddened eyes were sure signs. He admired her, in a way. These feral men and women of the streets made no agreements with the civilized life of apartments and beds and hot meals. They stuck to their park benches, their concrete seats on the traffic islands of Broadway, their standpipes around Times Square, their Greenwich Village phone booths. They preached, or screamed obscenities, or slapped passersby with folded newspapers. Somehow they managed to stay alive, sustained by forces of endurance that baffled the man. On his walks through the city he watched them, hoping he might learn something from them; for all he knew, he might go feral himself in his old age.

As he left the park, the man, whose name was David Hart, checked his watch. It was about 7:00 a.m. and, since he had a long walk ahead, he had to maintain a regular stride.

His rate was about a block a minute, and so he would have to be in Times Square by 7:20, at Thirty-fourth Street by 7:28, in Greenwich Village by 7:50, and on Canal Street by 8:20 in order to arrive at 125 Worth Street, where his office in the Department of Health was located, by around 8:30.

He knew he was crazy to be so precise, but walking and sticking to exact schedules had kept him going throughout the summer, the worst summer of his life. If he let himself forget his plans, he lost his will. He fell into an abyss where everything stopped but the endless, noisy train of words in his head. Hearing that mechanical jabber split him apart, and made him want to give up.

The past weekend had been especially bad. Almost everyone he knew had fled to the beach or the country-side, leaving the city, with its heat wave and its gar-bage strike, to the poor, the diseased, the old, the mad, and the heartsick. He had refused invitations from friends with country houses, choosing to remain among the abandoned and see out the last spasm of a summer he wanted to forget.

David Hart's wife had died in June. She had died and he had lived. He was a physician and he had not been able to heal her. No one had. Now he hated life but did not know how to stop it. He strolled in Central Park at midnight and drank recklessly in black bars on Lenox Avenue. But nothing happened to him. Young matrons were strangled, promising artists were blud-geoned, children were burned up in tenement fires, and yet he continued. His wife had been quick with her thoughts and words, well-loved by many people, mild and good-humored. They met at a party; he was drunkenly punching out window panes and she had stopped him and bandaged his hand. After that, ev-erything was different. For a few years. Then she was gone, and he, the useless one, was still around. He couldn't sleep much, and he walked the streets of Manhattan night after night until his legs ached, just to keep himself going. He constantly checked his pockets, thinking that he had lost his keys, or his wallet, and when he walked over a subway grating, he would worry that his wedding band might slip from his finger and be lost. Finally, on this morning that officially ended the summer, he had removed the ring.

It was a hot bright day. Columbus Circle was filled with the noise of traffic and the underground rush of the subway. At the New York Coliseum, where the marquee announced a hardware-salesmen's convention, he passed a five-day-old heap of garbage.

This garbage on the streets is nothing, Hart thought. It smells better than the mess inside my head. But the garbage outside was really piling up. So far the Board of Health had not declared a health emergency; that would probably come at the end of the week if the sanitation strike continued. The Commissioner of Health, Vincent Calabrese, would appear on TV with a soothing statement. The garbage looked worse than it actually was. It was something of a fire hazard, true. The rats might wander farther afield than usual, and kids might get hurt scaling the mountains of tin cans and broken bottles, but the piles were more upsetting to the eye and the nose—of a hardware salesman, for instance—than to the physical health of the people of New York. Because Hart was a New Yorker, and because he had lived in the city almost all his life, he was sure that even if the garbage were never collected again, people would survive and adjust. They would mine the piles. They would walk to their jobs in midtown over hills of coffee grounds, through valleys of shredded newspapers, beer bottles, and fishheads, and fear no evil. They would regale one another with tales of narrow escapes from the rats and they would show each other their scrapes. They would just keep going.

He was now in Times Square. PRESIDENT LEAVES

THE BLACK DEATH

CITY AFTER PARTY FUND-RAISING DINNER AT WALDORF, proclaimed a band of glowing words racing around the second story of the Allied Chemical Building. PREZ TO MAYOR: NOT TONITE, SID announced the headline of the *Daily News* at a magazine stand. PRESIDENT LEAVES NEW YORK AFTER BRIEF VISIT, noted *The New York Times* in a headline of more modest size, adding: "Says He Will Not Speak with Mayor Weinstein Regarding Metropolitan Fiscal Dilemma." HOTTEST FASTEST JUICIEST DOUBLE MIXED COMBOS EVER AT THE WORLD'S FIRST AND ONLY SEXATORIUM said a theatre marquee. KICK OF DEATH and DRAGON FIST said another. SIDNEY POITIER in A BOUQUET FOR THE TEACHER, said another. DO IT WITH ANIMALS AT ZOOLAND! urged a black-and-yellow sign over a dark doorway.

Hart automatically read sign after sign as he moved along, scarcely retaining the words after they had registered. He passed a seedy record shop blaring soul music and an emporium that sold fake oriental carpets, phony silver urns, and wristwatches. In its windows were the same posters that had been there for as long as Hart could remember, declaring imminent bankruptcy. "EVERYTHING MUST GO!" He shook his head to a hooker in a red wig and a miniskirt who invited him to "check it out," and started walking more quickly.

He was slowed down at Thirty-fourth Street by commuters pouring out of Pennsylvania Station, briefcases and newspapers under their arms. Some of them reminded Hart of soldiers in an endless, bitter war. Others looked worse, like galley slaves. By forty they were defeated; they had moved to the suburbs of Long Island, Westchester, and Connecticut because life in the city was too difficult.

He was glad to reach Twenty-third Street, and the hodgepodge of tenements, brownstones, and bodegas of Chelsea. He saw a girl talking in Spanish to a man who lounged on the hood of a car. Her bare brown midriff, glazed with perspiration, gave Hart a deep pang. New York was filled with beautiful women, but all summer he had forced himself to forget about them. Feeling horny made him want to cry.

This lovely girl, talking casually, her bare legs stretched out in front of her, disturbed him more than most. She made him think of Dolores, and he did not want to think about her. And now her image, her warm, ripe body, her Mayan cheekbones, floated through his mind and numbed him. He could have telephoned her over the weekend. He could have. At one point, after half a bottle of scotch, he was ready to call her up with some story about research on hepatitis he was doing and did she have her field notes on the outbreak in the West Village? . . . But he was always able to rescue himself from desire by being rational. He was a cold fish, a Wasp, and why would she want him? Maybe she had a hulking boyfriend, or a brother with a knife who would turn him into kitty litter if he so much as touched her. But the real reason was much simpler and much harder: she was a woman, and if he were ever to arrive at her softest parts and enter there, he might forget his plan, his schedule, and come upon the pain, the loss, the old nightmare. Better to forget the whole thing.

His stride was more purposeful now, and his legs were tense. He looked up and was struck by the colors and the depths around him, made sharper by the clear sunlight. The polluted haze would come soon, and by noon the sky would be a sulfurous yellow, but right now the light wrapped itself around the skyscrapers of midtown and gilded the curlicues on the facades of the brownstones on the side streets of Greenwich Village.

When he looked and listened to everything going on around him, his mind grew quiet. That was one reason he walked so much. Whatever had been bothering him in Chelsea was gone, or at least set aside, by the time he passed Sheridan Square in the Village. Two drag queens dozed on a bench in the dusty little park. From the smashed wine bottles, squeezed-out tubes of K-Y Jelly, and the clumps of Kleenex, Hart concluded that the night there had been a busy one.

Hart started organizing his mind for the work day. School was opening next week. Things would start picking up at the office then. Hart was the Director of the Bureau of Preventable Diseases, and his job was to keep track of outbreaks and epidemics. Once the children were back in school, there would be reports of measles, rubella, mumps, and flu. Flu was the worst. The virus that was coming this fall would be bad. New York would be hit hard, especially the old people. There was not much that could be done. Antibiotics were useless against flu.

Hart had once dedicated himself to public health in the belief that nature could be turned around. Now he believed in nothing. You worked as well as you could; you kept your eyes open; you used every tool. You isolated the contagion, you gave out medication, and you waited for the epidemic to run its course. The fact that he believed in nothing actually helped him work harder, free of sentiment, and he made it his business to learn everything he could about every outbreak of every infectious disease in New York. His curiosity and effort had brought him the job of chief epidemiologist at an early age, and he was willing to put up with the city's bureaucracy and low pay. Most of his friends from medical school were now earning six to ten times Hart's salary, but they earned it by taking money from sick people, and Hart could not do that.

He also liked his work because he never knew from day to day what might turn up.

At Houston and Varick, he paused to watch Con Ed workmen chalk a triangle on the pavement and then attack it with the blades of their jackhammer. He turned eastward, and before he knew it, he had passed the old warehouses in SoHo, with their ornate cast-iron facades and high lading docks, and the Chinese grocery stores of Canal Street. Now he headed south, toward the huge, reticulated towers of the World Trade Center. He was behind schedule. He walked faster and faster, and his thoughts—lists of tasks, mostly—sped up, and he noticed less and less around him until suddenly he was in Foley Square, with its pillared temples dedicated to federal and municipal justice and its ponderous WPA fortresses, like the Department of Health and Hospitals.

He gave a nod to the gold Art Deco eagles on plinths who guarded the door to 125 Worth. As he passed under the lintel, on which was written in gold CITY OF NEW YORK, he thought: *Home free again.* Now his craziness would leave him alone until it was time to return to his dark apartment.

6

ONCE IN his office, a corner room in a suite of high-ceilinged, narrow chambers, Hart went through the other papers in his in-box. Brochures from a medical society offering a winter vacation and "cruise seminar" in the Caribbean. Into the wastebasket. A memo from the Commissioner: Why have the tuberculosis rates gone up in the first nine months of this year as compared to last year at this time? Probably the cutbacks in the outreach workers, but Hart would have to think of some less controversial reply. A citizen's letter complaining that the Tropical Disease Clinic on 168th Street was dirty and crowded. It was, and probably would be closed down within six months if the President again refused federal aid to the city. A report from the Quarantine branch of the Public Health Service's Center for Disease Control in Atlanta: "Angola is free of cholera." So what? He was surprised that the CDC hadn't managed to take credit for this farflung accomplishment: that was the style of those guys. They flew in for a day, took a look at an outbreak or an epidemic, and then rushed back to Atlanta to wait until it was over. Then they wrote up the results. Epidemic mavens.

There was a commotion in the outer office, and Sam Andrews, Hart's assistant, appeared at the door.

"Bomb scare. We have to evacuate."

"Who is it this time?"

The young man, whose skinny form made him look more like a teen-ager than a United States Public Health Service Epidemic Intelligence Officer, shook his head, a lock of red hair falling over his forehead. He had a wispy beard he had begun growing upon his arrival in New York two months earlier, and a Georgia drawl. "Ah'll never get the hang of this place. If it isn't garbage, it's bomb scares."

"Today you get both—aren't you lucky?"

"And it's not even ten o'clock!"

"Dr. Hart! Aren't you coming with us? Don't you know there's a bomb scare?" It was Dolores Rodriguez, the woman of his fantasies, and she was looking unusually beautiful this morning. Her mouth was smooth and red, like a succulent tropical fruit, and her straight, shiny black hair was tied neatly behind her ears. Her scent and her reddish-purple dress made him think of roses.

He reminded himself of the brother with the knife. "I'll be coming in a minute."

"We'll miss you if you don't."

The bomb scare was making her reckless. Usually she avoided his gaze, kept her eyes dark and unreadable, and became silent and tense whenever they had to work together for very long.

Stay with me! he wanted to say. Stay with me in

the abandoned building. His hand on the firm rise of her brown thigh, that voluptuous mouth parting . . . Please linger awhile. "You'd better run along, Dolores." He started to pat her on the shoulder, but stopped his hand in mid-air so that he was waving instead. What a fool he was! "If the police find a Puerto Rican in the building during a bomb scare— well, you'll be in bad trouble."

She cocked an eyebrow at him and swiftly turned, following the others out into the corridor.

It was too much trouble to evacuate. Nothing ever happened anyway. He liked to think that all the bombs the police never found during these scares were piled up in some forgotten closet in the building, maybe down in Pest Control, or Sanitation. One day, they would reach critical mass. There would be an enormous explosion, and the contents of his office would whirl out the windows. The medical textbooks, the diplomas, the maps of the five boroughs, the glass-fronted bookcases and their dusty old binders recording every city epidemic for the past one hundred years, the bulletin board with its Immunization-Action-Month poster and the framed, yellowed front page of the *Daily News* (FORD TO CITY: DROP DEAD)—all of the contents of the entire Department of Health would be blown high over Foley Square. All of lower Manhattan, in fact, would be buried under birth and death certificates, vaccination certificates, mayoral health proclamations, several hundred thousand unread reports, a million memos in triplicate, and the vital statistics on over twenty million people. The works. He imagined the entire building blasted to pieces, its frieze of heroic names (MOSES JENNER RAMAZZINI HIPPOCRATES PARACELSUS PINEL LIND) and its bronze medallions commemorating great moments in public health flying apart, leveling the trees in the square and somehow—miraculously—hurling him to safety.

He would simply walk away without looking back. He would start a new life—but as what? The notion made him feel very good, especially when he coupled it with the daydream of tenderly pulling Dolores into an alley, lifting her skirt—

The telephone rang. It was the director of the Health Department's Bureau of Laboratories.

"What can I do for you?" Hart peered out his window at the hundreds of civil servants milling around in the square.

"Shapiro, the micro chief at the lab at Metropolitan, called me this morning. He's got a Gram-negative coccobacillary bacterium up there, in a sputum culture. It came from a fatal case of pneumonia."

"Did he say what he thought it was?"

"He said it could be an unusual bacteroides, or, more likely, a *Francisella*. Shapiro usually knows what he's talking about. He even thought it might be a *Yersinia*." There was a pause. "If it is, I'm not going to touch it."

"I have the morning free. I'll go up to Metropolitan and take a look."

Hart's staff was clustered around a row of park benches opposite the building. Sam Andrews stood a little apart from the group. They were all listening to Gayle Jefferson, one of the nurse epidemiologists.

"We were the only blacks in the whole campground," she was saying in her gravelly voice. "And what do you s'pose they have on Labor Day but a *watermelon-eatin'* contest!"

The other nurses, who were mostly black and Puerto Rican, screamed with laughter. "I did not want my kids to participate, but they were pullin' on me, sayin' 'Why, mama, why?' Finally, I gave in. Figured it wouldn't do them any harm. Well. I am here to tell you that my Tyrone came in first and little Gloria came in second."

One of the nurses spotted Hart approaching. "Oh, Dr. Hart," she called. "We're having a watermelon-eating contest on this hot day. You want to join us?"

"Not on your life," Hart said. "I'd lose hands down —to Dr. Andrews here."

Andrews looked surprised.

"Do *crackers* eat watermelon?" Jefferson asked, rolling her eyes in disbelief.

"Sure. They eat the seeds and throw away the rest," Hart replied, straight-faced. He thought he saw Dolores Rodriguez beam approvingly at him, but maybe she was just squinting in the bright sunlight.

There was more laughter. Andrews looked around at the dark faces, smiling uncertainly.

"You know why they call 'em crackers?" Jefferson asked. "Because they're *white* and *square.*"

Andrews pulled at his beard and blushed. He seemed to be thinking hard. Finally he said, with a strong drawl, "You watch yo' mouth or I'll send Gorilla Woman after you!"

It was a genuine threat. Gorilla Woman came to the bureau about twice a month, and no one liked the task of talking to her. She had been referred to the BPD by the Bureau of Pest Control and Animal Affairs, and her complaint, which no one in the health bureaucracy could resolve, was that she was turning into a gorilla and that her condition was contagious.

"Don't worry, Gayle," Hart said. "I'm going to take Dr. Andrews up to Metropolitan."

"That should fix his wagon but good," the nurse replied.

7

THE HEAT and the din of the uptown express train were overpowering. Hart and Andrews clung to a pole, hemmed in on all sides by men, women, and children who looked as if they were being driven mad by the shriek of the metal wheels against the rails and by the hundred-degree temperature. They grimaced, they sucked on their lips or bit them, and they tried to make themselves as compact as possible, pulling in their chins and pressing their arms to their chests.

". . . don't think it's *Yersinia*," Hart said, yelling through the subway's roar and clatter.

"What?" Andrews looked up from a creased piece of paper he was studying.

Hart saw that it was a puzzle he had composed for the nurse-epidemiologist training program. It was a statistical description of a famous "epidemic" that had occurred sometime in the last hundred years. It was given out to test one's ability to interpret figures and to reason out the cause or causes that would explain all the facts on the sheet. Andrews had been looking at the sheet for over a week now, and his most recent guess—that the "epidemic" was due to the earthquake in Italy in 1976—was wrong. Rodriguez had stayed up all one night trying to identify that epidemic, and had been the first to get it right. She never let go of a case until she was satisfied that all possibilities had been exhausted, and even then she would pull out old files of unsolved cases and go through them.

EPIDEMIOLOGICAL CHARACTERISTICS OF AN
EPIDEMIC BY SOCIAL CLASS, SEX, AND AGE

Socio-economic Group	Male	Female	Total	Adult	Children	Total
Group I (High)						
Population at risk	172	132	304	293	11	304
Number of Deaths	111	6	117	117	0	117
Death Rate per 100	65%	5%	39%	40%	0%	39%
Group II (Middle)						
Population at risk	172	103	275	267	8	275
Number of Deaths	146	13	159	159	0	159
Death Rate per 100	67%	13%	58%	60%	0%	58%
Group III (Low)						
Population at risk	504	208	712	645	67	712
Number of Deaths	419	107	526	477	49	526
Death Rate per 100	83%	51%	74%	74%	73%	74%
Total (All Groups)						
Population at risk	848	443	1291	1205	86	1291
Number of Deaths	676	126	802	753	49	802
Death Rate per 100	80%	27%	62%	63%	57%	62%

"Excuse me, what did you say?" Andrews asked as the train pulled to a stop at Fourteenth Street.

To Hart's astonishment, Andrews removed a small pink lump from each ear. Earplugs! Hart had been riding noisy trains for years and had never dreamed of using them. "You nut!" Hart exclaimed. "Never mind."

People poured out of the car onto the platform. A loud blast of *salsa* music from a record store in the underground arcade was cut off as the train roared northward again. At Forty-second Street, Grand Central Station, most of the people got off and a new batch got on, two Japanese businessmen, a dwarf, three toughs with "Savage Shadows" stenciled on their black denim jackets, a transit policeman, a covey of middle-aged Puerto Rican women. At Eighty-sixth Street, Hart and Andrews changed to the uptown local which was crowded mostly with blacks and Puerto Ricans, then got off at Ninety-sixth. Climbing the stairs, they passed a torn poster announcing the Rolling Stones' summer tour. Between Mick Jagger's legs was an inscription in Magic Marker:

> Get satisfaccion in everywhere
> because the life is large
> so much in the earth and the space
> so be nice soda
> Lalo

Hart was impatient to get to the hospital, but they had to walk slowly because of Andrews's limp. He had gotten polio when he was two, just before the Salk vaccine was developed. Hart assumed that Andrews had gone into epidemiology because he had been a victim; but then most people didn't know why they did anything, so Andrews probably thought he was in epidemiology because it was interesting and he was good at it.

They walked along Ninety-sixth down a hill from Lexington Avenue to Third Avenue. The street was the border between the white, upper-class Upper East Side and Spanish Harlem. Hart pointed out Metropolitan, a series of tall, buff-colored buildings resembling the housing projects that surrounded it.

"How many beds?"

"About seven hundred."

"It's a lot smaller than Bellevue, then."

"And a lot nicer, I think. As city hospitals go, it's a good one. It's even been in the movies. Ever see *Hospital?*"

"Oh, yes. George C. Scott." Andrews was pleased. That was something he loved about New York, no matter how much he hated the dirt and the noise: you could actually see places that were in movies, and you could sometimes run into real actors.

Once inside the hospital, it was as if they had entered another country: the only language to be heard was Spanish. Children were crying and wandering around, their mothers yelling at them. Old men moaned. A janitor, an old black man, mopped away, oblivious to the tumult. "This is the screening clinic," Hart said. "But the nurses call it the 'Screaming Clinic.'"

The Microbiology Lab was on the second floor of the hospital. In contrast to the broad, clean corridors of the hospital proper, the lab seemed worn, heavily used, and dingy. In the bacteriology lab, women in white jackets busied themselves among stacks of Petri dishes and trays of test tubes. Some of them stopped their work to listen to Dr. Shapiro talk with Hart and Andrews. They discussed the blood culture, sputum cultures, and various fermentation tests.

"We would have gotten through to you sooner, but our night shift has been cut out, and after a long weekend like this we really get backed up," Shapiro said. "I've got the slide on the microscope."

Hart peered through the lens.

"Interesting, isn't it?"

On the slide, Hart saw grapelike clusters of red, elongated ovals. The color came from the process of Gram-staining, which was used to classify bacteria into two main groups. Some bacteria, such as staphylococci and streptococci, would turn blue when stained; they were labeled "Gram-positive." The organisms of typhoid, dysentery, and gonorrhea, among others, would turn red; they were "Gram-negative." By knowing the staining characteristics of the bacteria—even without knowing which bacteria was present—physicians could decide on which antibiotics to use until further test results were reported. The red ovals Hart saw looked simple, but each one contained dozens of organs for carrying on digestion, replication, and excretion, and 60,000 genes to supervise and maintain a way of being in the world that had worked very successfully for four billion years. The particular bacteria he was observing might be over a million years old; many types were practically eternal. He thought about how to label it and kill it. "Coccobacillary, Gram-negative, bi-polar staining," he said to Andrews. "Take a look."

"It could be a lot of things," Shapiro said. "It looked funny enough to make me call the Bureau of Labs."

"How about a Fluorescent Antibody test?" Andrews asked. "Did you do an FA on the sputum? That's the only quick, definitive test for *Yersinia*."

"You must be kidding," Shapiro said. "Nobody in New York can do that. Even before the budget cuts we didn't have that. The Bureau of Labs doesn't even have a control to compare it to. When you come to think of it, why the hell should they?"

"Because you've got to be prepared for every epidemic contingency!" Andrews exclaimed, straightening up from the microscope.

Poor kid, Hart thought. He keeps hoping he'll come across some kind of well-stocked, futuristically equipped, smoothly run public-health facility in this city. But he runs into the same old story each time— the financial crisis, the budget cuts, the reduced staffs— and gets mad all over again.

The bed that had been occupied by Jane Doe was now being used by an ancient, toothless black woman. The respirator hissed. The fan turned. The window shades rustled.

Across the corridor, at the nurses' station, Hart leafed through Jane Doe's chart. Thirty-eight documents—some spattered and smudged, some messy with hurriedly scrawled notations, others neatly printed or typed—comprised the final record of the girl's passage.

"What about the interne on call yesterday?" Hart asked the nurse on duty. "Can I discuss this case with him?"

"Well, Dr. Lipsky went home early this morning," the nurse replied. "He was really exhausted—he'd been on duty since Sunday morning."

"Was there anyone else?"

"Bergman, a medical student. He went off yesterday."

"It says here the girl died from complications possibly resulting from an overdose. Did you call the Medical Examiner on this? Has the body been taken down there for an autopsy?"

"Dr. Lipsky reported the death to the ME," the nurse said. "But the body may still be in the hospital morgue."

8

THE BODY of a sixteen- or seventeen-year-old girl, waxy, cold, hard, lay in an open steel drawer in the basement morgue, a tag on the big toe saying, "Doe, Jane." Hart regarded the matted long brown hair, the cupid's-bow mouth, the round, freckled face. He took a Polaroid print of her face with the morgue camera. "The ward MD said in his report that she had needle tracks." His voice echoed on the white-tiled floor, walls, and ceiling.

"Well, I see she's got scratches on her arms and legs, and some small excoriations." Andrews put his hands in his pockets and shivered. The air-conditioning in the rest of the hospital did not work too well, but down here in the morgue it was very chilly.

"They look more like insect bites than needle tracks to me," Hart said. "And you can see from the long fingernails that she could have done a good job of scratching."

"Here are a couple more bites on the left ankle. I

don't see how these could be mistaken for needle tracks."

"Metropolitan gets junkies every day—ODs, hepatitis cases, abscesses from dirty needles, pneumonias. They see so many needle tracks that they forget there could be something different."

"Anyway," Andrews said, "you can see she got a tan wearing a bikini. I've never heard of a junkie with a tan." He was about to say something else but he stopped abruptly. "Dave."

The two men looked at one another and at the body.

"Bites?" Andrews pulled on his beard nervously. "Death from pneumonia? It couldn't be—"

"Ahh, they're probably just mosquito bites," Hart said. He was worried that Andrews would persuade himself prematurely of the diagnosis they both feared the most and then accidentally communicate his fear to others. He was, after all, a green kid.

To a morgue attendant who waited in the doorway, Hart said, "Get the body to the Medical Examiner's, and make sure everyone who has anything to do with it wears masks and gloves. I doubt that there's anything to be concerned about, but until we get the autopsy results, it's best to take precautions."

The attendant nodded sleepily.

"See, Sam, in this game, big things always seem to turn out to be little things." Hart spoke briskly as they went to the elevator. "This is probably like the adult chicken-pox cases. Every winter a couple of them turn up, and the people get scared and think they're dying of smallpox."

As they rode up in the elevator, Hart fell briefly into his private void. He forgot where he was. He clenched and unclenched his jaws.

Andrews thought he might be angry about something. "What are you thinking?"

"I'm thinking—I'm thinking I'm glad I'm alive." Hart was startled by his own words.

"Wal now," Andrews exaggerated his drawl. "That's a mighty odd thang to say."

"I'm a mighty odd fellow."

"I doubt if this is anything serious." Dr. Whitney Emerson showed Hart and Andrews into the small suite of offices of the hospital's Department of Preventive Medicine. It was next to the contagion ward. They sat down in a small room taken up by a long conference table. "We get these bacterial pneumonias from time to time," he went on. He was a soft-spoken, gentle-faced man in his sixties. "Derelicts or addicts who pass out, vomit, and inhale the wrong way. The lungs get infected, and that's it."

"But her X-rays don't conform to that diagnosis, Dr. Emerson," Hart said. Emerson reminded him of his father, who had been a successful plastic surgeon. The comparison did not reassure him. As his father had aged, he spent more and more time playing golf and growing roses out in Southampton, and less and less time keeping up with the latest advances in medicine. This always infuriated Hart, who had gone to medical school in the hope of at last being able to have a conversation with his father.

Hart repeated to Emerson the facts of the case as they had emerged so far: "The ambulance picks up a Jane Doe, passed out in the lobby of an apartment building on Fifth Avenue. She dies eighteen hours later of pneumonia with complications. The sputum culture shows a suspicious Gram-negative bacteria. I've requested an autopsy, and Dr. Andrews and I are going to pack up the culture and have it flown to the Center for Disease Control in Atlanta for a Fluorescent Antibody test. Now, I agree that it is probably nothing serious, or even contagious, but I think I'd better do some investigating, and I'd like you and the hospital administration to cooperate."

Dr. Emerson regarded the two young men with

grandfatherly indulgence. "What would you boys like to do?"

"If you could lend us an office and a telephone, we'll send for some of our nurse epidemiologists. We've got to trace all the contacts with the girl that occurred here in the hospital. And we'll also try to get an identity on the girl."

"Well . . . " Emerson's gaze wandered past them and rested on an amateur watercolor of an old red mill and a curving stream. "Seems to me you fellas are in a big hurry to go nowhere. Why don't you just wait until you get an autopsy report and the results from Atlanta?"

Andrews could contain himself no longer. "What? What? We can't wait!" His face reddened. "We have to stay on top of this—it could be big."

"Sam—hold it," Hart said. "It could be little. In either case, Dr. Emerson, there could be a paper in it for you, perhaps."

Emerson ruminated. "I doubt it. A seminar, maybe. Well, tell you what. My secretary's still on vacation, so you can use her office today if you really need to. As far as getting cooperation from the hospital administration—you're on your own."

"ETIOLOGIC AGENTS," the bright red label declared. "BIOMEDICAL MATERIAL. IN CASE OF DAMAGE OR LEAKAGE NOTIFY DIRECTOR, CDC, ATLANTA, GEORGIA." Next to the words was a warning symbol of red, interlocking crescents superimposed on a red circle.

Sam Andrews pasted the label on the package. "Merry Christmas, CDC," he said.

The bacteria grown from the sputum and blood of the dead girl were in vials wrapped in cotton batting, inside an unbreakable jar sealed with a gasket. The jar was inside a collar of dry ice, which was inside a core of shock-absorbent styrofoam, which was inside a heavy cardboard box. The assemblage made Hart think of a bomb.

"We didn't use to have to make all this fuss when we shipped a culture," Gayle Jefferson said.

"It's a new law." Andrews said. "Some airline people got exposed a few years ago to some polio virus that wasn't wrapped up properly. Now all etiologic agents have to be packaged so that there's no possible leakage, even if there's a plane crash. Does anybody have enough cash to pay my taxi fare to LaGuardia?"

"You'll be an old man before the city reimburses you," Hart said.

Dolores Rodriguez, who had been quietly watching them, opened her pocketbook. Hart sorted through his pockets and found $3.10 and a subway token, but by then Jefferson had shoved a ten into Andrews's hand. "Here, boy!" she said. "Get your ass in gear!"

Rodriguez smiled when she saw Hart emptying his pockets and not finding much. When he did things like that, he seemed more accessible to her. She was quite taken by his pale, wavy hair, his formal expression, his contained tension. She liked every way that he was not like her, not Puerto Rican. And because he was so different from her, she had decided that they would never get together. He looked up and met her smile, which she promptly made cool and mysterious.

We'll wrap this thing up by the end of the day and I'll take her out to dinner, he thought. But then his stomach sank. How could he ever be with someone so liquid, so alluring, so elusive, so wrong for someone of his upbringing—and so different from his wife? And now he was about to send her away again. He would never change. He would always be like this. What a dismal prospect.

"I got the ambulance report," she was saying. "They picked up Jane Doe at 1009 Fifth Avenue. I checked with the property office. All they have is a cashmere coat with a Saks label. She wasn't wearing anything else."

"She must have had a bad chill." Hart added with a professional edge to his voice, "I'd like you to go

47

through the hospital now and find out who was exposed to the girl, from the time she was picked up until now. That includes morgue attendants. We're going to have to track down every contact and examine each one. The girl's chart shows she received Keflin and gentamicin. Maybe she got the medication too late. If this is what I think, we'll have to make sure everybody exposed gets big doses of tetracycline."

She nodded and disappeared.

"Gayle," he continued, handing her the Polaroid print of the Jane Doe, "I want you to get over to 1009 Fifth Avenue and see what you can find out. You know, sweet-talk the doorman, ask the other doormen on the block if they noticed a girl wandering around delirious on a hot afternoon in a heavy wool coat. That sort of thing."

"You think this might be somethin' bad, Dr. Hart?"

"Well, I don't know. We have to work fast, that's all."

Hart knew that neither Gayle nor Dolores would stop working until they had turned up the information he had asked for, and he knew they would work as fast as they possibly could, and, if necessary, call in the other eight nurse epidemiologists. Meanwhile . . . He checked his watch. It was now 2:45, about twenty-four hours since the girl's death. Time was beginning to matter more and more, and it was beginning to move too quickly. His mind began speeding up; for the first time in months he felt wide awake. Maybe the girl had just come from India, or Vietnam—someplace where this thing was endemic. Or maybe from out West? There had been reports . . . No, he was jumping to conclusions. It had to be bacterial pneumonitis. And what about the contacts the girl had had before the ambulance pick-up? Maybe he should put a notice in the papers and call the TV stations. No. That would unleash the reporters—too many complications. Panic. God knows what would happen. The attending physicians—if he could just question them.

He picked up the phone and asked the switchboard to find Lipsky and Bergman.

"Dr. Lipsky's answering service said they would give him the message to call you when he checks in with them," the operator said. "He's ill and has asked not to be disturbed."

"And Mr. Bergman?"

"His mother says he's sleeping. She said if he felt better when he woke up she'd have him call you."

Hart put down the phone and stared at the wall. Good God. The two guys who did the trach were flat on their backs. Maybe a coincidence. There was a galloping crud, a vague, sniffling malaise that was always ricocheting around hospitals from patient to doctor to nurse to orderly. Not unusual for two doctors to be sick at the same time. He paced the room. There was nothing he could do until some results came in. Maybe the autopsy had been done by now. That would settle a lot of questions.

He phoned DeLuca, the Medical Examiner.

"Look, Hart, you know I can't do an autopsy on that Jane Doe. She's clearly a minor. I should have a permission slip from next-of-kin."

Hart silently ran through all the permutations of replies, counter-arguments, and bureaucratic ploys he could haul out. He took a deep breath. "I've got to have autopsy results on that case immediately."

"Sorry. Can't. You show me a permission slip and I'll do it. Otherwise I'm not taking any risks. What if she turns out to be orthodox Jew, or some other religion that's against mutilating the dead? I could be sued. Believe me. Her parents could show up and get very nasty. It's happened before."

You motherfucker, Hart thought. I'll rip your cheekbones out! Evenly, he said, "This is an emergency. I'll take full responsibility for this. I assure you. Just do the post and call me as soon as it's done."

"You'll put this in writing? Send me a letter?"

"Yes, yes!"

He put down the phone just as Rodriguez appeared in the doorway. "I've been checking around the hospital," she said. "Counting the lab technicians exposed to the blood and sputum cultures, the stretcher attendants, the orderlies, the aides, the nurses, and the doctors, fifty-five people were exposed to Jane Doe on Sunday." She spoke impersonally, trying to cover her accent, appearing to be absorbed in the figures she was reading. "You can figure there were some people who rode up with her in the elevator from the Emergency Room—say three unidentified exposures there. Of all those exposed, I guess that at least twelve people had close exposure to the patient and thirteen had intimate exposure. On Monday, seventeen more were exposed, one closely and fourteen intimately. And then, after she died, five more had intimate exposure, including the morgue attendants. The grand total is about eighty-two, with seventy-seven identified."

"I was afraid it was going to be like that," Hart said. "That's a pretty big number."

9

IN THE contagion room in the rear basement of the office of the Medical Examiner, an old black man with hair like cottonwool wheeled the stretcher bearing the girl up to a stainless steel table.

"Thanks, Jerry." The pathologist's words were muffled by the mask he was wearing. He wore a paper surgical gown and rubber gloves.

"You are most welcome, Dr. Chakarian," the attendant said. He and the pathologist lifted the body onto the table. Around its edge was a small lip to catch liquids and prevent them from dripping on the floor.

As the attendant was leaving, Dr. Malcolm, the second pathologist, entered, putting on his mask. "I don't see why we have to do this now," he said. "It's almost quitting time."

"DeLuca said we had to."

"That's good enough for me."

"He said the Department of Health wanted a post on this girl stat. He said it might be an infectious case. The girl had pneumonia. A Gram-negative."

"Well, if it's not TB, why the hell are we wearing these masks?"

"DeLuca said to."

"OK."

"We'll do a good job. Let's check the exterior first."

Each of the doctors began to run his gloved hands over the arms and legs, squeezing muscles and fat, occasionally bending a stiff joint. They looked between toes, under the arms, in the groin. They turned the body on its stomach and palpated the head, the base of the neck, the spine, the rib cage, the buttocks, the thighs, the legs, and the feet. They turned the body back over. The Medical Examiner's Office did about two dozen autopsies a day. The work load was excellent experience: between them, these two pathologists had performed twenty-three thousand autopsies. They worked as a single mind, like a left hand and a right hand, each anticipating the next move of the other.

"Standard IV marks on the arms. Extensive purpura on arms, legs, abdomen, torso. Looks like they did a cardiac puncture here." Chakarian pointed to a small dot on the chest with a trickle of blood oozing from it.

"A coagulopathy, maybe."

"Doubt it; probably just a post-mortem thing. But we'll see when we get inside."

Malcolm bent down to look carefully at one of the

ankles. His glasses began to slip off the end of his nose. "What do you make of this? See this welt? It has some scratch marks here and here." He pointed to the skin around a small, raised area the size of a match-head.

"Looks like a mosquito bite. Maybe a bee sting. I've got one here, too." He pointed to a similar bump on the girl's left forearm.

"No," Malcolm said, adjusting his glasses. "A bee sting would leave more erythema. It wouldn't cause the girl to scratch. Certainly isn't an injection or needle tracks, though. More like a mosquito bite or a mite."

"Let's open her up."

Chakarian picked up a scalpel and pierced the skin above the pubic bone. He drew the scalpel straight up over the lower abdomen, around the umbilicus, to the bottom of the rib cage. A trickle of blue-black blood appeared in the wake of the blade. At the bottom of the rib cage he cut towards the left armpit and then toward the right, following the outer margin of each breast. The blade went up to and underneath each arm and stopped. He had etched a large, neat Y.

"Excellent, Herr Rokitansky," Malcolm said to Chakarian. Rokitansky was a famous nineteenth-century pathologist who had developed this method of post-mortem examination.

"Saw, please."

Malcolm handed Chakarian a small electric saw with a circular blade. In Chakarian's hands, it sprang to life and buried itself in the left armpit of the body. Metal against flesh, then bone. The saw slowed as it cut downward into each rib, spewing a powder into the air. There was an odor of singed bone. After re-tracing the scalpel's path across the chest with the saw, he turned it off.

"Finish the cut and we'll pull the organs out."

"You want the tongue, Petros?" Malcolm asked.

"DeLuca wants the tongue."

"He'll have the tongue."

Malcolm lifted the sternum open, reached into the thorax, and wrestled with the inside of the girl's neck. He had a scalpel in his hand and was cutting something. He withdrew his hands, now covered with blood, and looked at the girl's mouth. His face expressionless, he put a steel rod into her mouth and pried her jaws apart. A quick cut at the base of the tongue, some pulling from below again, and the tongue disappeared down into the girl's throat.

The two men wrestled with the body, which began to split apart in the middle. Then the organs of the neck and chest began to rise out of the thorax. The doctors were ripping the viscera away from their attachments to the bones of the chest. The tongue, long and slender, attached to the trachea and thyroid, the lungs, light pink with glistening purplish-red patches of pneumonia, the heart, reddish-brown, encased in a shiny transparent sack . . . They allowed the collection of organs, bound together by silvery fascia and ligaments, to drop back into the body cavity with a splash.

"Cut the diaphragm on your side. I'll tie off the esophagus and the ligament of Trietz."

"Fine, let's get the viscera out."

"Wait, let's check the nodes first."

They both put their hands into the chest cavity again, then into the groin area, at the top of each thigh.

"Better eviscerate her and feel again. I think we got something in the left inguinal region."

"And here." Chakarian palpated the right armpit. "I got a big one—no, two—up here."

They lifted the white tangle of entrails out of the body cavity and placed them next to the body on the table. Then they put their hands back into the dark shell and began pulling and yanking at something.

"Christ!" Chakarian examined a golf-ball-sized piece of flesh he held in his hand. "This is one node!" He turned it in the light, peering at it. "And there's one more. I'm going to put on another pair of gloves. I'm going to wear two pairs. I'm putting on a second mask, too."

Malcolm held a similarly sized lymph node he had extracted from the groin.

The two men looked at each other in silence. Then they went to a cabinet against the wall and took out rubber surgical gloves. They changed their masks.

"She had pneumonia, you know," Malcolm said.

"Yeah." Chakarian did not want to talk now. He just wanted to finish up and get out of the room. The two worked swiftly with a minimum of professional conversation.

"Lungs: 1500 grams, firm, serosanguinous. Pneumonic infiltrations bilaterally, all lobes involved. Fluid aspirated for culture for fungi, TB, and bacteria."

Within twenty minutes, all the organs had been weighed and placed in bottles of formalin. Specimens of each organ would later be examined under the microscope.

The attendent came back as they were finishing up. "That was fast, you guys. You usually take an hour."

"Get the fuck out of here, Jerry!" Chakarian snapped.

Jerry backed out of the room. Something was up. Dr. Chakarian and he had known each other for eleven years. They were friends. "You want anything?"

"Yeah. Put on a mask and gloves, you stupid bastard. Then come help us. I think we got something here."

Jerry smiled. Something was definitely going on and he was in on it with Dr. Chakarian. Something really big.

10

HART SAT in the office Emerson had loaned him and waited. He hated to wait; his attention dulled and he slid into daydreams. Now he remembered how he had sat on the blanket watching her narrow, tapered hand hold down the stream of her gold hair. It was a bright autumn day, and the breeze had a cool, smoky edge. Clouds skidded overhead, and the light jumped and flickered. He loved the light: it glazed the square tower of the Cloisters, it glossed the leaves, it struck off the wide blue curve of the river below, and it made sparks in the champagne they drank. Her hands, he could remember her hands. Her hair. The red skirt tucked around her knees. Her face—no. Far away, easily mistaken for the rush of the river and the wind in the leaves, were the sounds of the hidden city. Then it was twilight, the sun red and huge on the horizon, and they were on the observation deck of the highest tower in the city. The view below reminded him that they lived on an island, an island that rested in the embrace of three rivers and a great harbor. It curved in and out like the body of a woman, tethered to the mainland by thin, silvery bridges. To the north, beyond the ridge of midtown skyscrapers, they could see the green expanse of the park, all the greener for the red that was washing over the sky. Let's live in the park, he said. She moved quickly to the other side of the deck. She did not like the city. She counted the ships and tugs in the river; their wakes were shiny ribbons extending past the Statue of Liberty through the neck of the harbor and far out into the ocean. They got married soon afterward. A few months later she found the lump.

He couldn't save the recollection of her face. He had played this film through too many times. It was getting flecked and worn. Whole patches were missing altogether. He had forgotten some secret: he reviewed, he considered, he walked, he talked, he kept working, harder than ever. But something was eluding him.

Hart stared at the vase of dusty plastic roses on the desk. They were eerily glazed by the fluttering fluorescent ceiling light. Deep in his mind was a faint swaying, almost a physical sensation at the base of his skull.

He was remembering the wrong things. He had been alert and now he was back in the pit again. He felt the way he did on restless nights when the wrong recollections would present themselves, the monologue would not stop, and he would be too weary to get up and go out and walk it to death. On those nights he would lie in bed and conjure up terrible organisms: they swam in the drinking water, they grew in the food, they wafted through the air. Typhoid. Tularemia. Anthrax. To take himself to the edge of sleep he would plan, step by step, the appropriate responses. He would review the disease's history and literature, the treatment, the isolation procedures, the resources available to combat the imagined epidemic. There was a part of his mind he had to keep busy that way or, he feared, it would destroy him.

And now, staring at the roses, remembering that he didn't remember his wife's face any more, he reminded himself that this time the organism was not imaginary. This bedtime story was real.

He had never used this one to make himself fall asleep. Other Gram-negatives, of course—viruses, fungi, bizarre toxins. But not the one he now suspected. It was too improbable, too medieval, too terrible.

A taste of an old memory stirred him. It was the smell and texture of boring winter Sundays during his adolescence. How he had longed for a nuclear war to break out, or for aliens to attack from outer space! He had made plans. He would leave his parents' apartment, somehow make his way north, into the forests beyond the Bronx, fight for his survival with a hunting knife, and live on roots and berries and pemmican. The world would be in ruins, everyone he knew would be dead, but he would survive, free from prep schools, tea dances, deadly dinners with his parents . . . He had longed for the worst more than once.

Back to the facts. If those seventy-seven contacts Dolores had identified had each made only one contact, that was one hundred and fifty-four people exposed. And if each of those had made contacts . . . Oh, God. It spread so fast—in a breath, a touch, a sneeze, a handshake, a curse. But even if it were the worst possible outcome, the unmentionable, it still could be taken care of. Tetracycline would work if you got it in time. Streptomycin would work in the early stages of the disease, but it required injection, and therefore the logistical problems would multiply. Those plastic roses! Dr. Emerson's secretary had tried to make the best of this cubicle; they must be her idea of cheer. What about the smallpox scare in 1948? He was a kid then and had gotten his shot. Of course in those days, people were still high on World War II. V-E Day, V-J Day, mass ecstasy in Times Square, everyone pulling together, serving the government. The smallpox crisis had been handled as though it were another war effort. When the city government ordered everyone in the five boroughs who had not had a recent immunization to have shots, everyone cooperated. Mayor O'Dwyer got a public vaccination. President Truman had one before visiting the city. Over six million people vaccinated in two weeks. Now, Hart knew, there would be no rerun of the miracle of '48. Decentralization, "community awareness," an infectious distrust of government, and federal indifference would all work against any "war effort." And the Health Department had been much bigger then. The money had been there to pay the per diem for the doctors, nurses, and overtime clerks who did all the vaccinating and paperwork. Now, thanks to successive budget cuts, the money and personnel to fight a major epidemic no longer existed.

A heavy orange object thumped down in front of him. It was a backpack. "That Jane Doe?" Jefferson began. "Well, her real name is Sarah Dobbs. She wasn't a street kid. She lived in that building on Fifth Avenue where the ambulance picked her up. A real fancy place, too."

"Wow, an identification that fast! Gayle, you're incredible!"

"You bet your ass." She grinned.

"So what did you find out? You talked to her family?"

"Well." Jefferson sat down on the edge of the desk. She lowered her voice. "I been a lot of places, but I never did see an apartment like that one! Looked like in some magazine or like in a movie, 'cause that gal's daddy is a *very* rich man. President of some corporation downtown? So the super, he's just the *super,* what does he know? *Nothin'.* He says the family's been away all summer, he thought in Europe. He didn't even know the girl had been in the apartment, but he recognized the picture, and he had found the Dobbs apartment door unlocked—she must have left it open when she went down to the lobby. The doorman identified her, too—the family's lived there since she was a baby. But just to make sure I got the right one, I brought this graduation picture of her to show you."

Hart looked at it carefully. He did not want to be mistaken. There was the long brown hair, drawn back at the neck. She looked like a lot of girls he had known when he was in prep school. They all had names like Bitsy and Muffy and they took riding lessons and had long straight tan legs. They were kind of dumb and laughed a lot, and married stockbrokers when they got out of Sweetbriar or Wellesley. "That's her," he said, an image of the pathologist's scalpel flashing through his mind. "The post results should be coming soon."

"The super wasn't very happy about me taking this, and I didn't get a chance to do much snooping around, what with him breathing down my neck. But I don't think she was living there. No food in the refrigerator, most all the curtains closed, the furniture covered up. Her bed was mussed up, though. Maybe she had just been there a little while. And I found the backpack in the foyer."

They unlaced the backpack and shook its contents out onto the desktop. Levis, a sweatshirt, a bikini, some T-shirts, underwear, sneakers, a camera.

"How about letters, a passport, an address book, telephone numbers? Was there anything like that around to suggest who her friends are, or where she's been?"

"Nope. The super's supposed to find out Mr. Dobbs's office phone number—it's in the owner's files —and call me back. But he's so pissed about the cop that he probably won't bother and I'll have to go over there again."

"Cop?"

"Yeah. I called up my old man and told him we had a health emergency. He sent a patrolman right over to stand outside the apartment. Orders of the Board of Health. I knew you didn't want the Dobbs people coming in without you knowing about it, and I knew you didn't want anybody else going in and out of that place. I didn't have time to get your official orders so I made some up. You can fire me."

"You're fired. Did you find out if anyone living in the building was friendly with the girl or had contact with her? How about the doorman who knew her?"

"Well, he didn't even know she was back from vacation. He hadn't seen her. The weekend porter was alone on the door when she passed out. He was the one who called the ambulance. Domingo Ortiz. I'd sure like to talk to him. But he doesn't have a phone. I did get his address—he's up in Spanish Harlem. My old man says he'll send some cops up there to talk to him."

"Your old man? Is he in the Mafia or something?"

"Shit no! You didn't know he was a lieutenant in th Twenty-third Precinct?"

"I guess I'd forgotten. Well, that's fantastic work. Now we have to figure out where the girl has been, and we've got to find her parents, *fast*. Try American Express, anything you think will work. Maybe the passport office could help. And if there's film in the camera, get it developed."

"Okay—I'll do that now." As Jefferson was leaving, Rodriguez came in.

"Dolores—"

"You want me to stick around?"

He rested his eyes on the creamy brown skin that curved from her throat down into the shadowy V of her bodice. She always made him feel strange; she was always able to distract him. He wanted to send her away because he wanted her to stay. His jaw tightened. This was ridiculous. Why did she bother him so much? "Uh, yes. I want you to call all the nurse epidemiologists in the Bronx, Brooklyn, Queens, and Staten Island right away, before they go home and tell them to report to the Bureau downtown first thing in the morning. They should set aside whatever they're working on and be ready for a long day."

Dobbs. Corporation president. It rang a bell somewhere. So much to work on, so much that had to be done. What breasts Dolores had! So plump and ready. He could not think. It made no sense. Why was he sitting here getting absurdly horny at a time like this? He stared at her softly pulsing throat. He stared at his open hands, spread out on the desk next to the dead girl's underwear. Then he had a very simple thought. An idiotically obvious thought. But it was what he had been trying to remember. It was only this: he was alive. It was his wife who had died, not him. He lived.

"Doctor?"

He cleared his throat. "Just thinking, uh, maybe you'd better plan to work late."

She nodded. "I can keep working on the exposures, too. We've gotten in touch with fifty of the people so far. We still can't find the other twenty-seven. But we've given everyone tetracycline."

"That's great."

"Doctor—you think the flu season is starting early this year? The employee clinic here at Met said that four people on the staff have called in sick. Two of them work in the emergency room."

"I don't know. Sixty or seventy employees were exposed to the girl, but it might be normal to have some small percentage of that number call in with the usual various complaints. Why don't you look at the employee absentee rate for the past couple of weeks and see what's typical?"

"Okay. Anything else?"

"Yes. We'd better bring in those people who called in sick and get a good look at them. Get some throat cultures for any bacteria, and blood cultures from anyone who's feverish. Whatever it turns out to be, we can document it better that way. Also, you'd better do cultures on the MICU staff—that includes the MD and the med student who handled the girl's case. They'll probably try to get out of it, so you'll have to scare them somehow." He paused. "Tell them your brother will cut them up."

"My brother wouldn't cut people up. My family is nice! My mother doesn't allow bad things, *mister*." She smoothed her silky black hair with a ferocious gesture that seemed to say, Sure, I'll fight you—name your weapon.

He watched the rise and fall of her breasts. "And

one, uh, one other thing, Dolores. Does your mother chaperone you on dates?"

"What are you talking about, you crazy or something?"

"No, Hart. Can't do it." Emerson chewed on his pipe, his gaze on the middle distance.

"Doctor, ambulances are bringing these suspicious cases in right now, and I am worried about spread. I hope they're not infectious, but if it turns out they are, then your Contagion Ward here is the logical place to put them."

Dr. Emerson appeared to be getting tired of Hart.

"Oh, I've got the beds all right. I just can't spare the staff. You'd better show me proof that this business is anything other than influenza. Then I'll see what I can do for you."

Hart looked at his watch. Almost six. Time was getting tight. This thing would spread fast if proved contagious. Everyone at the Health Department had gone home, so he would have trouble mobilizing extra staff right away. He had an impulse to knock Emerson across the office.

Emerson must have read his face, because he said, "Listen, son, this isn't in my hands anyway. You have to talk to Garson. He's the one who runs this place, not me. It's his responsibility to help you with your problem."

Arthur Garson, Chief Administrator of Metropolitan Hospital, was big, fat, and gray. He wore a gray suit and gray suede shoes, and Hart guessed that the man carried a gallstone, a kidney stone, or some other precious accretion that he would not give up, along with his store of paper clips, ballpoint pens, and petty privileges. He had run Metropolitan for the past five years with little interference from the City Health and Hospitals Corporation. The corporation had been formed under the Lindsay administration as a semiprivate enterprise in order to attract the brighter executive types to the city. Garson had been one so attracted. He knew how to say no, and when staffs and budgets were halved throughout the city, he got to say no all the time, and got promoted for doing so. He knew that the less his superiors downtown at Health and Hospitals heard about his hospital, the longer he would survive. And that was why he did not like the look of this outsider, this doctor from the Health Department.

The two assistants who flanked Garson smelled their boss's dislike and glowered at Hart.

"Look, Hart, I'd love to talk to you about whatever you've got on your mind, but I simply can't." He had a high-pitched voice. "People are waiting to see me on important business. I know you doctors always think what's going on in your little area is important, but somebody has to keep the big picture in mind." He wiped his sweaty neck and forehead with a tissue and then carefully tucked it in his breast pocket. "My air conditioner is broken," he explained.

"Mr. Garson, what I have to say is very important, and I think it would be better if we discussed it alone," Hart said.

"They can stay." Garson waved at his assistants as though they were matching file cabinets. "They are my coordinators, and they'll need to know anyway. *If* it's important."

Hart considered giving up. He could walk out of Garson's office, call the Commissioner of Health at home, and explain everything. The Commissioner of Health would then call the President of Health and Hospitals. He in turn would have to call Garson. Under optimum conditions, this process would take two hours. Now that it was past quitting time, it might take half a day. No: he had to get through to Garson right now.

"You had a young girl die here in the MICU yesterday," he began. "She seems to have had an unusual

Gram-negative pneumonia which may be infectious to others. Very infectious, perhaps. Quite a few people at Metropolitan may have been exposed. The body is already at the Medical Examiner's office, and he should be phoning me with the post-mortem results any time now. But we won't know the exact cause of the pneumonia until we hear from the Center for Disease Control in Atlanta. I sent them some cultures from the girl earlier this afternoon. In the meantime, on clinical grounds, we think she may have a very infectious disease."

The door opened, and Garson's secretary came in, quickly slamming the door behind her. "It's the representatives from 1199 and DC 37," she said. All the workers at the hospital belonged to 1199 or DC 37, two very powerful unions. "They're threatening to call the Mayor's office and Birnbaum if you don't see them right away. I think they're very upset, sir."

"Good Lord," Garson said. "If there's a strike I'll *never* get this air conditioner fixed! Hart, I'll have to talk to you later—"

"Sir—" the secretary began.

The phone buzzed.

"Come back another time," Garson told Hart. "Can't you see how busy I am? I happen to be the only one in charge, can't you see?"

"I have a call for a Dr. Hart?" The secretary looked vaguely around the room.

"I'll take that." Hart grabbed the phone.

"This is *my* office," Garson said. "You can't just barge in here and—"

At that moment the door opened and several people entered, talking loudly. The two assistants rose in unison and surged forward, and the shouting grew louder.

Hart plugged his free ear with his finger. "Who? Sorry, I can't hear you. Dr. DeLuca?"

11

"HEY, FLASH! Open up! It's your Sweetie!" The woman was wearing a purple satin miniskirt, a lowcut, ruffled scarlet blouse, platform shoes six inches high, and a fluffy platinum-blonde wig, which made her fair skin look dead white. She knocked on the door with growing irritation. She knew he was in there: she could hear the TV. "Flash!" she finally bellowed. "I know you can hear me! Let me in! You mad at me or something? C'mon, come *on*."

What if he had turned off on her? What if he had figured out that she was holding out on him? What if he'd just set her up for this, telling her she was his Number One Woman and making a real date for this evening—just the two of them, he'd said—and then making her wait outside like this? Just to show her he was hip to what she was doing behind his back? But usually he would just belt her—some place personal, some place where the Johns wouldn't see the marks.

Maybe this was a test. He had given her a key, but only to use in an emergency. She pounded and yelled some more. Suppose he was in there with another girl. What about that? "That's nothin' new," she snorted to herself.

She decided to wait him out. She sat down on the thick carpeting in the hallway, and lit up a joint. Flash was one rotten son-of-a-bitch. But she loved that dude more than anything. He took good care of her. Didn't he give her a mink chubby-coat on her birthday? Didn't he say he had dumped Betty as his Number One

Woman in favor of her? Didn't he say he loved her and that he would love her more and more every day as long as she lived by the rules? No holding back on money. No lying. No lesbian stuff. No he-say she-say with the other women. She had behaved herself, most of the time. She was no dope. That was how she got to be Number One. That was why she was going to the fights with Flash tonight while old Betty would be out flat-backing.

She got to her feet, took a deep breath, and knocked again. "Darling Lover, I'm coming in. Rhoda Sue is coming in now! I'm sorry! I can't wait any longer!"

She unlocked the door and stepped into a blast of cold, foul-smelling air. The six-foot projection television set was blaring *The Flintstones.*

Flash lay face down on an enormous fake leopard-skin sofa.

"Oh, is my Babycakes asleep?" She sat down next to him and stroked his ears and the back of his neck. She kissed his cheek. "Wake up, Sweetie! Wake up, Flash! We got a date, honey!"

He did not move.

On an end table, next to a lamp with a base in the shape of a crouching panther, was an empty glassine envelope, a hypodermic, some burned matches, and a bent spoon.

"Aw, Flash. You didn't go and OD now, did you?" she moaned, rolling him over. He slid to the floor like a bag of sand, blood from his slack mouth bubbling along the upholstery and the carpet.

"Flash!" she screamed. "You stupid fucker! You *asshole!*"

It took her less than ten minutes to pick over the cluttered apartment. She took a vial of cocaine from a bedside table, a big wad of hundred-dollar bills from the inside breast pocket of his bright green suit, and a diamond pinkie ring from his finger. And then she left, moving as fast as her heavily shod feet could carry her.

12

"WOULD YOU repeat that, please? I'm in a noisy office." Hart's jaw muscles worked in and out. He pressed the receiver harder against his ear.

There were six people in the room now, all talking and shouting at once.

"Inguinal nodes, axillary nodes . . . Yes, I got that. Hemorrhagic pneumonitis, all lobes . . . Repeat that, please. Yes, the nodes. They were missed up here by the interne and the residents. Probably deep, not palpable on the physical exam. Yes, yes . . ."

Suddenly the arguing men fell silent. Hart realized they had all turned and were looking at him.

"No, but thanks for the offer," Hart said. "If I do need help, I'll let you know. Yes, give your people streptomycin, two grams, stat, then a gram a day for the next few days. Yes, all of them. They had very close exposure. Otherwise I would just recommend tetracycline."

Garson and his assistants pushed the three men out of the room and slammed the door. "You can talk on the phone later!" Garson said to Hart. "These gentlemen want to speak with you right now!"

"Beg your pardon, Dr. DeLuca?" Hart continued, holding the phone away from Garson. "Right. And please call my office and give my secretary the names, addresses, and phone numbers of all your people who were exposed—from the pick-up people at Met to the pathologist. Everybody. We'll follow them up." Hart listened and nodded. "Thanks, Dr. DeLuca, right, yes,

I think we got the real thing here. I'm glad we agree on the diagnosis, although I wish to hell it was something else. Yes, thanks."

In the few seconds of silence that followed the click of the receiver, Hart held the phone and pretended to himself that he had misunderstood the ME's report. Then he saw what he should do next if he were in his right mind: Go immediately to his bank, draw out all his money, rush to the airport, and get on a jet bound for New Zealand. There were beaches there, and unexplored mountain ranges . . .

"Those union representatives say there's a dangerous flu going around and they want to know what is going to be done about it," Garson said. "They're hearing a lot of nasty rumors. Well? What are you going to do about it? This problem is a public-health matter—scarcely *my* responsibility!"

"Yes, there *is* something going around, and it is very infectious, as I said, but we can quickly take care of it. We need to set up a station down at the emergency room and announce that all personnel can pick up medicine there."

"What medicine?"

"Tetracycline."

Garson and his assistants exchanged looks of relief. "We have jars and jars of that in the pharmacy," one of the assistants said, as though the problem were now solved.

"Okay," said Garson, "I'll go out and tell everyone about the pneumonia and that they should all take tetracycline."

"Better wait until the station is set up before you make the announcement. Otherwise, people will just get the tetracycline from the wards. We have to make sure they come to the station for it so we can keep a roster of personnel who have received it. That way we can be sure that everyone is treated. Now, if you'll excuse me, I have some urgent business—"

"What the hell? Roster?" Garson began.

A burly man wearing a blue paper cap with "DC 37" printed on the brim pushed through the door into the office. "Mr. Garson, sir, we want to talk to you. Now!"

"Mr. Stein, Mr. Stein, I do not like it when people walk into my office without notice. Please get out of here right now. I am conducting a meeting, as you can see. I told you I would get back to you. Please leave."

The man in the cap stared at Garson with disgust and slowly walked out. "You'd better get out there and talk to us damned soon," he said.

"Look at this, Hart!" Garson exclaimed.

"I told you just what we're going to do. My nurse epidemiologists will set up a station in the ER, and people can come and get tetracycline. Tell the staff and union representatives that a diagnosis is pending, and in the meantime the best thing is to take the medication."

Hart went to Garson's secretary's office and told her he had to make a private call immediately. After she left, he called Vincent Calabrese, who was Commissioner of Health, and told him everything he had learned in the past few hours.

"Why don't you arrange a meeting up there for eight o'clock?" Calabrese's voice was quiet. "Then an organized procedure can be put into effect. The Mayor is still tied up with settling the garbage strike, so I'd prefer to hold off telling him for now." There was a pause. "Dave, you really think it's *that?*"

Hart wanted to say no. He wanted to go home: it was time to knock off, have a beer, go to a movie. Dolores. Instead, he had to face down ten thousand questions, phone calls, plans, contingencies, scenarios. Whether the diagnosis was right or wrong, the next few days were going to be pandemonium.

"Yeah, Vincent, I do. I'm not entirely—"

Garson burst into the room. "Who's this woman, Hart? She claims she works for you."

Rodriguez stood behind Garson. She looked very troubled.

"See you tonight, Vincent." Hart hung up the phone.

"Mr. Garson, there will be a meeting here at eight tonight with the Commissioner. You come. Meanwhile, the best thing you can do is remain calm and play this down."

"Low-profile it?"

"Yes."

"Dr. Hart," Rodriguez said. "I started taking cultures in the ER as you said. There was one person who had been out sick, a nurse from the maternity ward. She came in. She had a cold, that's all. I cultured her anyway." She continued to look worried.

"Anything else?"

"I think you better come to the ER and see."

In the green-tiled emergency room, a man lay on a stretcher shouting at a nurse. "Look here, I don't care on whose orders I was brought here! I demand to be taken to New York Hospital! I have rights! Somebody! Get me out of this pus pocket!" He stopped to cough into a tissue.

"It's Dr. Lipsky," she told Hart. "They just brought him in."

"Poor mon," said a nurse with a Jamaican accent. "He be outa his poor head. Usually be as sweet and nice as they come. He don't even recognize me!"

"Dr. Lipsky," Hart said softly.

"I won't tolerate this sort of treatment!"

"Dr. Lipsky."

"Are you an MD? Get me out of here. Good God, don't you *see?*"

"Dr. Lipsky, you've been exposed to a potentially contagious disease, and I've ordered you to be taken to MICU for treatment." Hart spoke firmly.

"Nonsense!" Lipsky went into a long coughing spasm. "This is just plain old grippe I've—"

He stopped, and looked with horror at the tissue, where a bright red stain had suddenly flowered.

13

PATROLMAN PATRICK LONERGAN and his partner, Manuel Maldonado, shooed the children off the hood of the patrol car and then drove slowly away from the Twenty-third Precinct Station House. This particular block, 102nd between Lexington and Third, was always a popular neighborhood hangout, but on hot summer evenings when the hydrant was open, hundreds of children gathered to tumble and shriek under the plume of spray. Occasionally the din was pierced by a sharp command in Spanish from a grandmother watching from a fire escape.

As Maldonado drove through the crowd, he kept an eye on the activity around the hydrant. Sometimes the older kids replaced the spray cap with a tin can open on both ends to make *la bomba,* a powerful jet of water they aimed at passing cars. As a kid he had done it himself many times. "Better roll up your window, Pat," he said, just before the car was sprayed.

"Jesus H. Christ!" exclaimed Lonergan, frantically pumping on the window handle. "Your people."

"What is this Health Department stuff? They think we're errand boys or something?" Maldonado turned on Third Avenue and headed uptown. "Can't they do this stuff themselves?"

"Jefferson said we had to, that's all I know."

"What do we do, bring the guy back to the station?"

"Nope. Find out if he lives at this address, and call the Health Department."

"Why?"

"Who the hell knows?"

"Is he a Bongo or a Banjo?"

"Bongo, I guess. His last name is Ortiz."

At 105th and Lexington they parked by a large red-brick Roman Catholic church.

"You think the car is safe from the piranhas here?" Lonergan asked. In El Barrio an unattended car, even a patrol car, would be stripped of hubcaps, antenna, radio, most engine parts, and the contents of the trunk in less than ten minutes.

Maldonado shrugged.

They walked to 118 East 104th Street, a decaying five-story walkup that was about eighty years old, built for the middle-income Irish and Italians moving uptown from the Lower East Side to escape the Jews. The Italians and the Irish had warred in the neighborhood until about the time Officer Maldonado was born, when Puerto Ricans began arriving in great numbers. After some bloody skirmishes in the early sixties, the Irish and Italians left, mainly for the suburbs. The few who remained were locked into the area by poverty. "Boy, what a dump." Maldonado looked at the explosion of garbage on the steps—banana peels, orange rinds, a rotting papaya, smashed bottles, an empty Pampers box, a broken doll. Several bulging plastic sacks ballooned with the foul gas of fermenting garbage.

The tenement looked just like the one Lonergan had grown up in, downtown under the Manhattan Bridge. No, this was worse, he thought. He didn't know how Maldonado had managed to reach manhood in El Barrio. "The garbage strike is supposed to be settled tomorrow," he said.

"There's always a garbage strike here," Maldonado said as they climbed the steps to the front door. In the dingy foyer was a stench of urine. All the mailboxes were broken. "Who's the individual we're looking for, again?"

Lonergan pulled a notebook from his back pocket and leafed through it. "Ortiz. Domingo Ortiz."

"No Ortiz on the mailboxes. Let's ask." Maldonado pushed all the apartment buzzers. Eventually a sleepy man in a t-shirt came out of one of the first-floor apartments and Maldonado spoke with him in rapid Spanish. No, he did not know any Ortiz; he was new to the building. Maybe the woman downstairs did. She was always home.

The well leading to the basement apartment below the steps was filled with more rotting garbage. Maldonado rang a bell next to an iron gate in front of the entrance. He could hear a baby crying, and the voice of a television actress speaking of *amor y la vida*. The face of a woman appeared between the rusted bars.

"Is there a Domingo Ortiz living here?" Maldonado asked in Spanish.

The woman frowned and rotated her lower jaw, pleating her face with wrinkles. She was perhaps fifty but she looked seventy. She shook her head.

"Amor es más importante que la vida . . ." the television was saying.

The woman kept glancing over her shoulder into the dim interior.

"Watching *La Usurpadora?*" Maldonado asked.

She nodded.

"My mother, she likes that one too. Are you also Puerto Rican, Señora?"

"Yes."

"Where in Puerto Rico are you from?"

"Arecibo."

"El Campbell's Manhandler, *el* Chunky Chicken *por todas las comidas!"* said the TV announcer.

"Well, if you hear about a man named Domingo Ortiz, tell him the Health Department wants to talk to him. Can I leave a phone number with you?"

She shrugged. "He does not live here. I do not know the name."

"Okay, thanks a lot." To Lonergan he said, "No soap."

14

HART SAT in the darkening hospital room and tried to trick himself into thinking there had been some mistake, some error in the diagnosis. What he again faced head-on was too sharp, too strong to look at for very long.

"Dr. Hart, would you like something to eat?"

The voice, though soft, made him start.

"Can I turn on the lights?"

When Rodriguez snapped on the light, everything changed for a moment. The change was so fleeting, so subtle, that if Hart had not been so tired and afraid he would have missed it. He saw the woman more clearly than he had ever seen her before. The sudden moist light on the curve of her cheek and in her eyes, the distinct ridge of her upper lip, the gloss on her hair. He heard the small rustling sounds of her dress as she moved, and her breath. He opened his eyes wider. There was nothing to think or to say.

In silence they ate the sandwiches she had brought and drank the coffee. A conspiracy of the we-the-living: we eat, we breathe, we see, we hear, we are with each other—what is all the rest about?

The phone rang. It was Patrolman Maldonado. "I was talking to Lieutenant Jefferson, sir? And he was saying like this was real important to find that male named Ortiz? He told me to call you because, well, I started thinking. Lieutenant Jefferson sent me and my partner up to that address and I talked to this old lady in the basement apartment. She said she hadn't heard of any Ortiz, and she told me she was Puerto Rican. But she wasn't no Puerto Rican. She had the wrong kind of Spanish. Sometimes you see these individuals, they're illegally in the country, maybe they snuck in through Puerto Rico, they got fake papers, stolen Green Cards or something. Well, I had the feeling that the old lady was covering up for him. She probably thought we were going to arrest him. I tried to explain about the Health Department but maybe she didn't understand what I meant. I might be wrong about this, but I live here all my life so I know the right Spanish, and she don't speak it."

"Where do you think she was really from?"

"Maybe one of the other islands. Or maybe some place in South America. Some country of that nature. Want me to go back there with a warrant?"

"Hold on a minute." Hart explained the situation to Rodriguez and then she spoke in Spanish with Maldonado.

"I told him not to scare the woman," she said afterward. "If she's got illegal aliens in the apartment and Ortiz is one of them, they'll hide him. They'll move him out at night if he's real sick and then we'll never find him."

"Maybe Colombia," Andrews said. "Of course. Ortiz contracts it in Colombia. It's endemic there. He immigrates illegally through Puerto Rico, gets a job as a porter in Sarah Dobbs's building, and infects her." He had not been so animated since the botulism outbreak in the Bronx in June; whole sections of textbooks seemed to be speaking in his brain. It was like final exam in med school and he was passing brilliantly. The proper handling of this situation would guarantee him a very good place in the CDC's hierarchy after his stint in New York was over.

"I don't know." Hart sat on the edge of the desk next to Rodriguez. "That sounds like quite a long shot to me. But we have to follow up every lead we can think of. Gayle is pulling every string she can, but we still haven't learned a thing about the girl or her family. If the girl contracted it in the city, then whoever gave it to her is already dead, and probably had managed to infect others. I've told Gayle to check with the morgues and emergency rooms around the city to learn if anyone is showing up with these symptoms. Meanwhile, we've got to get results on sputum cultures from Lipsky, Bergman, and the other new cases." Hart checked his watch. "No results before the meeting, though. It's ten to eight. The people will be coming any time now."

"The people are here." A tall, tanned, gray-haired man dressed in a crisply tailored cream-colored suit and a red polka-dot shirt strode into the room. He was Vincent Calabrese, the Commissioner of Health. He was followed by a small, thin man with thick glasses, an indefinite mustache, and an attaché case. "This is Irving Kaprow, from the Mayor's Task Force for Emergency Preparedness. He's here to assist us."

The small man grimaced and looked at the floor.

Calabrese pulled Hart aside. "Anything new?"

"Lipsky's dead. He was the interne who took care of Sarah Dobbs the night she was admitted and did the trach. He must have gotten quite a thorough exposure from the trach. He died of a massive pulmonary bleed. Almost like he popped a Rasmussen aneurysm. Suffocated in his own blood."

"God. And the others?"

"The head nurse on the MICU, an ER nurse, an aide, and a fourth-year medical student are all sick. The nurse is delirious, the medical student is comatose, and the ER nurse and MICU aide are showing acute respiratory distress. We've got them on streptomycin and Chloromycetin. We're giving everyone in the hospital tetracycline."

"Are you sure it's the real thing?"

"I'm afraid so." Hart looked around. Jefferson had arrived, but Rodriguez had disappeared. "The nurse epidemiologists are doing a good job of handling the hospital contacts. Miss Rodriguez and Mrs. Jefferson here have a rundown on exposures and I think we'll be able to cover them—if and when . . ."

"Anything else I should know about?" Calabrese asked.

"Well, if this thing turns out to be big and bad, we'll need some muscle. We need money, police support, and cars, and carte blanche on everything. I hope that guy from the Mayor's office can provide it."

"Dave, he's young. He's scared shitless, frankly. We'll be nice to him and he'll whisper in the Mayor's ear. You'll get what you want. And what about our friends at the CDC?"

"Sam Andrews sent the specimens down on a four-o'clock flight to Atlanta. We should be hearing the results of the FA tests any minute now. One other thing, Vincent. There's been some bureaucratic nonsense with the administrator here—Garson. I suggest you chair the meeting. There are too many Indians here who think they're chiefs."

Emerson's office had been selected for the meeting because it had an air conditioner that worked. Emerson led them all in and they took their places around the conference table. Hart looked from face to face. Calabrese, Kaprow, Jefferson, Emerson, Garson and his two assistants, Andrews. Where was Dolores?

15

THE TOWER of the New York Hilton was very sharp against the night sky. The faces of the men and women hurrying along Sixth Avenue were also very clear. The air around them was compressed and glittering. Rhoda Sue didn't feel a thing; she had enough cocaine freezing her brain against her sinuses to keep her numb for a long time, and more in her purse when the icy sensations wore off.

A girl in black vinyl hotpants and a pink halter walked toward Rhoda Sue. She was smiling. She had a gap between her two front teeth and wore a platinum-blonde wig.

"You seen Flash today?" the girl asked Rhoda Sue.

It took Rhoda Sue a long time to recognize the girl and hear the question. "Huh?"

"Hey, you! You spaced out on somethin'?" The girl's thin, dark, curved eyebrows drew together.

"Hi, Betty!" Rhoda Sue said. "I'm fine. How are you?"

"Oh, man, are you gonna get it," Betty said. "You're full of coke, I can tell it a mile off."

"No, no." Rhoda looked up and down the avenue, a march of tall rectangular slabs, all identical, all hard and clear. "Um, see, Flash and me, we had a date tonight. We goin' to the fights tonight, and he was suppose to pick me up at his place. I been waiting for him but he be late." Rhoda Sue and Betty were white, but they spoke the language of their black pimp.

"Well, honey, you *know* how absent-minded ol'

Flash can be." Betty, formerly Number One Woman, now Number Two, was pleased. "You know, he likes Carla a *lot*."

"Ah, she's new. What does *she* know? I think maybe Flash went to Florida. He always talkin' about going on a talent hunt."

"Aw, shit, Rhoda Sue! Don't be so fuckin' dumb. All he has to do to find new youngbloods is hit the bus terminal."

Rhoda Sue knew this, having met Flash herself in the Port Authority terminal after running away from Blue Earth, Minnesota, on a Greyhound. A soft-spoken, beautifully dressed black man had helped her carry her suitcase out of the bus station. He bought her dinner. They rapped: he somehow knew all about the way her daddy beat her up and threw her out of the house, and he was kind and gentle. He took her to a boutique run by his friend and bought her a hundred dollars' worth of new clothes. Just like that. They had a wonderful honeymoon for a week in a hotel on Lexington. Then he turned her out, and by her sixteenth birthday, in June, she was earning him $5,000 a month on the street. Betty's suggestion that Flash might be out with his new girl, maybe making her Number One, made Rhoda Sue mad. Then slowly a recollection chipped its way through her frozen mind: he was dead, blood on his face.

"He probably just scored some smack and forgot all about his little Rhoda Sue," Betty said. She turned and flagged down a man in a green-plaid sportscoat who was passing by. "Check it out, Baby?"

"How much?"

"How about partyin' with me and my friend here?" Betty asked brightly. "Seventy-five bucks."

But Rhoda Sue shook her head, waved, and walked quickly away.

16

"Now WAIT just a minute, Hart." Emerson was tired
and had missed a dinner party to come to the meeting, and he couldn't get around Hart's one-track statements about a possible epidemic. "Why do you jump
to all these dire conclusions? First of all, you don't
have any sort of confirmation on this from the CDC
yet. Our tests point only to a Gram-negative organism.
That's not conclusive evidence at all. We come across
lots of unusual pneumonias caused by weird bacteria.
We've had pneumonias due to every damned organism
in Bergey's Manual, and so has every other hospital
in the city." He looked around the table. "I'm confident, gentlemen, that what we have here is just
another version of the same old thing. Oh, more serious than usual, to be sure, but not really any different
from what we find in drunks and addicts who nod
off and then aspirate their own vomit. Bang—aspiration pneumonitis." Heads nodded thoughtfully. Emerson was an expert on childhood diseases, renowned
for his text on chicken pox.

"Very well put, Dr. Emerson," Garson said.

"But I don't follow this." Irving Kaprow drummed
his fingers on his attaché case, which he had placed
on the table. "I honestly don't know what you fellows
are talking about."

"I'll explain," said Andrews. "There are certain
kinds of bacteria, Gram-negative bacteria, that live
in the guts of certain fleas. The bacteria multiply
rapidly, choking the flea, so that when it sucks the

blood of the host animal—a wild rat, say, or a ground squirrel—it vomits the bacteria into the rodent's bloodstream. The rodent gets sick and dies, and its fleas, carrying the infection, hop onto the nearest warmblooded animal and bite it. Most of the time the nearest animal is another rat or squirrel. Diseases get passed around in rodent communities all the time. A disease like this can smolder for a long time in a particular area. That's what 'endemic' means. But sometimes, like when there's a drought and the rodents leave their usual habitats in search of food, the nearest animal the flea finds might be a domestic rat, or a human. Then suddenly the infection spreads very rapidly, with many animals and even people getting sick, and you have an epidemic."

"And the fleas jump from person to person? But people in New York City don't have fleas!"

"More people have fleas in New York than you think," Jefferson said.

"But you don't need fleas to spread the infection among humans," Andrews said. "If it becomes pneumonic, all it takes is one cough. Even breathing in an infected person's exhalations. It spreads faster than any other disease."

"So, if the girl had it, how did she get it?" asked Kaprow.

"That's what we're working on," Hart said. "We know she had a backpack and outdoors clothing, and a tan. We're guessing that she was in a wilderness area somewhere and got a flea bite. The autopsy indicated possible insect bites as well as suppurative inguinal nodes—"

"What?" Kaprow was scribbling notes.

"Buboes—big swellings of lymph nodes in the armpits and groin. That's the primary form. But the infection got into her lungs—and that's the secondary form, *pneumonic*. And its incubation period is short—about twenty-four hours. That means it spreads more rapidly than the flu!"

Calabrese observed the questions and answers with no change in his easygoing expression. Unlike Emerson, who had spent his time in pediatric clinics of university hospitals, Calabrese had lived for years in Africa, treating malaria and smallpox. He was one of the few physicians ever to have even seen smallpox cases, and he had been responsible for wiping out the disease throughout Africa. He had reluctantly accepted his present job because he felt he was getting too old to work in the bush. "I believe that almost anything can happen in epidemiology, including the outbreak in New York City that Hart is predicting," he said. "But I've also seen many disasters shrivel up and miraculously disappear. And I've seen—and made—many pessimistic diagnoses that turned out wrong. I'd just like to know why you're so sure of your diagnosis, Dave. Why are you so reluctant to entertain other speculations?"

"Sutton's Law, I guess."

Calabrese nodded thoughtfully.

"What? What? You have to explain all this medical jargon." Garson sighed impatiently.

"The term comes from med school," Hart explained. "Someone once asked Willie Sutton why he robbed banks, and he answered, 'Because that's where the money is.' When you hear hoofbeats, you think of horses, not zebras. The hoofbeats could be from a herd of zebras, but the first thing you think of is horses. The culture results we've got, the symptoms, the deaths, and the autopsy findings all point to only one diagnosis. It might add up to something less likely. I hope it does. Meanwhile we have to keep in mind that there were twenty cases in New Mexico and California last year. *Yersinia pestis* began spreading throughout the world again in the nineteenth century, and in this country has been moving eastward from the coast for seventy years. The fact that it's not endemic in the East is meaningless in an age of large-scale travel. Remember, smallpox is not endemic anywhere in the U.S., and yet we nearly had an epidemic of it in 1948."

"There's only one disease that's worse," Andrews said.

"No sense in scaring us, son," Emerson said. "It's highly irresponsible to go around spouting things like that."

"Well, people, I've got news for you," Garson said. "Personnel are already getting scared. The union, the staff, I don't know who all! Just before I walked in here, I got a call from the *Daily News*. Some *individual* at the hospital called them and told them we were battling a flu epidemic at Met and that people were dropping like flies. I told him I simply didn't know what he was talking about. Because I simply didn't know what to tell him. Will somebody *please* explain what I'm supposed to do?"

Once again Hart had the instinctive impulse to do the sensible thing—escape. But when he thought it through, he knew he did not want to abandon the city; this dirty, many-tongued, deranged place was his home, his island. He also saw that he really did not care what the final outcome was to be: it was the problem and its unraveling that interested him so, the hunt for the killer, the trial, the execution. He knew he would remain as long as the mystery lived. If he abandoned the city, he would be abandoning his curiosity. Probably that was what kept him alive, in fact. He knew he would stay—with himself, with the city, with these people. That knowledge made him happy in a way that he had never been happy before. It made him indifferent to whatever was going to happen next.

And he knew something was about to happen, because a nurse fetched Andrews from the room.

"Well?" Garson frowned at Hart.

"I think . . . I think we should make sure everyone in the hospital gets enough tetracycline to knock out trouble right off the bat. All the potential exposures have gotten it already. We should alert police and ambulance drivers throughout the city to be on the lookout for suspicious illnesses and deaths. We should get all emergency rooms to report any cases with these symptoms. And just give the media a calm, very simple statement. Tell them: 'Some personnel at Metropolitan have been exposed to an unusual bacterial ailment that is being treated.' "

"We can't trust the press," Garson said. "Remember how they handled the hospital-workers' strike? We can't tell the press *one single thing*. We can't make waves."

Garson's assistants and Emerson nodded vigorously.

"Mr. Kaprow here might have some useful suggestions about epidemics and the media," Calabrese said. "Irving, what does the Mayor's Task Force for Emergency Preparedness advise in this situation?"

The small young man cleared his throat and snapped open his attaché case. "This is what the Task Force is all about, Dr. Calabrese." He lifted out a stack of bound documents and sorted through them. "Ah, here. Gentlemen and uh—" He nodded toward Jefferson, who screwed up her mouth. "If I may quote from our report on preliminary hazard analysis?"

"Please do, Irving," Calabrese said.

"First, some background on New York City." He began to read. " 'New York City, located on the eastern coast of the United States, is 320 square miles in area. It is a highly organized area comprised of five boroughs: Manhattan, Bronx, Brooklyn, Queens, and Staten Island. The most unique geographic factor is its easy access by water which makes New York City one of the largest and busiest seaports in the world. Some of the major waterways in and around the city include the Atlantic Ocean, the Harlem, Hudson, and East Rivers, Upper and Lower New York Bay, Arthur Kill, Raritan Bay, and Long Island Sound. New York City is the most densely populated city in the United States. The latest Census has identified 7,867,760 residents, and this does not include an estimated one and a half million illegal aliens. Population breakdown for the five boroughs is as follows: Manhattan, 1,524,541; Bronx, 1,472,216—' "

"Irving—" Calabrese began.

Hart looked at his watch. Sam Andrews had been gone five minutes.

"Well, I guess I can skip those statistics. You get the idea. Just remember that most of the population is heavily concentrated in high-rise and multifamily dwellings."

"No shit," muttered Jefferson.

" 'During planning stages for the Task Force's effort,' " Kaprow continued reading, " 'the staff considered a wide range of potential disaster situations which could confront the City. Because of its high concentration of people, bustling port and waterways, many miles of subterranean subway and overland rail systems, and complex of industrial activities, *New York's potential for major disasters is high*. Combined subjective judgments were made on a variety of emergency situations which could tax city resources to the extent that a) many lives would be endangered or lost, and b) significant loss of property would occur. It appears that an Emergency Operations Plan for New York City should, as a minimum, consider the following hazards—' I won't read the details of these, I'll just summarize: 'A. Tornadoes. B. Hurricanes. C. Earthquakes (there is an extensive subterranean fault cutting into Manhattan at Fourteenth Street, slanting northwest to the Hudson River at 86th Street). D. Floods. E. Blizzards. F. Fires. G. Air accidents. H. Highway tie-ups. (A major problem exists as a result of the ease with which major highways can be completely blocked, thus affecting the ability of emergency vehicles to reach disaster sites. This situation is compounded by the total lack of helicopter evacuation capabilities in New York City.) I. Bridge collapses. . . .' "

As Kaprow read on in a monotone, Hart glanced around and saw that almost everyone was lulled by the recital and preferred to listen to bureaucratic prose rather than to struggle with the problem at hand. Except for Jefferson, who was taking a catnap. But wait until he gets to the part about epidemics, Hart thought. They'll be jolted out of their chairs.

" '. . . There are four major motor-vehicle tunnels in New York City. They are the Queens-Midtown, Brooklyn-Battery, Holland, and Lincoln Tunnels, Statistics indicate these facilities handle in excess of 87 million vehicles per year. M. Power failure. . . .' "

Rhoda Sue was dancing in a discotheque with a man who was very drunk. He was a hardware salesman from Pittsburgh, and he had five children, a wife, a house trimmed with aluminum siding, a station wagon, and no one who loved him. Rhoda Sue, with her darting pink tongue, her half-open mouth, and her big, bouncing breasts, held the promise of something between sin and love, something he had never experienced before but had dreamed of quite often. Watching her glisten and writhe under the flashing colored lights, he knew that she was going to give him an experience far more exotic and potent than anything he had ever imagined.

Kaprow kept on reading. The people around the table begun to shift in their chairs. Hart hoped that this background information was building toward some kind of usable solution the Emergency Preparedness Task Force had worked out. He knew that in any case, no one who wanted to survive in the bureaucracy would dream of interrupting an official from the Mayor's office. As he half-listened, he again wondered why Andrews was taking so long and why Dolores had disappeared.

" '. . . Water resources. New York City consumes an average of 1600 million gallons of water per day. It flows from upstate watersheds through City Tunnels One and Two and the New Croton Aqueduct. All of these structures are fifty years old or more. Water

Tunnel Number Three has been dug through bedrock five hundred feet underground, is 20 feet in diameter, and extends from Westchester down into Central Park and from the reservoir there to Ridgewood Reservoir in the Salem Field Cemetery in Queens. It would alleviate the strain on the older structures if funds were ever budgeted for its completion. At present, construction has been halted on Number Three, and the collapse or malfunction of any one of the old conduits would precipitate a water crisis of major proportions. Even a temporary drop in pressure—which could occur if a power failure hit the pumping stations—would be extremely dangerous, creating a serious health emergency as sewage backed into the supply system. P. Air pollution. Q. Explosions of volatile substances produced, stored, and distributed throughout the City consitute a hazard. R. Civil disturbances. New York City experiences daily mass protests in response to its fiscal crisis, decisions of the United Nations, and many other current issues. Unless the conditions and social climate which cause civil disturbances are eliminated, it is the opinion of this Task Force that comprehensive plans be prepared to meet the exigencies of civil disturbances of disastrous proportions. S. Strikes. T. Terrorism. There are a multitude of terrorist acts which could seriously affect the City: a) damage or destruction of utility installations, both power and communication; b) sabotage of national headquarters of major industries located in the city; c) blockage or attacks on bridges, tunnels, and roads which could effectively cripple traffic throughout the city; d) bombings and sniper attacks using munitions stolen from armories in the city.' "

Kaprow looked up and took a deep breath. "Last of all, 'U. Default. The consensus among governmental and financial authorities is that default is likely to be felt nationally as well as worldwide. The effects of a default on the City are likely to be catastrophic, with widespread disruption in vital municipal services, and possible severe civil disorder.' "

There was a long silence.

Finally Hart spoke. "What about epidemics? Did the Task Force examine the effects of an outbreak of a highly contagious disease on the city?"

Kaprow shook his head. "That was deemed beyond the scope of the Mayor's Task Force for Emergency Preparedness."

"But what about the press?" Garson asked. "Does your study say how we handle the media?" Garson pouted like a man who had been cheated.

Kaprow sorted through the piles of paper on the table. "Yes . . . Here. 'Information: Plan, supervise, coordinate, and disseminate all official announcements about the emergency. Instruct public on lifesaving measures. Provide emergency telephone service. Coordinate with all media.' "

"Irving, is that all?" asked Calabrese.

"Yes, Dr. Calabrese. And I am pleased to add that we received a letter from the Director of the Defense Civil Preparedness Agency in Washington commending us on the study. The DCPA also gave us a quarter-million dollars to do this study. We're very proud of it."

"Coordinate with all media?" Garson asked one of his assistants. "What does *that* mean?"

Sam Andrews returned and sat down next to Hart. His face was drained and his freckles stood out like spatters of brown paint. Hart gave him a questioning look. Andrews nodded like a frightened child.

"Excuse me," Hart said.

"How are we supposed to 'coordinate with the media' when all they do is shaft us?" Garson wanted to know.

"Excuse me," Hart said, this time a little louder.

"I am in a difficult position. You all can appreciate that," Garson went on. "I have my responsibilities, and I am responsible for keeping track of what lies within my scope of responsibilities and what does not, and I feel that Mr. Kaprow's report here—"

"Mr. Garson," Calabrese interrupted. "Mr. Garson, please let Dr. Hart speak."

There was a slow moment in which voices stopped and eyes again turned toward Hart. "Dr., uh, Dr. Andrews has just spoken to the Director of the Special Pathogens Laboratory at the Center for Disease Control. The specimens—the specimens from the dead girl that we sent them earlier today have been given the Fluorescent Antibody test and the result—the result, the result is positive. We—"

"We have *Yersinia pestis* in New York City!" Andrews burst out.

"Your-sin-ee-ahh? *Now* what are you talking about?" Garson asked.

"The plague," said Hart softly. "We have the plague in New York City."

17

THE NIGHT was hot in the streets and even hotter in the small basement apartment.

"Your son is very sick," Rodriguez told the old woman in Spanish. "He must go to the hospital."

The woman pursed her mouth and shook her head. She looked at the man stretched out on the bare mattress on the floor. He wore only a pair of trousers. He was breathing very rapidly and his chest gleamed with sweat. His chin was smeared with dried blood. Two small children in diapers played on the dirty, cracked linoleum floor nearby. Three men and two women sat on a sagging sofa drinking beer and watching television. From time to time they glanced over at the pretty young woman in the red-and-beige uniform.

"You must keep the babies away from him or they'll get sick, too. And all of you have to have medicine." Rodriguez opened a black bag she was carrying and brought out a hypodermic.

The old woman went into the kitchen and stood by the stove. It was encrusted with stains and crawling with roaches. "Adelaido, come in here!" she called over the noise of the television. One of the men got up and went into the kitchen.

Rodriguez gave the man on the mattress an injection and then spoke quietly to the children.

"He can't go to the hospital," Adelaido finally told Rodriguez.

"If he stays here, he'll die," Rodriguez said.

The old woman began to cry.

"Mama, mama!" Adelaido said.

"Leave," one of the men on the couch told Rodriguez.

"You don't understand." She filled another hypodermic and lifted one of the babies onto her lap. "Domingo here has a very dangerous disease and you're all going to get it if you don't let me help you. You all have to get medicine or you will get very, very sick and die."

Adelaido suddenly had a knife in his hand. "The police told you to say that, didn't they?"

"Adelaido, what are you doing? You crazy!" One of the women on the sofa came over and grabbed for the knife. Adelaido pushed her away.

Rodriguez finished giving the baby an injection and the child began to howl. She handed him to the old woman and prepared another hypodermic for the next shot.

"You listen to me, woman!" shouted Adelaido. "You get out of here, or I'll cut you!"

Rodriguez gave the other child an injection and

then stood up. "Okay, I'll leave." She fixed him with a furious stare. "But when you cry on the grave of your poor dead mother here, you will remember this moment!"

"Adelaido, put down the knife," the old woman said. "Don't be crazy."

The two men on the sofa got up and stood next to Rodriguez. "Don't worry about my brother," said one of them, a man in a green mesh undershirt. "Just leave."

"Sure I will," she answered. *"I'm* happy, *I'm* healthy. You're the ones who are going to be really sick, not me. Just remember *that* at your mother's funeral."

"Don't talk about my mother!" yelled Adelaido. "Let's take her outside," he said to his brothers.

"Police! Open up!" There was a rattling at the iron gate that barred the entranceway.

Everyone in the room froze.

"Listen," Rodriguez whispered to the old woman. "I know Domingo is here illegally. And I know that you're Cuban. Nobody has to know that but me. You all must come to the hospital. You won't be sent to jail or deported. I promise!"

"You promise?" The old woman was crying.

"I swear on the soul of my mother in heaven I won't tell," Rodriguez said.

One of the women opened the door and Maldonado and Lonergan came in, followed by Hart.

"We've got an ambulance outside," Hart said to Rodriguez. "I came as soon as I got your message." He pointed to the man on the floor. "Is this Domingo Ortiz?"

Rodriguez nodded. She looked very relieved to see Hart. "He's in bad shape. I gave him strep, but it may be too late."

Hart looked around the room. It was like dozens of others he had seen when he had made rounds as an interne. There were the brightly painted plaster statues of saints on the television set, faded photographs of grandparents with Indian faces; and a picture of John F. Kennedy. The floor was strewn with broken toys and bits of food. In the hallway was a row of paper bags stuffed with garbage.

"Dolores, how did you find him?" Hart asked, stepping into the hallway to let the stretcher attendants in.

"This is the same place the cops came earlier. You know how Maldonado had a hunch something funny was going on? Well, my cousin runs a bodega on 106th Street. He knows everybody around here, and he knows all their business because they all charge at his store, and everybody comes in every day. I just asked him what the real story on the people in this building was, then I left the message for you at the hospital and came over."

Attracted by the sirens, neighbors began crowding into the apartment. They shouted as the stretcher attendants carried Domingo Ortiz out to the ambulance. He looked around, uncomprehending. His eyes had the dry luster of fever.

"They wouldn't let me in," Rodriguez said. "But then I heard him coughing and just pushed inside."

"Oh, shit!" Hart muttered. He pointed to the quick shadow of a rat.

"Oh, no!" Rodriguez said.

The cops started shooing people out of the apartment.

"Cordon off the whole place," Hart told Maldonado. "Don't let anyone in this apartment. Dolores, make sure all of the Ortizes are taken to Metropolitan, examined, and medicated. See that everyone in the building gets tetracycline. The police, too. You make damned sure you take some yourself." He grabbed her wrists and squeezed them hard. "I'll see you back at the hospital."

He pushed through the knot of onlookers around the

basement entrance, waded through the garbage, and jumped into the back of the ambulance.

As the sirens started up and the ambulance sped toward Metropolitan, Hart turned on the overhead light and examined Ortiz. "Ortiz, Ortiz, listen to me!" The man had blotches on his chest and belly. "Ortiz! We're going to make you feel better. Do you remember the girl who got sick, and you called the ambulance? Remember?"

The man rolled his head slowly back and forth on the stretcher. Bloody foam dribbled from his lips.

"Diga me, diga me! Muy importante que hablamos!" Hart yelled. Then he calmed down. "It is very important that we learn who you have been with," he continued in broken Spanish. "Do you remember the sick girl at the building where you work? Were you sick before you called the ambulance? When did you start getting sick?"

"Madre de Dios," Ortiz murmured.

"Ortiz!" In exasperation, Hart picked up the man's arm to shake him conscious and then dropped it. Near Domingo Ortiz's wrist was a rash of red, raised marks identical to those Hart had seen on the body of Sarah Dobbs.

18

As HART waited with Ortiz and a stretcher attendant for an elevator to take them to MICU, he saw a notice posted above the elevator buttons.

On Sunday, September 3, a patient was admitted to Metropolitan Hospital with a diagnosis of pneumonia. At present the organism that caused the pneumonia and the death of the patient is unknown. However, it appears to be highly infectious. The Department of Health, in conjunction with the administration of Metropolitan Hospital, has identified all the people who may have been in close contact with the patient. However, because of the possibility that a few Metropolitan Hospital personnel may have been omitted from this listing, a decision has been made to offer antibiotic treatment to all workers. The antibiotic treatment will consist of tetracycline, one gram four times a day for two days. Tetracycline should be picked up at the pharmacy on the first floor. Any hospital employee, after giving his or her name, can pick up an appropriate dosage.

Hospital personnel SHOULD NOT DEPLETE WARD STOCKS OF TETRACYCLINE, since a roster must be kept of all people receiving dosages. If all personnel take this antibiotic, there is no need for concern about coming down with the disease or spreading it to your families.

If you develop a fever of over 99° (oral) a clinic has been set up on the fifteenth floor to evaluate you.

> Mr. Arthur Garson
> Executive Director
> Whitney Emerson, M.D., M.P.H.
> Director, Preventive Medicine

The same bulletin was repeated in Spanish.

Two aides going off duty paused in the corridor to read the notice.

"Humph!" one of the women snorted. " 'No need for concern'? Jessie up on MICU told me that Dr. Lipsky died of that pneumonia just after she came on duty."

"You going to get your tetracycline tomorrow?" asked the other woman.

"I got a whole handbag *full* of it already from Jessie. For me and the kids. I ain't takin' no chances."

"Ortiz won't talk," Hart told Andrews. "He's delirious."

Andrews paced around the small office and drank coffee from a plastic cup. "Jesus, this is a mess. I combed through the Dobbs apartment with a couple of police detectives. We didn't turn up the slightest clue about where the girl had been. Rich people seem to do a good job of keeping everything about their lives hidden."

"That's because there are usually servants around all the time," Hart said, thinking of his parents' household.

"Well, the fact that there's no passport for her means she hasn't been out of the U.S. And we do have the film from the camera that was in the backpack, and as soon as that's developed we might have more to go on. I contacted Interpol and told them to find her folks in Europe." Andrews fidgeted with his beard. "I wonder . . . Do you think bubonic has been endemic up in Spanish Harlem for a while, and that Ortiz just got bitten by an infected flea and then gave it to the Dobbs girl?"

Hart looked out the window; the sky was getting light. He shook his head. "I don't think Ortiz was bubonic. I couldn't feel any buboes when I palpated. It's primary pneumonia, but if the marks on his legs are fresh flea bites, then he's been bitten since he got sick —they had him on a mattress on the floor—and the fleas have probably gone on to other hosts. If the fleas are the right kind, then their next hosts will get bubonic. The Dobbs girl had bubonic *and* pneumonic. I think she passed pneumonic on to Ortiz, not the other way around."

Rodriguez appeared. She was tired; her guarded look had softened. "I got a list of all the Ortiz family's contacts," she said. "Ten people live in that apartment.

Most of them just hang around the neighborhood. Domingo and his brother Adelaido are the only ones with jobs. That cop was right about them not being from Puerto Rico. They're from Cuba. They got out just after Castro took over. Except for Domingo. He escaped only about two months ago on a freighter. He hopped islands and finally made it to San Juan. He got into the U.S. with forged papers and a borrowed Green Card. But please don't put that in any reports! I *swore* I wouldn't tell the authorities about him."

"No reason to," Hart said. "The disease might be endemic in Cuba, but there's no way he'd be sick now if he was exposed to it two months ago. I'm certain that the Dobbs girl infected him."

"Well, the real problem is his crazy brother, Adelaido. He didn't look so good, so I sent him up to the Contagion Ward. He's a busboy at the Waldorf Astoria."

"Just what we needed," Andrews said. He slumped into a folding chair. "Someone with pneumonic plague to cough on all the petits fours. By the way, the CDC boys have invited themselves up. They'll be here on the first morning flight from Atlanta."

"Good," Hart said. "They can come to the meeting the Commissioner is having at ten. There's nothing else we can do now. We'd better grab some sleep while we have the chance."

"I don't know if I can," Andrews said, leaving. "This is pretty near the biggest thing that's ever happened to me." He looked pale and solemn. "Except," he added, "the time the Braves almost won the pennant."

After Andrews left, Rodriguez lingered, her expression full of emotion, but just what emotion Hart could not interpret.

"You'd better run along home," he said.

"You, too."

"Well, I thought I'd stay here in case Ortiz came around. I need to talk to him."

"He's not going to come around."

Hart nodded.

She came close to him and tilted her face up to his. "What about us, are we going to get it?"

"Did you take some tetracycline?" She was so small!

"I will," she said. "But I mean—a lot of people could get this, right? It's very contagious, right? Like, my family. We live right on Madison at 106th Street. Are my parents and my little brother going to be okay? Does tetracycline really work for this?"

He wondered why she was playing dumb; she usually had the right answers. "Sure, of course. You know as much as I do."

"Well, it means a lot to me, because lots of my relatives—they live right around that neighborhood."

He did not know what to say. He put his arms around her and gave her a brisk squeeze, a professional, bedside-manner hug.

Something came alive in both of them at that moment; she leaned against his chest. Hart felt a spinning inside his head. She was so soft; he had not held a woman since . . .

He cleared his throat and stepped back. "Well, kiddo, see you down at the department at nine o'clock!"

She did not move. "Hey," she said. She was looking steadily into his eyes. She suddenly patted his fly and then vanished.

19

As THE limousine joined the great inward pump-stroke of the Washington morning rush hour, General Daniel Cosgrove, the President's National Security Advisor, listened intently to the tiny female voice nestled in his ear. "The President wants to reschedule this afternoon's briefing for 1445 . . . Mr. Marks's office has confirmed your lunch with him today at the Sans Souci . . . Colonel Watkins has obtained the Class B files you requested from the Defense Intelligence Agency . . ." Cosgrove was glad to be back in his daily routine. He hated to travel, and he especially hated to travel with the President, and worst of all he hated to accompany Mr. Decency to New York. Fortunately the trips were infrequent, and fortunately they were brief; most of this one had been spent in Chicago and Atlanta. Now that he was back in his own limo, with its soft leather seat and its blue interior, enveloped in the familiar milky odor of the air-conditioning, he once again felt comfortable and organized.

He checked his watch. He might be as many as eight minutes late today. As few as three. Worst case— eight. No, make it ten. He would operate on the assumption that he would not get to his office until 0910. He could dock ten minutes from his lunch with Marks so that he didn't get behind; in fact, if *he* determined the length of the lunch rather than Marks, it would be a subtle indication to the man about which of the two was in command. Marks, the Director of the Central Intelligence Agency, required greater vigilance than anyone else in the entire government.

Cosgrove had no trouble getting the President to evaluate developments within the proper parameters, but Marks was dangerously independent in his thinking, and, like all spooks, hopelessly secretive. More secretive, probably, than Cosgrove himself.

As he listened to the tape that his secretary sent to his house every morning in order to prepare him for the events of the day, he flipped casually through *The New York Times*. He hated the *Times* for its snobbish, liberal, complaining tone, its endless petitions for federal aid for the city, and most of all, for its occasional needle jabs at Cosgrove himself.

SANITATION WORKERS' STRIKE CONTINUES. Good Christ, what a nasty city New York was! The stinking wall of black garbage bags had been piled up into the side exit of the Waldorf, the very exit the President had been forced to use in order to foil the usual sniper threats. New York City was worse than the entire State of California when it came to terrorist groups. The Puerto Rican Liberation Front, for instance. Marks might have some useful intelligence on them—if he deigned to share it. On the affirmative side, the sniper threats always had the effect of persuading the President to limit his visits to New York to once or twice a year.

As Miss Milam's voice crooned on, he sighed. So much to watch for, so much to take care of, so much to anticipate. His mind always worked very fast, faster than anyone else's; he saw what was coming before anyone else did. And in the end, everyone relied on him. Even that Marks bastard. He was still an ungrateful son-of-a-bitch, but he would wind up calling Cosgrove two or three times a day, just as his predecessor had. Everyone in the administration eventually came to him. He made sure of it. The Pentagon, the Justice Department. In fact, the whole goddamned government, the parts of it that worked, counted on him. Why did he do it?

The answer was too close to being religious to share with anybody. Although he had personal ambitions, they were harnessed to a larger drive, which was to shape the events of the United States as a historical entity. His duty was to keep the nation front and center in the eyes of the world through the centuries to come. This mission had sustained him through the worst days of Watergate, the Senate investigations, those goddamned Army intelligence hearings. The image had made it possible for him to stomach the necessary arrangements with the Mafia and the Hughes organization, the obscure liaisons between the CIA, the Defense Department, and the White House. The mission justified tolerating gangsters, Cubans, doubledealers, and weak sisters. In order to carry out his life's work, he had, from the earliest days of his career, aligned himself with the permanent government.

Even back at West Point he had kept his nose clean and his ass covered, and although he had left there on the military track, his reputation soon reached the civilian establishment and he switched to the intellectual track: special graduate work at Princeton, attentive grooming by the Deputy Secretary of Defense. Then the phone calls from Haig, Kissinger, and Scowcroft started coming in. That was when he began to see that while administrations came and went, and presidents were elected, reelected, shot, or hustled out of office, the tacit, invisible center of power in the nation seldom shifted. He cultivated a military, good-ol'-boy delivery to mollify rival officers, who stood ready to do him in, and he devoted most of his energy to finding out all he could about everything and everybody in Washington. He did liaison work between the Army and the CIA; he became the eyes and ears of the Secretary of State. He planned covert actions that were carried out in

Cuba, Vietnam, Latin America, Africa, and the United States. While cabinet members and presidents passed through, Cosgrove had consolidated his power, and now, as the electronically operated wrought-iron gates of the White House swung open and the guard saluted, he reflected on the fact that he probably felt more at home here than the current tenant.

Carpenters from the General Services Administration were busy knocking new oak paneling into place in Miss Milam's office.

"How *yew?*" Miss Milam shouted over the din, patting her pearl-blonde bouffant coiffure. "So glad y'all are back. How was your trip?"

"Terrible."

"I see where they're still havin' that garbage strike in New York."

"Yes. It was pretty disgusting. Did the decorator finish up my office?" He was always expanding his office; he never seemed to have enough room.

"Oh, yes, General! You won't believe how fabulous it looks. Much better than the last time around."

Cosgrove went into his office and closed the door. The decorator had done a fair job. Everything looked exactly the same, except that the office was now five feet longer and three feet wider. The green paint was a shade darker, perhaps, but the woodwork was still ivory white.

He sat down at the long, brilliantly polished desk. There was an ashtray with the presidential seal beside the intercom, a pen set, a picture of his mother in a gold oval frame, and a picture of his wife, taken in 1964, her last sober year. He picked up a little piece of white thread, probably left there by the maid's dust-cloth, and put it in his pocket.

Miss Milam brought in several folders. "The top one has a memo that was just sent over from the Surgeon General's office, General," she said.

Cosgrove took the folders and glanced at the memo from Christine Shore Lewis, the Surgeon General. It reported an outbreak of plague in New York City. Two deaths. "The Center for Disease Control informs me that the source of the contagion is still being investigated. Meanwhile, I thought I should alert you to the potential gravity of the situation," the memo concluded.

He reread the memo. As National Security Advisor, he was accustomed to receiving reports from the various Departments regarding exceptional occurrences. But this memo touched on a preoccupation that had disturbed him for nearly two decades, and he felt as though he had just been punched in the stomach.

He stabbed the intercom button. "Miss Milam! Where's my coffee? Good Christ, this place falls apart when I'm gone for a couple of days!"

20

HART SAT in his sunny corner office. With amusement he looked around at its dingy baseboards, dirty linoleum, spattered windows, and the hole in the wall where the air conditioner had been removed and never replaced. He had kept watch on the contagion ward all night, and he now wondered whether the loss of sleep had done something to his brain. He suddenly loved this stupid place. He fished some scraps of paper out of the pockets of his wrinkled suit jacket—at some point, he told himself, he had to go home and shower, shave, and change clothes—and spread them out on the scratched surface of his desk. Each piece of paper had some fact or number or name on it, and now he had to assemble all these items into a story to tell his staff and the Commissioner's emergency meeting. He began typing.

Around nine, the "Blackhawks," Hart's nickname for the nurse epidemiologists, began coming into the map-lined room outside his office. Their crisp burgundy-and-beige uniforms made them resemble airline hostesses on some exotic flight. They ate doughnuts and studied the maps of the five boroughs. There were maps with hepatitis cases plotted by month; tuberculosis cases; measles and rubella; food poisoning; syphilis. Each map was studded with pins—a different color for each disease—to mark the location of each case. On this particular morning in early September, the maps were alive with color. The yellow pins on the hepatitis map clumped together in the West Village, where homosexuals transmitted the disease, and in the northern sections of Staten Island, where junkies passed it around on dirty needles, and in the Williamsburg section of Brooklyn, where a kosher butcher had managed to infect his Hasidic clientele. TB and syphilis chose other neighborhood groupings, as did measles and rubella. The nurse epidemiologists, who seldom gathered at the central office of the Bureau, also looked at wall charts showing pneumonia deaths, gonorrhea cases, and salmonella outbreaks, and they leafed through medical journals and newsletters from health departments in other cities. But mostly they traded gossip and speculated aloud about why they had been summoned.

Rodriguez came in and sat down in a corner, her back to Hart's questioning gaze. His heart sank: he had lost her. She had taken a risk and he hadn't followed it up; she would never come that close again, he was certain.

"How was your night, Dave?" Andrews asked, coming into Hart's office.

"What made you think that last night was different from all others?" Hart replied.

Andrews did not pick up on the old joke. He sucked his cheeks in and fidgeted. "Any news?"

"Domingo Ortiz died this morning, Bergman, the medical student, is dead, and so is Penrose, an ER nurse," Hart said as they went into the map room.

"If you liked the anthrax scare we had, you'll love this one," Hart told the group. They smiled.

The Blackhawks had never made a mistake. Hart had recruited the team of nurse epidemiologists from the Bureau of Public Health Nursing early in the Seventies to replace physicians who had done epidemiological work for the Bureau of Preventable Diseases and whom the Health Department could no longer afford. His plan had been opposed by several health officials and by the physicians themselves, but he had persisted. Out of four hundred candidates he picked the ten women with the best academic records and the most experience. Because they were swift, intelligent, and almost all dark-skinned or Oriental, he had nicknamed them "the Blackhawks," after some comic-book heroes he had always admired. But the women objected to the label, which they thought was undignified, and so it was used only when they were not around. Because most of the women had grown up in the poorest and roughest neighborhoods in the city, they moved with ease through the worst streets in the boroughs. The ghetto communities knew these women were there to help. They were treated with respect and trust wherever they went. Street-hardened, knife-scarred toughs often escorted them on their rounds among junkies sick with hepatitis, gonorrhea-ridden prostitutes, syphilitic drag queens, and tuberculous alcoholics. They were never hassled or mugged.

From the start, the Blackhawks investigated cases and outbreaks with a thoroughness that surprised and angered the few part-time physicians who had not yet retired from the Bureau. The nurse epidemiologists' reports were much more complete and accurate than those scratched out by tired old men counting the days until their pensions began. And they were faster. Once, two cases of botulism had appeared in the South Bronx. In only six hours, the two Blackhawks assigned to that borough had confirmed the diagnosis, found the contaminated foods, informed the Commissioner of Health, the Food and Drug Administration, and the Center for Disease Control, and had prepared a statement for the media. There were dozens of other instances in which the Blackhawks had saved lives and averted panics: typhoid in the Haitian neighborhood in Brooklyn, encephalitis in Chinatown. There had been a near-riot in the South Bronx when a schoolboy contracted meningitis, and Rodriguez had walked unaccompanied into a schoolyard jammed with angry, frightened parents and managed to calm them down and explain the facts so that they would no longer have to worry. The Blackhawks had become a crack troop of medical detectives.

Even after Hart told the women that the meeting had been called because of an outbreak of plague, some of them remained smiling. They knew that he enjoyed straight-faced jokes, and they assumed that this was a new training exercise that he had dreamed up.

"This for real?" asked Margie Pindere. She was a Jamaican from Queens.

Rodriguez and Jefferson nodded. "For real," Andrews said.

The women stopped smiling. They had had lectures about the plague. The bubonic form did not frighten them. It could be spread only by rats, there was a vaccine for it, and the mortality rate was only thirty percent. But the pneumonic form, which often sprang out of the bubonic form, was another story. They knew that it spread much faster than the worst flu, that there was no vaccine for it, and that it carried a one-hundred-percent mortality rate if not treated early. They also knew how severely the annual influenza epidemics in the city strained the Bureau, and how

19,000 New Yorkers had died in the 1918-19 influenza pandemic. What an epidemic of pneumonic plague would do was almost beyond their imagination. Hart could see worry in their faces.

"You don't have to work on this with us if you don't want to," Hart said. "I want only volunteers. But we need all the help we can get for the next few days to bring this thing under control. I think we've identified almost all the exposures, but we won't know for the next few days. Once this gets to the media, we're going to be swamped by calls. That's where all of you can really help." He read the typed summary aloud and then answered their questions, which were all brief and direct.

"What do we do?" Darleen Jones, from Brooklyn, asked.

"Okay, here's the countdown," Hart replied. "Adelaido Ortiz is a suspicious case. He works as a busboy at the Waldorf. Gayle, you call up the manager and find out when he was last on the job, what Ortiz's functions are, whether he has direct contact with food and people. Don't scare the manager—just tell him the guy has a suspected case of hepatitis.

"We need one nurse in each of the borough offices to wait for instructions. Forget about your routine field assignments. Stay in the office. If and when this gets to the media, you'll be answering the phone continually. We'll have a general information sheet on the situation that you can read to anyone who calls. But, for God's sake, don't mention the word 'plague' to anyone until the official release comes out. We have to be extremely careful about that: we don't want to create a panic. We all have to stay coordinated and to speak with one voice.

"One of you has to go over to the VD Division and get a big bottle of tetracycline. Enough for all of us in case we have to go into the field. Someone else should contact the Tuberculosis Division. We'll need five thousand doses of streptomycin here at the central office, just to be on the safe side. We'll use it if any one of us comes into intimate contact with a case, although I don't think that's very likely."

After the Blackhawks began sorting out their tasks, Hart and Andrews went back into the Director's office. Andrews pulled four green-and-yellow capsules from the pocket of his faded workshirt. "Two for you and two for me," he said.

"Tetracycline." Hart had been too preoccupied to think of giving himself the medication he had warned everyone else to take.

"Yup. From Metropolitan. Got them last night. You better take two right now—don't wait for the bottle from VD."

"Give them to Dolores. She probably took some last night after she was exposed to Ortiz, but she should keep up the dosage. Do you have any more?"

Andrews pulled out a handful of capsules. "Plenty."

Hart washed two of the pills down with some lukewarm coffee. "Remind me when six hours are up to take some more," he said, but Andrews did not hear him. He was in the map room giving the capsules to Rodriguez.

"Dave, two blue-haired women meet in the lobby of the Fontainebleau in Miami." It was Alan Katz, the Director of the Bureau of Pest Control and Animal Affairs for the City of New York. He was a short, broad-shouldered man with a nimbus of black curls. He wore a sports shirt open at the collar. His gaze was calm, and he had a way of standing with his chest and head a little forward so that he conveyed an impression of rootedness: no one would ever take him by surprise. Hart thought Katz's stance was probably the result of his having grown up in the most violent section of the South Bronx, in the precinct the police had named "Fort Apache." By joining a street gang known and feared all over the city, Katz, a Jew, had managed to survive in a neighborhood crowded with poor blacks, Puerto Ricans, Jamaicans, Haitians, and Dominicans. He had worked his way up to being leader of the gang while he was still in high school at Bronx Science. Even after he had earned his doctorate in zoology from City University, he had stayed in touch with his street brothers, and in fact had hired a few of them for his Bureau. "The women haven't seen each other in ages," he went on. "The first one says, 'Ida, how ya been, darlink?' The other woman says, 'Well, I got *tsuris* and I got *naches.* I just found out my son's a homosexual!' The first woman says, 'Ah, Ida, now that's *tsuris!* So what's *naches?*' The other woman said, '*Naches* is, he's engaged to a docteh!' I heard today you got *tsuris,* Davie."

"Who told you?"

"Calabrese. Man, I can't believe you got *plague.*" He whistled and pulled up a chair.

"Would you like to tell me everything you know about rats, Alan?"

"Frankly, no. You probably know as much as I do. These days I'm dealing with dogs, Dave. Dogs and their droppings. I just humbly try to cope with the two hundred thousand pounds of dogshit deposited on the streets every day. Ratshit is not a problem, ergo I know very little." He smiled and folded his arms across his chest. "Ratshit is ratshit but dogshit is my bread and butter."

"Wonderful," Hart said. "Just tell me what you learned in grad school about rats."

"You want good news or bad news?"

"Good news first, always."

"New York City rats are the wrong rats for transmitting the plague effectively. Our rat is the Norway rat—*Rattus norvegicus*—also known as the brown rat, although it can sometimes be gray. Norway rats invaded Europe in the 1700s, supposedly after an earthquake had driven them westward from around the Caspian Sea. Who knows? Anyway, there was a huge build-up in the Norway rat population, and in 1727 they swam across the Volga in search of food and set up housekeeping in Russia and Europe. They drove out the rats already in residence there—*Rattus rattus rattus,* a.k.a. the roof rat, a.k.a. the black rat—a very cute little guy with silky fur who lived cheek-by-jowl with humans. *Rattus rattus,* as we can call him for short, harbors *Xenopsylla cheopis,* also known as the oriental rat flea, which is the most effective carrier of the plague bacillus."

"Isn't that why plague died out in Europe in the eighteenth century?" Hart said. "When the Norway rats drove out the black rats?"

"Yeah, that's possible," Katz said. "But I got news for you. The black rats have been staging a comeback in Europe for some time. The predominant rat in London is now the black rat. But anyway. The Norway rat is still number one in New York—I guess they came over on the Mayflower with your people. And the Norway rat's favorite flea is *Nosopsyllus fasciatus,* which doesn't harbor plague too efficiently."

"There were rats all over the apartment where we picked up the guy with pneumonic plague," Hart said. "He was on a mattress on the floor, and it looked to me like he had flea bites on his arms."

"Okay. If you assume the worst, that fleas bit the sick guy, then hopped on a rat and bit the rat and infected it, then you got some problems. In a few days the rat will die of the plague and the starving rat flea will leave the body of his natural host and probably jump on another rat. Or a human, if one happens to be convenient."

"The human gets bubonic, which gets into the bloodstream and then becomes pneumonic," Hart said.

"And you got a tight little cycle going," Katz said. "But you should remember that we don't have many oriental rat fleas here—maybe two percent of the flea population of New York is oriental rat flea, the kind that spread plague in the Middle Ages. Our kind,

Nosopsyllus fasciatus, can also spread it—but not as well. The rest of my good news is that city rats travel only fifty feet in any direction from their nests. They're not nomads—they have a very small territoriality."

Hart thought about the Ortiz apartment. He had seen rats out in the open, in the hallway among the sacks of garbage. That meant there had to be rats behind the walls, under the floors, in the cellar . . .

"And now for the bad news," Katz went on. "Rats have killed more people in the world than all the wars and revolutions put together, and they're very hard to get rid of. Despite their limited territoriality, they have intercourse, so to speak, with other colonies. One colony almost always touches another, and so on. There are about seven point eight million rats in New York City—about one for every person. The sewers are the rats' rapid-transit system. That's where they pass along their diseases and their ectoparasites and generally get together and jam."

"Shit."

"Yeah. Under ideal circumstances, the rats could transmit the plague in Manhattan very quickly." Katz seemed unperturbed by this fact.

"What's ideal?"

"I'm sorry you asked. Hot, humid weather, close crowding, people living in basements and cellars, a good food source for the rats—"

"Like a garbage strike?" Hart asked.

"Like a garbage strike."

"So what do we do, Alan?"

"I'll dust a twenty- or thirty-block area around the Ortiz tenement with a safe insecticide. And then I'll go capture some rats and examine them for plague, comb them for fleas, examine their fleas. Just to be sure. Even if I don't find anything, I'll go back the next day after the fleas are all dead and come in with a quick-kill rodenticide. You don't kill the rats until you're sure the fleas are all dead."

"Sounds good," Hart said. "Except we have to remember that if this hits the papers—and sooner or later it will—then people are going to automatically get excited about rats, especially up in Harlem, where people see them all the time. There's going to be a lot of pressure to kill the rats immediately."

"Big mistake, big mistake!" Katz exclaimed. "If the rats are given a quick-kill, they'll all come pouring out of their nests and die all over the place, and their fleas will leave them and seek out human hosts. Not only will people get plague if the fleas are carrying *that,* they'll get rat bites from the dying rats. There'll be more ratshit around than usual if they come up out of their holes, and you know what happens when ratshit and urine get on food."

"Leptospirosis."

"You have to explain to everyone that under no circumstances can the rats be killed until we've killed their fleas with DDT."

"Okay," Hart said. "You're the boss in the rat department."

"Okey-doke. One other thing, Dave, when you get this thing licked."

"Yeah?"

"Then I wish to hell you'd help me out on my problem."

"Your problem?"

"Yeah, Calabrese said it's top priority. Dogshit in the Mayor's wife's garden."

As Hart gathered up the notes and papers he would need in the Commissioner's meeting, the phone rang. Hart's secretary buzzed him. "There is a gentleman who wants to talk to you. He won't tell me who he is."

"Tell him to leave a message and I'll get back to him."

"He refuses to talk to anyone but you. He says he's from the government."

"Tell him to drop dead. I'm on my way to a meeting with the Commissioner."

Hart started out the door.

"He says he'll come over."

"No," Hart said. "If he won't say who he is, I don't have time to bother—now *or* later." He pulled on his suit jacket, tightened the knot of his tie, and hurried to the elevator.

"Wait!" Jefferson shouted, running up behind him. "I just finished talking to the manager at the Waldorf Astoria. He told me Adelaido Ortiz brings in trays and clears tables in the dining room and that he hasn't been there since he was called in for a special banquet job on Monday."

"Did you find out what his contacts were?"

"Well. The manager was pretty upset about the hepatitis story."

"Figures," Hart said, stepping into the elevator.

"Yeah, but, oh boy, was he hopped up," Jefferson said, holding the elevator door so that it wouldn't close. "That banquet the Ortiz guy served at was for the President."

21

RHODA SUE sat up in bed and sniffed. She couldn't remember where she was or why. She had a banging headache. She rubbed her nose.

Next to her slept her escort of the previous evening. Slowly, she began to remember. They were in a room at the Holiday Inn. Flash was dead, her sweetheart was dead, and now she had a purse full of coke and hundred-dollar bills, and she had partied all night for free with her friend the hardware salesman. Except that they hadn't really partied. Just as they were really getting it on, she had cracked an amyl nitrate popper under his nose and he thought he was dying. She had had to give him three Valiums to calm him down. He wouldn't wake up for quite a while.

She got up, wiped the rings of mascara from around her eyes, applied fresh mascara and lipstick, snorted some coke, and got dressed. She went through the man's wallet and removed his credit cards and eighty-six dollars. Even though she was rich now, it didn't hurt to have a little extra. She checked her watch. Ten o'clock. The stores would be open now.

Meetings in the municipal bureaucracy were always about the same. Hart found them boring unless he was called upon to speak. The lifers in the Health Department had been in these meetings for so many years that their appearances blended in with the monotonous landscape of scratched wooden conference tables, gray metal folding chairs, and faded mimeographed documents; their manifestations of personality had been reduced to little facial tics, finger-twiddling, and stentorian breathing. Because even the direst conferences required only half of Hart's attention—everything was repeated at least once and followed up the next day with at least one memorandum—Hart had used the droning hours to study his colleagues. Every one of the bureaucrats there was attached to a bigger bureaucrat, who in turn . . . all the way up to the Commissioner and the Mayor. Then there were the two men who had flown up from the CDC. Andrews sat with them, speaking in a deferential manner. The feds had their own ad-infinitum going, a maze which Andrews hoped to penetrate, headed by the Surgeon General, who ran the U.S. Public Health Service, and who answered to the Secretary of Health, Education and Welfare, who in turn answered to a gentleman who had recently dined at the Waldorf, the President. Who answered to—whom? The American people! Hart suppressed a laugh and took a sip of coffee.

"Let's get this thing started," Calabrese said.

The Commissioner of Health had managed to reach his post, one of the most impressive in the public-health establishment of the country, without suffering the bureaucratic erosion of many of his fellows. His face was alert as he addressed the officials from the Health Department and the representatives from the Center for Disease Control. "We're going to have to work together. Dr. Hart, why don't you tell us what you think should be done?"

As Hart began to speak, he had an eerie feeling of separation from himself. He could hear his own voice as though someone else were talking. That sensation was not new to him; he had noticed it other times when he had been extremely tired. What was new was the view that all this must be happening to someone else, happening to David Hart, Director of the Bureau of Preventable Diseases, whose wife had died, who trudged through the city on sleepless nights and imagined epidemics to help himself fall asleep. He was not that person, it seemed; true, he had done all those things, but very possibly he was someone else. Someone who just breathed and looked and listened, slept, and ate . . . Now, he was supposed to act like someone who could stop an epidemic. Okay, that's how he would act. He took a deep breath.

He went on to give the numbers of those exposed, identified, and already treated. Last of all he told the gathering that the plague had taken five lives. "Jesus Christ!" someone muttered. "Like Forty-eight—maybe worse."

The two MDs from the Center for Disease Control sat back and puffed on identical pipes. They both wore plaid shirts.

"We have to identify and treat all people exposed to the girl," Hart went on. "Our nurse epidemiologists have located most of them. I think if we get some help on this from the Police Department, we can probably locate the rest."

"You'll get it," Calabrese said.

"We also have to treat the known secondary cases and make sure we get all of them. The municipal hospitals, like Metropolitan, should set up special isolation wards."

"Fine," Calabrese said.

"We have to go public on this one, I think," Hart continued. "If we don't, it's bound to leak out anyway. But before we make an announcement, we have to set up facilities in the district health centers to cover people who think they have the disease. There's probably going to be some degree of panic no matter what we do, but if people know that they can get medication, the panic can be greatly reduced. We have to offer them something . . ."

"What about a vaccine?" someone asked.

"We don't have any vaccine. The Army might have a little. During the war in Vietnam, soldiers got plague vaccinations. But we can't really count on any vaccine to work. First of all, it takes at least two weeks to build up some sort of immunity after receiving the vaccine, and secondly, the vaccine is worthless for *pneumonic* plague. Completely worthless. I'm already worried that some local MD is going to pull out his dusty Cecil and Loeb and read that there is a vaccine and raise hell about why we aren't giving it out. We have to be able to tell the public that it's not good for the pneumonic form, but if we do that, it will probably create more anxiety. I'd like to ask Dr. Ilfeld whether the CDC would recommend using the vaccine or not. If not, then we can say that the feds are backing us up. A CDC statement would counteract the instant experts who will be demanding vaccine."

Turner Ilfeld, the epidemiologist from the Center for Disease Control, had tinted eyeglasses, a beard, and a midwestern twang. "Let me say," he began, "that you will have all the cooperation you need from us. We won't do anything or make any announcements without an okay from you. Now, we'll go along with the bit about vaccine. Vaccination is not the way to tackle this. I also would like to say that giving out tetracycline to anyone on demand is also not indicated. The press should inform the public that the Center for Disease Control suggests that only known contacts of the patient or the Metropolitan Hospital personnel receive evaluation for treatment and—"

"Where did you do your training, Dr. Ilfeld?" Calabrese asked.

"Is that relevant?" Ilfeld peered over his glasses at Calabrese.

"Yes, it's relevant," Calabrese replied. "This is not Des Moines or San Antonio. There are a lot more people here and they occasionally think for themselves. We can't control what they think, and even with the cooperation of the press, this thing is going to explode. I think we have to offer something like tetracycline, or, as Dave says, we'll have riots. George, can we set up something in the district health centers?"

George Johnson, the Deputy Commissioner for District Health Services, frowned. "We're down to ten health district centers in the city now. If the reaction is large, people will be lining up all over the place. We'd have to screen people, make sure that the women aren't pregnant, get consent forms so we can't be sued. We'd have to pay overtime for the staff and find some docs—God knows where—to look at all the people who think they have it. And where in the hell are we going to get the tetracycline? We're talking about twelve to twenty caps per person. If only twenty percent of the city's population show up, that's still over two and a half million capsules."

"We could raid the VD clinics for it," Calabrese said.

Johnson shrugged and maintained a dour expression. "Okay, we might have enough, but probably we don't. What happens if people patiently wait their turn and we run out of medication? They'll tear down the district health centers. Why not use the hospitals for this?"

"The hospitals will handle the sick ones, but we're not set up for mass distribution of anything," Jeffrey Strohman said. He was President of the Health and Hospitals Corporation.

"Looks like we use the centers, George," Calabrese said. "We have a slush fund of about $500,000 here in the Department for emergencies like this, and I think the Mayor will find some spare change. He'll *have* to."

Several of the men shook their heads. Strohman laughed without smiling.

"If we stress in the press release that spread of the disease is unlikely and that cases have occurred only in Manhattan," Hart said, "we might be able to cut down on the number of people coming to the health centers in the other boroughs. That would save on tetracycline and we could ship the extra supplies into the Manhattan centers."

"Good idea," Johnson said. He seemed to cheer up.

"Anything else, **Dr.** Hart?" asked the Commissioner.

Hart thought for a moment. Gayle's news that the President might have been exposed seemed too sensational to pass on just yet; anyway, Adelaido Ortiz may not have become infectious until the next day. "We have to find out more about the Dobbs girl's whereabouts before she was admitted to Metropolitan. She might have picked up plague outside the U.S., but since we haven't found a passport for her, we assume she got it here. We're checking anyway with the passport office to learn whether she's ever been abroad. According to Dobbs's firm, the parents are expected back soon—apparently they're traveling in Europe without a fixed itinerary. We have Interpól looking for them. If she got plague from a domestic exposure, then we have to alert health officials in the area where she picked it up. But right now, let's worry about the city."

"She may have picked it up in a foreign country and I wouldn't rule that out," Ilfeld said. "But there are foci in the Southwest, and plague is traveling eastward in the rodent population at the rate of one meridian a year. The CDC is checking right now with the health departments around the country for reports of rodent die-offs. Identifying the source may not help the situation in New York, but it will certainly be important to the other states."

"Of course," Hart said. "But here in New York we've got to stop this thing here before we get any more secondary and tertiary cases. About forty-two hours have passed since the girl died, and to judge from the report of her condition when she was taken to MICU, she was probably contagious for forty-eight hours before her death—give or take twelve hours either way. Anyone she infected became infectious as early as twenty-four to thirty-two hours afterward. So there's been plenty of time for the disease to spread. The number of cases we've already turned up shows how fast it can multiply—"

"But," Ilfeld interrupted, "sooner or later these epidemics do all the damage they can and then just die out. That's what happened with the Black Death: a third or so of the world population survived it, and some never got it, even though they were exposed. But the evidence shows that Hart's 'scare' will stop before it gets started. You simply use the media—put a picture of the Dobbs girl on the six-o'clock news tonight, put her in the papers, and ask for people who have information about her to get in touch with you. You get medication to the exposed people and that wraps it up. It's simple, really."

Rhoda Sue was not feeling well. The new hit of coke did not take her headache away, and she was getting a cough as well. To cheer herself up, she bought a floor-length mink coat at Lord & Taylor and paid an astonished saleswoman with a stack of fifty hundred-dollar bills.

Then, the coat over her arm, she walked up Fifth Avenue. She decided to get a facial and massage at a fashionable salon, but the salon's receptionist took one look at Rhoda Sue, with her red, runny nose, her platinum blonde wig, and her purple hotpants, and shook her head.

"We're all booked up."

"Well, fuck you!" Rhoda Sue shouted in the woman's face.

22

WHILE BRYCE MARKS, the Director of the Central Intelligence Agency, ate his cheese soufflé, Cosgrove watched him and thought about how he could bring the conversation around to the Surgeon General's memo about plague without seeming to give it undue weight.

Marks had straight, thin lips, a narrow, blunt nose, a pointed chin, and small eyes that were hidden by tortoise-shell-rimmed glasses. He had managed to reach late middle age without acquiring a single line or wrinkle along the way. He had the demeanor of a person to whom nothing has ever happened, but Cosgrove knew that this was not the case, and assumed that Marks had probably been very careful to arrange his exterior so that he resembled a vice president in a midwestern public-relations firm. Before taking over the CIA directorship, Marks had been, among other things, a lawyer in the Justice Department, ambassador to Iran, and Secretary of Labor. After the reorganization of the intelligence community, the President had been under considerable pressure to appoint a director whose past was impeccable, or at least inaccessible to Senate investigation. Cosgrove himself had picked out Marks, although he had come to regret his choice. The man was quiet, circumspect, and thoughtful; he went to Episcopal church every Sunday with his wife and daughter; and he spent his free time at home in his basement making salt and pepper shakers and candlesticks on a wood lathe. Cosgrove had discovered that he did not understand Marks at all.

"Say, Bryce, I was just wondering about those sniper threats in New York yesterday." Cosgrove sliced into his well-done steak. "What does the station chief up there say?"

"Routine," Marks said. "Nothing we don't already know about. Just a terminated Cuban asset."

"Can't you control those maniacs?"

"Well. We've got about twenty thousand terminated Cuban assets living in the New York area, and only one hundred ten live Cuban assets working for us."

Thirty thousand terminated assets, you lying bastard, Cosgrove thought. One hundred *fifty* live assets. There was about a thirty-percent chance that Marks had also just been lying about his intelligence on Sheikh Nuri's dealings with the Soviets. Raise it to fifty percent. Christ, if a man is telling you something that's fifty percent off, you sure as hell better figure it's a hundred percent off. Maybe he'd take Marks away from the Agency right now. Put him back into an ambassadorship; those jerks were *supposed* to be able to lie well. "Well, it's of no real importance, I suppose." Cosgrove shrugged.

Marks nodded.

Marks would love to put it to me, Cosgrove thought. He knows I want to get rid of him, and if there's one person in the world in a position to do me genuine harm, it's the Director of the CIA. The trick here would be to keep Marks viable until it could be determined down to the finest detail why he concealed and distorted information. And what did he know about old covert operations? Marks's predecessor, hastening to his ambassadorship, may have not briefed him on ancient history. Cosgrove decided to be fairly direct. "Just to change the subject, Bryce," Cosgrove asked in a kindly drawl, "what do you know about plague?"

Marks was about to light a cigarette. He stopped. The match he was holding burned down almost to his thumb. A waiter rushed up with a lighter and lit the cigarette. When he had gone, Marks said, "What kind of plague do you mean?"

"Oh, I don't know. Bubonic, pneumonic."

Marks was silent. "As you may know," he said at last, his voice as toneless as ever, "there's something going on up in New York."

"Yes?"

"The station chief is worried that one of our assets was exposed. The asset and his whole family are in the hospital, and I just got word that his brother died this morning."

"The brother was not an asset?"

"No. We're running a check on him right now. It's a little confusing. They live up in Spanish Harlem—"

"Your man is black?"

"Cuban."

Cuban. Aha. The *Aha* went off like a phosphorus flare in Cosgrove's brain. Why didn't Marks mention the girl and the doctor who died of the plague? And did Marks know that the presidential party had been exposed to hepatitis at the Waldorf banquet? Was Marks perhaps trying to accumulate enough secrets to make Cosgrove look like an ignorant fool at the next Forty Committee meeting? A possibility. A definite possibility. No. A probability. Worst case: a certainty. "Another Cuban? First there's a sniper threat from a terminated Cuban asset, then another Cuban asset gets the plague. Interesting, isn't it?"

"It's just coincidence. The would-be sniper and the live asset whose brother just died were both in the Bay of Pigs, but I doubt that they even knew each other. I wonder if it's really even plague."

"Well, if it is, there's a vaccine for it, isn't there?" Cosgrove pushed his plate away and leaned back in his chair.

"I think so. I understand there were two other deaths, but the Surgeon General doesn't seem particularly worried that the disease will spread."

Cosgrove allowed himself a brief look of disdain. The Surgeon General was a forceful black woman, one of the few appointees the President had chosen without Cosgrove's advice, and her zealous campaigns about stricter antipollution devices on automobiles and tighter control over the pharmaceutical companies were something of a joke around Washington.

"Didn't they call plague the Black Death in the Middle Ages?" Cosgrove asked offhandedly.

"I think so. But nothing like that could happen now. This is the twentieth century."

Either Marks was lying again, or no one had ever briefed him about Operation Visitation.

23

IN AN appliance store, Rhoda Sue bought a dozen tape cassettes of soul music and a cassette player. A small chord organ caught her eye. She picked out "Ring Around the Rosy." "I used to know piano," she told the clerk. Suddenly she started coughing, and coughed so hard she had to let her packages and her mink slide to the floor so she could catch her breath.

Nearby, a bank of televisions, all tuned to the same channel, gave out the noon news. "An unusually virulent form of influenza is going around. City health officials say they have not yet identified it but suggest—"

Hart found Rodriguez in the outer office. A new map of the five boroughs had been put up, and she was putting black pins into it.

"New cases?" he asked.

"Yes," she said, keeping her attention on the map. "Both of the little Ortiz kids, Adelaido Ortiz, Mrs. Ortiz, and one of the daughters-in-law. Two nurses are in critical condition and one of the nurse's kids is sick. Also, an aide, a morgue attendant, and a pathologist from the Medical Examiner's office. Eleven cases."

"Deaths?"

"Daniels, the head nurse on the MICU, died about an hour ago."

"Six deaths and eleven cases."

"And a lot of rumors going around East 104th Street, my cousin says. I called him up, he told me they got the police outside the Ortiz place, guys in Pest Control Department vans all over the place. They're wearing weird protective outfits and spraying, and also catching rats and putting them in cages. Everybody's talking. See, with the Ortizes being Cuban and all, there's a lot of gossip."

"What kind of gossip?"

Her eyes widened. She was going through some kind of intense emotion, but again Hart had no idea.

Fury at him? She had made a pass at him and he had not followed her up on it. Or maybe she was upset about the epidemic . . . but why keep speculating?

"Well, my cousin—I told you he knows what everybody on that block is doing. He knows how much money they get from the welfare and everything. Because everyone has an account at his bodega, and they come to the store every day, and charge stuff. Everybody does. 'Cause the A&P won't give credit." She hated having to talk about the way her people lived to this clean white doctor, and she did not mention her cousin's numbers racket. She spoke to the map, and kept her voice formal. "But some of the Cubans, they don't just get money from the welfare and from their jobs. They get it from someplace else."

"Drugs."

"Well, sure, a lot of people do. But they also get it from the government, the U.S. government. They just have to tell some guy who comes to see them every few weeks what's going on, what their relatives in Cuba are writing to them about, what the other Cubans they know are up to. Then the government guy, well, he gives them money."

"And the government was giving the Ortizes money?"

"My cousin thinks so. He didn't know much about Domingo. He was new. But everyone knows Cubans are really crazy. And everybody is wondering about the tetracycline the people in the building were given. Everybody wants some."

"We're going to try to give it out at the district health centers." Hart checked his watch. "Let's grab a bite of lunch and then get uptown. I want to see what's going on at Metropolitan."

"No," Rodriguez savagely jammed a pin into 104th Street.

"I beg your pardon?" Hart could feel heat spreading across his face as if he had been slapped. He heard his phone ringing.

"No."

He saw that her cheeks were flushed, and she kept her head turned away. "What's wrong?"

"Nothing." She pronounced it "naw-theen."

"Goddamn it, you are going up to Met with me and that is an order!"

She walked away. "I will go up to the hospital. But forget the lunch! You mother!"

His phone was ringing. It was the manager of the Waldorf.

"We are all terribly, terribly worried," he began.

"The hepatitis case is *suspected*," Hart said, "not confirmed."

"We'd be terribly, terribly upset if this got in the papers."

"It won't—at least not until we know more. Can you give the nurse epidemiologist, Gayle Jefferson, a list of the people at the banquet?"

"Yes. That will be easy to do. I did take the precaution of notifying one of the President's aides. He wants to talk to you."

Andrews came into the office and waved to get Hart's attention. "The chance that Adelaido Ortiz was contagious on Monday is very remote," he whispered. "He was not exposed to his brother until Monday morning. He started feeling sick on Tuesday and so he didn't go back to work."

Hart nodded at Andrews. "Don't get so upset," he said to the manager. "This may amount to nothing. If anyone else calls in sick, contact Mrs. Jefferson. I'll talk to this aide and set him straight. 'Bye."

Hart's other line began ringing. "Sam, can you talk to those turkeys? I want to get uptown right away."

"What do I say?"

"As little as possible at this point."

Hart and Rodriguez, who had not spoken a word during the ride uptown, went up in the elevator to MICU with an orderly and an old woman on a stretcher. Her irises were opaque, her bony hands crumpled inward against her chest. She was whimpering softly. "MICU?" Hart asked the orderly.

The orderly nodded, tucking the sheet around the woman's legs.

There was a sleepy guard sitting in a chair by the

door to MICU, near a sign that said: RESPIRATORY
PRECAUTIONS. STRICT ISOLATION PROCEDURES MUST BE
OBSERVED. ALL PERSONNEL MUST WEAR GOWNS AND
MASKS. Hart and Rodriguez put on masks, gowns, and
gloves.

"Mrs. Ortiz, Adelaido Ortiz, and one of the kids
are in critical condition," the head nurse told them.
She was wearing a cotton mask. "The other kid died
at noon. The others are resting comfortably. We had
some trouble with Miranda. She was the aide on duty
when they brought the Jane Doe in. She started wandering around and screaming and banging her head
against the wall. She's a small woman, but it took
a couple of orderlies to hold her down until the resident could give her a shot of Valium. What do these
people *have?*"

"A very infectious pneumonia," Hart replied. "Have
you and everyone who works on the floor taken tetracycline?"

"Yes, sir."

The resident appeared, wearing a mask. "It's another one of those pneumonia cases," he told the head
nurse. "I wish someone would—"

"Hart, Bureau of Preventable Diseases. Who is the
woman, do you know?"

"Sure I do. Mrs. Bergman, the mother of the medical student who died here during the night."

Arthur Garson had the look of a man who had
been half-strangled. "What are you going to do about
this mess?" he moaned, following Hart down the corridor. "Thirteen cases!"

"All personnel are getting the proper dosages of
tetracycline?"

"Yes, but we've also had a number of medication
thefts. People have gotten wind of something bad,
Hart. Ward stocks of tetracycline are suddenly way
down. The union men keep coming in. And the papers
keep calling me up. They want to know about *this*—"

He pointed out a window overlooking the courtyard. There were long lines of people filing slowly into the Emergency Room. "Everybody and his brother is coming in for free medication."

"Good. What are you telling the papers?"

"Nothing. I told them to call the Health Department. But they just go ahead and interview other people here without my say-so. Somebody is bound to blab!"

"Excuse me, Hart." It was Turner Ilfeld and his colleague from the CDC. "We just stopped in on our way to the airport. Andrews told us you'd be up here."

"You want to go up to the MICU and take a look?" Hart asked.

Ilfeld shook his head. "Nope. Nope. Say, what's all the commotion out there in the courtyard?"

"That's people demanding examinations and tetracycline, which we are rapidly running out of," Garson said. "I'm Arthur Garson, chief administrator of Metropolitan, and I certainly hope you people are going to help us with this—this—"

Ilfeld nodded and chewed on his pipe. "This will be reported to the Surgeon General. She will report to HEW and the World Health Organization. I think if Dr. Hart follows my suggestions, this thing will be whipped."

Hart said nothing. He was anxious to get over to the Dobbs apartment. As Ilfeld and his friend left, Hart heard Ilfeld remark, "You should get a good paper out of this one, Bob."

"Telephone," Rodriguez said. "It's Sam."

Hart had the sensation of swimming in sand. Every time he made a move he was interrupted. He took the call in Garson's secretary's office. "Your CDC pals just left," Hart told Andrews. "Extremely helpful fellows."

"Aren't they, now? Listen, Dave, stuff is bustin' loose down here. You won't *believe* who's been calling. Some guy phoned from the *White House!* The

President's physician wants more information on the 'hepatitis' at the Waldorf."

"Why don't you tell him that it was not hepatitis after all but a bacterial pneumonia? Tell him we're just doing a routine check on who was in the dining area of the hotel that day. Tell him to give the President tetracycline."

"Joanie Chen has been examining the staff over at the Waldorf," Andrews said. "So far, everybody's fine."

"That's great news. That's wonderful. Let's keep a close watch on everyone there just to be safe, and you can tell the White House to go fuck itself."

"I'd just love to," Andrews said. "I'll give the dude some kind of story when he calls back. Next thing: the newspapers and TV stations have been calling. We're telling them that there will be an announcement later on this afternoon and that there's no cause for concern."

"I gather that Calabrese and Public Relations will have something we can look over before it's sent out?" Hart asked.

"All I have so far is a draft of his recommendation to the Board of Health."

"Can you read it to me?"

" 'The Health Department has confirmed five deaths from the plague—' "

"It's now seven."

"The streptomycin isn't working?" Andrews asked, his voice fading.

"I don't know. The antibiogram shows that the thing is sensitive to strep. We might have gotten to the Ortizes too late for it to do any good. Daniels, the nurse, the ME aide, and the doctors were pretty far gone by the time they were brought in; they were all exposed Sunday night. Daniels just held on longer than the others. I think maybe the strep *is* working. We just have to wait and see. Go on."

" 'The Health Department has confirmed *seven* deaths from the plague and a few people may have come in contact with these cases,' " Andrews read. " 'There is no reason to believe that the disease has spread further than a few blocks between 96th and 105th on the East Side, and all known cases have been hospitalized. However, anyone developing fever over ninety-nine degrees, chills, and shortness of breath, should report to any of the thirteen city hospitals. In Manhattan, these are Bellevue, Harlem Hospital, and Metropolitan Hospital. Special wards should be set up in all city hospitals and strict isolation procedures should be observed. Schools should postpone opening the fall session until further notice. Those private schools that have already begun the fall session should close. Public events, like baseball games and concerts, should be postponed for at least one week. People should be educated regarding symptoms and the dangers of contagion; they should be warned to avoid public transportation and crowds. The Governor should be alerted, and the National Guard should be put on stand-by alert. We must warn health workers throughout the city to anticipate the possibility of a major epidemic.' "

"I hope this convinces the Board of Health to ask the Mayor to declare a state of imminent peril," Hart said. "I hope the Board of Health is meeting right away."

"Not a chance. The members are scattered all over the city. Some of them are out of town. They're going to try to meet late this afternoon to approve this. Calabrese will be there rooting for us. Then the Mayor—"

"Yeah, yeah. Let's hope the Mayor gets to it before the papers do."

"Then I got an insane call from a total lunatic," Andrews continued.

"That sounds refreshingly normal."

"Yeah. He wouldn't say anything. Then he came over and he had a little card that said he was from the Secret Service."

"What did he want?"

"I don't know. He didn't say much, and he was very evasive when I tried to ask him. He asked about the Ortizes, and you."

Hart recalled what Dolores had said about Cubans being paid informers. "Oh, brother. Just what we need. What did you tell him?"

"That they were a Puerto Rican family who were in the hospital with bacterial pneumonia. I would have told him more but he was too creepy. A bad case of flattened affect, if you ask me. Have you ever talked to a shower curtain? He wouldn't answer any of my questions, and he managed to talk without using any nouns. No sense of humor. It was very strange. He wanted to know what you did, what you were like. I told him that as far as I knew you had never engaged in pederasty or mopery."

Toward the end of the afternoon, Rhoda Sue reached the upper Fifties. Her fever and her drug told her she had arrived in a paradise. Tall, burnished women in clinging, diaphanous summer dresses slid into waiting limousines and handsome couples strolled arm and arm down Fifth. She paused occasionally in front of a window. Gucci. Godiva Chocolatier. Elizabeth Arden. With their scalloped canopies and polished brass doors, they resembled fancy bonbon boxes. She pressed her nose against the thick-paned glass of Tiffany's and imagined living in a miniature landscape with a lapis lazuli pond and coral trees whose branches were hung with diamond fruit. In the windows of Bergdorf's, thin, contorted mannequins, their limbs rigid and pale, slowly began to dance. Rhoda Sue coughed. Her eyes filled with liquid. She sank down against a standpipe. The reflections of moving cars and people in the window moved too quickly, hurting her eyes. But she had every right to be here—she, too, was rich.

The Dobbs apartment resembled the home where

Hart had grown up. The ornate little tables, antique mirrors, faded oil paintings of dead relatives, and dull colors were in keeping with his mother's ideas about tasteful decor.

Sanitarians in full decontamination gear—white uniforms, masks, peaked hoods, and gloves—moved slowly through the apartment searching for fleas, animal hairs, or any other clues that would reveal what Sarah Dobbs's actions had been in the days before her death.

Hart removed some color snapshots from his breast pocket and flipped through them for the third time. They were from the dead girl's camera. One showed an older couple on a sunny lawn; another, a twisted cypress jutting out over a rocky beach; another, a small furry animal with bright black eyes.

The phone rang.

It was Rodriguez. She still sounded unfriendly. "We got five new suspected cases from the Ortiz neighborhood. I sent them all over to the Emergency Room at Met. Joanie Chen has finished examining the Waldorf people—no one's sick. I guess the rich are immune."

"No. This time they just happened to be extremely lucky. Anyway, a rich girl started the whole thing."

"You certain about that now?"

"I think so." He looked at the snapshot of the animal.

"My mother called me and told me some guy came by, like from the Secret Service or something? She was kind of confused. Anyway, he wants to talk to me. I didn't do anything wrong." She sounded irritated.

"They're pestering Sam, too. Did you find out whether those new cases are connected with the Ortizes?"

"Yes, all of them had been in contact with the family in one way or another." There was a silence.

"Dolores?"

"Including my cousin! They came into his bodega every day. Now he's coughing and sick."

"You made sure he was getting the right treatment."

"You bet I did."

"It's good that we're finding these cases soon enough to cure them. Domingo was only infectious for about a day before you found him." He looked at his watch. "Listen, Dolores, it's almost five. Why don't you go home and get some sleep? There's nothing more you can do right now."

"The Secret Service, or whatever kind of guy he is, said he was coming back there for me when I got off work. I might as well keep busy."

"Why don't you just go over to my place and get some rest?" Hart had forgotten that she was angry with him. Maybe she had, too.

There was a pause. Hart heard some noise in the foyer. "How do I get the keys?"

Smiling, he said, "I have to check on things at the office. Meet you there in an hour."

"Just what exactly is going on here?" demanded a deep voice. A well-dressed, middle-aged couple stood in the foyer surrounded by their luggage.

Hart hung up. The sanitarians stopped their work and peered at the newcomers through the clear plastic visors of their hoods.

Hart quickly pulled out his wallet and showed the man and woman his badge and ID. "I'm from the Health Department. I must know at once where your daughter has been for the past ten days."

"I'm not answering anything until you can explain to me what you and these—these—" Mr. Dobbs waved at the sanitarians.

"Tell me where your daughter has been," Hart said firmly, without emotion. "I have to know. It's official business. I'm a physician with the Department of Health."

"Why, she's in California," the woman said, smiling mechanically and pulling off her gloves. "She's in

Carmel with her aunt and uncle. Why, is something wrong?"

"Please give me the phone number in Carmel."

"I—I suppose, if you insist . . ." Mrs. Dobbs fumbled in her purse and pulled out an address book. "Is my daughter all right?"

Hart did not reply until he had taken down the number. He looked at Mr. Dobbs. "May I speak to you in private?"

"It's Sarah! *What* is the matter?" Mrs. Dobbs asked.

To Hart, everything seemed to slow down. He felt this had already happened, that he knew exactly what each person was going to say and do. Déjà vu. He was going to say, Your daughter contracted a very serious disease. I am sorry to have to tell you she died yesterday morning. The woman would put her hands over her face and her knees would buckle. She would fall against the wall. The man would look as if he had been slugged in the gut. I am very sorry.

As he stepped into the elevator, he would hear a long, full-throated wail.

24

RHODA SUE was loaded down with packages: Bergdorf's, Azuma, Saks, Tiffany's, Lord and Taylor, Korvette's, F.A.O. Schwartz, Bendel's, Van Cleef & Arpels. Around her neck she wore six new gold chains and two ropes of pearls. Despite the thick, still heat of the late afternoon, she had the chills and the energy from the cocaine was leaking away. She buttoned up the long mink coat and stood by the fountain in front of the Plaza Hotel. Should she go back to her hotel apartment downtown on Lexington? She didn't know. She felt horrible. Her mouth tasted of rust. What if she just checked into a room at the Plaza? The hotel swam in front of her eyes, a block of molten gold, a fairy-tale palace, the faces of dead babies at the windows . . .

Best to get out of there. Her head was killing her. She went into Central Park and found a bench. She sank down on it and arranged her packages around her. Then she coughed for a long time. The only cure was more coke. She glanced around blearily: no one was looking. She took the vial of white powder from her purse, stuffed the tip into her nostril and inhaled deeply. Immediately she felt better.

A hot-dog vendor wheeled his cart past, and she stopped him and bought a can of soda and a hot dog. When he handed them to her she sneezed. "Oh, excuse me!" she cried, afraid he would hit her.

"Nyaaah, watch it!" he said through his nose, waved her off, and pushed on.

The hot dog writhed in her hand and she threw it to the ground. The soda tasted like blood.

"California ground squirrel," Hart said, showing the snapshot to Andrews and Rodriguez. "Taken at very close range."

"Either very tame, or too sick to run," Andrews said.

"A cute little wild animal," Rodriguez said. "Just the thing a girl would like to hold and pet."

"And one of the biggest carriers of plague on the West Coast," Hart said. "We have to find out if they've got reports on any unusual die-offs in the rodent population out there. I talked to Sarah Dobbs's aunt and found out that last Wednesday they went to Point Lobos—where Sarah found this sick squirrel. Sarah got on the bus in Monterey that night, and she arrived in New York at six in the evening on Saturday."

Andrews whistled. "Oh God. Oh God. The Port Authority Bus Terminal on Labor Day Weekend. You can't do much better than that. But why hasn't the CDC heard of any other cases? Somebody along the route must have been infected. What about the poor bastard who sat next to her on the bus?"

"Gayle's checking health departments all across the country wherever the bus stopped, and the bus company is trying to get in touch with the driver. CDC is doing the same. He's probably okay—he's out on the road. It takes a couple of days for bubonic to become pneumonic. I bet she didn't become contagious until late Saturday."

"What a fantastic piece of luck that would be!" Andrews said. "In the smallpox scare of Forty-eight, the guy who was the carrier got off the bus and just stayed in his hotel room. Maybe she took a taxi home and just stayed in the apartment. The bulletproof shield would protect the taxi driver, and—"

"And she would breathe or cough on Ortiz when he helped her out of the taxi," Rodriguez said. "Or when he called the ambulance the next day."

"We have to see if any unpredictable cases turn up —people who were in the bus terminal. But it looks good, doesn't it?" Andrews was buoyant. All three of them beamed with relief.

"If she was so rich, that Sarah Dobbs, why did she take a cross-country bus to get to New York?" Rodriguez asked. "Why didn't she fly?"

"Her aunt said she just wanted to see the country. Her parents had been against the idea, apparently, but they were in Europe."

The telephone rang. "Hart here."

"Dr. Hart, please hold for General Daniel Cosgrove." It was a woman's voice with a strong Southern accent. Another voice came on the line. It was deep, also with a slight Southern tinge. "I'm calling from Washington and I'd like to ask you a few questions."

Hart was surprised. He knew Cosgrove's name from

the newspapers. Wasn't he the President's Security Advisor or something? "Shoot."

"I apologize for taking up your time, but anything like this that touches on the safety of the President automatically becomes a matter of national security."

Hart said nothing. He waited. Cosgrove waited.

Cosgrove leafed through an Army 201 File with "HART, DAVID T. 129-30-9098 MAJ MC USAR MC 3005B" stenciled on the margin. He shifted the telephone receiver under his chin. "What did that busboy at the Waldorf get sick with?"

Hart decided to be truthful. Why not? "First let me emphasize that the busboy—his name is Adelaido Ortiz—"

Cosgrove picked up a CIA folder, on which was stenciled "ORTIZ, ADELAIDO FULGENCIO JM/WAVE 2199 AM/DESK."

"—was *not* infectious at the time that he was serving at the presidential banquet. He eventually came down with a bacterial pneumonia."

"Not hepatitis?" Cosgrove made some notes on a pad.

"No. I told the nurse epidemiologist who talked to the manager of the Waldorf to say that so that she could learn what she needed to without causing undue alarm. We sometimes have to do that. Otherwise people get panicky. The manager got panicky anyway, and called the White House. Let me repeat: it's not hepatitis, and Ortiz was not infectious until later on. No one at the Waldorf has come down with anything."

Cosgrove waited. That's how you got liars to trip themselves up. You just gave them enough rope.

"Look, you seem to know what Ortiz was exposed to and so do I. And I assure you I do." He couldn't tell whether this Hart was a pawn for someone else or whether he was actively involved.

Hart listened to a faint buzz on the line. He wondered if it were tapped. Why were these people so insistent and so unnecessarily mysterious? Cosgrove's silences and his clipped sentences made Hart feel as though he himself were lying. Even if there is no plot, he thought, the mere presence of a paranoid is enough to create one.

There were some clicks on the line. "Hello?" Hart said.

"Hello," Cosgrove said.

"Are you calling from a phone booth?" Hart started laughing.

"What about Domingo Ortiz?" Cosgrove finally said, tonelessly.

"That's Adelaido's brother. At least I think that he was. He died this afternoon."

"What of?"

"I can only answer that in strictest confidence."

Silence.

"You know a lot about epidemics, Dr. Hart?"

"Middling." Hart again felt he was lying.

"What?"

"My job is to know a lot."

Silence.

"Look—there's no danger to the President. Dr. Samuel Andrews, who's the Epidemiological Intelligence Officer assigned to New York by the Public Health Service's Center for Disease Control, has already spoken with one of the President's staff members. He has advised that the President take a particular dosage of tetracycline. That's because there's an extremely remote chance, an extremely small possibility, that the President and the others at the banquet were exposed to this sick busboy. But—and let me repeat this again—*the boy was not contagious at the time of the banquet!*"

"Where did Domingo Ortiz get the disease?"

"He worked as a weekend porter at an apartment building, and a girl who lived in the building gave it to him."

"How do you know he didn't give it to her?"

"We've established that she was the index case. The

girl gave it to Ortiz, and the way it spread from there —well, I don't think the girl was maneuvering to give it to the President."

Andrews and Rodriguez stared at Hart. Who could he be talking to?

"One-hundred-percent certainty on that?"

"On what?"

"That she gave it to him, and then he gave it to the other one, or was it that he gave it to her and to the other one?"

"General Cosgrove, I don't understand what you are saying."

Silence.

"We're not communicating," Cosgrove said.

"Sir, there is no such thing as one-hundred-percent certainty in medicine. But we're ninety-nine-percent sure that she infected Domingo Ortiz and Ortiz infected his brother Adelaido."

"What did *he* have?"

Hart was silent. Give the jerk a dose of his own medicine.

"Where was this Ortiz from?" Cosgrove finally said.

"Which Ortiz?"

"You know what I am talking about."

"No sir, I don't. I told you that the President is not in danger."

"How many persons could a contaminated individual infect?"

"It depends, General. If you're lucky—as the President was—and the infected person doesn't breathe or cough on someone or have an intimate contact in a restaurant or crowd, maybe no one at all. If the person was coughing in, say, a crowded bus terminal, it could be worse."

"Ten?"

"More."

"Fifty?"

"Maybe. Those exposed would in turn expose others . . ."

"Doctor, I read a paper of yours on zoonotic disease distribution. I gather that Latin America is a fairly active region for this kind of thing."

"For what kind of thing?" Hart was staggered. He had written that paper for the *Journal of Tropical Medicine* eight years ago, when he was traveling through Central America on a public-health fellowship.

"What do you mean?" he repeated.

Silence.

"You didn't mention Cuba in your paper," Cosgrove said.

"There are some countries that don't report cases to the World Health Organization," Hart said, dreamily. The conversation was having a hypnotic effect on him. Too many hours without sleep.

"I know you're very fond of the Ortiz family and want to protect them," Cosgrove said. "I don't want to see them get in any trouble either." His voice grew harsh. "But you have no idea how big this thing is. You don't have any way of knowing—of knowing what we know. So I want you to cooperate to the fullest extent and tell me what you know. Don't try lying to me. It won't help either one of us."

Hart was taken aback by this outburst. "Well . . . I know as much as you do. Or less, apparently."

"You know they're Cubans, you goddamned well know that!"

"I know that they're ill with a serious disease and that three members of the family are dead from it. As a doctor, that is what I know. That's it."

"Dr. Hart, I realize that you are very concerned for their welfare, as a good doctor should be, but don't try covering up. We know that you were with Domingo Ortiz in the ambulance and at the hospital. What did he say to you during that period in time? What did his mother say? His brothers? Their wives?"

"He was delirious. My Spanish isn't too good, but I got the impression that he was praying."

139

"What were his words?"

"Mother, mother of God—something along those lines."

"That's all?"

"Yes sir."

"Thank you very much for your cooperation, Doctor. If we have reason to converse again in the future, I want you to be more straightforward with me. Do you understand?"

Hart made an obscene gesture at the telephone. "I have to hang up, General. I have a great deal of work to do."

Cosgrove made a few notes and slipped them into Hart's folder. He mulled over the facts. Domingo Ortiz was a Cuban who had slipped into the U.S. from Cienfuegos and had somehow, against all odds, escaped being reported to the Agency by the live assets in the New York Cuban community—one of those assets being Adelaido Ortiz, his brother. According to the CIA file, Adelaido Ortiz had been interviewed by a Freedom Flight Debriefing Agent in Miami in 1960, assigned the code name DESK, and recruited for various covert CIA attacks on Cuba as well as for the Bay of Pigs invasion. When the hidden war deteriorated and JM/WAVE was dismantled, Adelaido had moved with his family to New York. And then, years later, Domingo Ortiz had suddenly arrived from Cuba and promptly died of the plague. Meanwhile, a teen-aged girl who lived in the building where he worked had also died of plague. And so had Adelaido . . . after serving the Presidential party on the rare occasion of a visit to New York. God, those hysterical Cubans. Can't be trusted an inch and they'll die for anything. That nut, another terminated asset, the doctor who fired the bazooka at the U.N. from across the East River. Good Christ! Adelaido Ortiz gets sick with the plague, but this Hart character first claims it's hepatitis, then bacterial pneumonia. Even though he's an experienced epidemiologist with a good reputation. Very, very fishy. An expert on Latin American and West African epidemiology, too. Widely traveled in Central and South America. Says here he worked at a clinic with Arnulfo Mendez, who later became Minister of Health for Allende! Three-month fellowship in Angola. That really stinks to high heaven. Angola, for Christ's sake! These public-health types were always suspect. If an MD chooses public-health work when he could be making far more money in private practice, he's probably got left-wing ideas. Maybe Mendez set him up with a Communist power. In Angola, he must have met Cubans . . . No police record. Marched in a Vietnam moratorium parade in New York in '69. Drafted after residency training. CBR training in the Army; Medical Corps Major in Vietnam. Registered Democrat but let his registration lapse in '72 . . . It would take only two or three people to wipe this country out with germ warfare, and if one of the people was the individual in charge of controlling epidemics in New York City . . . Hart isn't wasting his time. He's isolated all the Ortizes, nobody could get in to talk to Adelaido. Meanwhile, twenty-two cases and seven—no, eight—deaths . . . And Marks is as silent as a goddamned tomb.

Cosgrove buzzed his aide. "Get me the New York office of the DIA."

"That's the most bizarre conversation I ever had," Hart told Andrews and Rodriguez. "That guy seemed to think there was something important about Domingo Ortiz. But he wouldn't tell me what."

"You think they're on our necks just because the President was at the Waldorf when Adelaido was?" Andrews asked.

"Yes. I guess they don't have much to do with their time."

"Remember that the government tested some kind of germ-warfare device, some kind of gas-dispersal thing, in the New York subway system." Andrews said. "Back in the early Seventies."

"That really happened?" Rodriguez asked.

"Absolutely," Hart said. "It came out in the Senate hearings on the CIA. Calabrese tried to learn more from Colby, who was head of the CIA then, about what they'd done. No one ever answered his letter, but funny little guys came around and asked him questions about why he was so interested in the public health threats to New York City. When he explained that he was Commissioner of Health, and that it was his job, his tax returns for the previous five years were audited."

"Well, how do we know this plague business isn't something the CIA cooked up?" Andrews was growing excited. "Or one of those other secret outfits?"

"Sam, Sam. I didn't realize paranoia could be transmitted over telephone wires. It's worse than the plague! Go home and get some sleep."

Hart thought for a moment about paranoia. It was like a microbe dropped into a rich culture. Fermentation began immediately: strands and interlocking geometric forms emerged from the sterile medium, and the overall pattern grew increasingly complex. But there was a difference. Bacteria grew and changed, and the constructs of paranoia were always fixed and dead. Hart had come across plenty of paranoids in the emergency room during his internship and residency, and this nosy Cosgrove sounded just like one of them. But luckily he was far away, and his weird ideas had nothing to do with the epidemic and its solution. Hart was sure of that. The spooks might poke around for a few days, but when they found nothing, and were forced to accept the facts about Sarah Dobbs, they would surely go away.

At twilight, a policeman found Rhoda Sue sprawled stiffly among her packages, her shoes kicked off. Near her bare foot a squirrel was placidly nibbling on a hot-dog bun. "Come on, lady, move along," the policeman said. She stared at him. He came closer and repeated the command. Then he saw that her mouth was bright red—not from lipstick but from blood.

"I talked to the CDC—no cases anywhere but Manhattan," Andrews said. "Dolores and I just finished calling most of the big emergency rooms in the city—no suspicious cases. I called the Medical Examiner's, and there have been no suspicious autopsy findings. The cops say that everything is quiet up in the Ortiz block, and no new cases have been brought in from up there." He grinned. "It's looking good, Dave."

"Any more from the California Health Department?" Hart asked.

"Just confirmation of the rodent die-off at Point Lobos, which the state officials have closed. Gayle says no one on the bus Sarah Dobbs took or along the route has been reported by any health departments. The Board of Health approved the recommendation to the Mayor, but now it looks like we can tell Weinstein to forget about declaring a State of Imminent Peril."

"Not yet, Sam," Hart replied. "Things *are* looking much better. Better than they have since we first got word of this thing. But there's still the contagion factor. If just one rogue case pops up, everything could still fall apart."

"Well, I guess the Mayor's going to make the announcement on TV tonight, so we probably couldn't stop it if we wanted to. But when you get the media going on something—" Andrews shrugged.

Hart was struck by how thin and pale Sam looked tonight. "Go home, lost waif," Hart said. "Go home and curl up with your teddy bear."

"Forget it—he might have little stuffed fleas."

25

From a wall safe concealed by a row of paintings of battles—Saratoga, Gettysburg, San Juan Hill, Ardennes, and the Bulge—Cosgrove withdrew a plump, dark-brown folder. Its weight and texture gave him a stomach tremor, the sensation of a terrifying but exciting ride at a carnival.

He sat down at his desk and began methodically to sort through the file. The documents inside were brittle and yellowing; most of them dated back to the early Sixties. He had carried this folder from one office wall safe to another for almost twenty years.

He thought of the file as his c.y.a. masterpiece. If you must cover your ass, then cover it to perfection.

During the Senate and congressional investigations of the intelligence community, he had had the file ready at a second's notice to present to some ambitious newsman. But the topic covered in the file had never come up, and he had never learned why. Any of his enemies, any of those aching to put it to him, would surely have had a perfect opportunity during those hearings. Afterward, he worked harder than ever to make the file even more impeccable; just because the bomb had failed to go off did not mean it had been defused. He continued to extract relevant documents from the files of the Defense and Central Intelligence Agencies whenever he was granted access to them on other pretexts. His folder also contained memos and directives initialed by two Presidents, a Secretary of Defense, a Secretary of State, two Attorneys General, a previous National Security Advisor, two Directors of the CIA, and the Chairman of the Joint Chiefs of Staff. Some of these memos were authentic; others had been written several years after their purported authors had died. There were also copies of memos Cosgrove had written to these men long after they had gone to their rewards. But the dates were right, and the seals and signatures were perfect.

The file also contained a report Cosgrove himself had written. Nothing in it had been altered. As he began to skim through it, he was sickened by a premonition of monstrous reversal.

His report, which had been rapidly assembled in the fall of 1962 during the Cuban missile crisis, was chiefly a study of the way epidemics and military operations have been intertwined throughout history. Until World War II, he had written, epidemics killed more soldiers than weaponry did. The war between the Israelites and the Philistines was decided by plague, which decimated the Philistines. Athens was well defended and had an excellent navy, but plague struck the city during its golden age when it was under siege by Sparta, and it killed most of the inhabitants. Sparta, the lesser power, finally defeated Athens as a result. It was not only disease that weakened Athens; her fighting spirit was crippled by the anarchy and licentiousness that arose during the epidemic.

Clearly there was a pattern, a rhythm to these catastrophes. Plague, the report continued, appeared to recur on a worldwide scale every several centuries, then to recede into the high plains of Central Asia, where it survived among wild rodents. By the middle of the sixth century, most of Western Europe had been overrun by barbarian hordes from the Asian steppes, and in 542 A.D., bubonic plague appeared in the Egyptian port city of Sin. Fever and violent delirium swept through the Middle East, Europe, and Asia. So many died that graves could not be dug: the roofs of towers were removed and the towers filled with the dead. Ships were loaded with corpses, towed out to sea, and set adrift.

Ten thousand died every day in Constantinople, and all the great cities of antiquity were horribly debilitated. The Byzantine empire of Justinian was the most powerful in the world, but by the end of his reign, his magnificent army was in ruins and barbarians had captured most of his cities. Shipping and commerce came to a standstill, piety and obedience were forgotten, and civilization entered the Dark Ages. When the Plague of Justinian, the first great pandemic, finally retreated, at least one hundred million were dead—half the population of the known world.

About eight centuries later, when cities once again prospered, droughts drove barbarian hordes to migrate from the steppes. The second great pandemic struck. The Black Death—so-named either because hemorrhages under the skin gave corpses a blackened appearance or because black meant terrible—was probably the most frightening event in all of human history. Men, women, children roamed the streets screaming with the pain of abscesses, swollen armpits and groins, and hemorrhages under the skin. The fever inflamed the brain, and a great many died raving and hallucinating. The Brotherhood of Flagellants went from town to town announcing that self-torture would distract God from His mission of chastisement; hundreds of thousands took to the road, beating themselves and spreading contagion into the remotest areas.

There were not enough survivors to bury the plague victims. Vast trenches were dug and the dead tossed in. At Avignon, the Pope consecrated the River Rhone so that corpses thrown into it could benefit from Christian burial. Morals degenerated. Parents refused to take care of their sick children, neighbors avoided one another, and the dying were left to themselves. Funerals became casual affairs, and people ceased to mourn.

Throughout Europe, Russia, and even in the Viking

colonies of Greenland, everything came to a stop. Whole towns were deserted, and the roads and fields were littered with human bodies and the carcasses of untended livestock. Grass grew in the main thoroughfares, and the major port cities were all but abandoned. All military activity ceased.

In one year, 1349, between one-half and three-fourths of the population of the known world died of the plague.

The survivors were completely disoriented. Jews, gravediggers, and priests were blamed and tortured to death. Repeated pogroms drove the Jews to seek refuge in Eastern Europe. Harvests rotted in the fields while the serfs reveled in the castles of their dead masters. Soldiers refused to fight, peasants revolted, and looting, orgies, and cannibalism were commonplace. The once prosperous feudal countries of Europe did not recover from the ravages of civil disorder for three centuries.

Plague, Cosgrove noted, flared up again on a smaller scale in the seventeenth century. This time the rich and the nobles fled to the countryside and survived. But the major ports and cities of Europe lost hundreds of thousands of their inhabitants. London, where 100,000 people died in the year of 1668, was one of the worst hit, but the Great Fire the following year appeared to stop the plague there permanently.

The third great pandemic did not yet have a name. It started in Yunnan, China, in the 1850s, when millions of rats rushed out of their holes and danced until they died. Chinese soldiers sent there in the 1890s to quell a local rebellion brought the plague back with them to the great port city of Canton. Within a year, at least 100,000 Cantonese were dead and ships had carried diseased rats, humans, and cargo laden with infected fleas to the ports of Australia, India, Africa, and America. Plague soon killed twelve million in India. The first casualty in the United States was a Chinese laborer who died in a hotel basement in San Francisco around the turn of the century. City officials anxious to conceal the dread diagnosis of the Health Department refused to institute a quarantine. As a result, one hundred fourteen died, and the plague spread into the rodent population of California and beyond.

Although Cosgrove had reread his old report once or twice since 1962, he had never been affected by its contents before. For him, history was like an ocean in which, at certain rare moments, a number of waves crossed one another. Whoever stood at their center would attain lasting power and recognition. Montgomery at Al Alamein, for instance. Patton crossing the Rhine. In order to step into that center of power at the critical moment, one had to understand the system down to its finest interconnections, to be thoroughly prepared, and brave enough to leap. This was his dearest belief, and with this report, he had tried to make that belief work for him. But he had been premature. He had hoped that Operation Visitation, which he had conceived and thrust into motion during the Cuban missile crisis, would catapult him into a much higher position. In fact, the project had failed horribly, the operatives had been caught, and Cosgrove had never ceased in his efforts to erase all records of the matter.

And now, staring at the old papers fanned out across his desk, he once again felt that he stood near a nexus of destiny. This time he would make the true leap.

He buzzed an aide on the intercom. "I want to put through a call on the scrambler phone to General Phillip Sheffield at Fort Detrick," he said. "He's the director of the Chemical-Bacteriological Center. He's probably gone home—it's past nine—so you'll have to get him to go back to the office and use the scrambler."

26

HART LOOKED out at the dark mauve and brown haze to the south where a flock of pigeons or gulls wheeled between the World Trade Center towers. He usually hated this time of day, when the air became thick and dim and the lights were not yet turned on, but this twilight seemed most welcome. He had now lost a great deal of sleep, but instead of feeling tired, he sensed that his body was tapping some new source of energy. It was a very subtle food that fed his eyes and ears, and even his sense of touch. He was in an alert, clear state.

Rodriguez had taken his keys and accepted his offer to go to his place and rest. During the day he had started once or twice to apologize to her, but then he stopped, because he had no idea what he was apologizing for. To ask what was wrong would have been a move of greater intimacy than he had the courage to make. Before he had met his wife, he had taken out many women—bright, articulate professors, account executives, physicians, biologists—and he had always been able to approach them boldly. Now he wondered and hesitated about everything—why? Why did the compact, sensuous presence of Dolores scare him so? Was it because he could not approach her in the glib, wordy ways he had always used before on women? He did not know.

As he was leaving to go home, his phone rang. It was Irving Kaprow, the head of the Mayor's Task Force for Emergency Preparedness.

"It's about that statement of Imminent Peril,"

Kaprow said. "The Board of Health met and ratified it and passed it on to the Mayor. But now he's changed his mind. He doesn't want to deliver it. He's afraid that if he asks people to avoid public transportation, there will be bad traffic tie-ups everywhere. We have two million commuters daily, you know. The highways in the metropolitan area can't take the strain of an ordinary rush hour, and if all those people bring their cars, it will be a nightmare. And he doesn't want to say it's the plague or that we should be prepared for a serious epidemic. He thinks those are scare tactics."

"But they aren't—that happens to be the truth," Hart said. "Why can't people just be told exactly what the situation is? There's no workable vaccine for pneumonic plague, but we do have tetracycline and streptomycin. There's absolutely no need to panic. If the district health centers are organized to handle this, and if the Mayor's office, the police and the media cooperate, then we should be able to stop the spread of this disease right away. In a few days everything will be back to normal."

"Let me be frank with you, Hart," Kaprow sounded much stronger and braver now that he was safely back in his cubicle in the Mayor's office. "The Mayor has been told that this is a stunt you and the rest of the Health Department are pulling. I mean, we know there are some real cases of the plague, but you people want to blow the whole thing out of proportion. He has reason to believe the Department is doing this to get attention and money, and that you're being pushy because you're bucking for the Commissioner's post when he retires."

Hart listened in disbelief. "Kaprow, you are out of your fucking mind! Who's saying that crap?"

"I'm not authorized to say. But I can tell you that Councilman Barnes wants to begin hearings on wasteful spending in the Health Department. He wants to find out why certain unnecessary bureau directors spend their time dreaming up phony epidemics."

Hart ran his hand through his hair. He was furious. "I don't believe this!" Barnes was always threatening to investigate one thing or another. "Listen, Kaprow, forget this political horseshit. If you want to see this city survive, you'd better think, man! This is potentially a major disaster, the kind you were reading about in the meeting last night. Can't you explain that to the Mayor?"

"Dr. Hart." Kaprow was delighted. He had never had a chance to push around biggies before. "Dr Hart. An earthquake is a disaster. A hurricane is a disaster. A subway crash is a disaster. A few cases of a curable disease up in Harlem—that's no disaster."

Hart slammed down the receiver. He picked up the telephone and hurled it against a filing cabinet. His chest was tight, his skin was burning, the muscles in his right arm—his punching arm—were taut. He decided to go over to Kaprow's office and beat the shit out of him.

Rodriguez was waiting by the elevator as Hart slammed out of the Bureau.

"You still here?" he asked.

She started to reply but stopped when she saw the angry look on his face.

"I forgot to lock up," he muttered, trying to conceal his rage at Kaprow.

"I'll go back and do it," she said.

"I will." He walked back down the corridor and locked the door. She followed him.

"Man, do you look mad!"

"It's just one of those days, I guess," Hart said. Then he burst out laughing. "Either I'm crazy or they are, what do you think?" He told her about Kaprow, and the Mayor, and Councilman Barnes. He said he supposed he ought to notify his superiors.

She said nothing. She fixed her big dark eyes on his. He felt a pull in his lower abdomen. He unlocked the door and went back inside the office and, while she perched on his desk, he got on the phone and tracked down Calabrese. He was with the Mayor at the television studio, but he listened carefully to Hart's story about Kaprow.

After Hart hung up, he sat and looked at her. She remained seated on his desk. He could see the firm curve of her inner thigh under her dress. Her lips were half-parted.

Too much was happening to him all at once. He couldn't control it.

He began kissing her, slowly easing his tongue into her mouth. She wrapped her arms around him. His mind stopped working altogether. They were just there, the two of them.

He leaned her gently across the desk and slid his hand up her thigh.

The phone rang.

"You'd better answer it," she whispered.

"No."

She sat up and picked up the receiver. "It's the Mayor," she said.

"Oh, shit." Hart took the phone.

"Dr. Hart, Dr. Calabrese has persuaded me that I must say *something* about this epidemic." Sid Weinstein was from Brooklyn, and sounded it. "Now, I'm going on television in a few minutes, but I don't want to tell the people that they are in a state of imminent peril when only a few people have come down with this disease, which you people are doing everything you can to treat, I know. And I don't understand how this epidemic is a serious threat to the entire city when almost nobody is sick. If I tell the citizens they are in peril, there will be a panic, which will happen especially if I mention plague. You see my point of view."

"Yes I do, Your Honor. But we have to educate the public properly and get everyone to cooperate. Otherwise, the disease could spread very rapidly, and we could have thousands of cases in a matter of days. I'm sure that won't happen, particularly if we can find the people who may have it and isolate and treat them."

"But do we have to blow it up all out of proportion?"

"That is not my intention. It's not the intention of the Commissioner or the Board of Health, either, sir."

There was a long silence. "Okay, I see what you mean. I don't want Barnes making a big stink about this, though, so how about I go along with the Board of Health's statement—but only on these conditions. First, I do not want to say it's the plague, which sounds very disturbing, like the Middle Ages, but call it something less scary-sounding. Okay? Second, the responsibility for this is all on you, and if anything goes wrong, then you are out on your ass."

"I'll take that responsibility," Hart said.

"Okay, great. I'll make the declaration tonight, then. Now, Doctor, what are we going to call this disease?"

Two patrolmen stood over the pimp's bloated body. The huge television was still on, blaring last bits of the ten o'clock news. An announcer was saying:

> Large crowds gathered around Metropolitan Hospital today to receive free medication for a highly infectious influenza sweeping the Harlem area . . .

"It's my old buddy Flash," one of the patrolmen said.

"You know him?" asked the rookie, preferring to stare at the television rather than at the corpse.

"Yeah," said the patrolman, switching off the TV. "He was a big pimp and a dealer. He hung out in the Times Square area, mostly, when he wasn't running around with one of his foxes in his Eldorado pimpmobile."

27

To Hart, Central Park was an island within the island of Manhattan. As the taxi wound uptown along the dark drive and Rodriguez dozed against his shoulder, he peered out at the dark, leafy canopy overhead and at the pink globes of light that lined the main paths. The park was almost empty, and the only sounds were the swish of the tires and the rush of the breeze, and, from far away—he might have been imagining it—the faint, mournful notes of a flute.

As they passed through the intersection where forty hours earlier he had listened to a woman with a bandanna tied over her mouth explain God and the government and the plight of the city to him, he thought about how swiftly his life had changed. Yesterday he had set out for work still raw and miserable from the long Labor Day weekend, convinced of the pointlessness of his life. The night before that he had wandered along the winding paths of the park until sunrise, losing himself in the overgrown Ramble, wading in the lake, feeding hamburger to the coyote in the zoo. He had passed a couple making love, skirted a grove where a band of Haitians were pulling apart a flapping, clawing white rooster, and had shared a bottle of sloe gin with a grizzled blues-harmonica player who had set up housekeeping on a park bench. He had felt great self-pity that these people all had reasons to live and he did not.

Now his mind was inside out.

He saw everything quite differently; his thoughts did not follow the old troughs carved out by past events. It may simply have been lack of sleep, or the fact that the crisis had demanded all his attention so that he had had none left to feed his self-pity and self-disgust, or maybe it was simply because he had his arms around Dolores. He did not really know, because the part of his mind that sought out causes and labeled them was not working very well.

He brushed his thumb across her cheek and his excitement grew. He was finally bringing her home to his bed; he no longer had the energy to be angry or afraid, and when those two emotions were starved out, all that remained in him was a powerful desire to make love. She was so lovely! How stingy he had been with his life, how cautious, how blind!

As the taxi turned up Central Park West, he studied her face as the light from the streetlamps passed over it. Her lips were slightly parted, full and placid. Her narrow nose looked Spanish and aristocratic to him, but her slanted eyes and high cheekbones made him think of the women he had seen in the villages of the Yucatán. She was always so present, so direct—maybe that was what had frightened him; his wife had always been more at home with abstract discussions. Dolores, instead of speaking, would simply smile at him and raise an eyebrow. He did not understand what he felt for her, but he did know that it was powerful.

There was much more work that had to be done on the epidemic; the worst was over, he hoped, but tomorrow—no, he would not think about that now. Tonight he would visit this mysterious island of a woman, and everything else would have to wait.

When the taxi pulled up in front of a brownstone on West Ninety-fourth Street, near the park, he awoke Dolores and led her up the steps.

"This is a nice house," she said, yawning.

"I just have a messy bachelor's apartment on the second floor," he said. He dug into his pockets for his keys. They were gone.

For an instant he was paralyzed by a strong current of fear in his chest. He suddenly felt a profound loss.

"Is something wrong?"

"Uh, keys. My keys. I've lost them—"

"Relax." She looked at him, her eyes and mouth deep shadows. "You gave them to me, remember?"

She handed him the keys and touched the small of his back as he unlocked the door. The fear went away.

It is over, he thought. That part of me is gone. I will never be the same again. He felt immense relief. They went up one flight and he unlocked the three locks on his apartment door and reached in and switched on the light. Then he bent over and kissed Dolores. "Please come in."

"David!"

"Oh, shit!" he groaned.

The place was a shambles. All the books had been pulled from the bookcases and dumped on the floor. Papers, notebooks, file folders, and envelopes were scattered on the carpet. The drawers of his desk had been wrenched open and overturned.

He was astonished at how much he had squirreled away over the years. His entire life had been suddenly coughed up before his eyes. "Jesus," he said, "look at all this junk! This garbage! I wish they'd taken everything. What do I have of value?"

"Well, at least they didn't steal your TV," she said. "Or your stereo."

"They probably heard a Puerto Rican coming up the stairs and scrammed." He patted her buttocks and bolted the front door.

"You just watch that talk, you guy, or I'll *keel* you!" She went into the kitchen. "Hey, is this little dish full of change yours?"

"They didn't even take that?" Hart found a bottle of wine in a kitchen cupboard and unscrewed the cap. "That's very strange. I don't see how they could have gotten in—the door was locked."

"Look." She pointed to the kitchen window, which overlooked a fire escape and was covered with a metal grill. The grill had been neatly sawed open, and a pane of glass had been removed from the lower half of the window. "No junkie did *that,*" she said.

"It does look rather professional. I'll call the cops in the morning. Not that they'll be able to do anything about this." He handed her a glass of wine. "Listen, I'm sorry for all this mess—" He tried to secure the grill over the window.

"You Wasps! Always apologizing! Even for things you didn't do! Boy, this wine tastes delicious."

He started laughing. "Yes, it does." She made such wonderful sense.

He led her into the bedroom. Clothes had been pulled out of the closets and tossed on the floor, and all the drawers of the dresser had been thrown on the bed. "I was hoping they'd left the bed alone," he said. He felt very giddy.

"They left your clock radio." She turned it on and tuned in a Puerto Rican station. "You want to dance?"

She began to shrug her shoulders and move her hips to the music, and at the same time, she picked up a corner of the bedspread and began to tug on it. Laughing, he tugged on another corner of the bedspread until all of the drawers and their contents—underwear, shirts, cufflinks, sweaters, mufflers, gloves—slid off the bed and onto the floor. She danced around him, encircling him with her arms, swaying and smiling and tossing her hair.

He switched off the radio. The night was very quiet except for the faraway whine of a siren. "You are so beautiful." He cupped his hands around her breasts and lifted them gently.

She gazed up at him, breathing deeply, her nostrils flaring slightly. Everything was right: he felt the way he did when he was absolutely sure he was about to make a blind bank shot in a game of pool. As he unbuttoned her uniform she began to tremble slightly. He lowered her onto the bed and looked at her for a long time. She pulled him down, and as he ran his hands and mouth over her taut, brown, supple surfaces, he had the dazzling sense of fantasy and reality becoming one. She was fragrant and silky and damp and open, and all that he had imagined about her tongue was true. She wrapped herself around him eagerly, and the ten thousand impressions of her that he had stored up rushed together into a long, exquisite shudder, from his groin to the crown of his head.

The more they made love, the more he wanted to make love. He wanted to make up for all the time he had wasted, all the stupid hesitations, all the miserly rationalizations.

At last they lay stretched out on the sheets watching the wind billow the curtains above them. "I've wanted to do this for a long time," he said.

"Me too. But I didn't think you were interested."

"Well, I always have been. But I was nuts, too."

"I believe it."

They made love again. "I am so happy," he said. But she was already asleep.

For several hours, Hart slept deeply, his mind and body completely silent and at ease. And then the sharp wire of a thought pushed its way up into consciousness and he bolted awake. It was still dark. Dolores lay curled against his side, her hair a dark cloud across his chest. Whoever had broken into his apartment had not been a junkie, and had been searching for something particular. Or just snooping thoroughly. But he could think of nothing important he had to hide.

Two days ago the robbery would have disturbed him a great deal. Now he was just glad he had his life. He was glad he had his arms and legs and head, and his spine, his penis, his heart, his brain. He could leave his apartment and never go back. As long as he could breathe and eat and sleep and make love—that was enough. It was all so simple. Much simpler than the tale he had been telling himself for so long.

He spread his palm on the firm half-moon of her belly. It was just this. It was enough.

28

"I WANT to thank everyone for doing such a terrific job," Calabrese said.

Hart watched Dolores. She sat tranquilly in the morning sunlight, her hands folded on her lap, her head slightly tilted to the left. She looked at him and covered her mouth with her hand. The corners of her eyes rose slightly and he knew she was smiling.

Calabrese surveyed the nurse epidemiologists, the sanitarians, the clerks who sat in folding chairs in his outer office. He wore a pinstriped blue suit and a yellow tie, and he looked unusually cheerful. "Dr. Hart tells me that since Tuesday afternoon you have examined and given medication to over five hundred people. You're all to be congratulated for your promptness and thoroughness. Do you want to just summarize the situation for us, Dave?"

Hart got to his feet a little too quickly and slipped into a brief eddy of dizziness. "We have gone over all the known contacts and it looks like the Dobbs girl wasn't contagious until she was alone in the apartment Saturday night. After that she probably was too ill to go out again. No new cases have turned up. There are thirteen plague cases being treated in isolation at Metropolitan. Some of the patients are still in critical condition, but most seem to be responding well to treatment. There have been eight deaths. Alan Katz has gotten a good look at the rats in the vicinity of the Ortiz tenement and they—and their fleas—appear to be happy and healthy. I think we should remain alert for new cases, but thanks to the Mayor's announcement last night, we should be able to sit on them immediately. I guess that's about it. I'd like to thank everyone for working so hard."

There was a little friendly applause and the meeting ended. Hart turned to Calabrese. "Vincent, thanks for talking to the Mayor last night."

"Don't mention it. As a matter of fact, I regretted it this morning when I was being driven to work and the FDR Drive was jammed with bumper-to-bumper traffic. Everyone is evidently taking the Mayor seriously and avoiding public transportation."

"Right," Hart said. "I rode down on the subway this morning and it wasn't crowded at all."

"*The New York Times,* the *Daily News,* the *Post,* the radio and TV stations, and the wire services have called this morning wanting to know the name of the disease," Andrews said, joining them. "I was tempted to tell them it was bourbourigmy."

They all laughed.

"An epidemic of stomach-growling!" Calabrese said. "I'll tell the White House physician that when he calls this morning."

"They still won't leave this alone," Hart said. "Why don't the feds believe us? That reminds me. The resident on MICU at Met told me that someone who said he was from the FBI tried to get in to see Adelaido Ortiz before he died. I understand that a lot of Cubans are recruited as informers and spies when they escape to the U.S."

"Doesn't Washington have something better to do with our tax money?" Andrews asked.

"Just be glad they waste their energies on petty activities." Calabrese lit a cigar. "If those secret-agent types had any brains, we'd all be in a lot of trouble. The whole country would be."

"Trouble? Gid oudda heah!" It was Alan Katz. "You played 'Beat the Reaper' and won!"

The telephone in the BPD office rang. It was DeLuca, the Medical Examiner.

"Uh, listen, Hart. I have a couple of autopsy reports I thought you should know about. Bilateral broncho-pneumonia with hemorrhagic pleural effusion . . . hemorrhagic rash . . ."

Hart felt everything in him and around him stop. The smiling faces of Calabrese, Katz, and Andrews seemed to freeze for an instant, their banter to hang suspended in the room.

"Cases from Metropolitan?" He heard the shiver in his own voice.

"No."

The word was like a crowbar blow across his chest. He retched on his palate. His mouth went sour.

"I have some police records here from a fingerprint check," DeLuca said. "They're not complete. One is Rhoda Sue Opdahl, also known as Marie Osmond, also known as Sue Osmond, also known as Marie Rhodes, arrested six times for disorderly conduct, three times for loitering for the purpose of committing prostitution, d.o.a. Roosevelt Hospital."

"Jesus," Hart murmured.

"The other one is George Brown, also known as Ritz Brown, a.k.a. Flash Ritz, a.k.a. Flash Brown. He was an addict, a dealer, and a pimp. He was found dead in his apartment on West Fifty-eighth Street."

After Hart hung up, he turned to the other men in the office. He thought he must look terrible, because they were all staring at him with great concern.

29

"Do you think the pleats in this jacket look all right?" Cosgrove turned so that his secretary could get a view of the side vents in his new uniform.

"Why, they're just so fabulous!" Miss Milam exclaimed.

"Do you think I look all right? I've got a new tailor, and I—"

"Why, General, I just *know* it's perfect. Everything about it just says—just says, 'Here's a *man* in *command!*'"

"You really mean that, now?" He cocked his head and pouted a little. "Maybe the old uniform was better—"

"General, I really and truly—cross-my-heart—think it looks fabu*loso*. It makes you look so—*Ah* don't know! So—*in charge.*"

"I'm going to lunch with the President and then I've got to stop in at a meeting over at HEW. When I get back I want to find that Defense Intelligence Agency report on David Hart on my desk. You hear?"

"Sure thing, General. Y'all have a nice day, now."

As Cosgrove sat in the Health, Education and Welfare conference room waiting impatiently for the meeting to begin, he noticed that the big capsules of tetracycline seemed to be sticking in his throat long after he had swallowed them. The drug made him somewhat sleepy. Interesting how the President had been the only one in the entire entourage who was advised to take medication. Very interesting.

Cosgrove stared at the people seated in front and in back of him on rows of folding chairs. These HEW types! The Secretary always bent over backwards to have just the right number of Negroes around. Christine Shore Lewis, for example, who was just now calling the meeting to order. That trouble-making twat —always in the news banning something or other. To Cosgrove's mind she belonged on a box of pancake mix rather than in the office of Surgeon General. A couple of Mexican-Americans were also present—sorry, "Chicanos." Jews weren't so bad. They tended to be slippery know-it-alls, but at least they didn't go around campaigning to be called Hebro-Americans or some such nonsense.

To make it worse, about half the gathering was female. A goddamned hen party.

The head of the Center for Disease Control, Carl Rader, went to a blackboard at the front of the room and began speaking. He was small and deeply tanned and spoke slowly to the gathering as if it were composed of children. "There is an epidemic of pneumonic plague in New York City," he said. "Until this morning, the outbreak appeared to be under control, with all cases and exposures identified and isolated. But then two new fatalities were discovered. One of those persons was a pimp and a drug dealer, and the other was a prostitute. The City's Department of Health does not know how these two were infected—whether they came in contact with the index case, Sarah Dobbs, or whether they were infected in some other way. We have no idea how many people may have been exposed to them. Pneumonic plague is transmitted very rapidly and easily. A single case can infect dozens of people with a sneeze, a cough, or even a breath. The latest word is that pneumonic cases have been cropping up all over Manhattan, with some midtown hospitals reporting as many as ten each. The count so far is a total of fifty-three cases, with fourteen deaths.

"According to the evaluation by two of our CDC

epidemiologists, who visited the Bureau of Preventable Diseases in New York yesterday, the Department of Health is not sufficiently well equipped or well staffed to handle routine outbreaks. An epidemic of something as critical as the plague would require considerable support from federal resources, in my opinion."

The people listened raptly, some of them with expressions of fear, others with faces filled with strain.

"What about quarantining the epidemic so the rest of the country doesn't get it?" Cosgrove asked.

"Quarantine is really a rather old-hat concept," Rader replied. "They used to practice it in the nineteenth century. Isolation wards for the sick are feasible, but a quarantine of an area, a neighborhood—or even, say, Manhattan—is just impossible."

"Thank you very much, Dr. Rader," Christine Shore Lewis said. "I am sure it's apparent to everyone present that we must act quickly and do whatever we can to be of help to the New York Health Department. The potential for crisis—for human suffering—is enormous."

Cosgrove listened as Rader and the Surgeon General outlined a plan: all available Public Health Service officers were to be sent to the city, sanitarian teams mobilized, Army doctors in the Reserve placed on active duty for the duration, medical institutions in New York, New Jersey, and Connecticut supplied with additional personnel and medicine.

"We have to go into the neighborhoods and talk to the minorities," said a woman with a Spanish accent. "They're always the hardest hit, because they're poor and because they don't understand what's best for them in a situation like this. They must be educated so that they know how to protect themselves."

"Amen," someone said.

"Gentlemen," Cosgrove said. "Uh, Mrs. Lewis . . . The President personally asked me if I would represent him at your meeting here. I would like to say, simply, that because of the potential threat to the security of the United States posed by the current situation in

New York, the President has directed a special committee, operating with the National Security Council, to take charge of government policy in regard to this matter. No actions will be implemented without approval by this committee. I suggest therefore that this meeting be adjourned. We will reconvene at the Executive Office Building at 1700 hours. Those of you whose participation is needed will be notified beforehand. Now, if you'll excuse me, I'm very late for another appointment, so good afternoon, gentlemen."

"Just a minute, General," Dr. Lewis said, getting to her feet. She was a tall woman with a broad face, a high forehead, wavy hair, and the relentless gaze of an ice-pick murderer. "You don't just walk in here and walk out like that! Every minute of postponement—every minute we sit here in this room, someone else gets sick. Babies, old folks. We have to act immediately. And we will. You go ahead and worry about national security. We have to save lives."

Cosgrove rose, keeping his face stony. "And so do *we,* Madame." Imagine, his father had once told him, that you are always walking on the bodies of your enemies. He tucked his hat under his arm and strode out, his chin jutting forward, his stride long and powerful.

30

"YOU TOOK your tetracycline last night?" Andrews asked Hart as they rode uptown on the subway.

"I can't remember," he replied. "But I'll take some as soon as we get to Met. I took the regular dosage all day yesterday, I think. Wednesday seems so long ago."

"Doesn't it?" Andrews shook his head and wiped

the sweat from his eyelids. "I feel like I'm in another dimension or something. Everything looks and feels the same, but somehow the arrangement is different."

"I know what you mean."

Andrews leafed through the afternoon edition of the New York *Post*.

Hart's stomach raced, he kept swallowing, he had shooting pains in his head. Fear. The same cycle of thoughts kept revolving in his brain: a clearly worded statement to the media educating people on how to get medication and how to protect themselves; police cooperation in controlling a possible panic . . . He tried not to berate himself. How was he to know that a pimp and a hooker had been spreading it around? Where did *they* get it? Some drifter in the bus-terminal area who gave it to Sarah Dobbs and to them, too? Where was *that* case? No—the evidence was strongly in favor of Sarah Dobbs as the index case. The shiny-eyed squirrel at Point Lobos. She must have had some contact with the pimp or the prostitute. Maybe she had used drugs, and bought them from the pimp? No, she had led a sheltered, straight life. Gayle's interviews with her parents and friends had not turned up anything tawdry.

"Oh, Jesus Christ!" Andrews yelled suddenly. Hart jumped.

"Look at this!" Andrews handed him the paper folded open to page six.

BLACK DEATH IN HARLEM?

There have been unconfirmed reports of five or more deaths from bubonic plague, the "Black Death," in Harlem.

City health officials have denied these reports and attribute them to rumors surrounding the current increase in pneumonia cases at Metropolitan Hospital, which is located on the edge of Spanish Harlem.

Bubonic plague is transmitted by rats, etaoinshrdlulargelumps inthe armpits and groin area.

Rev. Booker Smith, Director of the East Harlem Community Awareness Program, stated that "We can get no response from the authorities on this dangerous matter. We have been begging for better rat-extermination programs for years. I think it's time the people get their own rat poison and deal with this menace once and for all." He added, "The Mayor has cut off every social program in Harlem over the past few years. He's just trying to create a crisis big enough to attract federal money to solve his budget problems. The bubonic plague deaths are just a part of this nefarious plan."

The crowd around Metropolitan waiting to receive medication completely filled the courtyard outside the emergency room and spilled out onto the sidewalks, the lawns, and the streets. Hospital guards held open a lane for ambulances, which passed so slowly that bystanders could peer in through the windows. Hart and Andrews saw a man with a bloodstained mouth lying in one ambulance. Others saw him too, and relayed the news: "He's got it, blood on his mouth, he's got it, too! Another one!" Men, women, and children pushed and jostled one another to see. Across the street from the hospital, a black man in a black suit stood on the roof of a car and shouted: "We got a dis-ease in Harlem! Who give us this dis-ease? The *man* gave us the dis-ease! We gettin' *sick* in Harlem! Hallelujah, we gettin' *sick* in Harlem! Who makin' us sick? The *man* makin' us sick! Praise God! The man tryin' to kill off all the black peoples of the worl'!"

There was a continuous mad symphony of sirens. Hart was tired. The faces pressed around him were angry and distorted. He kept blinking. I am cracking, he thought. Cracking under pressure. I can't handle this.

"Dave, hey Dave?" Andrews gripped Hart's shoulder. "I don't think we'd better try to get through this crowd. We'd better go directly to Gracie Mansion."

"No," said Hart. NO. The word ran along his bones, opened his eyelids wider. NO. No cracking up. No copping out. This is just a shitload of hard work, no different from sleepless weeks as an interne, or in a bush clinic. The important thing was to keep alert and keep going and do what needed to be done. He shouldered his way through the crowd and Andrews followed.

"We are frantic!" Garson shouted. "Just *frantic,* Hart! We need extra staff and Strohman is dragging his feet on sending in reinforcements!" Garson followed Hart as he moved swiftly through the corridor. "We don't have enough personnel to handle all the cases that are coming in! Many of them need respirators and intensive care!"

"Do what you can, do what you can," Hart said. "I understand. I'm going to see the Mayor and I assure you that I will see that you're given enough extra staff to cope with this. The other city hospitals are also in the same situation. Hysteria won't help. Stay calm and set a good example."

The contagion ward was filled with plague cases. Behind the glass partitions of room after room, Hart could see beds filled with men, women, and children. Many were connected to respirators and intravenous bottles. Nurses ran through the corridor carrying syringes and basins. The sounds of groans and deep coughing were everywhere. An orderly wheeled a stretcher with a covered corpse.

Suddenly a toothless old black woman burst out of a room. "Oh Lord a Mercy I see the Beast at the endin' of the World!" she shrieked. Blood streamed from the corners of her mouth and her hands danced like bats. The orderly firmly pushed the woman back into the room, where she continued to rave. "I see his horns, I see the fire! Oh Lord God a Mercy!"

Emerson emerged from his office looking withered and cowed. "Hart, I never thought I'd see my ward turned into a—a pesthouse!" There were tears in his eyes. "I can't believe this is happening . . . it's just not . . ."

"You must rest, Dr. Emerson," Hart said soothingly. "You've been taking the tetracycline dosage?"

"I started today. I didn't believe there was any epidemic until I came in today and saw—"

Hart kept moving until he found Rodriguez. She was at the bedside of a man who was gasping and thrashing. His arms and legs had been strapped to the bed. "My wallet! She took my wallet! My credit cards!" he screamed.

"I'm trying to learn who he's been in contact with," she told Hart. "He's not making any sense. He thinks he's at the Holiday Inn or someplace. I've interviewed twenty-two people so far. Gayle is over at Bellevue doing the same thing."

"Lots of contacts per patient?" Hart asked, lightly touching her shoulder.

"Oh, David." Her mouth turned down. "It's so hopeless. We treat one case and five new ones crop up. My cousin—"

"I'm sorry, Dolores. I really am sorry. You are doing a very good job here." His tone sounded mechanical to him. "Just keep it up, do one thing at a time, pay close attention. And take the tetracycline. You'd better get some more strep too, since you've been in intimate contact with these patients. We'll all just keep working as hard as we can. The government, the Army, somebody will send in more medical help—Sam and I are going over to Gracie Mansion to meet with Calabrese and the Mayor right now. If anything comes up, you can contact me there."

He looked at her for a long moment before turning away. He wanted to memorize her face.

The Mayor tried his best not to look rattled. That was good, Hart thought. He was a tall, thin man with a full head of white, wavy hair, a trim moustache, and the manner of a good dentist. Hart felt immediately at ease with him.

"Dr. Hart, Dr. Andrews, thank you for coming. I know you are extremely busy with this grave situation, which I know we can overcome."

Hart extended his hand to shake the Mayor's, but Weinstein drew back. Hart and Andrews exchanged quick glances. "We're not contagious, Your Honor. Don't worry," Hart said.

The Mayor laughed with his teeth closed. "Oh, well, yes, just instinct I suppose. Such a scary word, plague is. But the point which we all have to remind ourselves of is not to panic, right?"

"Right."

The Mayor sat down at the head of the table and Hart and Andrews sat down next to Calabrese. As the other officials, including Councilman Barnes, filed into the room and took chairs, they all chose the opposite side of the table.

"Your Honor, I have some suggestions," Hart said. He did not feel like waiting for protocol now. "Your Statement of Imminent Peril last night has helped us today. Now we have to go on TV immediately and state very explicitly what's going on and also send out a call for volunteers. In the tri-state area there are enough nurses, doctors, and paramedical personnel to help in the clinics and hospitals."

The Mayor did not appear to be listening. He was reading a note a secretary had just handed him. Goddamn these politicians, Hart fumed. His face grew hot. Politics always comes first. He'd better understand that if he doesn't act quickly, there won't be any voters left to vote.

"Excuse me," Mr. Weinstein said. "I've just been informed that the unions—police, firemen, sanitation workers, and hospital workers—have all agreed to call a work stoppage at midnight unless we guarantee that if they come into Manhattan they won't be sent into

Harlem or any other infected areas. They also want medication."

"We can definitely give them medication," Calabrese said. "Medication that will protect them when they go into infected areas. They *must* go in—"

"Have you seen *this?*" Councilman Barnes held up the early evening edition of the New York *Post* with the headline, in big type: PNEUMONIA EPIDEMIC IN CITY: 32 DEATHS. "The editorial asks whether this has anything to do with the plague rumors in Harlem. They want to know why the Health Department is sitting on its hands."

"Listen, Your Honor," Hart said, speaking quietly but with force. "I suggest that you go on TV and explain this. And you should start talking to the union leaders immediately. But meanwhile, since we can't rely on the outcome of those talks, the declaration of a State of Imminent Peril is no longer sufficient, and I would respectfully suggest that you arrange for the declaration of a State of Emergency right now and ask the Governor to call in the National Guard."

"Yes, David is right, Sid," Calabrese said. Hart had never seen his boss look so tense; his facial muscles, normally smooth, were knotted, making him look much older. "I'll go talk to the union representatives with you if you like. They have to be made to understand that tetracycline will protect them. They must understand that this is exactly like a war, and that they are our army. But since they might not buy that, I agree that we must persuade the Governor that she has to call in the National Guard."

The Mayor rubbed his chin and stared at the table-top. "I am extremely reluctant to do that on account of the fact that when a State of Emergency is declared, people get very excited. The law is that in a State of Emergency, all insurance policies are automatically voided. The business community would go into a turmoil, which would have a ripple effect. The threat to property—"

"Goddamn it!" Hart exclaimed. He slapped the table. "Your *life* is the best personal property you own! And the best way to protect it is to bring in the Guard, and even Army medical personnel, and solicit volunteer nurses and doctors. The resources of the Health Department have been exhausted. We are not sitting on our hands! We've been working day and night. The hospitals are barely able to manage, and the cases are still coming in. When I left Metropolitan Hospital a few minutes ago, there were sixty-two cases jammed into a small isolation ward. Many of them require intensive care, and special machinery that we'll have to bring in from the other boroughs. And outside the hospital there's a large, worried crowd."

"Whatever happened to quarantine?" Barnes wanted to know. "Why can't the infected areas be cordoned off and guarded? Or maybe a kind of triage approach: we save the parts of the city that we can, with all the help we can muster, and in the infected parts, let events just . . . take their course."

"Dr. Hart?" The Mayor appeared to be pleading.

"Your Honor, I know that we can stop the epidemic right now, within the next few days, if we're given enough help and cooperation. Politics has to be put aside; otherwise, more people will die in a mass panic— caused by conflicting reports and terrible rumors—than would ever die of the plague.

"Furthermore," he went on, "we should immediately start giving tetracycline out on demand at all of the city hospitals and district health centers. We also must set up receiving centers and wards to isolate and treat all cases. Some of the hospitals and clinics that have been closed in the past few years could be temporarily reopened. Streptomycin should also be given on demand, although that has to be done by injection and will take more time. And let me repeat what I said earlier: You and perhaps Commissioner Calabrese should hold a conference with the most responsible members of the press and give them a clear, truthful statement, and you should also educate the public by going on television. If people learn that there are precautions that they can take and that treatment is available, they won't panic."

"I strongly endorse everything Dr. Hart has just said." Calabrese seemed somewhat surprised that Hart had taken over.

"Your Honor," Kaprow began, "I have a report here—"

"Does it have to do with what is going on right now?" asked the Mayor.

"It's about bridge and tunnel egresses in Manhattan, and I—"

"Save it for later."

The Mayor's secretary signaled to Hart from the doorway. He got up and went toward her but she backed away, whispering, "The Surgeon General is calling from Washington. I'll show you which telephone to use." She led him past her office to a small room with a stool and a phone on the floor. Hart was puzzled; then he realized that she was avoiding him, like the plague.

31

THE NATIONAL Security Council met in a long, bone-colored, low-ceilinged room in the basement of the Executive Office Building. It was enclosed in an electronic membrane that prevented sounds from being transmitted to outside eavesdroppers. Cosgrove watched the members of the Council enter the room one by one and take their places around a polished teakwood table.

Most of them fixed their gaze on a blank movie screen set up at the end of the table.

Even before Cosgrove had been appointed head of the National Security Council, he had looked upon its members as so many logs. They all ran important outfits, like the National Security Agency, the Defense Intelligence Agency, and the State Department, but all their time was spent sitting through one meeting after another, and they were no longer particularly useful for anything, to Cosgrove's mind, except as totems. Over the years, Cosgrove had been able to refine the membership of the council until most of the incumbents reflexively favored his directives. He never let any of them forget that they owed their status to him and that they were mere transients. Cosgrove, of course, remained secure in the arms of the permanent hidden government of the United States.

Dr. Christine Shore Lewis, the Surgeon General of the United States, was not a log, and for this reason she seemed quite out of place. She was too interesting, Cosgrove thought. She was too vehement, and too dedicated to be anything but a hindrance to the smooth operation of the meeting. Cosgrove had not wanted her to attend, but the President had insisted upon it. In small matters like these, Cosgrove was quick to give in. It kept the President from feeling his genuine weakness on those occasions when important decisions had to be made by Cosgrove and the other permanent people. And, if she were completely excluded, she would probably not hesitate to slander Cosgrove in the media and stir up a great deal of annoying public sentiment about New York.

Cosgrove opened the meeting and introduced Dr. Lewis.

She had a deep, musical voice and Cosgrove half-expected her to break into the opening bars of the national anthem. All in all, in the hushed, white room, filled with white men in dark suits and uniforms, she looked very odd. "I've requested that the epidemiological units of the Army Medical Corps to be flown to New York," she was saying, "but I understand that they're in Fort Bragg, North Carolina, and Fort Backer, California, and that it will take some time for them to assemble. I've also set up a network for coordinating and allocating volunteer medical personnel who want to go to New York. But in addition to the spread of the disease itself, there's the very serious problem of panic. City authorities have made some vague statements to the press, and the State of Imminent Peril the Mayor declared yesterday remains in effect, so that people are avoiding public transportation, schools are staying closed, and so on. However, the sanitation workers are still on strike, and the other unions are refusing to return to work tomorrow. The police, firemen, and hospital workers are refusing to report tonight. This alone may start a panic. In summary, gentlemen, we have an enormous crisis on our hands.

"I realize that many of you here are concerned primarily with defense. But I would urge you to keep in mind that our objective here is to save lives: our only enemy at the moment is the plague."

"Of course, Mrs. Lewis," Cosgrove said. "Thank you very much for your briefing. I'm sure you will understand that because the rest of our meeting concerns classified information, we'll have to ask you to leave now."

"What? This is an epidemic! I don't see how this can be 'classified.'" She frowned. "We don't have a lot of time! We don't know if this epidemic can be contained."

"We're all aware of these problems, Mrs. Lewis. Now, if—"

"And there's something else you should be aware of, *Mister* Cosgrove," she cut in. "If this epidemic spreads, it could quickly become a *pandemic*. Not only America but the rest of the world, particularly the underdeveloped countries, could be decimated. I'm serious. Food shortages are so severe now that resistance to infection in backward countries is practically nil—the time is ripe for a pandemic. If we act promptly and intelligently, we—"

"Colonel Watkins," Cosgrove turned and addressed his aide. "Would you please escort Mrs. Lewis to the—"

"I won't be shut out of this!"

"Perhaps Dr. Lewis could assist us in working out the public-health aspects of this," Bryce Marks said.

A ripple of mutters passed around the table.

When Cosgrove asked someone to leave, he—there had never been a she before—left. Cosgrove looked at Marks. "Mr. Marks, we have before us a problem of national security. I don't think that Mrs. Lewis should be troubling herself about our affairs when she has so much to attend to over at HEW. I will see that she's briefed on any unclassified matters we may be covering today."

Colonel Watkins, looking as if he expected Dr. Lewis to strike him, stepped forward to escort her to the door.

"If you boys don't wise up," the Surgeon General said loudly, "if you boys don't make sure that all the federal relief you can possibly get together goes to New York City in the next twenty-four hours, you're going to regret it as long as you live. I can guarantee that. People are dying up there, and we have the power to help them. I'm going to do everything I can. I'm going to go to the President and sit him down and tell him the straight life-or-death facts." She glared at Cosgrove. "Just once, just for a change, I hope you decide to apply a little of your know-how toward helping people." She brushed past Watkins and slammed the door.

There were a few low, uneasy laughs.

Cosgrove wondered if they were intended for him; had he handled this farce of a woman in a suitably stern way? "Before this meeting," he began, "I spoke with the President, and he asked me to remind all of you that we're here to make emergency decisions on this multidimensional national security crisis. We're at a critical juncture in regard to preserving the United

States government's ability to act. Particularly since we are confronted with implications on an international level. For this reason, I've invited some gentlemen who don't normally attend our meetings—the Attorney General; General Sheffield from Fort Detrick; Doctor Gould from the Treasury Department; General Burlingham from the Office of Emergency Preparedness. Each of them will be briefing us on his field of expertise."

General Phillip Sheffield sat forward to speak. He was a short, bald-headed man who smiled frequently, although his eyes always remained cold. His face was round and waxen, and he made Cosgrove think of a nun. Sheffield was as immaculate as any single person in government. He had a doctorate in biochemistry and had been Director of the Technical Services Division at Fort Detrick, Maryland, before going on to his present position as head of the Chemical-Bacteriological Center there. He probably knew more about chemical, biological, and radiological warfare, or CBR, than anyone else in the country. His views on the subject coincided with Cosgrove's, and in fact, they had collaborated on a number of projects. Nevertheless, Cosgrove reserved for himself a few percentage points of doubt: if the CIA had engineered this epidemic, or had a hand in it in any way, then they might have co-opted Sheffield. *They*—Marks, perhaps?—might be exploiting Sheffield's close ties to Cosgrove. *They* might even know of the one secret whose exposure neither Sheffield nor Cosgrove could endure. Operation Visitation. The thought made Cosgrove swallow involuntarily.

"I would like to begin," Sheffield said, "by quoting Marshal Zhukov, who stated in 1956 that 'Our future wars will not be won with nuclear weapons and mass airpower alone; biological and chemical weapons will be used to augment conventional and atomic weapons.' Khrushchev also said, shortly before his retirement: 'All available weapons will be used in the next war, and this is the logic of war, the logic of struggle.' And, finally, I would like to quote from a report made in

178

1960 by the Committee on Science and Astronautics of the House of Representatives: 'Chemical-biological-radiological—CBR—warfare is toxic warfare against man, his animals and crops, rather than explosive warfare which destroys both man and his material possessions, such as buildings and machines. Much emotion and political portent are associated with these forms of warfare, but they are very real and very likely to be used against the United States.'" He spoke effortlessly and quickly, as though he had made this presentation many times before. "And so we must definitely consider the possibility that New York City has become the target of CBR.

"Now, in the case of biological warfare," Sheffield continued, "living microorganisms which cause disease are employed to reduce man's ability to wage war. They can be used to attack his crops or domestic animals and reduce his resources. At Fort Detrick we've worked to anticipate attacks of this nature from every conceivable form of dangerous microorganism. Biological agents include not only bacteria, but also the rickettsiae, the viruses, the fungi, the protozoa, and the microbial toxins. Slide, please." A kaleidoscopic image of red, blue, and purple photomicrographs of these organisms stained the screen. "There are about one hundred sixty serious diseases that can be caused by biological agents. These antipersonnel agents may be classified as either lethal or as incapacitating. Plague, for example, is lethal, as are anthrax, smallpox, botulism toxin, and the various kinds of encephalitis. The agents that incapacitate are brucellosis, Q-fever, and staphylococcal poisoning—but those are not our concern on this day. Now, potentially lethal agents must lend themselves to efficient dissemination and predictable effects. The enemy would also desire that his agent be treatable by his forces while going undetected and being difficult to treat by our forces. Certainly the situation in New York fits these requirements.

"Now. A biological weapon requires disseminating

munition and a delivery vehicle. Two of the most effective means of dissemination are by way of the aerosol form and by the use of infected insect vectors. In the case of bubonic plague we have infected fleas; in the case of pneumonic plague, the transmission is via aerosolized secretions. Dissemination by insect vectors provides certain capabilities which do not exist when using the aerosol form. The insect vector is truly a search-type weapon. Some insect vectors specifically seek out humans, while others, like rat fleas, will take humans as their second choice."

Sheffield spoke without looking at anyone, as though he were alone with a tape recorder. "Now, we've developed a bomblet the size of a baseball that can contain several billion effective doses in aerosolized form; two or three such bomblets would produce a satisfactory casualty level over an area of one square mile. The evidence does not support the notion that such a bomblet may have been released in Manhattan, but I mention it anyway to give you an idea of how effectively the aerosol form can work on an unprotected population. Should we ever decide to retaliate in this manner, we're prepared. We've also recently made the Rotocraft monocopter part of our potential delivery system. Slide, please."

On the screen flashed a picture of an object resembling a single blade of a helicopter rotor. "The aerodynamic design of the Rotocraft monocopter is taken from the samara, the winged seed pod of the maple tree." Sheffield smiled. "The monocopter is rather like a very small, unmanned helicopter, and it lets us spray areas without actually sending in manned helicopters. Now, this model is about two feet long, weighs two pounds, and can carry a payload of five pounds. It's powered by a compressor. It has a flight range of twelve miles, a flight duration of about twenty minutes, and an air speed of fifty knots. It's equipped with two sensors, one for ground and one for obstacle orientation, and it has a heading accuracy of ten degrees and a twenty-foot range collision system. It was developed to provide a cheap and safe method of dispensing insecticide on the battlefield at the point of contact of troops and disease vectors, like malaria mosquitoes. The monocopter is quite versatile, and, as you can see, it would be the ideal vehicle for maneuvering among tall buildings and through narrow streets. An enemy could put a payload of some aerosolized biological agent in a monocopter and launch it from a distance of twelve miles. Say it were targeted for Times Square . . ."

Sheffield paused while the men studied the picture of the strange white blade. "There's a children's toy on the market that employs the same concept," Sheffield said. "My boy has one."

He continued his briefing. "There are several factors bearing on the conduct of biological operations. One: A biological attack can occur without warning, since its agents can be disseminated by undetectable weapons systems, like infected fleas. Detection and positive identification, as we have seen in the cases in Manhattan, require appreciable time.

"Pneumonic plague further has the advantage of complicating preliminary diagnosis beyond recognition. In the index case in New York, the patient was diagnosed as having pneumonia. By the time it was determined that the patient had plague, many others had been infected.

"Other factors are—Two: Nondestruction of material and structures. Three: Penetration of structures. Four: Agent decay, which affects how much decontamination will later be necessary. In the case of plague, once the epidemic has run its course and burned out, the organism will remain in the reservoir provided by rats and other rodents. If New York City is severely affected, then decontamination measures will necessarily be extremely stringent, since all fleas and other carriers would have to be destroyed." He paused, as though he were considering his next remarks.

"I'm sure that Mr. Marks has supplemental data in regard to the use by foreign powers of plague as a biological agent. I would just like to conclude with a few historical facts.

"The Tartars catapulted plague-infected bodies into the city of Caffa, near Constantinople, during a siege; they won the battle, and then most of the population of Europe died in the period of one year from the Black Death, which spread outward from the Black Sea region.

"During the Sino-Japanese war in the Thirties, the Japanese tried introducing plague-infected fleas among the Chinese. No one knows whether this ploy was a success.

"And, as I'm sure most of you gentlemen are aware," Sheffield said, surveying the room, "there were experiments concerning the spread of plague among rodents in guerrilla-occupied zones in Vietnam, Laos, and Cambodia in the late Sixties."

Cosgrove tensed. Was Sheffield going to touch on Operation Visitation? But Sheffield leaned back and folded his hands. "In conclusion, I would like to remind everyone that plague as a means of biological warfare is already a reality, and that we should consider the epidemic in New York, which is a region never before afflicted by the disease, a possible foreign adventure."

With the exception of Marks, Cosgrove noted, the men around the table appeared stunned. He wondered if any of them had sufficient control of facial muscles to do that on cue. Marks, of course, always wore exactly the same calm expression. But then he probably knew about Operation Visitation.

Cosgrove looked at Marks, who sat opposite him. "Do you have any intelligence that might augment General Sheffield's excellent report?"

"Yes. In the last three hours we have drawn up a Preliminary National Intelligence Estimate from relevant information in our files and from recent surveillance." Marks's voice was even and light. He sat with his palms together and his fingers pointing outward, toward Cosgrove. "Plague is on the increase among humans and rodents in many countries. The World Health Organization lists a total of two thousand ninety-three cases for last year, with sixty-three deaths. Forty-seven of those deaths were in Vietnam alone. However, many—"

"Excuse me, Mr. Marks," Cosgrove said. "Do any of those cases in Vietnam relate to those plague experiments?"

"We have no way of knowing that," Marks replied. "Even prior to our operations in Vietnam, there were pockets of plague there. All our troops received anti-plague vaccine; that was one reason we confined those experiments to a disease we were certain could debilitate the enemy without affecting our men. While incidents of plague appear to have increased in Vietnam, we can't be sure why. It may be simply due to the decline in Western medical practices since the pull-out. As I was saying, it's difficult to determine true statistics concerning plague, because systems of reporting differ from country to country, and usually cases are underreported. This is partly because only confirmed cases are reported to the World Health Organization in most countries, and partly because many countries conceal cases for economic and political reasons. So we have no accurate picture of the extent of plague in the world, although WHO estimates it is more prevalent by a factor of three than the figures show.

"Now—" Marks paused, then resumed. "—we've also investigated the use of plague as an instrument of warfare among hostile foreign powers. To our knowledge, it's never been used. According to our best research, however, thirty-eight world leaders, hostile to increased surveillance on the part of the United States, have embraced CBR—chemical, biological, and radiological warfare. Several countries possess this sort of capability: ourselves, Israel, West Germany, Iran, the U.S.S.R., Britain, France, China. All these governments

deny they possess biological-warfare capability, but—
and this is extremely classified—they're quite well
equipped. We also suspect Iraq, Uganda, Syria, Egypt,
South Africa, and Brazil."

"What are your grounds for suspicion?" Cosgrove
asked. He suddenly wondered whether Agency operatives might have gotten to Hart's apartment and
cleaned out hard evidence of the man's foreign connec-
tions before the Defense Intelligence Agency boys'
break-in.

"Well, those countries like Iraq and so on have hidden nuclear capability, so we assume they also possess
CBR capability."

"You mean you don't *know?* You don't have *facts?*"
Cosgrove asked.

Marks's mouth tightened. He inhaled sharply and
started to speak. Then he stopped. Finally he said,
"No. We don't know. But as it happens, the technology
of producing plague is so simple that the most primitive
country could do it quickly. In any hostile country with
plague cases, the enemy could simply have a victim spit
into a vial and then convey the contents into this country, aerosolize the spit in a crowded place—and an epidemic would start. We have no evidence that this has
ever happened, but it's a possibility we can't rule out.
During the Fifties, the Agency spent a great deal of
time and money on studying U.S. vulnerability to
bacteriological warfare. It was concluded then that the
New York subway system was one of the best ways to
introduce a biological agent into a metropolitan area."

"Yes," Sheffield said. "We tested a gas in the subway
system that could have borne an active biological agent
throughout the entire system, infecting everyone who
rode on the trains."

"There are several classified reports on potential
outcomes," Marks went on. "All of them suggest that
the immobilization of the island of Manhattan through
bacterial warfare would gravely endanger the entire

country. New York is the one city whose paralysis could immobilize the country."

"Manhattan would be the primary target of a hostile power reluctant or unable to use nuclear warfare, then," said General Charles, Secretary of the Joint Chiefs of Staff.

"Perhaps."

"Mr. Marks," Cosgrove began, "in your opinion, could a terrorist group use plague to blackmail us?"

"We're anticipating that terrorist groups will rush forward to take all the credit for the New York situation whether they had anything to do with it or not. We've ordered increased surveillance on possible terrorist suspects: the Puerto Rican Liberation Front, the Jewish Defense League, the Weather Underground, the usual Palestinian and Arab terrorists . . . And of course we're actively surveilling the diplomatic communities in Washington and at the U.N."

"Any unusual movements?" Cosgrove asked.

"Well—yes and no. There's a heat wave and a garbage strike in New York, and so several diplomats have prolonged their vacations outside the city—the General Assembly doesn't open until later on in the month anyway. The Nigerian ambassador was recalled two days ago, but that appears to be in line with a domestic shakeup."

"What about the Cubans?" Cosgrove asked. "How many Cuban assets do you have targeted on the U.N.? How are they behaving?"

"All the major Cuban officials are still in Cuba, on summer vacation. But they take leave at this time every year. Three out of ten of our assets are also on vacation."

"I find that quite interesting, Mr. Marks," Cosgrove said.

"I should like to make it clear that we've found no evidence of work on the part of a foreign power in regard to this epidemic. What does concern me is the vulnerability of the United States while we're preoccupied with New York. That would certainly be the aim of any hostile foreign power. All overseas military and intelligence missions have been ordered to cancel all leaves and file hourly reports on suspicious movements. Israel is already fearful. There is the question of what bearing the Sino-Soviet détente has on all this. And we should notify the Shah—"

"I think it's important to let all our allies know that we'll continue to honor all our commitments as vigilantly as ever, despite the crisis," Cosgrove said.

"I have a question for Mr. Marks," said General Charles. "If the plague were introduced by a foreign power, I understand—from your remarks and General Sheffield's—that the best vehicle might not be a plane, or a bomb, but rather a person."

"An unwitting human agent, perhaps," Marks said. "Or a witting human agent carrying a properly prepared dispersal device."

"What intelligence do you have on the first victims of the plague in New York?" General Charles asked.

"Not much. The girl's best friend has an uncle who is a lawyer with the American Civil Liberties Union. In 1936, the girl's mother belonged to the Rosicrucian Anthroposophic Society. She was a member for a month. It became a Communist Front in 1939, when it relocated in Chicago under a grant from the FBI. The girl's maternal grandfather subscribed to *The Nation* for fifteen years. As for Domingo Ortiz—he was a Cuban refugee—"

The word "Cuban" caused a subdued commotion. The Secretary of State whispered something to the Attorney General. General Charles, who had a pinched, red face and a dyspeptic expression, leaned across the table. "Mr. Marks, that's very interesting information. Do you have any evidence that Ortiz was in G-2?"

"According to our assets in the Cuban Directorate General of Intelligence, no." Marks remained still, his palms together, his mouth a straight line.

"Was he with us?" asked General Charles.

"No."

"What information *do* you have on him, then?" asked Cosgrove.

"He appears to have escaped from Cienfuegos some time in mid-July and to have joined his family in Manhattan. The others all came over to the States after the revolution. His brother, Adelaido, worked with us on the Bay of Pigs and on JM/WAVE, and remained a live asset after he moved with his family to New York."

"Did he report the arrival of Domingo Ortiz to his case officer in New York?" asked Charles.

"No."

"What about Domingo Ortiz's Freedom Flight Debriefing Report?"

"We have Freedom Flight Debriefing Reports on all the other Ortizes . . ."

"You mean to tell me you boys have interviewed every single Cuban who has set foot in the U.S.A. since 1960 but yet you *don't* have a report on the one guy who brought plague into this country? Don't you think that's odd? Don't you think that's *unusual?*" Charles glared at Marks.

"We have no evidence, General, that Domingo Ortiz brought plague into this country," Marks replied.

"Well, with all due respect, Mr. Marks," Cosgrove said, "I would have to say that these are very suspicious circumstances, and I don't think you have thoroughly checked them out." Humiliate the little bastard. Let him squirm.

"I think we should be scrutinizing Castro very intensively," General Charles said. "In the past few years he's mysteriously come alive. Angola. Jamaica. Agitation in Puerto Rico—I mean, Jesus Christ, we *know* he's supporting the Puerto Rican Liberation Front! Ever since Angola it's been one unpredictable stunt after another. The more I hear, the more I'm persuaded that it would be very wise to partially mobilize our troops in the South just in case Castro is trying something. Goddamn it, I don't want to get caught with our pants down!"

"With all due respect, General," Cosgrove began, "I'd like to warn that if the military leaks anything regarding a foreign power using plague as a weapon, or if the military leaks anything regarding mobilization of troops—then Castro will become alarmed and he will certainly try something."

"This whole plague business has thrown the entire upper echelon of the government off balance," said General Charles through his teeth. "If this action is a preparatory attack, sir, then it has indeed succeeded!"

32

HART ANSWERED his ringing phone for the tenth time in as many minutes.

"What's the hardest job in a Polish town?"

"I give up, Alan." Hart had trouble focusing his attention on Katz's voice. A television in the outer office jabbered away; other phones rang continuously.

"Riding shotgun on the garbage wagon. But that's not what I called to tell you. I'm in a phone booth and this is my last dime. I wanted you to know that I'm widening the area we're spraying for fleas. We've turned up a couple of dancing rats."

"Whereabouts?" Hart's mind reeled at the thought: Bubonic plague had hit the rat population, just as he had feared. Hart's bones ached. His tongue worked dryly against the roof of his mouth.

"One on East 106th, another near 103rd and Park. Listen—what happened to the Health Department's press release? It's time to get an accurate statement to the media—the papers and TV stations have got to explain this *chozzerai* with the spraying."

"The Mayor is supposed to make some kind of announcement tonight on television," Hart said. "But he hasn't wanted to use the word 'plague.' Even so, we're already getting calls from the press."

"Calabrese better wake the man up," Katz said. "Already the community leaders up here are hassling me about the spraying. I'm uptown since early this morning. Everyone here is dying to set out rat poison. I can't seem to make anyone understand that you gotta kill the fleas first. People are giving my boys a hard time, ganging up around the pest-control vans—"

There was a click and a silence and then Katz's voice returned. "Sorry—we were automatically interrupted by the phone lady."

"You want police protection?" Hart asked.

"You kidding? My boys can take care of themselves." Katz's staff was recruited from Project Wildcat, a methadone-maintenance program. "The head of the Young Lords was giving me some shit today—"

"What did you tell him?"

"I told him to be very nice to me because I scare easy. No, I only mention this to give you an idea of why we got to get the media informed on this—look, the phone lady is going to cut me off. The point is, the people in East Harlem are scared. They know something is going on. Rats they know about. They know rats are big and mean and bite their kids. When people get scared, and the weather is hot, and the garbage is worse than usual—"

"I get the picture, Alan. Calabrese and I had better talk to the Mayor right away."

"Beautiful. Listen. Three Popes walk into a bar—a Catholic Pope, a Jewish Pope, and a Protestant Pope. The bartend—"

There was a click and a buzz. Hart sat holding the receiver and absently listening to the dial tone.

"Whew!" Jefferson came in and collapsed into a chair next to his desk. "I thought I'd never get back downtown. Everything's tied up. The trains are barely running. You suppose we're having a brownout or something?"

"The trains might not be running too well because the transit workers have started to call in 'sick,'" Andrews said from the outer office, where he was watching television. "Ditto the Manhattan police, most of whom live out in Long Island and up in Westchester. Ditto the firemen, all of whom seem to live in Queens, and ditto the sanitation workers. *They* live in Staten Island."

"Well, my old man ain't calling in sick." Jefferson kicked off her shoes and massaged her toes. "He's working overtime up in the Twenty-third. You heard about the trouble?"

"Trouble?" Hart started laughing and nearly choked.

"Calm down, boy!" Jefferson thumped him on the back.

Finally Hart got his breath. "I just swallowed the wrong way," he said. "Which trouble do you mean? When you have an epidemic of plague going, it's hard to keep your troubles in order, you know."

"Well, yeah, *that* trouble. But I'm talking about the trouble with the crowds up around Metropolitan. That's why my old man's got to work overtime."

"Oh, Jesus. Just what we need. Is Dolores back yet?"

"From Metropolitan? I haven't seen her."

"The Mayor is on the tube," Andrews called from the outer office.

"You go watch," Jefferson said. "I can't move."

The Mayor was pale. His voice was jerky, as though he were reading unfamiliar cue cards, and he kept tapping his lip with his forefinger. "We have not been given the federal funds we so desperately need to keep this great city going. A direct reflection of this problem is the current spread of pneumonia, which I'm not going to call an epidemic. The Commissioner of Health tells me it's not that serious. But—"

"Way to go, Sid!" Andrews exclaimed. "You know, he's a nice guy, a wonderful politician—but he's in over his head."

"I can't watch this." Hart went back to his desk. He took four aspirin. "Headache," he explained to Jefferson.

"I understand," she said. She massaged her own temples.

"Do you have a headache, too, Gayle?"

"Naw! Just a tight scalp. Now, honey, do you want to hear about the exposures at Bellevue we tracked down?"

"Okay. How many?"

"One thousand, two hundred and eight."

"God. How many cases?"

"When I left they were just bringing in number seventy-six. So far, twelve deaths. But they got quite a few who aren't going to make it. They're bringing in respirators from Queens, and they still don't have enough to manage the intensive-care patients."

"Same at Metropolitan. I did talk to the Surgeon General—"

"Of the U.S.A.?"

"Yup. She's flying in the Army's epidemiological units, and she's coordinating volunteer doctors and nurses and flying them in. Says there are a couple thousand volunteers. They should start arriving soon, and I'd like you to stay here and direct them to whatever hospitals need them the most."

"Hey!" Andrews called. "I just talked to the Medical Examiner. He says two more of his pathologists are sick, so they're way behind on autopsies. But so far they've found four bodies with incipient or fully developed inguinal and femoral nodes." He came to the doorway.

Hart stared at Andrews. A bubble of light encased

Andrews's head. It was veined with red and blue and it came to a point about six inches above the top of his skull. Hart blinked. The bubble remained. He brought his hands to his eyes and dropped his head. A red sheet descended over his vision.

"Bubonic," Andrews went on. "People are getting it from rats, too."

Hart broke into a heavy sweat. He was afraid to open his eyes.

"Don't you think," Andrews was saying, "that it's time to get the Mayor to declare a state of emergency, insurance policies be damned and full speed ahead?"

"I thought it was time to declare a state of emergency yesterday," Hart said. "What you saw on TV —the bid for federal aid—is the result of a three-hour meeting." He opened his eyes and looked around. Everything appeared normal. Gayle's black Afro had a phosphorescent glow, but that was not unusual, was it? "I think we'd better go back to Gracie Mansion and twist the Mayor's arm. I'll get Calabrese to come along. Gayle is going to mind the stone, I mean the store."

"I think *you* the one who's stoned, honey!" She put her arm around Hart's shoulders. "You better get some rest."

Hart phoned Calabrese, and they arranged to drive up in Calabrese's limousine. Then Hart phoned his father.

"Hi, Dad. How are things in Southampton?"

"Well, it's been fairly warm. Starting to get cool at night, though."

"Really? Already?"

"When are you going to come out for a visit?"

"Well, I've been pretty tied up, and I will be for a while. I just wanted to warn you." He spoke rapidly. So little time! "There's an epidemic of plague here, and—"

"What did you say?"

"Plague. A lot of people are getting pneumonic plague. Some even have bubonic."

"That can't be. It's never been in this part of the world."

"I know, Dad, but—"

"It's some other thing. Influenza."

"No, it's plague."

"Can't be. We would have heard about it, from the authorities, or on the television."

"The Mayor's been trying to keep it a secret to prevent a panic. But it really is the plague. Now, I want you to set things up so you're in good shape in case things get bad. Do you have some tetracycline?"

"That stuff turns your teeth yellow and ruins your kidneys. Wouldn't have it in the house if you paid me."

"You *have* to take it, Dad. It's the only thing—"

"Goddamn it, I'm a physician, too. Or have you forgotten?" His voice turned cold.

"I don't have time to get into an argument with you, Dad. Please. You have to do what I say. I *am* the authority. Remember? I'm the Director of the Bureau of Preventable Diseases for the City of New York."

"You think I'm senile? You think I don't know that by now? Hell, you're always telling me about that crap."

"You'd better stock up on food. But the most important thing is the tetracycline. Five hundred milligrams four times a day for the next week. I'm warning you. This is the plague."

"Well, we'll see what the television says."

There was a click. "I hope you drop dead," Hart said.

33

As THE limousine carried Andrews, Calabrese, and Hart up through Chinatown, along the Bowery, and through Little Italy, Hart leaned back and gazed out the window through half-closed eyes. The streets were crowded with pedestrians avoiding the buses and subways. There were Chinese grandmothers in brocade jackets lugging shopping bags, plump Italian women in black dresses, bums with paper bags containing bottles of cheap wine. They all blurred together in the thick twilight, their foreheads flickering in Hart's vision like candles.

"I'm pretty sure the National Guard can handle this, and along with the assistance we'll be getting from the Army, we can stop this before it gets any bigger." Calabrese's voice was strong and clear.

"I'm not so sure," Andrews said.

"Well, it's still contained in Manhattan—that one case in Brooklyn was brought into Bellevue and there weren't any untreated exposures out there. We have the medication, we're getting the manpower. It seems to me the federal government has been slow to react —not a peep from the President on this yet—but that's not unusual."

"Don't you think the feds would like to kick the shit—pardon my language, sir—uh—I know I am technically a fed, but—"

Calabrese laughed dryly. "Sam! You're in New York too long! The CDC must think you've gone native.

Sure, the feds *would* like to kick the shit out of New York. But they won't. This country can't make it without New York. Even if the place is a pesthouse."

The counterpoint of Andrews's Georgia drawl and Calabrese's flat Little-Italy delivery was soothing to Hart. He didn't care what they were talking about; the sounds of their voices felt good in his ears. The limousine moved slowly, from one traffic jam to the next, the driver calling out from time to time that he was making a detour.

After they confronted the Mayor, Hart would go over to Metropolitan and escort Dolores out. She deserved some rest. Then he would go back to the Health Department and work out what the National Guard, the Army epidemiological units, and the volunteer medics would do at each hospital and clinic. It would be important to get mobile medical units moving through the city to give out tetracycline, strep, and—why not?—plague vaccine when it came in. The Army was well supplied, no doubt. Enough nurses with each mobile unit to do examinations, bring the sick back to the hospitals. The hospitals! God. Talk to Strohman, reopen Sydenham Hospital, a couple of the others. Use stretchers on the floors. . . . And the dead —the morgues must be filling up. Cremation. Make a note, a not, a knot, an ought, the lights, the lights, too bright, his mind was sliding sideways, the headlights bled over his eyes . . . he was right, he was right, his father would not listen, he was right, he would write, in the bright, write in the bright book of life . . .

The mayor was not at Gracie Mansion. He had gone up to Spanish Harlem, followed by television crews from the networks and the local stations, to speak to the rioters.

Back into the black limousine. It pressed on, slowly, a barge in a human river. People thumped on the roof, on the hood, cracked against the windshield with their knuckles. They hooted, they screeched, they screamed. There was chanting. It echoed over and over in his inner ear, in his chest cavity. Better not to explain this to anyone.

"Those people are going plumb insane!" Andrews said.

"I think they're very sensible," Hart said thickly. His mouth was full of saliva and his tongue was sluggish. He spat into a tissue and stuffed it in his pocket.

"What?"

"What?"

Calabrese and Andrews turned and looked at Hart. The light on the planes and angles of their faces from the street lamps and the headlights of oncoming cars made them into divine statues, gods, in a pharaoh's tomb.

"Well, they're very man—er, *mad*—and afraid, and that's how they're acting. Not like us, sitting here with our hams in our lamps."

"We're mad and afraid like they are?" Andrews said, baffled.

"Yes."

"Are you feeling okay, Dave?" Calabrese looked at Hart closely in the dark.

"Yes."

"But we're trying to do something sensible and they're just—just rioting!" Andrews exclaimed.

"It comes out the same."

The lights from the television trucks had turned a portion of the block adjacent to Metropolitan Hospital into day. The shadows to each side and above the lights were so deep and sharp that they abraded Hart's skull. The sheet of light was a scintillating scroll that seemed to roll and unroll continuously as he blinked. There were sounds of bottles smashing, and more shouts.

The Mayor was at a microphone next to a television

truck, and police on horseback kept the area around him cleared. "We are bringing help to you, to everyone," he was saying. "Now, it is important for your own sake, which is the most important of all, and it is important for our great city, which is the greatest city in the world, to pull together. To help one another. Which is a simple, small thing to do, but the only thing that will make it possible for us to help the sick. And the federal government has promised aid."

"You stupid motherfucker!" someone shouted. "Give us the medicine and shut up!"

"We have medication right here in the Emergency Room of Metropolitan Hospital—enough for everyone. Wait your turn, line up, you will all be taken care of! I am going to take mine right now!" The TV camera swung toward the Mayor's face for a close-up. A woman handed him a glass of water.

The glass, the golden cup, Hart wanted to stop him, wanted to shut him up. The mayor could have said "soda water bottle" over and over and it would have been just as useful. State of emergency. Hart had to get to him, to warn him not to drink from the golden cup.

He fought his way toward the burning scroll.

Faces and bodies spurting blue and white flames surged around Hart and divided ahead of him like water.

"We might as well try to talk to him as soon as he's through with his speech!" Calabrese yelled over the noise.

"It's okay as long as we stay along the police line here," Andrews said.

Calabrese told a mounted policeman who they were and the man reined his horse back so that they could pass into the cleared circle where Mayor Weinstein stood under the lights.

Hart was coughing now, and his arms and legs were

trembling. His shirt was soaked with perspiration. The headache was gone. He felt nothing. He was as weightless as light itself. He could fly in waves of energy toward the Mayor, no, past the Mayor, toward Dolores . . . O Dark Lady! She filled the night sky, a ship's prow, a face on an Olmecan vase. His legs and arms loosened in their sockets and flew outward from his body.

He turned to Calabrese, but Calabrese was listening to the Mayor.

"I can't declare a state of emergency," Weinstein was saying. "I just can't. We're going to do okay without that, aren't we? We'll get the National Guard in anyway. I already called Albany. They can run things until the unions come to their senses—"

"Sid, the Guard isn't coming. I just talked to Barnes back at Gracie Mansion. He was looking for you to tell you. The Guard refuses to come into the city."

The Mayor shriveled. He grew smaller and smaller until he was the size of a doll. Hart watched in horror. A TV newscaster approached Weinstein with a microphone in one hand and a newspaper in the other. "Your Honor, I am from WPIX and I would like to know if you have any comment on this headline." He held the paper up to the camera and then to the Mayor, who could not read it because the lights were directly in his eyes. "It's the midnight edition of the *Daily News.*"

The shouting and jostling of the crowd was growing louder. It sounded like the tide coming in.

" 'BLACK DEATH IN NYC'," Andrews read aloud. " 'SIXTY DIE!' "

Hart stepped forward to speak to the Mayor, who was still squinting at the front page uncomprehendingly. "Your Honor," Hart began, extending his hands toward the tiny figure. Then followed a long sentence that began as a brilliantly illuminated cloud flowing from Hart's mouth and ended in black.

As Hart pitched forward he could feel the light

ebbing away and the red shadows dropping over his face, and he knew that his head would not strike the pavement because his two friends were there to bear the fall.

34

THIRTY-SIX hours earlier, droplets containing the organism had been drawn into the momentary vacuum created by a single inhalation. In one breath, an invisible force had entered Hart's body and begun to work. The tidal respiration of inspiration and expiration had carried the droplet nuclei deep into the traceries of the bronchial tree.

Some landed on the cells of the larger bronchioles and were immediately caught in the swaying forest of microscopic cilia. As though bent by the wind, these hairlike structures passed the small particles slowly upward until they reached the larynx. In a subliminal reflex, Hart swallowed the collection and it was passed down to the stomach. There, pools of antiseptic hydrochloric acid destroyed the invader.

Other droplet nuclei penetrated the barrier of cilia and slid down into the smallest tubes to the air sacs, the alveoli. The droplets settled on the fine mucus of the air sacs and dissolved, releasing the organism. The carpet of mucus was rich in sugars, proteins, salts, and water. Each new breath brought in oxygen. The organism began to adapt to its new environment and to assimilate the nutrients it needed for reproduction.

Approximately every one-and-a-half hours the organisms divided and two clones appeared. Within twenty hours, wherever a droplet had come to rest, fourteen generations had sprung up. Scavenging white blood cells, the last defense of the lungs, found the invader and tried to attack and devour it. But there were far too few white blood cells, and the aggregate number of the organism was now in the millions. An alarm rippled through the microenvironment of the body. In a few hours, more white blood cells from reserves in the bone marrow and spleen would arrive in the lungs. These new cells would slow the invader for a time, but alone they would not be able to prevent a fulminating spread throughout the body.

35

As COSGROVE entered the White House Situation Room, two secretaries were chatting near a Telex machine. They had to raise their voices to be heard over the cacophony of a dozen scrambler teletypewriters, several wire-service teletype machines, television sets tuned to different networks, radios, ringing telephones, and people talking.

"Ah caint b'leeve it's four a.m. and ah'm still heah," one of them said.

"May I get through, please?" Cosgrove brushed past the two women. Then he ordered one of them to put a call through on a scrambler phone to the Joint Chiefs of Staff.

Cosgrove found a vacant desk. Next to it was a metal stand with a red telephone in a clear plastic box, which the secretary unlocked.

"I just spoke with the President," Cosgrove said. His words were electronically scrambled as soon as they registered in the telephone receiver and were shielded from decoding until the electrical impulses reached General Charles's scrambler phone in the War Room of the Pentagon. "The Governor is no problem. She called up the Guard, but they refused to go into the city. Conditions there are deteriorating very rapidly and she's ready to agree with anything we suggest. The Attorney General is worried about the danger of civil disorder spreading beyond the city and he wants to go with a declaration of a State of Emergency, and put the Guard on active duty in the suburbs to prevent vigilantism and a breakdown of order around gun, food, and medical supplies. But the Guard can't enforce a containment—the Army will have to do that. Now, a couple of hours ago, the President consented to the Alpha Echelon Contingency List evacuation, so I think we'll be able to secure martial law before noon. The riots in Manhattan have spread beyond Harlem and the areas around the hospitals, and they appear to be increasing in scope and violence, and the bridges and tunnels are already badly jammed. There seem to be two waves of panic —one in Manhattan, with everyone trying to escape the plague—not many have been able to get off the island because of the tie-ups at the egresses—and then a secondary wave in the suburbs. Everyone there is attempting to leave before plague reaches them. If we permit the residents to fan out from the infected area it will only spread the plague and further provoke vigilantism. The media, as usual, is our worst enemy in this. But I've persuaded the President to ask the networks to cooperate and to emphasize that a number of medical personnel have volunteered to go into the city. And the Army epidemiological units are on the way."

"Did you discuss invasion contingencies with the President?"

"We talked about it, and concluded that any invasion would be unwise at this point in—" Cosgrove was distracted by the hoarse, weary voice of Walter Cronkite emanating from a nearby television.

. . . and this just handed me . . . In addition to the riots and arson in East Harlem and around the hospitals, where plague has reached epidemic proportions on this grim September night, several large explosions have rocked the Wall Street area and midtown. We do not yet have—

"Good Christ," Cosgrove said. "Did you catch that?"

"We'd better step up the Alpha Echelon evacuation and get our quick-response Strategic Units ready to go," Charles said.

Colonel Watkins, Cosgrove's aide, appeared with a Telex report from the Center for Disease Control.

The Center for Disease Control has been notified of six cases in Brooklyn, fourteen in the Bronx, and ten in Queens. All of them are in strict isolation, in hospitals with armed guards. A few cases were actually shot by vigilantes as they tried to come to hospital emergency rooms. The last report from the Bureau of Preventable Diseases gave the plague death toll in Manhattan as three hundred and twelve. The estimate is that four to ten times that number are infected. Over six hundred medical volunteers have been brought into the City. If there are no further cases outside Manhattan within the next twenty-four hours, and if none of the cases in Manhattan is allowed to leave the island, and if more medical personnel and equipment can be sent in, then we will be able to contain the epidemic.

—Carl Rader, Director
U.S. Center for Disease Control

36

"AH'D SAY you just had an average week in New York City." Andrews pushed the plunger on the syringe and Hart winced. "Garbage strike, your apartment gets broken into, you go to a riot, you pass out right there on TV. Look out you don't get mugged, now."

"It's happened in hospitals before." Rodriguez slid an extra pillow under Hart's shoulders.

"Yeah." Hart kept dozing off every few seconds.

A low rumble rattled the partitions of the contagion ward. Hart closed his eyes and he was in Vietnam, the field hospital. The continuous clatter of Hueys, the smell of mildewed canvas and alcohol. Severed limbs, blasted faces, fixed, wide stares. He forced his eyes open and saw Dolores smoothing the sheet across his chest. He was so cold.

"What's—?" *Going on? Going on?* a voice in his head chanted. He searched for his will. It lived, in the center of his abdomen; he knew he had to hold on to that point or he would fly apart, turn into a billion particles, collapse into a permanent dream.

"Those are helicopters," Andrews said. "A lot of them. Hey! I'll bet that's the Army medical people, the epidemiological teams—they're probably going to land in Central Park. I'd better get back to the Bureau and find out what's going on. Dave, you don't worry. We'll be back to check on you again. I'm going to look after everything, and Dolores is going to help me, and we have Gayle and all the others, and Calabrese and Katz too. You just get better real fast, you hear now?"

Hart moved his head slightly but he was not sure what Andrews was saying.

Andrews vanished. Dolores pressed her long fingers against Hart's cheeks. She kissed him on the forehead. She seemed to sense that language was now beyond him, and instead of speaking, she gave him a long look.

As he looked at her, tiny beads of ·light shot out from her forehead, her eyes, and the top of her head; she was a carved angel, a dark madonna.

37

"YOU'VE BEEN examined, I hope?" Cosgrove asked the man who sat next to Marks on the sofa in his office. "You've had the proper medication? You're not sick or anything?"

"I'm fine," the man replied. His name was Randolph Smith and he was the New York station chief for the Central Intelligence Agency. He had long, graying sideburns and close-cropped curly gray hair, and he wore a dark blue suit and a Princeton Ivy Club necktie. "I've been taking tetracycline since the very first intelligence on this, and the medics at the quarantine station took a look at me, too." He talked in a low monotone and, like Marks, maintained an expressionless demeanor.

"Good," Cosgrove said. "We don't have much time —it's already ten, and I have a meeting in an hour —so we'd better get on with the debriefing."

"Fine," Smith said. "I'll give some background first. Tensions were high even before the epidemic. Unemployment has been high, the usual recreation programs for teen-agers in the ghettos were not funded this year . . ." Smith spoke as though he were testifying before a Senate committee and had carefully memorized his version of events.

"In any case," he continued, "the blacks and Puerto Ricans have been more restive this summer than any summer since the 1960s. We know that the usual domestic subversives have been at work—trying, and failing, to organize the ghettos. We also have been aware that some of these terrorist groups have stockpiled weapons and explosives in Manhattan. Last month a National Guard Armory was robbed of two hundred M-14 rifles, sixty grenade launchers, twenty shoulder rocket-launchers, and at least half a million rounds of ordnance for these weapons. Several Claymore mines, too. The bombings last night were the work of the Puerto Rican Liberation Front—we have an asset targeted on them. We can expect some of the other terrorist groups to also exploit the current panic with similar bombings and arson."

"You don't have reason to believe these terrorist attacks and the plague epidemic are part of a coordinated effort by an outside hostile power?" Cosgrove asked.

"Well, it's possible. But it seems to me that everything that's happening in New York is quite characteristic of the city. That is, all the elements of this crisis have been present for some time."

"Except plague," Cosgrove said.

"Yes," Smith said evenly. "On Thursday morning, because of the mayor's declaration of a State of Imminent Peril Wednesday night, the traffic situation was very bad. People were asked to avoid public transportation. There are something like two million commuters, and God knows how many of them brought their cars into the city. The streets were absolutely jammed, no movement at all in most places, well into the night. There were a lot of pedestrians, including a lot of male teen-agers with nothing to do but roam around. So you had traffic jams, altercations, restless gangs. And that was when the panic about plague really hit. The word started spreading.

"Plague itself was the most disruptive phenomenon of all. By the time I was able to get out, the cases were no longer confined to the hospitals and the lines outside the emergency rooms. I saw a number of delirious individuals wandering the streets. Apparently, toward the final stages of the disease, the victims get extremely restless and agitated, and start running amok. They hallucinate and they scream and they cough blood." He paused, and his upper lip twitched.

"You say these people are wandering around?" Marks asked. "No one is treating them, or keeping them in bed?"

"Even if someone could help them to get to a hospital, there are crowds around every hospital, riots— how could a person get in? In any case, these delirium cases are quite horrifying to look at, they scare people, some of them are violent, and of course they're extremely contagious. And from what I was able to observe, they add considerably to the atmosphere of hysteria. Some of them have religious visions, and they point at the sky and scream, and that excites the crowds, too."

"Isn't anyone up there trying to maintain order?"

"At first I saw people—volunteers—trying to direct traffic and calm down the crowds, help put out fires in trash cans, that sort of thing. But—they're in the minority. The smart ones have tried to get out, I should think. That's another very grave situation though."

"I think I can supplement that," Marks said. "The latest reconnaissance report came in at six-thirty a.m. It says every bridge and tunnel leading out of Manhattan is blocked by stalled traffic. Vigilantes in the neighboring areas—New Jersey, the Bronx, Queens, Brooklyn—deliberately set cars on fire, and overturned buses and trucks. They don't want this thing spreading beyond Manhattan."

"How about pedestrian egress?" Cosgrove asked.

"It was blocked a few hours ago by police and vigilantes in the other boroughs," Marks said. "I suppose some people are still getting out—on small boats or whatever. There have been incidents in other boroughs, where relatives and so on are trying to get past the vigilantes and rescue people trapped in Manhattan."

"I would assume that those Strategic Units General Charles sent in will be able to tighten up the de facto blockade," Cosgrove said. "Containment is everything at this point."

"From what I saw," Smith said, "I don't think many will be capable of making an effort to get out. After I received the Alpha-Echelon contingency notification, around one a.m., I walked from my apartment down through midtown to the office to get the code books and do the shredding. All the streets were jammed with traffic, people on bicycles, people in wheelchairs, and mostly people running. Some were part of a mob that kept surging back and forth on Fifty-seventh Street for no reason that I could make out. They smashed store windows, clubbed people, trampled one another —like so many cattle. But those who hadn't gone berserk and just wanted to stay out of the way were running toward the subway stations. Every subway entrance I passed was packed with a wall of screaming people—they were wedged in so tightly that no one was moving, and then more people would rush up and push from behind. I hate to think what it was like down below. Grand Central was worse. There was a mob outside the station on Forty-second Street. I couldn't even see the doors of the building—people were knocking one another down, walking on top of other people, over the roofs of cars, using umbrellas and canes and sticks—whatever they could grab—to beat their way through. I saw a great many casualties. I would estimate a large number of casualties inside simply from suffocation. And there were plague-infected individuals mixed up in the crowd, too." Smith stared absently at the military oil paintings.

"How did the evacuation go?" Cosgrove asked.

Smith returned his gaze to Cosgrove, crossed his legs, and lit a cigarette. "I was supposed to report to the park next to the U.N. General Assembly Building, which I did. The U.N. guards and some Army personnel who had come via helicopter had set up a barricade, and they were making people line up and show their Alpha-Echelon identification. There were a lot of U.N. diplomats with their families. The Secretary-General was there with some of his staff, Mikhailov was there. So were several Agency people. Some of the men who were Alphas, but whose families were not, chose to stay behind. Or they tried to bribe the soldiers to take their kids out instead. There was a lot of trouble about that. I would recommend that future contingency lists be reviewed for potential troublemakers. But anyway, at the U.N. the atmosphere was initially—I won't say it was pleasant, but it was orderly in comparison to what was going on in midtown."

Cosgrove found himself admiring Smith and suspecting him at the same time. The man had amazing composure. He was sufficiently urbane to win a good job in State some day. But his presentation was just a little too slick—as though he might have trained himself extensively for just this occasion.

"You didn't investigate the subways, then?" Cosgrove broke in.

Smith lifted an eyebrow slightly, as though Cosgrove might have committed a slight gaffe. "General, as I thought I had made clear, it was not physically possible to get into the subway once it became known that dozens of plague cases were springing up all over the city. The transit workers called in 'sick.' I think the subways probably stopped working shortly after midnight, even though people continued trying to get in. I suspect people might have tried walking through the tunnels to Brooklyn and Queens."

"You were talking about the evacuation," Marks said.

"Right." Smith thought for a minute. "As I said, at first there was no trouble. Oh, a delay, and some diplomat or other yelling at a guard, but basically things went well. Finally the helicopters started landing. You couldn't board until your name was checked off the list the head guards were carrying. I was way at the end of the line and I was concerned that I wouldn't get out. They were Army choppers, and soldiers got out of them carrying bayoneted rifles—that worried a lot of people, especially the Soviet-bloc missions and the Africans. The Angolan ambassador wouldn't board. All foreign-mission staff members and their families were Alphas, so they were permitted to board. But other Alphas, some of them federal people, had brought wives, babies. It began to get chaotic, with women crying, people yelling in various languages. Then, outside the barricade, another crowd began forming. I'm not sure who was in that crowd—I saw some people delirious with plague, a large proportion of blacks, and then people with suitcases and kids who had been attracted by all the floodlights, guards, soldiers, Army helicopters. There must have been a lot of rumors. Right away they deduced that it was an evacuation and began pushing the guards, knocking them down, trying to get their guns. A guard right in front of me was stabbed in the chest." He shut his eyes and sighed.

"People started offering money to the diplomats and other Alpha-Echelons inside the barrier. Women were pulling off their wedding rings and handing them to the guards, and others were screaming hysterically. Children would break loose from their parents and get stepped on. Some people who had gotten guns—either from the guards or maybe they were carrying their own—started shooting at the helicopters as they took off. Nobody understood what was going on. I tried at first to help people and explain that it was a temporary evacuation, but no one wanted to listen, and some son-of-a-bitch slugged me in the stomach, so I just tried to keep my place in the line. About the time the sun was coming up, the last two helicopters landed, big Chinooks. By that time the guards were just shooting people. They didn't care. When the last Alpha-Echelons were starting to board, the U.N. guards started pushing them aside. I heard one say, 'We're getting out of here—you bastards can rot!' Yuri Ouspensky, from the Soviet mission, practically threw me into the helicopter. The U.N. guards shot several of the soldiers and took their rifles. They jumped in and told the pilot and the co-pilot they'd murder them if they didn't lift off immediately. We barely got out of the park, because people were clinging to the runners and pulling the chassis down. The last helicopter didn't make it. The mob had broken through the barricade into the park and dozens of people grabbed on to the runners, and more people grabbed the people who were holding on to the runners, and the weight of all those people pulled the helicopter down and over on its side. God." Smith shook his head. He seemed to forget himself. "Jesus. Those blades slicing through the crowd, people running, screaming. It was a goddamned nightmare and I hope as long as I live I never have to see anything like that again."

"Anything else?" Cosgrove asked.

"The ride was insane. The pilot had a gun to his head all the way to Fort Dix. Yuri kept singing and laughing and hugging me. He was drunk. He kept saying, 'So this is America's Saigon!' So I didn't see all that much. It was just before the sun came up, and it was very murky. The main arteries were all clogged with traffic, hundreds of thousands of pedestrians. And fires. I noticed a lot of fires."

"How were things at Fort Dix?" Marks asked.

"Not too bad. A lot of people milling around, but plenty of medical personnel to screen everyone, Red

Cross ladies with coffee, that sort of thing. Everyone is getting antibiotics, and those who show any symptoms are being isolated. The evacuees who were taken out by the Navy and Coast Guard vessels hadn't arrived yet. I assume it'll get pretty crowded out there when they do."

"Thank you very much, Mr. Smith," Cosgrove said. "I'm sure we'll be able to utilize this intelligence."

"You're quite welcome," Smith replied. "I might add one thing. I don't know what it's going to take to recover Manhattan—I don't know if it can be done."

38

In HART'S body were globules of specialized protein created by his immune system to neutralize the enemy organism, but it would take days for his spleen and lymph nodes to manufacture enough of these antibodies to devour the killer. However, his body had received another substance from the outside, a byproduct of a mold. It was made up of key-shaped molecules with twenty-two carbon atoms arranged in a cyclical fashion: tetracycline. It had been absorbed through his stomach and small intestines, filtered through the liver, and passed into the bloodstream, which carried the chemical to all the organs of the body. Billions of molecules of tetracycline floated through the spongy cellular maze of the lungs and came in contact with the hostile organism. Because it ate any potential nutrients that happened to wash by, the organism consumed the tetracycline. The organism did not comprehend that the artificial molecules were not there to nourish but to sabotage. They keyed into the genetic apparatus of the organism and jammed the reproductive process. The machinery stalled and the next generation did not appear. Every six hours a new wave of tetracycline molecules swept through Hart's bloodstream and prevented the organism from cloning.

Then, tetracycline stopped coming in from the outside, and the number of molecules dispersed in the lung tissues dropped to a low level. The organism's reproductive machinery came back into action and the organism soon resumed rapid growth. But precious time had been gained, and the first small wave of antibodies came into the lungs and began to eat at the organism.

Hart remained suspended between dreaming and thinking. Finally the clatter of the helicopters stopped and he no longer dreamed of Vietnam. He had to get to the Health Department to give a lecture. It was a lecture for a course he did not know he was responsible for. He did not have all the facts. If he performed badly, he would be in serious trouble. On his desk was a big black book, but he could not open it. Invisible forms crowded around him; one put its knee on his chest so that he had difficulty breathing. *Adieu, farewell earth's bliss.* Swords of fire coughed from the throats of demons as tall as the clouds. Flames fell around his bed. *This world uncertain is.* He had to get to the Health Department.

And what was the subject of the lecture? The men around the table waited, their faces wreathed in flames. *Fond are life's lustful joys,* he told them, *Death proves them all but toys.*

There was a shriek in the ward. "O God, I am a murderer! I have killed! O God, please forgive me!"

"Will you shut the fuck up!" someone shouted.

Hart opened his eyes and then quickly shut them. The light was too painful; it scratched his eyes and sent darts through his brain. *None from his darts, none from his darts can*—He would fail. He hadn't even known he was responsible for this. *I am sick,* he explained. *I must die. Lord, have mercy on us!*

"David, David, look who's here!" Dolores's voice. She was at the other end of a tunnel. Too bright, as bright as a trumpet note, too much light. Dark and cool, that was what he wanted. "Gayle is here. She's going to be right in the next bed."

I can't help her, he thought, the words dropping very clearly through his mind. I can't help anyone. I am sick. Keep the focus on the abdomen, that was where the will lived. Forget the lecture. Fires burned day and night in the palace of the Pope. He did not want to study. He had not signed up for the course. Abracadabra, quicksilver worn in a hazelnut, a sapphire talisman. He had to get downtown to the Health Department. The book would not open. His head ached. The cure: a good pair of boots used until they wore out. A needle slid into his arm.

He tried to sit up but was pressed down. He coughed and kicked his legs. "NO!" he shouted. "I WON'T TAKE THE TEST!"

"Our Father which art in Heaven," Gayle began. "Our Father which art in Heaven. Our Father which art in Heaven. Oh, shit! Can't remember how it goes!"

Hart had to urinate. He got out of bed, feeling disembodied, and staggered to the bathroom adjoining the ward. On his way back to the bed, he looked out the window. The entire city was dark except for an occasional flicker of light in a high window. Fires burned everywhere, poinsettia blossoms, orange, red, yellow. He found it quite pretty. He wanted to go for a walk. Get downtown to the Health Department. Find Dolores.

"Dr. Hart! You get right back in bed!" A flowing figure carrying a candle materialized behind him. She shoved him back into bed as if he were a five-year-old. Meekly, he obeyed.

"Oh, please forgive me," Gayle whispered. "I didn't mean to live so bad. I meant to live good. I tried."

"It's all right. You are good." The figure with the candle vanished.

He fell asleep, washed with perspiration, panting against the pillow. He dreamed he was running, downtown to Worth Street. He ran and ran and ran. His legs turned to sand. He kept running but he did not move. Red-stained shapes throbbed in his head; every microscope slide he had ever seen danced past. Black silhouettes of animals, rats and mice and squirrels, squeaked around his bed and scampered across the sheet. Oh Lord have mercy on us, they whispered.

39

COSGROVE TURNED on a small portable television set in his office. "That son-of-a-bitch Cronkite!"

"I thought the President told the networks to stop fanning this panic," Marks said.

"So did I," Cosgrove said.

". . . and this just handed to me," Cronkite was saying. "National Guard divisions have been called out in New York State, Connecticut, New Jersey, and Pennsylvania to protect gun stores, supermarkets, and pharmacies. There have been a number of incidents at shopping centers on this second grim night . . . We have been asked to caution everyone that there is no need for alarm. There is no need to panic.

Army troops have been stationed around Manhattan. The military is going in to restore order, martial law is in effect. The lights are back on in most of Queens and Brooklyn, although Manhattan and the Bronx are still without electricity. Telephone service in the metropolitan area has not yet been restored, but as soon as it is I hope to be talking with Mayor Weinstein about the tragic events that we have witnessed on this grim night. Plague, ladies and gentlemen. The Black Death has struck the United States of America—"

"Good Christ!" Cosgrove shouted. "This has got to stop!"

"As I mentioned earlier," Cronkite continued, "we were off the air for about an hour but only in the New York area. The CBS news department has relocated in Newark, and we'll be continuing to provide up-to-the-minute—"

Marks switched off the television. "What do you think we should do?" His mouth was tighter than usual, and his suit was wrinkled. Otherwise there was no change.

"Several things about this are very mysterious and disturbing."

"Yes," Marks said. Cosgrove hoped he would go on, but he got up and went to the window, then stood there looking out.

"Listen," Cosgrove said. "What do you think the real story is?"

"Either this is exactly what it seems to be on the simplest level—a natural epidemic and a panic reaction, which we may be able to turn to our advantage," Marks said slowly, "or we have been quite badly kicked in the balls."

"And *you* don't know which it is?" Cosgrove dropped his voice almost to a whisper.

Marks did not respond.

40

ONE WEEK after Sarah Dobbs had arrived in the city, Hart opened his eyes. It took him some time to realize that the dim expanse above him was the ceiling of a large room. He was able to focus on a bank of fluorescent light fixtures that were not on. They crossed his field of vision on a diagonal. Over the next few minutes the room began to fill with light. It was either getting lighter outside or his eyes were becoming accustomed to the darkness. He made no effort to lift his head or to shift his gaze.

He began to sense pain in his left hand and forearm. He tried to lift his arm and found it very heavy. The pain worsened. At last he was able to raise his arm so that it was directly in front of his eyes.

His forearm and wrist were swollen and pale. He lifted his other arm and began to palpate the wrist. His probing fingers sank into the flesh, leaving deep depressions. Edema, he thought to himself. Edema from an intravenous feeding that had infiltrated. The IV fluid had gone into his forearm and hand instead of a vein. He closed his eyes again, satisfied that his diagnosis had been correct, and fell back into sleep.

41

"I THINK, gentlemen, that as of tonight we are in a positive atmosphere to initiate a program of epidemic termination." Cosgrove spoke quietly and crisply to the men around the conference table. The only other sound in the white-carpeted, windowless room was the whisper of the air-conditioning system. "I have met with the President again today, and he has requested that we formulate specific response options to effect a speedy restoration of the critical financial, port-oriented, and general decision-making activities of New York City.

"The current disruption of the economy and world trade must end. We're already under extreme pressure from all the nations in the free world, who are deeply concerned about their gold reserves—a total of eighteen billion dollars in gold bullion—in the Federal Reserve Bank in Manhattan. And the short-term erosion of the credibility of the strategic posture of the United States is unacceptable. I suggest that we address ourselves to the business of compiling action scenarios to present to the President.

"According to the last bulletins we received before the phone circuits went out, deaths on the order of eighty thousand to one hundred thousand have occurred," Cosgrove went on. "Between a thousand and two thousand of those deaths are probably from the plague and the remainder, from secondary causes—mostly related to panic. We also estimate that an additional one hundred thousand of the surviving inhabitants of Manhattan and possibly as many as two hundred fifty thousand are short-run fatalities—due to untreated wounds, contaminated water, loss of power supply, continuing violence and crime levels, and on-going spread of plague. It appears to me, gentlemen, that either the epidemic will burn out in Manhattan and we can count ourselves very lucky, or it will spread beyond Manhattan and cause fatalities in the high-kilodeath to low-megadeath range—comparable, in other words, to the results of a limited nuclear spasm. General Sheffield, does that sound correct to you?"

"I think that's a reasonable estimate, yes. An eastward spread to Long Island could be contained without excessive loss of life, although certain key defense industries would be affected. But a south or westward spread would definitely pose a grave risk to the entire country and result, in my opinion, in a fatality rate on the order of ten to thirty megadeaths. These projections are based on bacteriological-warfare scenarios put together at Fort Detrick, and the figures can therefore be considered accurate to a factor of two."

"Thank you, General Sheffield," Cosgrove said. "There are some aspects of this crisis working in our favor, however. All twenty bridges and tunnels are blocked on the Manhattan side by stalled and wrecked vehicles, and on the opposite sides, some troops, policemen, and vigilantes have created blockades which they are assiduously patrolling. Thus the infected area appears to be sealed off to a large extent. But we cannot leave this ad-hoc quarantine in the hands of vigilantes and other anxious civilians. They are not effective enough. This committee should recommend to the President that the Army establish a perimeter around the entire island."

"That's not a bad idea," Attorney General Slater said. "I don't like having to call in the Army. But from where I sit, I'm faced with the problem of a major breakdown in order in the entire Northeast. Not just in the Northeast, actually—the whole country is in a state of hysteria. Everywhere people are buying guns, hoarding food, setting up vigilante blockades on the interstate highways . . . I'm worried about the banks and the art treasures in New York, and I am worried about the raids on gun stores in the suburbs that are going on. We're already getting stories about innocent people being shot just because their cars have New York plates. But we also have to keep in mind the medical nature of this crisis. As the Surgeon General says, this is a health crisis, not a war, and if you bring the Army in, you should land a couple thousand troops in Manhattan with medical supplies."

"That's commendable thinking," Cosgrove said. "All precedents show, however, that we can't cure or help anyone until some kind of order has been established." Cosgrove quickly went on, ignoring Slater's throat-clearing and other signals that he had more to say. "Now, in the event that it proves impractical to maintain a perimeter along the Hudson and East Rivers, we will simultaneously establish a fall-back perimeter along the right-of-way of Interstate 287 from Port Chester to Suffern and the Garden State Parkway from Suffern interchange to Perth Amboy. We will be operating under martial law, and any persons attempting to cross the perimeter lines will be interdicted.

"The 82nd and the 101st air-mobile divisions are on standby, Wright-Patterson is on a qualified alert, and the Coast Guard has six cutters standing off the Verrazano Narrows beyond visual shore contact. All the ships that would normally be in the harbor are now anchored beyond the Narrows. They're about ninety minutes from the Battery. The carriers *Forrestal* and *Constellation* are proceeding to their rendezvous at Ambrose Light. Two battalions of the Second

Marine Division are on the *Constellation,* and the 12th and 57th Air Rescue Group augmented by forty-four helicopters from the 14th and the 21st are on the *Forrestal."*

"But what about Manhattan?" asked the Attorney General.

"We estimate that the per-diem die-off rate is five percent, with ultimate casualty rates of sixty to seventy percent minimum after the projected elapsed-time for the disease to run its course—that is, between sixty and one hundred and twenty days," Sheffield said. "Allow another ninety before the city can be opened and reoccupied."

"I thought we had agreed that a stoppage of the financial and communication structure lasting beyond two weeks was unacceptable, given the economic disruption we're currently experiencing," the Secretary of the Treasury said.

"Yes, sir," Cosgrove said. "I'm only offering hypothetical figures. There are several of us who think that, given the dislocation in world trade caused in only two days by the high rate of refusal of shipping to call at any East Coast ports, even two weeks is unacceptable."

"Yes, of course," the Attorney General said. "Mrs. Lewis has been telling me about a plan over at HEW for major intervention by federal agencies to assist New York. I understand that several hundred nurses and doctors from around the country went into the city before it was sealed off, and that thousands more have volunteered—"

"Sir, I'm sure you're familiar with the concept of triage—concentration first on those who can be saved and abandonment, if necessary, of the hopeless cases," Cosgrove said. "Rather than expending time and efforts in a fruitless attempt to save those who won't survive in any event, it is considered more useful to focus on the cases where likelihood of survival is greatest. That, in my opinion, sir, is the nature of the situation in New York. Our first responsibility must be to the rest of the nation. We can't endanger two hundred million Americans to try to save fewer than one million. Studies prepared at Fort Detrick as part of our defense planning in a bacteriological-warfare context indicate that even heroic efforts would have only a marginal effect on the ultimate outcome. Dispatching thousands of medical experts, and the tens of thousands of troops needed to ensure a sufficient level of order to permit their effective operation, would merely result in extensive loss of personnel. I'm sure you would agree that we can't spare doctors who may be required to contain a further spread of epidemic, and we most assuredly cannot waste combat units that may be essential to the security of the continental United States in the event an adversary seeks to exploit this current health crisis.

"I might add, sir," Cosgrove went on, "that we can't rule out the possibility that the New York outbreak represents the use of bacteriological warfare by a hostile power, and that further attacks are being contemplated.

"As for now, there have been no *overt* attempts by the Soviet Union or China or any of their client states to exploit our present difficulties, except through propaganda. The Chinese and the Soviets made a special point of communicating their support of the Canadian decision to seal their border, but there have been no unusual military movements in the latest packet of satellite photos, which are current to within three hours. Nevertheless, in our current weakened state, we can't forget for one second the Sino-Soviet détente and the Middle East. I think we should stay on alert for the duration."

"We already have one quarter of our Strategic Command ringing New York City," General Charles said. "If we have to widen the perimeter, it's going to be over a third. If I were a North Korean, I'd get awful tempted to make a move. The Russians, no, I don't think so. They know we're on DefCon Three, just as we were during the missile crisis, and they know it's a goddamn chancy business doing anything overt when we're on a hair trigger. But now they're talking to China. And they can't keep their crazies, like Castro, in line any more than we can."

"Mr. Marks, do you have any new data on Castro?" Cosgrove asked.

"Let's assume for the purposes of discussion that Castro is behind the present crisis," Marks said. "What are his motives? One, he could be carrying out the orders of another power; since Mao's death and the beginning of the Sino-Soviet conferences, we know that Communist agitation has been magnified in every country. Castro may be only a pawn of the Sino-Soviet détente. Two, Castro could be impelled by internal upheavals in his own government. In the past there have been occasional challenges to his leadership, and he has tended to generate some foreign adventure during those periods. Third, and most problematic, is the possibility that his motives are atavistic. His sudden renewal of intervention activities in the mid-Seventies was unpredictable, and his fluctuations in the last two years have bordered on the irrational."

Cosgrove slowly lifted his hands from the table and dropped them to his lap. He gripped his thighs and tried to make himself calm. Was Marks extremely naive, or extremely cunning? "Do you have any hard evidence to support one or more of your speculations, Mr. Marks?"

"No conclusive evidence, General. But if I may indulge in a small recollection . . . There was a Corsican proverb that Sam Giancana was fond of repeating: 'If you seek revenge, wait twenty years to take it, or you act in haste.' "

Cosgrove swallowed. Marks was trying to make him writhe—but what was behind that attempt? Why did he choose precisely this moment to quote a dead Mafioso who had been a key operant in Operation Visitation?

During the vast, covert war against Cuba that was initiated in the early 1960s by the White House, run by the CIA, executed with the help of an army of Cuban exiles, and partially financed and encouraged by the Mafia and the Howard Hughes organization, dozens of operations had been set into motion. In addition to the official economic embargo, the commando raids on oil refineries and sugar mills, acts of sabotage, and the establishment of a major CIA base in Florida (also used by the underworld for drug-running), there had been an assassination workshop called "Executive Action." Cosgrove had been the chief aide to the Secretary of Defense at the beginning of those operations, and he now recalled White House meetings when McGeorge Bundy, General Landsdale, Robert MacNamara, and the Kennedy brothers would discuss how useful it would be to the United States if certain leaders were removed from power. Cosgrove immediately dedicated himself to advancing his career by researching refined methods of executive action, and over the years his handiwork had taken him far. He had quickly gone on to become liaison for the Technical Services Division at Fort Detrick, the CIA and the Pentagon. Sheffield was then director of the Technical Services Division—a body created by the CIA and the Department of Defense—and the two of them had originated a number of elegant devices for removing Castro from power. While Cuban exiles took potshots at Castro from the decks of CIA-run fishing boats, using arms the Mafia had stolen from National Guard Armories, Sheffield and Cosgrove and several technicians were working overtime to design suitable delivery systems for certain substances. These substances, stockpiled by the CIA and the Army Biological Laboratory, and occasionally supplied by the U.S. Public Health Service, could cause tuberculosis, anthrax, encephalitis, valley fever, salmonella food poisoning, smallpox, kuru, and plague. The two men also studied the most effective means for administering cobra venom, strychnine, cyanide, curare, shellfish toxin, botulinus toxin, and hallucinogenic drugs. They became experts in the physiological processes of paralysis, asphyxiation, convulsion, anesthesia, amnesia, stroke, cardiac arrest, nausea, mental depression, hallucination, and brain damage. They developed a wetsuit contaminated with fungus for Castro to wear skin diving; a tiny poison dart the diameter of a human hair that a Mafioso was to fire at Castro from a gun concealed in a cane; a fluorescent bulb that spread a mycotoxin when the light was switched on; an untraceable poison to drop in his chocolate malt; cigars tipped with botulinus toxin; a shoe-polish that would give off a chemical to make his beard fall out; and a comb impregnated with a slow-acting brain virus. For years, the demise of Castro was Cosgrove's greatest goal, and his work had been lavishly supported and rewarded not only by successive political administrations but also by the permanent government—the complicated organism made up of enduring public servants, like J. Edgar Hoover; businessmen, like Howard Hughes; and underworld leaders, like Meyer Lansky.

But nothing happened. If anything, Castro had flourished. Still, Cosgrove had assured the permanent government that soon Castro would fall ill, go insane, or die, and the second invasion of Cuba could be ordered.

Some time after Castro became involved in the Angolan war, Sheffield had dropped by Cosgrove's White House office and they had reminisced about the intensity of the old days. Sheffield remarked on the apparent irony: perhaps Castro had contracted a brain virus from their specially treated comb after all. But now that he had become erratic and vulnerable, the times were wrong. Nixon was gone, the intelligence community was undergoing an intensive Senate investigation, frantic shredding was being carried on by the Defense Department and several other agencies, the

Warren Commission Report was undergoing Congressional scrutiny, Howard Hughes was dead, the Syndicate and the Mafia had given up on the recapture of Cuba and were concentrating their gambling and drug operations on other Caribbean islands. Sheffield and Cosgrove had agreed that anti-Cuban action was now inopportune. They had to try to hold on to the high positions they had managed to attain by other means.

All these recollections rushed through Cosgrove's mind as he listened to Marks and Charles discussing Castro. "If we can substantiate the details of this epidemic," Cosgrove said finally, rubbing his wet palms on his trousers, "and satisfy ourselves that this is yet another of Castro's covert attacks for which he has spent years laying the groundwork, then I recommend immediate invasion, before he tries something worse."

42

ANOTHER FOREIGN molecule had appeared. This one came from depots within the muscles of his arm and thighs, where it had been injected through a hollow needle. It was streptomycin. Like tetracycline, it was the by-product of a mold. The organism absorbed the streptomycin and then mistook it for an essential component of the genetic material needed to make new cells, new enzymes, and new protective membranes. The organism formed new cells, but misread the genetic code so that the cells grew incomplete walls, nonfunctioning enzymes, and harmless toxins. When the organism attempted to split apart in order to reproduce, the two new clones were incomplete. Wrongly formed and vulnerable, the organism was now surrounded, suffocated, digested, and absorbed into the white blood cells. Every hour, more white cells arrived from the lymph nodes and new antibodies were created to cleanse the lungs of all traces of the organism. The antibodies would live on in the lungs and in the blood stream for years to come, remembering everything about the organism. Now that the immunological system was fully forewarned, it would turn aside any new attacks of the organism with ease and speed.

43

THE LAGOON was a flat, glittering turquoise under the noon sun. Hart pulled off his sticky boots and his clothes, which were soaked with sweat, and stripped down to his bathing trunks. He threw himself into the clear water and rolled and twisted and splashed and ducked. In the clear depths, a school of bright yellow and fluorescent-blue fish flashed past his knees.

Then he was in a dining room with big arched windows facing the ocean. A girl with long black shiny braids, almond eyes, and big breasts appeared with a glass and an ice-cold bottle of beer. Hart was not thinking or planning anything. He was just living. Everything was very clear: the light reflecting the ocean up into the shadowy corners of the room, the easy grace of the girl as she set the beer on the table. Hart caught her staring at him, and he knew for sure that he would make love to her before tomorrow.

She brought out an enormous tray heaped with oysters, each one rough and black and about the size of a man's hand. They were the biggest and most succulent Hart had ever eaten. He looked at the ocean, and ate, and listened to the surf. His skin felt tight from the salt and the sun. Then he smiled at the girl. She smiled back. It was good to be alive.

A fly buzzed around the table. It landed on one of the empty oyster shells, and Hart watched it drink the juice.

Hart awoke to the sound of low buzzing. The sound had also been in his dreams, and so he was unsure whether he was actually awake. When he was certain that his eyes were open and focused on the bank of light fixtures overhead, when he was certain that he was really awake and not just dreaming that he was awake, he had a powerful sensation of loss. He had lost something or forgotten something.

He slowly raised himself until he was sitting. Everything around him seemed extremely well defined. He saw that his bed was not parallel with the walls; it had been pushed at a slant into the center of the room. He saw another bed, empty, with its sheets stained brown. There was a powerful, cloying odor in the room. He looked down at himself. He was wearing green pajamas that were wet and wrinkled.

He swung his legs over the side of the bed. Dizzy, he took a deep breath. That made him cough, and he noticed that his chest was sore.

The bed was unusually high. He slowly lowered his feet. His left foot touched the smooth tile of the floor. His right foot came to rest on a cold, hard, irregular object. He looked down. It was a human hand.

It was connected to a sprawled corpse. As he quickly withdrew his foot, flies arose in clouds. An empty IV bottle was still attached by tubing to the arm of the corpse. The head, swollen to twice its normal size, was dark brown and puffy, like a thoroughly rotten apple. Must have died with his body hanging over the edge of the bed, blood collected in the head. Finally fell to the floor. Dead for perhaps two days. The features were still recognizable. It was Whitney Emerson, the man who had reminded Hart of his father, the man who had been head of Preventable Disease at Metropolitan.

Dozens of flies crawled on Emerson's face, buzzing around and alighting on the eyelids, nostrils, and mouth, which oozed a brownish, bubbling fluid.

Hart put all his weight on his feet. His knees were wobbly but he could stand without holding onto the bed for support. He had a fleeting recollection of being a year old, the moment of bodily delight when he had first found his own center of gravity and could stand alone.

He listened for voices. There were none but the constant, atonal chorale of the flies. No human sounds came from the other wards or from the corridor. He would have to help himself.

He walked to the window, taking care to avoid the broken bottles, tangles of intravenous tubing, shattered glass, and sticky black patches. And he avoided the corpses. There were two others in the ward, embraced by the morning sun and covered with hundreds of flies.

He leaned against the windowsill and looked out. He must have been about fifteen stories high. He could see towers, a shining river, the lacy span of a bridge, a broad, curving highway along the river's edge, strips and squares of green set among rows of low, red-brick buildings. Plumes of smoke rose here and there. The sky was hazy over the rooftops, but overhead it was a transparent dark blue, filled with the clear, dry light of early fall. He opened the window and drew in a deep breath. He caught the sweet autumnal smell of bonfires.

He was alive, he was alive on a sunny day. He could see everything. And now he felt very hollow and light, as though he had left his body behind along with other burdensome luggage. But his body was there: he was breathing, his heart was beating, his eyes were taking in light.

His lips were cracked and dry, and he was very thirsty. He made his way into the bathroom and turned on the faucet. There was a sputter and a hiss but no water. He urinated in the toilet and pressed the handle. It did not flush.

Touching the walls from time to time for support, he went out into the corridor. There was another body. A black woman, face down, her Afro matted and clotted with blood. It was someone familiar. His mind shut off. Water—that was what he was looking for.

He came to a door marked TREATMENT ROOM and pushed it open. A swarm of flies buzzed into his face. The room stank of putrefaction. He saw three corpses. One had apparently died on the examining table. A man wearing a white coat spattered with blood slumped at an awkward angle across a chair, and another man lay on the floor. He, too, wore green hospital pajamas. The rictus of death made him grin.

He found an unopened bottle of distilled water, cracked the metal-foil seal, and tipped half its contents into his mouth. The lukewarm liquid dropped straight to his stomach: he had not eaten or drunk anything for a very long time. He poured the rest of the bottle over his head.

He was in a hospital. It had obviously been abandoned, or at least this floor had been abandoned. The water was shut off. He tested the light switch—no electricity, either. It seemed to him that he ought to know the reason for all this, but he couldn't think what it was.

He picked up a clean linen hand towel and dried himself with it. Then he tied it in a triangle over his nose and mouth to keep out the stench.

He went again to an open window. The sky in this new direction was a thick, smoky yellow. Black and brown clouds veined with fire billowed up from tenement rooftops: whole blocks were in flame. Now he saw why the view from the other window had seemed so tranquil: there was no human motion anywhere. All the streets were filled with traffic, but it was frozen.

He returned to the room where he had awakened

and leaned against his bed to rest for a moment. In a small bedside cabinet he found a light-blue seersucker suit, a white shirt with sweat stains, socks, shoes, and a pair of glasses. The glasses seemed to improve his vision. He dressed slowly and carefully and then folded up the pajamas and put them in the cabinet.

He went down the corridor to find an exit, pausing at the Treatment Room. There was something in there he ought to have. He looked around the room and noticed that his gaze kept returning automatically to a shattered glass cabinet in the corner. Finally he focused on boxes in the cabinet labeled "Streptomycin." He found an unused syringe and another bottle of distilled water. He mixed the contents of one box with water, drew the mixture into the syringe, and pushed the needle through his clothing into his upper buttock. The syringe sank into the muscle and bobbed there as he rearranged his grip to work the plunger. The injection stung him; for a second he wanted to cry like a baby. He withdrew the syringe and threw it on the floor.

With several boxes of streptomycin in his pockets, he made his way through the debris and corpses along the corridor to the exit. He found the door locked, and he had to ram it open with the iron headboard of a wrecked bed. The effort took all his strength.

The stairwell was also littered, but the smell was not as bad. He slowly made his way down flight after flight, holding on to the banister. He began to hear a sing-song that occasionally rose above the rejoicing of the flies. It sounded like a voice, and it was accompanied by a rhythmical slapping.

As he descended he began to distinguish words: ". . . in Him trust (*slap*) . . . shall deliver thee from the snare of the fowler (*slap*) . . . and from the noisome pestilence (*slap*) . . . He shall cover thee with his feathers (*slap*) . . . thy shield and buckler (*slap*) . . ."

After five flights, he began coughing. He sat down on a step and slowed his breathing. The recitation continued to echo up the stairwell: "Thou shalt not be afraid for the terror by night (*slap*) . . . nor for the arrow that flieth by day (*slap*) . . . Nor for the pestilence that walketh in darkness (*slap*) . . . nor for the destruction that wasteth at noonday (*slap*)."

When his chest seemed quiet, he resumed his descent, following the chant. ". . . thousand shall fall at thy side, and ten thousand at thy right hand (*slap*) . . . but it shall not come nigh thee."

It was an old black man. He was mopping the landing with distilled water. "Only with thine eyes shalt thou behold (*slap*) . . . and see the reward of the wicked."

"Good morning."

"Good mornin' to you," the man said. He stopped his work and smiled.

"Looks like a really nice day today."

"Yup, I expect so. Gettin' coolish nights now, though."

"Well, I guess summer is over. I don't mind the cool weather—I like fall."

The old man thumped his chest. "Any time of year is just fine if your mind ain't no trouble."

"Yes." He started laughing. He felt very happy. He looked into the seamed black face: another life!

"Excuse me, I best get back to work."

Hart waved and continued down the stairs, laughing. He had been telling himself the story of his life for years, telling himself everything he ever heard, saw, thought, and felt, and it all had been *wrong!* Completely wrong! It was a story he could not possibly take seriously. It was a hilarious joke. *You've been a lovely couple, but now it's time to play You Bet Your Life.*

The Screening Clinic was dark, and there were dozens of corpses on the floor. He picked his way around them and headed toward a row of office doors. Papers were strewn everywhere, and dried spatters and blood covered the papers and the walls. He bent over the bodies. Some were riddled with reddish-black holes; others were bludgeoned. One of the corpses was of a nurse. Her skirt was pushed over her hips and a large pool of black, clotted blood spread beneath her pelvis.

The glass door of the Administrator's office had been shattered. Hart peered inside. File cabinets had been overturned, desk drawers pulled out. Bloodstains were everywhere. Then he saw the shoes, gray shoes. They were on the feet of a fat body in a gray suit. The body was stretched out on the floor and its head placed on the base of a big paper-cutter. The wide, curved blade had been brought down through the neck until it had been stopped by the cervical vertebrae.

Hart found a part of the corridor free of bodies and sat down on the floor. Something in him wanted him to give up, to go to sleep, to let gravity take him back into dreams. The window overlooking the sea, the open smile of the girl in the black braids—that was a good place to go. If he just lay down . . .

He bolted awake. He was *here*. There was no way out of *here*. He drew in even, deep breaths. His mind began to work very rapidly, in single, coherent arcs.

There was another woman, another smile. The impression of her hand on his cheek remained. He suddenly had a full, rich sensation of his entire body, inside and out. It worked, he would make it work. He had an aim, and he could make it work. He could make everything follow that aim if he kept his will.

He was going to find her. Nothing else mattered.

Moving with care but without stopping, he went through a maze of corridors to a set of double doors leading to the Emergency Room. More bodies, more wreckage. Machines, stretchers, cabinets, bottles, and linen had been violently flung about, and there were at least a hundred corpses, many of which were in a heap in front of the doors leading to the main ER entrance. Trying not to step on bodies, he took a second exit that led to an inner courtyard.

He pressed open the large glass doors and stepped outside. The air was clean. He took a deep breath and felt a sharp pang in his right chest. His breathing was fine, but there must be some pleuritic involvement inside.

Several red ambulances were parked in the courtyard. He walked to the rear of one, opened the doors, and climbed in. Among the canisters of oxygen and other emergency gear was a big, black wooden box. He opened it and found an orderly arrangement of medicines, surgical instruments, syringes, tubings, bandages, splints.

He went around to the front of the ambulance and discovered that the keys were missing. He went to the next ambulance. No keys. The third ambulance had keys dangling from the ignition and an intact emergency kit.

He climbed into the driver's seat and started the engine. The grind and whine were painfully loud. He spent a few minutes trying to figure out how the gears worked before he found reverse and backed toward the driveway. When he got to the high gates he saw that they were bolted shut. Slowly he backed through them until they broke open. The tires bumped over objects in the driveway: he did not want to see what they were. As the ambulance lurched out onto the street, he saw many more bodies—the greatest number lay in contorted poses around the entrance to the Emergency Room. Many had bullet holes; many more had mouths and faces caked with blood. His eyes stung from the fetid odor.

On a wall near the Emergency Room entrance had been splashed VIVA US. The last letter dripped down to the sidewalk, where the ambiguous slogan ended in a puddle of dried blood. Nearby lay a flaccid plastic blood-bag that had been squeezed empty.

Then he saw the rats. They crowded in the gutters

and prowled among the cars, their restless, curved backs forming one writhing, streaming mass. One rat the size of a tomcat lumbered in front of the ambulance, indifferent to its noise and motion, and began feeding on the face of a corpse.

Hart found the horn and honked it. The rat stopped, twitched its nose, and then trotted away from its feast and took refuge under a car. The other rats also turned toward the source of the sound, their attention passing on down the street from one rat to the next until they all froze and stared at him with black, shining eyes. He honked again. A few rats nearby scattered, but most of them remained still.

He kept his foot on the gas pedal and threaded his way among the cars, honking from time to time to scare the rats closest to the wheels.

Gusts of smoke sprang up from among the projects and tenements into the soft light of the morning like black genies out of magic lamps. He could not make sense of anything. It was probably a dream: he had walked out of the room of one dream into the room of another dream, which in turn had led into this room . . .

He was jarred by a sudden rush and clatter. He stopped the ambulance and craned his head out the window. Overhead hovered a helicopter with US NAVY stenciled on its fuselage. It was less than two hundred feet away, and he could feel the strong wind generated by the rotors. In the cockpit were four men in blue. Hart leaned out the window as far as he could—he did not want to step down because of the rats—and waved both arms.

One of the men pointed out Hart to the others. Hart kept waving. The helicopter dipped lower. Suddenly there was the loud report of a rifle shot. Several shots followed. The helicopter quickly pulled straight up, flew toward the East River, and then veered south until it disappeared behind some tall buildings.

Hart drew back into the ambulance and scanned the rooftops and fire escapes for the source of the gunfire. He saw nothing.

He hunched down to protect himself and kept driving.

The intersection at Ninety-seventh and Madison was jammed. Two ambulances lay overturned, their windows smashed, their drivers beaten faceless. An empty bus blocked the avenue at a diagonal. And the dead lay everywhere, nourishing the squeaking horde of rats.

The sidewalk at one corner was piled high with plastic bags stuffed with garbage. Using the front of the ambulance to bulldoze the mound aside, he drove over the sidewalk and turned north, keeping the ambulance half in the gutter and half on the sidewalk. As the wheels rose and sank over soft bumps, he tried to keep his mind blank.

The woman, the woman. He remembered his aim: To find her. When he kept her image in focus, the horror around him faded. He tried to avoid seeing the faces of the dead—when they had faces—because he did not want to find hers among them. They stared fixedly from the windows of cars, blood on their faces; they gestured rigidly with stiff fingers, from the gutters, and some of them seemed to stir as he passed.

At Mount Sinai Hospital, he was forced to stop and get out. There were so many bodies and vehicles that not even the sidewalks were passable. And over everything swarmed the rats.

He wondered whether they preferred live flesh, and he hoped that they were too busy at their gruesome banquet to bother to attack him. As he climbed through the wreckage, he kept an eye on his legs. The rats retreated from his path only a pace or two at a time. He was glad to find a broken baby carriage from which he wrenched the aluminum handle and used it to beat the rats further back.

The woman he was looking for lived in a building that was part of a housing project at 105th and Madison. The sidewalk in front of the development was heaped with more black plastic garbage bags. He saw a black foot poking out of one of the bags, and when he examined them more closely, he realized that most of them contained bodies.

Across the street the Sophie S. Cohen research building of New York Medical College gave out puffs of smoke dissipating into the overall haze.

From a building further up the street, a banner fluttered: PUERTO RICO LIBRE, it said.

Puerto Rico, Puerto Rico. She was small-boned, with round breasts. She had a half-humorous way of speaking with one eyebrow cocked. Full lips, white teeth. She had appeared in other rooms, other dreams, her hand on his. He stood in the foyer and stared at the row of names by the buzzers. Name, she had a name.

Hart grew excited: he was on the edge of remembering. At the same time he felt a heavy pressure in his head and sat down on the floor. The pressure seemed to push him forward into sleep. If he slept, the dead would rise up, live and whole again, the rats would return to their holes, the air would grow sweet, the streets would be cleansed . . .

He fought to remember why he was here.

His efforts were interrupted by a deep thunder that rattled the building. He stepped out onto the stoop and saw four small jets in low formation dart across the sky like silvery fish in murky water. The roar of their passage tore a hole in his mind, and he gazed upward, trying to piece together the shattered train of thought.

That was when Hart saw the angel. It whirled lazily over the rooftops, like a falling silver leaf. Then it stopped and moved from side to side, dancing against gravity, turning and flashing in the sunlight that glinted through the haze as though it were searching for something. He heard the pop of distant gunfire but the angel placidly continued its descent until it dropped behind some buildings about a dozen blocks to the north.

The sight of it filled him with deep dread. Nothing else he had seen since waking up had frightened him so. There was something quite familiar and terrible about the angel.

The shock dissolved the pressure to fall asleep. Hart continued searching the sky for a long time but the angel did not reappear. The gunshots stopped. He was flooded with a rapid series of vivid thoughts, emotions, images, ideas, all completely and subtly interconnected. For an instant he grasped exactly what was going on.

And then he went unconscious for a few seconds. There had been too much. The inner tide rushed away.

He had lost it all. He knew only that it had come and gone. He understood nothing. He only knew he must find the woman who was so precious to him. He had been ill for a long time; he could not expect miracles. He went back into the foyer and stood in front of the buzzers. Marquez, Blanco, Zuniaga, Rodriguez, Conforte . . .

Rodriguez. 6B.

44

No ONE answered his knock. The door was unlocked and he stepped inside. The living room was tidy: a green velour sofa and armchair, a brown rug, a stereo, a television. A row of geraniums blossomed on a window ledge. On one wall was a picture of John F. Kennedy and three framed certificates. He looked at them. They all bore the same name: Dolores Rodriguez. The first was a diploma from Mabel Dean Bacon High School. The second was a diploma from the Harlem Hospital School of Nursing. The third was a notice of congratulations upon having completed the special training program in epidemiology at the Bureau of Preventable Diseases. It was signed by Vincent Calabrese, Commissioner of Health, David Hart, Director of the Bureau, and Virginia Hinkley, Director of Public Health Nursing.

He went into the kitchen. Everything was white and polished. Red curtains flapped softly in the breeze. On the counter was a basket filled with blackened plantains. In the refrigerator was a bowl of black beans and a pan of stew. The beans were covered with a white, fuzzy mold, but the stew looked all right. He found a fork, removed his mask, and quickly ate several bites. It was spicy and quite delicious. Better not eat too much right away.

He immediately felt much better.

He found some framed photographs arranged on a

starched lace doily on the television set. An old couple by a palm tree. A portrait of a young man in an Army uniform. A beautiful woman with wide, dark eyes, a serene, full-lipped smile, and glossy black hair.

He trembled. He picked up the picture and studied it. She was real.

Three doors lined a hallway off the living room, and they all were closed. Behind two of the doors he found similar scenes: in one room lay the bodies of an elderly man and woman in a double bed; in the next, the body of a young man—the uniformed boy of the photograph—with bloodstains on his mouth and throat. The hands of each of the bodies had been folded over the chest and the eyes closed.

He stood, the woman's portrait in his hand, before the third door. He did not want to open it. He wanted to keep the photograph and go away. To a white beach with turquoise water . . .

Abruptly he opened the door. The room was very simple: a narrow brass bed, a dresser, and a mirror. A faint fragrance hung in the air, giving him a sudden recollection of her neck against his lips. On one wall hung a black silk shawl embroidered with red roses; on another, a crucifix. Taped to the mirror were several snapshots. Most of them were evidently of relatives, including those who lay dead in the other rooms. But there was also a photograph of a clear-featured man of about thirty-four with blond hair, blue eyes, and wire-rimmed eyeglasses sitting at a cluttered desk in a sunny office.

He looked at the photograph of the woman in his hand and he looked at the picture of the man taped to the mirror.

Then, for the first time since he had awakened that morning, he looked at himself in the mirror. He was gaunt, with deep lines around his mouth and eyes, his skin was white, his hair tangled, his face covered with a red stubble.

He scarcely recognized himself. A vast gulf separated the man in the mirror from the man in the snapshot.

Hart left a note on the door of the apartment telling Dolores he had been looking for her and was now going to stop at Gracie Mansion to look for city officials and then go on to the Department of Health. As he walked back to the ambulance, he kept his mind busy with calculations to distract him from the rats.

It seemed to be early morning and he was at 106th Street, about fifty blocks from midtown, ninety blocks from the Village, about 120 blocks from 125 Worth Street. Six miles. If all the streets were like the ones around Metropolitan, he would have a great deal of trouble driving. If he were in good shape, he could walk a block a minute and get to the Bureau in two hours. But a large amount of energy was still tied up in the processes of recovery; it was important not to get overtired. He would pace himself, then. Drive as far south as he could in the ambulance, rest frequently, keep calm. He would have to find more food eventually, too. He should be able to reach Worth Street by noon.

He climbed back into the ambulance and started the engine. He listened to the roar of more jets overhead, the squeaking rats, the buzzing flies, and thought about Dolores.

45

THE DRIVING went very slowly. Every street was filled with abandoned vehicles, garbage, dead dogs, and always corpses and rats. He had chosen to stay on Park Avenue because it was wider, and therefore it would be easier to make his way around the obstacles. There were fewer fires toward midtown; most of the burning had occurred in Harlem. He witnessed a repetition of an earlier scene: a helicopter filled with uniformed men—this time it was an Army chopper—dipped low to get a look at him and then pulled away when shots rang out.

But this time Hart saw the snipers. The barrels of their guns poked out of the windows of the top story of a high-rise apartment building on Park Avenue. From one of the windows hung a sheet on which had been spray-painted HQ PEOPLES UNITED LIBERATION COALITION ARMY.

He assumed he had probably been unconscious for no more than three days, and the city's rapid and profound change astonished him. Surely there were survivors who were not members of peculiar little armed fronts. Surely not everyone had been killed by the plague or by riots and mass panic. Surely the federal government had set up a base of operations. And where was the National Guard? Why all the aircraft whizzing back and forth overhead and why no soldiers in the streets cleaning up the bodies?

Perhaps he was still not perceiving things clearly and

had missed some important observation. No. He felt extraordinarily lucid. Some fatigue, but that was to be expected. He had been quite ill.

He must have taken enough tetracycline to keep from being killed by the plague, and he had probably been pumped full of streptomycin at the hospital before it had been abandoned, but on the other hand, he must have forgotten to take regular dosages. He did not wonder about this long. The point was that he had survived.

Hart turned east on Ninetieth. At Lexington he found a grocery store. It had been looted and the clerk shot in the head. Hart sorted through the debris on the floor and found a jar of peanut butter, a can of anchovies, a jar of apple cider, a box of crackers, and a bag of lemon drops. He ate as much as he could, then went back to the ambulance, his mouth crammed full of lemon drops.

As he approached Gracie Mansion, Hart began to realize there was no nucleus of order here. The gates to the grounds of the large, white Georgian mansion were open, but the conspicuous lack of the usual guards and police barricades made him decide to park outside.

He moved cautiously toward the mansion, using the trees and shrubs for cover. Three dead German shepherds lay in the drive, and he saw several corpses at the doorstep of the mansion, all of them policemen. Papers and briefcases were scattered over the pebbled driveway. He thought he heard music, but it turned out to be voices singing drunkenly in English and Spanish. There were shouts and the crashing of glass. Hart hid behind a limousine in the driveway. Presently a man appeared at the front door carrying a shotgun in one hand and a bottle in the other. He lurched against the door and then regained his equilibrium. "I proclaim this to be a day of jubilation an' hard drinkin'!" he yelled at the dead policemen. "I urge all

citizens to par-tee-cee-pate to the best of their ability!"
He saluted the dead men with his bottle, took a swig,
and stumbled back inside.

Hart wondered how many more of these men there
were. He had not seen anyone else alive—except for
the old orderly at the hospital and the snipers. Had
there been a mass evacuation? But bands of looters
must be roaming the city, along with every crackpot
who had a gun and a cause, every little "front" and
"army," all the madmen who were usually kept under
control by the everyday life of the city.

But there had to be some sane survivors—somewhere. They probably kept themselves hidden. And
the military was obviously keeping Manhattan under
continual surveillance. There *had* to be a rescue operation.

He tried to work out which neighborhoods would
be the safest. The most damaged area he had seen so
far was Spanish Harlem and around Metropolitan.
Park Avenue had seemed almost serene by contrast.

He drove down York. The ambulance made all too
good a target. But it was safer than walking out in the
open. At least for now.

He wove in and out of the motionless traffic and
tried to avoid running over bodies, although the tires
were already red and shiny.

On the corner of Eighty-seventh Street he passed
stacks of bodies, and he drove around the remains of
a funeral pyre that had only partially consumed its
fuel.

At Eighty-sixth Street, York Avenue had been barricaded by several buses. It was the first purposeful
arrangement Hart had come upon. He turned west on
Eighty-sixth and drove through Yorkville, the German
section. He kept having to back up, detour, turn
around, and try new tacks in order to get back to
Park Avenue.

He was concentrating so much on the driving that

he did not notice the people until it was too late. Five men emerged from the doorway of a bar and ran toward the ambulance. Two of them had rifles pointed at Hart.

46

THE MEN seated around the conference table were subdued. Three days of crisis had tightened their jaw muscles and darkened their eyesockets. Cosgrove, despite a continual inner alarm that would have sounded like a siren if it could have been loosed into the air, was pleased to find that his sense of personal power was intact. He felt he was thinking faster, and that he was more persuasive than usual.

Bryce Marks, General Charles, and General Sheffield also appeared to share in this enhanced energy the crisis had generated. Sheffield was speaking now, and though his voice was hoarse, he was still fluent and forceful. "The United States has renounced first use of chemical and bacteriological weaponry since becoming a signatory to the Geneva Convention. But there is nothing in the Geneva Convention forbidding retaliatory measures. However, whether or not the epidemic in New York represents the use of bacteriological warfare by a hostile power, particularly Cuba, is really of little concern at this point, in my view. The decision to retaliate can be made at a later date. And it is possible that the index case *was* the Dobbs girl and that she was accidentally infected by a California ground squirrel. Now, in a limited-infection situation, the ideal response is isolation and a hands-off strategy coupled with zone-by-zone decontamination. If, however, there is a commanding time consideration, then we would be compelled to resort to a process of animate suppression."

47

HART WAS not afraid of the rifle trained on him at point-blank range, but he stopped.

"He's white!" one of the men yelled. "Get outta there, Mac."

Hart got down from the cab.

"I'm a doctor," Hart began. "I'm with the Department of Health. I'm just trying to get back down there."

There was laughter. A big, burly man grabbed Hart's arm. "You a Jew?"

Hart shook his head.

"Doctors are Jews! They did all this! They started the plague so they could get even richer! You *sure* you're not a Jew?"

"I'm just a doctor. I have to get downtown. So if you'll excuse me . . ."

"Let's kill the son-of-a-bitch!"

A big man with two revolvers in his belt appeared and told the others to shut up. "ID, please," he said to Hart.

"It must still be up at Met. I was a patient up there. I just recovered." He added, "I work for the Department of Health."

"Your name?"

"David Hart."

"Never heard of you."

The man was tall, and weighed well over two hundred and fifty pounds. He wore a grimy sports shirt, khaki pants, and brown shoes, and his manner of inquiry suggested to Hart that he might be a policeman.

"Are you with the Police Department, by any chance?" Hart asked. "I know Commissioner McClelland slightly, if that's any help."

The man squinted at him. "How well?"

"I'm the Director of the Bureau of Preventable Diseases and sometimes we have to work with the police—"

"Preventable Diseases?"

"Yes."

"You want some advice, Mac? I'll give you some advice. Don't go around telling people that. What's the address of the Health Department?"

"One-two-five Worth Street."

The man made an OK sign to the others. Relieved, Hart began asking him questions about the city.

"Above Eighty-Sixth it's very bad," the man replied. "You got your no-man's land between here and Harlem. Very dangerous. Sometimes we go a few rounds with perpetrators who try to come down to loot, but most of the time they stay there and we stay here. We hold our own down here. We got a vigilante crew keeping order, plus we're trying to clean things up a little, burn the dead, help people."

"Were most of the people evacuated?"

The policeman shook his head. "You came down from Met, right? Well, everybody up there is dead, and those who could get out of that area scrammed two days ago—the plague is really bad up there. Your colored element, they really got rats. And what I've seen, the people down here—there are plenty of them up in the buildings, but they won't come out. First of all, they might be too sick to move, you understand? Or, if they're not sick, they don't want to get the plague, so they don't want to have nothing to do with anybody. Or, they're afraid someone's going to take a potshot at 'em. Those individuals come out at night, mostly, sneak around to the grocery stores to get food and something to drink. It's a problem. We need more help to get this area working again, but we don't want to go into the buildings and get people to come out—because they might infect us, you understand? I figure we just have to hang on until help comes. I know they must be planning something."

"I don't get it," Hart said. "When I passed out on Thursday night, there was some trouble—riots around the main hospitals. But the Mayor was still around, and he was getting the feds to come in. I thought it might get pretty ugly, but nothing like this. What day is it?"

"Sunday." The policeman spat on the ground. "I don't rightly know myself what's been going on. And the stuff on the radio don't help much." He shifted his weight. "I went off duty Thursday evening. I'm with the Twentieth Precinct. Went home and watched the TV, something on the news about plague in Harlem. I figured that they must have medicine against something like that, and I figured we'd been through worse in this town. You live in New York, you learn to take it. Then I go to sleep, but horns and yelling from the street wake me up. Right under the fucking window, steady honking. I go down to the street and there's a mob scene. People going nuts. I really mean that—guys running around in circles, beating their head against walls. Lots of screamers, too. Real weirdos. They'd carry on for awhile, then just fall down. Well, someone said that was the plague that was doing it, it made you insane and killed you, and we would all be in the same boat if we didn't get out. Plague was sweeping down from Harlem, your blacks, your PRs all had it, and so on. I got my gun and tried to quiet people down but then I just got out of the way. People were really going berserk, running in all different directions, pushing themselves along in wheelchairs, trying to drag their bikes over the hoods of cars. Guys on motorcycles knocking down people on the sidewalks. The unions weren't working, you understand. Only a couple of cops stayed around to maintain law and order and they immediately got the shit beat out of them. At first I was trying to help out, off-duty, you understand. Then I says to myself, 'Mike, you can't put the whole city in cuffs.' See, suddenly you got perpetrators all over the place, breaking into the banks, stores, you name it, Doc. Everybody had the same idea. Grab something valuable and get out, anywhere, leave."

Hart watched the policeman as he spoke. The man seemed to have a great need to deliver his report and justify his actions. "Sounds like you did a good job," he said.

"Well, I got a woman, my Esther. Works in a bar on Seventy-second, you understand. Night shift. I waited for her to come back. I went back inside and watched the TV. NBC had a special on the plague thing. Frank Field goes on telling people to cool it, that there was no reason to panic, that you could get medicine if you just went to a hospital or health station and waited your turn. I guess they didn't know that people were already panicking. And the Mayor came on and said help was coming—the Army and volunteer nurses and doctors. And the Commissioner of Health—you know him, right?—told people how to take care of themselves. They all talked about how everything was under control. That was a lot of bullshit."

"What about Washington? What about the Army? Have they sent anyone in, any troops, or the National Guard? Somebody must be doing something."

"Well, Doc, we got a transistor radio, and all we know is what's on that. They say the Army has surrounded the city. They say help is on the way. We see helicopters a lot—they stay high up. Every crummy punk who ever wanted to be a sniper is up on a rooftop with a gun. At first, I kept thinking I'd see troops marching up Park Avenue to rescue us, but nothing happens. We just keep waiting. We're just trying to stay alive and keep some law and order going." He fell silent and chewed on his lower lip. "I'm waiting for Esther to come home. She hasn't been home since Thursday night. I went down to the bar Friday morning but it was closed. There were people jammed into the streets—you could barely get through. People with shopping carts ripping off the supermarkets. I saw two bank robbers. I didn't care. I was looking for Esther."

"Maybe she got out of town," Hart said.

"No, she wouldn't leave without me. I know that. Something happened to her. I'll wait for her right here. You married?"

Hart thought for a second. He recalled that once he had been married. In the past he had either answered that question with an embarrassed "no" or had replied that he was a widower. Too complicated. "Yes," he said.

"What's her name?"

"Dolores."

"Nice name."

"Yes. That's who I'm going to meet. She's downtown at the Health Department. I have to see if she's okay."

"Then you better get your ass down there, fella," the policeman said. He pulled one of the revolvers from his belt. "Better take this thing along. Thirty-two snub-nose, better than nothing—what with these maniacs running loose. I call it my 'equalizer.'"

"Thanks." Hart checked the safety and tucked the gun in his belt. "By the way—don't try to burn the dead. Better to get some quicklime from a hardware store and sprinkle it on the corpses, then bury them in a vacant lot."

"You'd better get rid of that ambulance if you don't

want to get shot." The policeman escorted Hart to a light blue Volkswagen. "This is your best bet. It's got a full tank, the tires are good, it's little so you can maneuver around in it. We were keeping it handy for an escape in case we were invaded. You can put it to better use."

Hart selected a few items from the ambulance's medical kit, and presented the remainder to the policeman. As he drove away in the VW, he heard the cop yell out to the man who had menaced Hart: "Who are you calling a Jew, Mac? You got something against Jews?"

Hart drove south on Park Avenue. The VW was much less cumbersome, and the downtown lanes were relatively clear of abandoned cars and corpses. He saw moving forms along the narrow strips of grass and shrubs in the center of the avenue. More rats.

Many of the side streets were in flames. The old brownstones and tenements burned easily: there must have been thousands of fires throughout the city. Even on a normal day in Manhattan, there were about a thousand conflagrations. It was noon, and the air was now thick and still.

Occasionally someone would rush out of a doorway screaming, clawing, leaping, pointing at the sky, gagging on blood. Some would clutch their heads, others would tear at their hair. They were beyond help and extremely infectious at this stage of the disease. No wonder he saw no ordinary pedestrians. The dread of an encounter with a lunatic whose very breath could kill would keep the hardiest of adventurers indoors.

Hart put the car into third gear and maneuvered around the empty cars like a skier in a downhill slalom. As he passed the high-rise apartment buildings of Park Avenue he suddenly noticed that the windows of most of the apartments were open, and he wondered why that should look so odd. Then he realized that he had never seen them open before—this was the first time the people living in these luxury buildings had had to do without air conditioning. The rooms of the duplex and triplex apartments must now be insufferably hot. He wondered how many of these people cowered in their plush apartments, afraid to leave their possessions behind. With the electricity off, what robber would walk up that many flights when he could simply break into a bank?

He guessed that, depending on what plans were being made to rescue the city, it might take two weeks or more to establish order. And the electricity, gas, the subways, bridges, and tunnels would be restored only after order had returned.

Meanwhile, people had to survive. Perhaps there were many families up in those apartments watching him pass. They might get their provisions from the large water tanks on the rooftops and from the well-stocked kitchens of neighbors lucky enough to escape. The water and food would last them for a week or so. Canned goods would be a premium item.

Suddenly he thought of Dolores, with longing and anxiety. Would she have enough to eat? She had to be at the Department. Had she been the one who laid out the family in the apartment? She had to be all right. His picture on her mirror—amazing! The whole dismal summer she must have been waiting for him.

Suddenly in his rearview mirror he saw another car approaching. It was a dark green Lincoln with a tall radio antenna bent back by a flapping flag. He slowed the Volkswagen and stopped. The car was now a block away and slowing down. The flag attached to its antenna might mean it was from some foreign delegation. It was a criss-cross flag of red, white and blue. He squinted in order to see better. A Confederate flag!

A man riding in the back seat stuck his head out the window, waved a can of beer, and yelled, "Hey, partner, friend or foe?" There were four in the car, and they all looked scruffy and drunk. They gave a rebel yell, and accelerated toward Hart's car.

"Hook 'em, Texas, hook 'em!"

A blast from a shotgun exploded in Hart's ears, and the rear window of his VW shattered. He felt sharp pins rain into his neck and scalp—glass splinters. The car was a hundred yards behind him and closing fast. He cut sharply to the right, hoping to turn into a cross street before they got off a second blast. He pulled up on the sidewalk and accelerated. Just as he cleared the protection of a church on the corner, he heard the second report from the shotgun. He found a taxi smack in front of him, halfway up on the sidewalk. He barely scraped past, bumping into a parking meter and bouncing off the poles of a restaurant canopy. The big car had made the corner behind him and was coming after him. In the rearview mirror he could see two of the men aiming their guns out the rear windows. At Madison Avenue, Hart cut the corner as sharply as possible, turning left down the avenue. The uptown clotting of stalled cars was bad, but the little car was able to navigate through them. He smiled. This was just like Dodge'm Cars at Coney Island. As he looked back, the Lincoln crashed into a parked car and stalled. Hart pulled away, floorboarding the accelerator, and veered left on a crosstown street and over to Third Avenue. Near Second Avenue he had to slow to a crawl to wedge through a knot of bicycles on the sidewalk. He stopped and selected an Italian ten-speed racing bike, put it in the trunk, and drove on. The new mall by the Roosevelt Island Tramway terminus was filled with corpses. Otherwise, it looked cheerful, even festive.

He looked toward the East River. Several helicopters hovered over Queens. He saw that the tramway had been dynamited. The pylons stuck up out of the water at crazy angles. The entrance and exit ramps of the Fifty-ninth Street bridge were clogged with cars, buses, trucks, some police cars, and even a hook-and-ladder fire engine. The traffic on the incoming ramp had been reversed; cars had tried to get up both ramps and over the bridge, away from Manhattan.

He saw about a dozen people picking their way through the jumble of cars up the walk ramps. Some carried shopping bags or suitcases. A fat woman in bright green slacks that had been torn and blackened by soot walked by him. He got out of the car and tried to talk to her. "I have to get home and make lunch for the kids," she said without emotion. She hugged the shopping bag she carried. "Jerry will love the tangerines." Her eyes were blank. She followed the others up the incline to the pedestrian lane. There was a distant popping sound coming from the bridge, the staccato of automatic rifle fire. There were screams and shouts. The people turned back, and ran down the ramp. "They're shooting at us again!" cried a young man wearing the black, straight-brimmed hat and long sideburn-ringlets of a Hasidic Jew.

"Why?" called Hart.

"We want to get out of the city and they won't let us. We don't have plague, we're healthy! They won't let us go. They barricaded the end of the bridge, and they're shooting at us." He started to sob. *"Oy vay's mir!"*

"Who's shooting at you?" Hart asked.

"People in Queens. They yelled at us to stay back. They said they didn't want plague over there, that they were protecting themselves. Barricaded. I keep trying."

"You'd better take it easy and stay away from bridges," Hart said.

A very tall black man wearing sneakers ambled up. He was at least six foot eight, and he sported a neatly trimmed beard. Hart thought he recognized him from the newspapers. Wasn't he a basketball player for the Knicks?

"Diamonds Springer!" the young man exclaimed. "You got caught in the city too?"

"Bet your ass I did, friend." He hooked his large

hands into his belt as if he were awaiting a jump ball. "Diamonds was lef' behind with all the po' folk and white trash. Only the rich ones an' the influential cats got air-lifted out of here. Wish I'd been traded to Phillie las' year, then I be out of this mess! We gettin' our ass kicked in this jungle. Bein' black an' tall ain't the bes' thing now days, as I make a good target fo' the vigilance boys cruising the streets. They like to put me on their fenders like a deer." He threw his head back and laughed deeply.

"Have you tried to get over the bridge?" Hart asked.

Diamonds squinted and pretended to be warily on guard. "I try the tunnels to Jersey first, as I live over on the Wes' side. Bof of them is dark and there's weird noises coming from them, like moans and some screams. No *way* am I going to crawl into them. For all I know they may be *leaking*." As he spoke, he began losing his easy drawl. "It looks like the Jersey folk have got us trapped. Same on this side of the town." He extended a long black arm toward the East River. "You know what I just seen?" He did not wait for a reply. "I seen a dude in one of them inflatable rafts out there in the East River paddling his ass off to Queens before the current carried him out to sea. He was more than halfway across and I started cheering for him 'cause it looked like the son-of-a-bitch was going to make it! Then I sees bullets, jumping around his boat like fish. Shit, they were taking potshots at him from those buildings on Roosevelt Island. The poor bastard didn't have a chance."

He shook his head. Then he held out his huge palm for the young man. He looked up at Diamonds and smiled, pulled his hand out of his pocket and gave him a soul slap.

" 'Bye now," Diamonds said, as he slapped Hart's extended palm. "I'm goin' *up*town to the Triborough."

The young man nodded goodbye. "I'm going to try the Battery Tunnel now. I live in Brooklyn." He gestured toward Queens. "They wouldn't do that kind of *meshugenneh* stuff in Brooklyn."

Hart climbed up on the roof of a Mercedes and looked up and down the avenue. He was about half-way through his journey. It was going slower than he'd hoped. If he paced himself he could probably reach Worth Street by midafternoon. But going by car was too slow. He returned to the VW and he pulled out the bicycle.

He began pedaling south among the cars and trucks. Frequently he saw bodies hanging out of car windows; many of the faces were smeared with blood. So it wasn't all violence. The plague had killed more. Many must have been too sick to leave their cars when they got stuck in the traffic. A man, dressed completely in black rubber, picked his way down an intersection.

As he grew nearer, Hart could see that the man was in full scuba gear, complete with an oxygen tank, and he carried a spear gun on his shoulder as if he were in some extraterrestrial infantry. Ignoring Hart, he plodded toward the river, his flippers slapping hollowly on the pavement.

Hart stopped to rest and took his pulse. It was about eighty, and regular. His breathing was good except for the pain in his right chest, but that seemed to be diminishing. He could conserve his strength by coasting and using the easiest gears. He looked at his hands. They were wonderful. So were his legs and his arms. He could have been dead. But he wasn't. He would take it easy.

The east Forties were uninhabited except by rats. They rose up out of cellars and drains, they surged out of piles of garbage and scampered around store fronts. There were many rat carcasses, too, the limbs projecting stiffly into the air, the fur soaked and blood-stained.

But they were not as terrible as the human corpses.

The bodies in midtown had been dead longer than the bodies uptown.

People had drowned in their bloody secretions. Some of the bodies resembled the black bags of garbage that were everywhere: he saw several corpses that were swollen so that the abdomens puffed out like caricatures of the grotesquely obese. It was the sun that did it, the heat. It speeded up decomposition, especially in the intestines. The belly of one corpse had snapped the buttons of the white shirt that was still tucked in at the waist. Hart saw other bodies which had exploded.

He had left his mask at Dolores's apartment, and now his nose, his throat, and his sinuses were assailed with the characteristic odors of gangrene and necrosis. They were the smells of aberrant amino acids which formed when protein broke down, the smells of decaying meat: Squalene putrescine, cadaverine.

He started to dry-retch, so he pedaled faster to create a wind around himself.

At Forty-second Street he took a left and coasted over a block to First Avenue. Going down First, he passed a man pushing a shopping cart filled with neat banker's packets of money and a small gang of grimy, half-naked children chasing rats with sharpened broom handles.

He kept going, kept his attention on his will. Twenty-third Street. Thirty-five blocks to go. He knew that if he stopped he would never reach Worth Street, never again see Dolores. His legs felt weak but he was able to rest going downhill. He passed Bellevue Hospital and the Medical Examiner's Office, where the remains of Sarah Dobbs probably still rested; Beth Israel Hospital; the Manhattan VA hospital. They all appeared deserted. The bodies were very numerous here. All plague victims.

He turned right on Fourteenth Street. The massage parlors on that street all had crowds outside their doors. One man carried a small gold brick in one hand, another a case of scotch.

"Keep in line, gents," a man in front of the Cleopatra Rap Session and Body Massage yelled. "The girls are still busy but you'll get your turn. Goin' price is a thousand dollars or the equivalent! Fast Fred here will negotiate any deals!" He pointed to a man holding a .45.

One last fling.

Hart coasted left down Third and the Bowery. It looked about the same, although some of the ragged derelicts prone on the sidewalk were probably dead rather than dozing. Others sat in the sunny doorways with dozens of bottles of liquor, opened and unopened, arrayed before them. They sang out warm greetings as Hart passed and offered him toasts and swigs.

He crossed Houston Street and prepared to turn right to reach Elizabeth Street. He always felt secure in Little Italy. The local families looked after one another, and the streets were always monitored by the old men who sat on folding chairs in front of the store-front social clubs during the day and furtively unloaded vans during the night. They did not care to have police snooping around, and so they policed Little Italy themselves.

Now all the streets of Little Italy were barricaded with trucks and hearses at the Bowery intersections, and sentinels watched him from the tenement roofs. He caught glimpses of bright banners, strings of lights, spangled arches, and garlands of stars looped across the streets. Decorations for the Feast of San Gennaro.

As he coasted, one worry began to repeat itself with growing frequency: What if Dolores . . . ? He told himself it was pointless to torture himself with that fear. At this moment, for him, she was not dead. Then he would go on to the next moment—she was still not dead. And so on. The progression of moments maintained her life for him. And kept his will firm and commanding.

At the edge of Chinatown, he began to see people searching around in the piles of corpses and the automobiles and he was reminded of all the photographs of disaster he had seen in newspapers. Something dreadful was always happening in China, and the pictures always showed the Chinese picking through the ruins with clear, unlined faces in which you could read anything you liked: terror, acceptance, shock, serenity. A man with a cleaver and a basket moved from car to car in the jam around the Manhattan Bridge. It was several moments before Hart understood that he was severing the fingers of the dead passengers to remove their rings.

Hart turned west on Canal, and south on Centre. The streets of Chinatown teemed with rats, but below Canal Street there were no corpses.

Hart passed a large family gathered around a fire in the middle of the street. A woman was stirring vegetables in a big wok on a grill while others heaped mounds of shining noodles onto platters.

He was now so close to the Health Department that the towers of the World Trade Center were surreally huge. He could hear the strains of a hymn. It was probably from the band that always played outside the Chinese funeral parlor on Bayard. "Standing on the Promises."

48

THE HIGH iron gates across the entrances of 125 Worth Street were locked. Hart went around to the side entrance. Broken glass and blood made a mosaic on the steps and the sidewalk, and the gates here were also closed.

His heart was pounding now, and a sickening knot tightened in his solar plexus. He had not thought about what he would do if the Health Department were abandoned and Dolores were nowhere to be found. He gazed at Foley Square. A light breeze moved the leaves of the plane trees. A squirrel scampered over a pile of bodies stacked like cordwood. He found he could not move.

If he went into the Square, he would be forced to look among the corpses for Dolores and his other co-workers. He did not think he had the strength to scale the gates and walk up the four flights to the Bureau of Preventable Diseases. He wanted to vomit, but then he went numb. Maybe it would be better just to lie down on a park bench and try to blot out everything that had happened. Finish the whole thing off. Give up.

He looked up at the office with the corner window on the fourth floor, right below where MOSES was inscribed. KOCH PASTEUR LEEUWENHOEK EHRLICH BILLINGS HARVEY. What would these men do if they were alive in the city today? He couldn't imagine. He looked at the two American flags flying from poles on opposite sides of an upper-story setback. They made even less sense than the names of the medical heroes.

He had traveled through a good half of Manhattan and had seen absolutely no evidence of help from the United States of America. It was hard to believe. If there had been an epidemic in Chad, say, or Panama, American aid would have been rushed in. If a defense contractor were going bankrupt, or a railroad, federal funds would be provided. It was not as though the federal government had forgotten Manhattan. The constant buzz and roar of military aircraft made him think of the resentful hovering of a stern parent who is always present to reprimand—*"I told you what would happen if you weren't good!"*—but is never able to provide real help.

But the rest of the country must know about conditions here, surely there had been television coverage! But maybe not—he had not seen any civilian craft. Perhaps the military had restricted all access by land, sea, and air, for fear that the plague would spread.

These speculations only made him angrier. Before he fell ill, he had talked to the Surgeon General; she had assured him that enormous volunteer teams and supplies were on the way. Had there been an enemy attack? No—the cop uptown had said radio bulletins kept promising a military rescue.

He sensed that he stood in a concentric circle of delusions. The widest one was a belief, going back to elementary school civics, that the federal government, like God, was good and helpful to all its citizens. The next was a belief, almost as old, that all Americans shared in the decision-making process of the government and were kept informed about all important events. And the next delusion was a sentiment dating back to when he began specializing in public health: New York would hold itself together, no matter what. And the tightest circle of delusion was that the world he was most familiar with—the everyday universe of his job, his apartment, his co-workers, and the woman he had begun to love—was eternal. It might change in small ways, of course: he might one day be promoted to Commissioner of Health, or find a big rent-controlled apartment on a good street. But basically nothing enormous would happen. He had been punished enough by his wife's death; he would never be struck that way twice. That idiotic assumption had given him the certain belief that Dolores was alive and that they would get together, and live happily ever after.

He threw the bicycle down and sat on the curb. A rat watched him cry.

Finally he had had enough.

Since he had nothing at all to do in the world, and since the world did not care in the least whether he lived or died, and since he might as well learn everything he could, he walked over to the gates across the entrance and slowly began to hoist himself up.

The muscles in his arms jumped. He could not do it. He lacked the strength. The gates were too high. It would be better to find some food, sleep for a while. He pushed himself a little higher. He clutched the bars to keep himself from falling back. Inch by inch, he worked his way up.

At last he was over the top. He sat astride the gate and rested. Then he lowered himself a few feet and let go. His knees twinged when he struck the ground.

At the door of the Bureau of Preventable Diseases, he broke into a sweat. His hands trembled as he pushed open the door and paused to listen.

He could have been the first one in to work on an ordinary Monday. The clutter of desks, filing cabinets, and tables stacked with papers and documents was unchanged. He held his breath to still the tremors of fear moving through his chest and stomach and looked around for bodies. When he saw there were none, he exhaled with a hiss.

The nurses' room was stuffy. The windows were

closed and the shades pulled down. In the gloom he discerned a small, dark-haired form in a dark red-and-beige uniform stretched out on a bed made from two desks pushed together.

His heart gave a terrible jump, as if he had been stabbed.

He wanted to back out of the room and close the door. He stood with his fingers still touching the door-knob, his eyes fixed on the motionless curve of the woman's body. Her face was turned toward the wall and her loose dark hair spread like a stain over her shoulders and the desk.

49

THE MEN around the conference table watched Sheffield intently. General Charles's face was flushed: he had probably been drinking during the lunch break. When the Secretary of State, a smoker of some elegance, lit his pipe, his fingers made the flame tremble.

"Let's return to animate suppression for a moment," Sheffield said. "In order to be in a position to reoccupy a given area quickly and regain access to installations, we would move to eradicate all living things within the zone. Since any kind of animal life is a potential harborer, carrier, and vector of the disease, it isn't possible to differentiate among life forms. War-quality bacteria are extremely pervasive and hardy. Even under controlled environments in laboratories, hostile organisms have penetrated the most invincible barriers and infected humans. The elimination of such organisms requires complete removal of the environment in which they can exist. It may seem like lighting a cigarette with a hand grenade, but there is simply no other way. In a sense, it's like guerrilla warfare: it's impossible to clearly identify the enemy—in this case bacteria—and hence it's necessary to concentrate on sanitizing the territory. The more speedily you wish to gain or regain effective control of territory, the less discriminating you must be in your use of the sanitizing agent."

Sheffield paused and lightened his tone of voice slightly. "I think it would be helpful to think of the process I am outlining as area-wide instant decontamination. In bacteriological warfare, there are only two kinds of life-forms: those which are infected—and hence have become unwilling agents of further transfer—and those which have not become infected, and hence are vulnerable to attack. Our strategy is to isolate, and if necessary, eliminate the first category to protect the second. I'm sure you can see that sentimental distinctions are useless. Once a man has become infected, he has, in essence, become an enemy soldier. If he is allowed to come into contact with other individuals, he will kill them as surely as if he had shot them with a weapon."

50

HART SLOWLY went toward the body as though he were swimming through a thick liquid. Her foot jutted stiffly out over the edge of the desktop and he could see the fan of blue veins in the instep.

He gently brushed the hair away from her cheek, which felt like marble.

It was Mia Thomas, the nurse epidemiologist from Staten Island. She must have returned to Manhattan to help out. Her lips were closed with clots of blood.

He backed out of the room and closed the door.

He had opened too many doors today. It was time to stop. His other co-workers, including Dolores, either lay behind other doors, or out in the streets. He was sure they would not have fled. They would have stayed, like Mia. He had seen so much death now that it was becoming meaningless. The thousands of corpses he had passed could have been so many dead leaves.

His office was the same. The map set up for the plague was black with pins. I was the director here, he thought. He leaned against the wall, tired and dirty and disheveled.

There was nothing to do but whistle, and as he began to whistle a Latin American wedding tune, "La Bamba," there was a shout from the outer office.

"Stay right there!"

He stopped whistling and put his hand on the gun in his belt.

"Don't move!" It was a woman's voice.

He turned and saw her. Her face was hard, as though it had been cut from brown stone, and the lines of her mouth and cheeks were as straight and deep as chisel blows. Her eyes were wide but the hand that held the .45 was steady. In her other hand was a black plastic bag.

He saw her startled gaze and the effort she was making to assimilate the sight of him, and he hurried toward her. "You're some tough Puerto Rican!" he said. "A gun and a garbage bag!"

He hugged her, crazy with joy and relief. He picked her up. For a moment he wondered if she were real. He ran his hands over her head and back. She was real. She was alive. Deep, dry sobs shook her body.

"Oh, David, you don't know . . . I can't believe it! I never thought . . ." She leaned against his shoulder and shook.

Then she drew back and looked at him. "Hey! You're really okay! Boy, you didn't look so good the last time I saw you! I didn't know if you were going to—"

She began to sob again, but there were no tears.

"Come on, that's enough."

"You mother! How come you got sick, *estúpido?* Some doctor, you are."

"If you hadn't seduced me like that I would have remembered to keep up the tetracycline dosage. You had me so addled—"

"None of that! Boy, I was really mad at you. You sure picked a dumb time to flake out. I told Dr. Andrews, 'If David dies, I'm never going to speak to him again, ever, not even in heaven!' "

"I'm glad you didn't come and see me in the hospital—you might have killed me."

"But I did," she said, her face growing serious. "See you up at Met, I mean."

"When?"

"Friday."

"Really?"

"Of course!"

He thought how strange it was for them to be arguing, as though nothing had ever happened but some silly mixup.

"Where is everybody?" he asked.

She looked at the black plastic bag she was carrying and her face hardened again. "I have to take care of Mia," she said quietly.

"I know about Mia," he said. "But the others?"

"I don't know—I thought you must be with them. Sam, uh, Dr. Andrews was supposed to check on you —did you see him?"

"No." He told her the story of how he had awakened

that morning and gone looking for her. "Your apartment, your family—"

"I know," she said, looking at him in a clear, resolute way. He read in her face that she had seen everything and understood it as well as she was able and did not care to talk about it.

She sat down on the desk and he pulled her close, his arm around her waist. He had an irrational fear that if he stopped touching her she would vanish and he would awaken to a new nightmare. He could feel the beat of her body.

She looked quite presentable. Her hair was brushed, her uniform was clean. She was the first decent-looking human being he had seen since his awakening. She had taken care of herself. The whole city had collapsed, people raved in the streets, her friend lay dead in the next room, her family had died, but she had made herself function and survive. Why?

"Even when I didn't think I would see you again, I still hoped I would, and I just tried to do whatever I had to and just kept going," she said. "After Sam and I took you upstairs at Met, and I made sure you were hooked up to the IV okay and had your medication and everything, I helped out on the ward for a little bit and then Sam and I came back here. Oh, man, it was really getting crazy. There was a big crowd in Federal Plaza and outside the Health Department. There were helicopters all over the place, and Sam and Dr. Calabrese thought they were the Army epidemiological units, but they weren't. They were picking up people, like down here in Federal Plaza, but we never figured out why.

"Gayle and Joanie and Mia and the others who could get back into Manhattan went through the crowd, giving out medicine. But everybody was too wild. Guys would just grab the boxes of strep and run off before we could mix it up and put it into hypodermics. Some people were eating it and they wouldn't listen when we told them that wouldn't help. There were also pushers selling tetracycline for ten dollars a capsule. And there were people who were really sick, really in a lot of pain, and we tried to get them to lie down on stretchers. But even with a lot of police who had stuck around to help and just regular people who volunteered, we couldn't do enough. When people saw that some guys were being taken away in those helicopters, they went crazy. We had to barricade ourselves inside the building the rest of the night. Then around the middle of the day the power went off and the phones stopped working. Dr. Andrews and Dr. Calabrese kept trying to get through to somebody —the CDC, or the Surgeon General. But it was no good. And all the radio would say was to keep calm, help was coming. I told Sam I wanted to do my job and try to take care of people. But I told him I had to get back to Met to see how you were. He was really against that, and so was Dr. Calabrese. They said you were in good hands up there. But then Dr. Calabrese saw that I really was worried, and wondering about my family, too, so he said I could go if Gayle went with me. We got a gun from a cop just in case, and two cops drove us up on the back of their motor scooters.

"When we got there, people were going crazy outside Met. The cops didn't think we should try to get inside, but we did. We started climbing up the stairs and Gayle started getting really sick all of a sudden. Oh, man. On the lower floors we could hear a lot of yelling from inside—we just stayed on the stairs—so I didn't want to take her in there. She'd rest for a while, and then she'd get a lot of energy and run up a bunch of flights—I couldn't keep up with her. And she was starting this crazy talk. Finally we made it to the fifteenth floor and there were only two nurses on duty for the whole ward, and they had the emergency generator keeping the power going in the hospital, but then I think the rioters got to it, because the lights went out and stayed out. So I put Gayle into bed and fixed

her up real good, and gave you some more strep—
you were really out of it, too. Whew." She grinned
and gave him a kiss. "Boy, am I glad to see you!"

"So then what happened?"

"Well . . . I went to my place, and—" the curious
look of determination came into her eyes again. "And
after that, I, uh—" Her eyes moved back and forth
as she went over her recollections, and her face darkened. She realized she was still holding the gun. She
laid it carefully down on the desk. "What was I saying?"

"After you went to your place. . . ?"

"Oh, yeah. I got back down here to the Bureau and
Mia told me that Dr. Andrews and Dr. Calabrese
decided—"

"How did you get back downtown, Dolores?"

The look returned again.

"Is there something bad that—"

She lowered her eyes for a long time. "It's okay.
It's taken care of. I'm fine." She gave him a brilliant
smile. "I take very good care of myself. And now I
can drive a motor scooter like a pro."

He felt awe. He understood that there were quali-
ties in her that he would never see. He had told her
about the rigors of his journey downtown with some
pride, but he realized that whatever had happened
to her during her journey belonged only to her. "So
Calabrese and Sam decided what?"

"They figured the Army epidemiological units might
have landed in Central Park and set up some kind of
health station there, so after things had calmed down
here and the crowds went away, they packed up a lot
of supplies and medicine—mostly in police vans or on
motor scooters, since you couldn't get through the
streets. Mia had stayed behind. She didn't tell anybody she was getting sick. When I got back downtown
she was alone here and I stayed with her. I was thinking that if you started getting better you would probably try to come down here. Sam *promised* me he would

go back up to Met and check on you and Gayle. Hey, how is Gayle?"

He shook his head. "She got exposed so early."

"Oh David! You know something awful? I can't cry anymore about anything! I used it all up."

He held her tightly. "I know what you mean."

51

"Now, IN IDEAL battlefield conditions, isolation and treatment based on triage would be used, since there would be no immediate problem of reoccupying installations. We would try to salvage what we could later on. But in the case of Manhattan, we're dealing with a fixed installation whose value if decontaminated immediately is immense but whose contaminated value is nil." Sheffield spoke with his gaze resting on an invisible point high in the conference room. "We have the capability to restore the value of Manhattan in about one hundred twenty hours by eliminating the entire animate environment of the plague bacteria."

"How would you accomplish this decontamination, General?"

"A powerful insecticide could be counted on to eliminate most fleas, and chlorine gas pumped into basements and sewers would eliminate most rats. But we are concerned here not with 'most' but with 'all,' and not just with rodents and their fleas but with nonrodent carriers. To achieve a simultaneous elimination of the entire bacterial infrastructure, agent VX would be the most effective means. Within twenty-four hours it will penetrate to all subterranean cavities and thus totally eliminate all rodents and any nonrodent life that has sought shelter. Its half-life is three days, after which the city could be safely entered. It is totally effective. No biological system that we have encountered can exist for more than fifty seconds after being exposed to VX."

52

"WHAT DO you think you're doing?" Rodriguez asked. "You're not driving that thing. You get on the back."

Hart looked at the small woman and at the large green-and-white New York Police Department motor scooter.

"It's okay, now, Dolores. I'm here—you can relax."

She pulled an elastic rope tight around the medical kit and the box of food lashed under the seat. "You're the one who needs to rest, not me. I'm healthy—I didn't go and get myself sick like you did."

"I'm never going to get any pity from you, am I?"

"Nope. If you're nice to people who harm themselves, they just hurt themselves worse. If you aren't good to yourself, if you don't take care of yourself and you get sick again—I'm not gonna bother with you." She glared at him. "I'm not kidding."

"My God, I think you're serious!"

"You bet I am. Anyway, I know how to drive this."

As they began to weave their way through the cars and piles of bodies on Worth Street, he realized he was glad of the chance to rest. The muscles in his chest were tight and sore, and his arms and legs throbbed with exhaustion.

The streets along Foley Square were packed with the now-familiar tableau of abandoned cars, piles of corpses and garbage, and the twittering, feasting rats. Overhead, Hart counted three jets and a large seaplane, probably a Coast Guard job. "Every outfit except the Girl Scouts seems to have New York under surveillance," he shouted over the scooter's noise.

"Yeah, I noticed that," she replied over her shoulder. "I can't figure it out. The last time I listened to the radio all they were talking about was some kind of rescue operation the Army was planning."

"Well, maybe up in the park."

Broadway was deserted. A car had been driven through the plate-glass window of the bank where he had an account. He found himself taking a slightly malicious pleasure in the sight: all the hours he had been forced to wait in line there only to be sent to some other teller, all the times his checks had been erroneously bounced . . . Perhaps he was not alone in his vengeful satisfaction; perhaps the feeling explained some of the destruction he had seen. On an ordinary day in New York City, a person was always vulnerable to some reduction of spirit. But the thought of vengeance and its satisfaction was quickly replaced by a sense of balance. He rested his hand on Dolores's rounded hip and gave it a gentle squeeze. He no longer needed to devote so much energy to petty hatreds.

SoHo, the section between Canal and Houston, was not as badly jammed. The afternoon sun slanted through the narrow crosstown streets and flashed off the tall arched windows of the lofts where painters and sculptors had lived and worked. Loud rock music drifted down from an upper story: "Let It Bleed." The Rolling Stones. Suddenly the music was interrupted by a screech.

"You're sick now—you have to leave the party!" someone yelled from above. A loud thud followed.

Rodriguez stopped and they looked back. A man lay crumpled on the sidewalk with his legs twisted under his back. He whimpered and tried to lift his head.

Two faces appeared at a sixth-floor window, and waved at the man on the sidewalk. "Sorry! You have to leave the party!"

"Dios mío!" Rodriguez cried, jumping off the scooter and running to where the man lay.

He wore a faded workshirt and had a Buffalo Bill moustache. He gazed sadly at Hart and Rodriguez as if to say, See how they treat me around here?

"Don't touch him," cried one of the figures in the window, a woman with short dark hair. "He has the plague and he didn't tell us!"

Rodriguez and Hart exchanged looks. The man was beyond help. They tried to make him as comfortable as possible without moving his spine, which was probably broken. He was mumbling, and blood trickled out of his ear and across his cheek. "If only I—"

"Yes?" Rodriguez gave him all her attention.

"If only I hadn't—"

"It doesn't matter," she said. "Look—look up at the sky!"

"If I hadn't sold my motorcycle, I—" His face settled into the grimace of a wronged five-year-old and he died.

53

"I THINK we should pursue other options for a moment," said Carter Fairleigh, the Secretary of State, "or at least establish to the satisfaction of the President that no other options exist." He lit a pipe and blew a gray cloud across the table.

"The only other option we've been able to formulate is a purely military one, Mr. Secretary," said Cosgrove. He had a sudden absurd image of himself as a symphony conductor. "General Charles will outline it."

"Mr. Secretary," Charles said, "the Army is capable of conducting a block-by-block forced evacuation of the city into existing designated Civilian Detention Camps. Our best estimate is that it would require the active participation of fifty infantry battalions plus support elements for a total of about one hundred thousand troops and would require eight to ten weeks. Given the resistance we have encountered in our aircraft operations over the city and the fate of our epidemiological units, the troop casualty rate would be about twenty percent. Remember, we're confronted with hardened terrorist groups who are extremely well armed and quite capable of prolonged guerrilla warfare in an urban setting with which they are quite familiar. Something on the order of twenty-five thousand civilians would become casualties, presuming light resistance to the operation. Street-fighting is a very messy business, gentlemen: my recollections of it from Bastogne are still very clear."

General Charles consulted a small notebook. "The FBI has estimated that there are one million handguns and rifles in New York City," he continued. "Furthermore, the National Guard armories there have been systematically raided over the last few years. We assume that most of these weapons remain in Manhattan. In the last raid, in August of this year, we lost two hundred M-14 rifles with ten thousand rounds of ordnance each; twenty M-60 machine guns with twenty thousand rounds of ordnance each; sixty M-79 grenade launchers, with four hundred rounds each; twenty-four thousand rounds of fragmentation-type grenades; twenty M-72 AT rocket launchers with four hundred rounds each; twelve 4.2 inch mortars, five hundred rounds each; and one hundred Claymore mines. This equipment can arm approximately three hundred forty men who would be fully combat ready for a week or more of heavy fighting. There are ten armories in Manhattan, gentlemen. At present, they all stand unguarded. The amount of weaponry and ordnance now in the hands of terrorist bands like the Weather Underground and the Puerto Rican Liberation Front—groups that apparently see the present situation as an opportunity to cripple this country or to seize a vast power base—is probably enough to severely compromise the restoration of order by our troops. And there are also ferocious gangs, like the Hell's Angels, and there are psychopaths, addicts, and felons. In addition, our men would be handicapped by protective gear, which they would need to avoid inhaling plague bacilli in the air or getting bitten by fleas. And of course there's the possibility of whole units becoming infected. You simply cannot rely on medication to protect them; it would be extremely hard to administer regularly to troops in a combat situation. We could end up weakening those battalions before accomplishing anything—weakening them at a time when we have to be alert to potential invasion threats from Cuba and a general erosion of law and order across the country."

Fairleigh frowned and chewed on his pipe stem. "But perhaps there's a strategy based on a clear ultimatum? For example, if it were announced through public-address systems on helicopters and leaflets that all citizens of Manhattan were to report to various debarkation points—say the West Side piers—to board ships for ultimate quarantine at some coastal point, and that anyone who remained in the city would be in deadly peril from powerful decontaminants, wouldn't it be possible to salvage a good percentage of the surviving population in a short time? The failure of such an effort would cost no more than the period allocated for the attempt. If there were a massive breakdown of order, and it proved impractical to effect a sea or airborne evacuation, we could then proceed with the sanitization program."

"I appreciate your humanitarian sentiments, sir," General Cosgrove said. "But such an evacuation effort is simply impossible. We already know that many people died during the riots that broke out around the Alpha-Echelon evacuation points. We could expect a replay of that—evacuees insisting on bringing their infectious relatives, for example. Another Saigon-type situation. The evacuation of two to four hundred thousand New Yorkers—and that's probably a conservative estimate—is unfeasible. That's equivalent to the population of a medium-sized city. Where could we possibly put that many people? Even if we could manage such an evacuation, the risk of at least one case slipping past quarantine is immense, and this would jeopardize the entire nation, the world. Only one or two cases infected and disrupted New York City.

"But say we did attempt to carry out an evacuation and it became known that the attempt had failed: a widespread sympathy reaction to the plight of the Manhattan populace would develop. At present, ac-

cording to the polls, Americans feel more frightened
and threatened by the crisis in New York than directly sympathetic. But if great sympathy were allowed to develop, what can now be rationalized—
with considerable but not fatal negative political conse-
quences—as a terribly difficult and unpleasant decision taken to ensure the survival of the entire nation,
would become premeditated murder in the public
mind. I think we've all learned the lesson that actions
which must be taken in the interests of national security but which would not enjoy even a sizable minority of public support, let alone legislative sanction,
are best taken unilaterally by the President, with a
minimum of notice, and then explained later. Only
the President has the power to act in the nation's
higher interests. Congress would surely interfere in
this process: ten percent of the House is from New
York State, and many people have friends and relatives in the city. Anyway, there's not enough time to
take this matter up in Congress."

54

RODRIGUEZ AND Hart made their way slowly northward on Fifth Avenue. It was the least jammed route
they could find. Hart had begun to feel much better
and at the same time to grow increasingly baffled and
angered by what he saw. On his trip downtown, he
had focused solely on reaching the Health Department and finding Rodriguez; he had not been very
interested in analyzing what he had observed. But
now he began to move his attention outward. He saw

that most of the casualties they passed were the result of human stupidity rather than of some blind force of nature. And the casualty of the city itself, wounded, burning, its vital signs faltering or absent, its inhabitants dead or in disarray, was almost incomprehensible to him. What bothered him most was that no one he saw appeared to be making any effort to improve matters. A great many people were sick or in shock and seemed to be kept alive solely by a retreat into deep instincts. They sat on curbs and doorsteps, paralyzed by intense fear, or wandered through the streets with their bodies rigid, as though they were carrying sheets of plate glass; their eyes were blank, as though they were no longer able to take in any images. Victims. And there were those who were in intense states of emotion, like the solemn crowd singing hymns with the Salvation Army band under Washington Square Arch, or like the ecstatic, inebriated couple who lounged in evening dress among the plastic ferns of a French Provincial living room in a window of W. & J. Sloane's furniture store, or like the determined throng emptying the Forty-second Street Library and feeding its contents to a bonfire on the steps between the stone lions, one of which now wore a hand-lettered sign saying: BURN ALL EVIL BOOKS! ONLY BIBLE HAS TRUTH!

In front of the massive doors of St. Patrick's cathedral was an altar displaying icons of St. Roch and St. Sebastian, patron saints of the plague; mounds of bills and coins were stacked around it, and priests sprinkled holy water and swung censers among the throng of supplicants gathered on the steps below. Across the street were faith healers, Hari Krishnas, and followers of the Reverend Sun Myung Moon, who promised the Kingdom of Heaven to all who accepted him as Savior and swore to defend South Korea.

And there were the ragpickers. Some came out of department stores onto Fifth Avenue, carrying garden hoses, peignoirs, cases of perfume, wicker baskets, and ten thousand other objects. And some filed out of the Museum of Modern Art with paintings and sculptures under their arms or in shopping carts. Rodriguez and Hart stopped to watch two bearded men carefully load a Brancusi marble and a Renoir oil into the sidecar of a motorcycle.

Many of the banks and shops along Fifth Avenue had been bombed. The block where two Gucci stores once stood was now a crater filled with charred rubble and twisted girders. Disorganized violence could not account for that much devastation. Hart began to wonder again about whether there had been a coup, and when they passed the Plaza Hotel, he thought he had the answer. From the second-floor windows hung a makeshift banner: LIBERATED BY THE PEOPLES ARMY. The entrances to the lobby were guarded by a shabbily dressed band of men and women with M-14 rifles and M-60 machine guns. The roof and the cupolas were also patrolled by armed guards. He noticed that low-flying military craft swerved to avoid the airspace over Central Park South.

At the intersection of Fifth Avenue and Central Park South, one of the guards summoned them. Hart put his mouth to Rodriguez's ear. "Step on it!"

She sped up as they passed the Plaza, and Hart raised his fist in a power salute. The salute was returned by several members of the Peoples Army, who, apparently assuming that the couple had liberated the New York Police Department motor scooter, let them pass into the park.

Hart tried to pull together everything he had seen through the long day, starting with Metropolitan hospital. He could find no particular logic or order to the way the city was now occupied. Some sections were completely deserted and rank with decay. Fifth Avenue, the spine running from Greenwich Village up to the park and on into Harlem, was the most populous stretch: but that morning he had bicycled downtown on Park and Lexington, only a few blocks to the east, and had seen only rats and corpses. He had also begun to notice many who appeared to be sick, but not from plague. They vomited on themselves, or defecated in the gutters. They were probably sick from contaminated water. Dysentery. That meant that typhoid and hepatitis would eventually be commonplace in the city unless something was done soon.

In the past, Manhattan had always seemed somewhat random to him. A steam explosion might blow manhole covers high over the street, or he might be knocked over by a man chasing a pickpocket. The city always had an atmosphere of imminent disaster: the screech of brakes, the hectic wail of sirens, the raucous horn blasts of the fire trucks. But in fact, Manhattan had been a coherent, working body—as coherent as a million or so people jammed together on a small island ever could have been. Crowds of rushing people, all of whom made use of the electricity, public transportation, water and sewerage systems, museums, theaters, concert halls, parks, thousands of different kinds of industries, businesses, and shops . . . it had all worked. But now the intelligence and the nervous system of the city had been damaged: the entity that had operated on a scale so vast that its sudden visible manifestations had seemed random had now disintegrated. Now events were truly random.

The sun, crimson, bloated by the haze, sank behind the cliff of buildings west of the park. The windows of the apartment buildings along Fifth were touched with flame, and Hart could not tell which buildings might actually be on fire and which ones were only reflecting the sunset. The park was dusty and littered. Cans, bottles, papers, and wrecked cars surrounded the pond; packs of dogs roamed and sniffed at bodies that lay in the grass like dozing picnickers.

As they followed the path through the zoo, they saw that all the cages were empty.

They had been forced open, and the coyote, the deer, and the gazelles had fled. The seals barked steadily, pleading for food. Although he had seen enough bodies throughout the day to saturate the reflex diagnostic mechanism in his brain, one body in the zoo did engage his attention. A man lay on the mall by the building that had housed the large African animals. The trail of dried blood on the sidewalk indicated that he had been dragged for some fifty yards before his right arm had been twisted from his torso. Hart peered around for signs of a large cat—a lion, or a tiger. If they had been freed along with the other animals, they were now stalking the park for food—or would be as soon as night fell. He decided not to mention that possibility.

"Dolores—listen!" From under the arch by the Children's zoo came soft tinkling music. She slowed the motor scooter.

"The steel-drum guy—he's still there!" she exclaimed. "He plays here every Sunday."

A tall, serene man smiled at them and continued tapping his arrangement of steel drums. The music reverberated under the arch and hung in the air like a waterfall.

"Thank you," Hart called to him. "Sounds wonderful!"

They rode up a hillside, around an abandoned taxicab, and into the Mall, where they stopped to stretch their legs. He gave her a kiss, and she pointed out a gazelle near the band shell nibbling on the lower leaves of a chestnut tree. The light was fading, leaving them in a dense sepia twilight. The faint sounds of the steel drums, the sight of the gazelle, and the firm curve of her body against his pleased him. In silence they looked and listened.

"What a date!" Hart said finally.

She laughed, her teeth white in the dusk. "Well—we're pretty close to your place." Then her face grew serious. "I keep trying to think of where Dr. Calabrese would set up the health station."

"Me, too," Hart said. "My guess is that they would

try to get close to the reservoir, where they could have a supply of water. It would need to be purified, but it would be safer than drinking whatever happens to trickle out of the tap."

"Let's have a snack from that bag and then keep looking until it gets too dark," she said. "And then . . ." She lifted an eyebrow and clicked her tongue.

As he was about to kiss her, he caught three dark silhouettes out of the corner of his eye, moving swiftly toward them. Then there were more shapes.

They were suddenly surrounded by a dozen or so young men. They all wore black denim jackets with the frayed sleeves cut off at the elbows and white T-shirts. Each had an automatic rifle slung over his shoulder. Some had loops of chain dangling from their belts. Others carried pool cues. One of the men came forward—he was about six feet tall and had a bushy Afro—and stroked the motor-scooter handlebars as if he were inspecting them for signs of rust.

Hart felt Rodriguez's shoulders hunch and her spine stiffen. He slowly moved his hand until it rested on the gun in his belt.

"You goin' somewhere?" the man asked. He was chewing gum.

"To the health station," Hart said, thinking it was best to sound definite.

"What you talkin' about, man? You think we estupid? Now why you say that?" The others shifted in their stances and laughed. "You want to see estupid people?" He pointed across the Mall, where a Lincoln with a shattered rear window had crashed into a tree. It had a tall radio antenna with a pennant attached.

"Got four estupid ones there, man, an' they all dead. We no estupid asshole, so don' say estupid things!" He thrust his face toward Hart's. He had a scar that ran across his forehead and cut deeply into the bridge of his nose. "And don't think you can give us the plague, 'cause we're *medicated.*"

"Look," Hart said. "I'm a doctor. I think my friends

are camping here some place, some nurses and doctors, and I want to find them." He was now wondering whether Calabrese and the others had made it up here.

"Santiago—you take care of the scooter," the leader told one of the other gang members. "I take care of the lady here." He suddenly gave Hart a shove. "Hey —some doctor! He got a gun!"

He grabbed Hart's wrist, squeezed it until his fingers released the gun, and then smacked Hart with the back of his hand, a sharp ring scratching Hart's cheek. "You'll get more, man. Now you tell us what you after here in our turf. This our park. The Savage Shadows control it and ain't nobody can come into it without our permission." He scowled and took Hart's chin in his hand. "You a fuckin' spy, ain't you? Man, we fix your ass." He pulled a length of chain from his belt.

One of the others pulled Rodriguez away.

"Watch out, I get her first!" The leader raised his chain.

55

"CAN WE formulate a believable adversary action to help create an external focus of public outrage?" Marks asked.

"An overt statement on the part of the President suggesting that Cuba was responsible for the plague is a constructive possibility," Cosgrove replied. "We would then have to make a *Mayagüez*-type response, and that could be an important source of political benefit. General Charles has formulated a plan under which Cuba can be reduced and occupied in ninety-six hours, and this option will be made available to the President. However, the evidence we have of Cuban involvement is not decisive, and the evidence which we can develop to improve the logic of the response will always fall short of being satisfactory in that the purported hostile action was not clear and visible. Certainly, though, some reference to the continuing investigation into the possibility of foreign involvement would maintain the option, and I am prepared to so advise the President."

"What will be the impact on a global basis?" asked Secretary Fairleigh. "We must address ourselves to that question."

"In my view," said Cosgrove, "those nations who have traditionally responded to strong actions taken by the United States will react as they always do, with Swedish-type moral responses for public consumption. The direct benefits to the North Atlantic region, both in economic and military terms, are so clear, however, that private response will be very positive. Our adversaries will be shown an extremely useful lesson which should convince them of our will and our credibility as perhaps nothing else could. I think this is an unarguable benefit of the current situation.

"The enemy of this country has always been and always will be a lack of willingness to take positive action at critical moments," Cosgrove continued. "One casualty worth considering is the image of our nation in the minds of people around the world. It can be strengthened or wounded; it can die as surely as a soldier can. So long as nuclear warfare makes an ultimate confrontation with our adversaries unfeasible, we're compelled to shadowbox on a world scale. But no one must ever doubt that it is a real and deadly match and the stakes are the world itself. I think today we can, in a single stroke, recapture every bit of ground lost because of Indochina."

56

HART WATCHED the chain swing back and forth.

The Savage Shadows were from the South Bronx, but they were notorious all over the city.

"I'm sorry we're on your turf," Hart said. "My friend is a public health nurse, and I'm a doctor—"

"Yeah?"

"Really! You'll find a medical kit strapped to the seat of the motor scooter. Oh, shit, listen, I am a doctor." He held up his arm and began to point out its bones. "This is my humerus, my radius, my—"

"Whaaat? Don' give me that shit! Don' give me no hooomerus!"

The Shadows laughed. "This motherfucker has flipped out!" one of them said. Several of them took their chains from their belts. One of them held Rodriguez by her neck. *"Tú loco!"* she shouted. She went on in Spanish. "This man is a doctor—you hurt yourselves if you hurt him! Where are your mothers? Are they sick? We can help them! How about your little sisters and brothers, and your girlfriends? We have medicine and we can help them. Don't hurt someone who can save your life!"

"If he's a doctor, they could have drugs," one of them said. "Or maybe they know where to get some."

The leader chewed his gum and looked at his captives. Finally he said, "We gonna take you to the Minister of War and let him check you out. If you lying, we fix your ass!" He put his chain back on his belt. "Chino, Kingbop, you. Take these prisoners to

Gato. If they telling the truth, maybe he want to use them for our wounded. Everybody else come with me."

The group quickly vanished toward Fifth Avenue, taking the police scooter with them, and Hart and Rodriguez were left with Chino and Kingbop. Hart recalled all the times he had wandered through the Park at night hoping to be killed. Now that wish was dead. He reached for Rodriguez's hand, but Kingbop, a wiry man with several gold medallions dangling from his neck and a head bristling with tiny braids, said, "No touch her, mon." He sounded almost friendly. He was Jamaican, and Hart concluded from the braids that he was probably a member of the Rastafarian cult, which worshipped Haile Selassie.

"Your neighborhood hit pretty badly by the plague?" Hart asked Kingbop.

The man grinned, revealing a big gold tooth. "No, we all be fine up deah. No plague in Bronx, mon! We come Manhattan rescue our brothers, but we havin' real fun." He shook the medallions on his chest. "Plenty good t'ings you can get here, and we workin' now for de Minister of War. We got ourself a nice clubhouse and ever't'ing." He patted Rodriguez's shoulder. "You like it, Miss."

She slapped his hand. "Drop dead!"

"Whew!" Kingbop drew back in mock fear. "You sure got a rude girl, mon," he told Hart.

"You really a nurse?" Chino asked her. "Like goes around to people's apartments?"

She nodded.

"Huh," Chino said. "I can remember these chicks would come around, with a blue uniform, really nice, you know. When I was like, little, and my mom was still alive, the nurse would come."

"Yeah, that's right." She smiled at him. "That's what I used to do."

They emerged from the Ramble on a hill, climbed down in silence, through abandoned traffic on the

Drive, and went up another slope. Hart recognized it as the hill behind Belvedere Castle. "Is your clubhouse in Belvedere Castle?" he asked.

"Naah," Chino said. "We got a real nice place, a mansion."

"On Fifth Avenue," Kingbop added.

"The castle is just headquarters," Chino said.

"Don't talk to the prisoners, mon," Kingbop told Chino.

"Right," Chino said. "No talking to prisoners."

Through the overhanging boughs, Hart got a glimpse of the Great Lawn, an open space which stretched out below from the pond known as Belvedere Lake almost up to the Reservoir. He saw tents, small bonfires, trucks, and people milling around under naked light bulbs strung from tree branches. His first impression was of refugee camps in Vietnam, and he was also reminded of pictures of detention centers and prisoner-of-war camps.

They reached the top of the hill, where the walk broadened into a stone terrace and an overlook beside Belvedere Castle. There were more light bulbs and a few spotlights, a card table, and a big overstuffed sofa. Several men with Savage Shadow jackets stood around.

Hart glanced at Rodriguez. Her face was set and her eyes were darting—she was taking in everything. He began to sweat, and the small cuts made from the glass splinters, the mementos of the Dixie boys, had begun to sting his neck.

Chino and Kingbop led their captives to the card table. Behind it sat a man in a Savage Shadow jacket. As the others began to notice Rodriguez, they gathered around her and whooped and whistled.

"Some piece of ass you guys find! Whoo-eee!"

"Cool it," Kingbop told them. "Manuel gets her first."

"Will you guys SHADDUP!" shouted the man behind the table. He was short, powerfully built, and his face was covered with black stubble. "When you gonna learn some manners, *creeps?* You treat a woman with respect! Unnastan'? You stink on ice!"

"Two prisoners for in-terro-ga-shun, Gato," Chino announced.

The glare of the bare light bulbs pained Hart's eyes and he doubted what he saw. But the build of the man was familiar, and so was the voice. "Alan? Alan Katz?"

"Jesus Christ, Dave! I don't believe it!" Katz reached across the table and gave Hart's shoulders a hard squeeze. Hart replied with an involuntary cough. "Dolores! Oh, man, am I glad to see you two. We thought you'd bought it, Dave. We figured Dolores was okay, but we thought you'd bought the farm."

57

COSGROVE, SHEFFIELD, and Marks sat drinking bourbon in Cosgrove's office.

"I wouldn't have said this at the meeting," Sheffield said, "but I don't see how we're going to sell this to the President, frankly." He removed his glasses and polished them with a white handkerchief.

"If the plague gets out of New York, hundreds of millions will die," Cosgrove said. "If hundreds of millions of people die, the United States as an entity will die, and take Europe with it. Western civilization —gone. All because the President didn't act quickly enough. If he follows our solution, he will be known throughout the world, throughout history, as a hero. He'll never turn his back on an argument like that."

"He might suggest an intensive medical program coupled with military occupation of the city," Sheffield said. "That's also heroic."

"But impractical—you can give him the figures for how rapidly epidemics always spread through armies and military bases. Show him how the Spanish-influenza epidemic was scattered throughout Europe and America by soldiers."

Marks watched Cosgrove and Sheffield playing devil's advocate to each other for a while, and then, putting his fingertips together, he said, "I'm surprised that both of you feel you have to rest your presentation to the President on those grounds. The arguments you've just been discussing are for the media, for public consumption. The President is already under intense pressure from the media—there are continual demands about why he hasn't done anything. He still believes he has a choice, that he's weighing the matter. In fact, that's not true. It's never been true. The President can do *nothing*."

Cosgrove looked at Marks with surprise and guarded admiration.

Sheffield made a dismissing gesture. "All right. We all know that the man is no genius, we know that he's a whiz at smalltown, backroom politics. We all know Dan here basically runs the country through the President. But he still *is* the President; he still has to be made to go along with what we recommend. He still has free will."

Marks said nothing.

"Do you disagree?" Cosgrove asked.

"Arguing like this is a waste of time," Marks said mildly.

58

KINGBOP GRINNED proudly. Minister of War Gato had performed an instant miracle—they had brought in a spy, a trespasser, and Gato had transformed him into a friend. "He okay then, mon?"

"Yeah, yeah," Katz said.

Hart suddenly felt overwhelmed by all the impressions he had taken in during the long day. Seeing Big Bird strolling across the terrace and waving casually to Katz before disappearing around the side of the castle did not help.

"My boys didn't hurt you guys?" Katz asked.

"No, not really," Rodriguez said. "They were pretty decent after they found out we were public health."

"I still don't follow all this," Hart said. "For instance, why are you wearing a Savage Shadows jacket and bossing these kids around?"

"Ahh, I knew these punks when they were little. I used to take out Chino's sister. I beat up on Manuel once a week for a year solid. The Shadows was always one of the best gangs going. I was Field Marshal when I was in high school. And now they make me Minister of War. You should see the clubhouse—it's the Frick Mansion."

"And they call you 'Gato' instead of Katz," she said. "I like that."

Hart put his arm around her shoulders. "This is all very strange," he said.

"To say the least." Katz lifted an eyebrow in imita-

291

tion of Rodriguez. " 'Ey man, ee-ho, I deedn't know you guys was, how-you-say . . ."

"Oh shut up," Dolores said.

"Well, you better powder your nose, because we're going to see the Mayor."

"The Mayor? The real Mayor or the mayor of the Savage Shadows?"

"I had in mind His Honor Sidney P. Weinstein," Katz said. "Did you think he left with all the other big cheeses? No, he's here. He'd never leave New York. No one beyond the city limits could ever unnastan his lang-wich."

"Evacuation? What about the health station? Why are these helicopters and planes constantly circling overhead? Maybe you'd better tell us everything that's been going on."

Katz led Hart and Rodriguez over to the sofa and they made themselves comfortable. "What do you want?" he asked. "You want beer? We got beer. Maybe you want a Martini? Dinner won't be ready for awhile. Dolores—how about some Ripple for you?" Katz snapped his fingers and Chino came over. Katz told him to fetch beer, and he saluted and disappeared down the path.

"First of all," Hart said, "I'd like to know about this business with the Shadows. Are they in charge now?"

Katz settled back. "The Shadows organized a big expedition *into* Manhattan from the Bronx while everyone else was trying to get out. They thought the plague might be fun—which shows you how much in touch with reality *they* are—and they figured they could rescue their brother Shadows who happened to be trapped here, too. They met up with several of their brother gangs from the Lower East Side and Harlem. The Mayor was trying to get back to Gracie Mansion from his office downtown, and a bunch of Shadows surrounded his car. Don't ask me how, but Sid actually convinced them to serve as his bodyguard.

They liked the idea because it was so crazy, and also he offered them a lot of bread. But then Sid realized they were the only real policing force in the city, so he made them the 'official' police force. There are some real cops, too, who more or less keep them in line." Katz looked around to see if any of the gang members were listening. "In truth, they're just about all we've got protecting us from the maniacs. I even saw some guys in Nazi regalia in Gramercy Park when we were coming uptown from the Health Department—you wouldn't believe how many nuts per square foot we got in this town."

"I saw a few myself," Hart said. "I actually don't think it's that many, but they get around, and they like to play with guns."

"Right. So we got the Shadows—they patrol the perimeters of our set-up here, and we've been trying to make them bring everyone in for 'interrogation.' That way we can medicate the sick ones and also keep the Shadows from getting too violent. At least we know they aren't killing anyone."

Hart thought of the wrecked Lincoln—he was fairly sure it contained the bodies of the good ol' boys who had shot out the back window of the VW. He decided it was not important. "Sounds like you have things organized here," he said. "What about Calabrese and Sam, and the other nurse epidemiologists? And did the Army epidemiological units ever land?"

Chino appeared with cans of cold beer. Hart opened one and took a deep gulp. It tasted so good that it sent a shock through his system. He quickly drank the entire can and opened another.

"Sam can fill you in on that—"

"He's okay?"

"Sure. You mean you didn't see him this morning at Met?"

"No."

"That's funny." Katz scratched his three-day beard. "He checked on you Saturday, and this morning he was going to go up with a couple of Shadows as body-guards to see how you were doing." He called King-bop. "Find Dr. Andrews and report back to me." He turned back to Hart and Dolores. "Sam can give you details. Basically, the units landed and insisted on doing things the Army way—they wouldn't listen to Calabrese or Sam. They put on protective gear—you know, the white peaked hood and the gloves and coveralls—and they drove some of the mobile vans from the TB Division up into Harlem, where the riot was going on. And that was that! Harlem stomps the Ku Klux Klan."

"They were all killed?"

"Not all of them. There were only sixty of them in the first place."

"The Surgeon General—what's-her-name . . . Dr. Lewis—told me she was sending in the full complement of Army LA, LB and LC units," Hart said.

"That *was* the full complement, Dave. That's it. The Army only *has* a few people trained for this kind of work. Now they have twelve—all good men, specialists. But they were really freaked after the episode up in Harlem, and I think that's one reason we haven't been getting any help from the feds. Oh, we get drops over in the Sheep Meadow—Spam, bandages, newspapers, medicine, and so on—they're pretty good about that. But I'm talking *real* help. The Army guys who didn't get killed up in Harlem decided to go home. Then they found that their helicopters were gone, and called up the Pentagon on the police short-wave radio and told them nasty things about our fair city. Between their stories and these moron liberation armies, I think the feds have been, shall we say, put off."

"Goddamn it!" Hart yelled. "What in the fuck are they doing, then? Why are these planes buzzing us all the time? Why don't they get some troops in here and help us out?" The anger he had been accumulating through the day was now spilling over.

Katz crumpled his beer can with one hand and threw it into a wastebasket several yards away. "Jeez, I don't know. The Mayor talks to the feds all day long and they just say they're organizing a relief effort. We do have a lot of volunteers who came in from all over before the Army put a stop to civilian aircraft. We even got doctors from Sweden. So the feds say, 'Come on, you got doctors, you got airlifts, what's the beef?' Or they say that we have to be patient, containment of the plague, et cetera."

"But doesn't the Mayor tell them that people are dying all over the place?"

"Yeah, yeah. They agree, and they drop in more strep and tetracycline. But frankly, Dave, I think the feds are so scared that they don't know *what* to do. They know bubonic is now entrenched in the rat population, and they're scared it's going to get out of the metropolitan area. We're told that the plague cases in the other boroughs are in strict isolation, but I think the feds are worried that we dirty New Yorkers will spread plague around if we're not watched and blockaded."

"What about the media?"

"There's a kind of a blackout, apparently. I mean, the Mayor, he's talking to Barbara Walters one minute and Walter Cronkite the next, but it doesn't get broadcast. The President has declared martial law and ordered the networks to comply with strict military censorship. All we get on the radio is noise about how the Army has everything under control, the National Guard is policing the surrounding area, Army doctors are at work saving lives in Manhattan. And lots of Mantovani."

"So how are the Mayor and Calabrese responding to all this?" Hart asked.

"You'd better see for yourself," Katz said. "They'll be at dinner."

Katz led Hart and Rodriguez to the edge of the

overlook and pointed across Belvedere Lake to the Great Lawn. "This is our city," he said.

Hart could make out tents of several different sizes, areas penned up with police barricades and lit by flood lights, lean-tos, Port-o-San outhouses, school buses with red crosses painted on their sides, and several thousand men, women, and children. "My God," he said. "First I thought it was like a Vietnamese refugee camp. But actually it looks more like Woodstock."

Katz clapped him on the shoulder. "I'm glad you made it."

59

As COSGROVE and Marks approached the Oval Office, Cosgrove was momentarily paralyzed.

The Surgeon General, Christine Shore Lewis, was just stepping out of the Oval Office. She wore a black dress, a black hat, and black gloves, and the President stood behind her, absently patting himself on the head as he bid her goodbye. Simultaneously, from another office, came the videotaped voice of the President calmly saying, "We have now successfully isolated the plague . . . rescue operations for the survivors and disaster relief are being . . ."

The scene intruded on the furious inner stream of arguments and plans that absorbed Cosgrove. He felt as if he were about to cleave in half along his spine.

He never cared to think about his body. He did his best work when it was totally absent as a factor. The fear of contracting the plague had reminded him all too well of his physicality.

"When are you going to cooperate?" the Surgeon General whispered to Cosgrove and Marks as she approached them. "When are you going to stop these conferences and get some help for New York?"

Cosgrove ignored her, but Marks was almost friendly. He appeared to have been cast out of some mysterious pale substance that crisis could not corrode. "We're preparing to discuss that right now, Mrs. Lewis," he said with a slight smile.

After the butler had served a round of drinks and the door to the Oval Office had been closed, the President set down his bourbon and said, "Bryce, Dan, why don't we pray before we get down to business?"

Cosgrove and Marks exchanged brief looks. Television religion was one thing—but the danger that the President actually might be sincerely religious was a problem Cosgrove had never considered. Perhaps it was a feeble power ploy—perhaps the President was maneuvering, trying to scare Cosgrove and Marks with unpredictable behavior.

But the solemnity in the boyish, rouged face of the politician, who had kept his television makeup on because of his frequent daily speeches, was eerily authentic. His expression was one of deathbed piety.

"Good idea," Marks said briskly. "Our father which art in Heaven . . ."

Cosgrove was relieved that they did not kneel, and he began to see what Marks was up to.

". . . for Thine is the kingdom and the power and the glory forever, Amen."

There was a difficult silence afterward, and then Marks, speaking softly, outlined the option that the National Security Council, after several hours of debate, had finally chosen.

"Everything has been worked out, Mr. President," Cosgrove said. "Down to the finest details. But you of course have to give the command."

The President looked into his glass. "I tell you what's stopping me, was just conferring with Mrs.—eh, Doctor—Lewis. She says often these epidemics just burn out. She thinks we can send troops in and—"

"They won't go in, Mr. President," Cosgrove said. "We've been over this. Our troops are not made up of scared draftees anymore; our men are mostly black, and they're tough and self-willed. They know what happened to the Army epidemiological units. They would rather be shot than risk dying horribly of the plague. Besides, say we *could* get troops into Manhattan, past the terrorists, et cetera. When it's time for them to leave, it's very likely they're going to bring the plague out with them."

"Even if they're vaccinated?"

"Some were vaccinated on Thursday, but it's useless—it won't start protecting them until two weeks from now."

"We can't allow New York to remain at a standstill that much longer," the President said. "The Secretary of the Treasury tells me that the business panic alone may cost several billion dollars and has already—"

"Exactly," Marks said. "We all agree on that."

"Okay," the President said. "Here's the next objection. Say we decontaminate Manhattan and get it working again. Our methods are bound to be discovered. I don't care to be labeled in history books as a . . ." He screwed up his face involuntarily. "This is so painful. I—"

"If you don't act promptly, and with full candor right now," Cosgrove said, "and if the plague is allowed to run its course, hundreds of millions will be dead within a year. Not only in the U.S. but in the rest of the world. And if anybody survives, they'll blame the President for the catastrophe—they'll talk about how he temporized during the first crucial days. They'll talk about how he failed to stop it."

"But it's not *my* fault!" the President said.

"That's enough, General," Marks said. "The President is under enormous tension. I don't even think it's necessary to trouble ourselves unduly with these matters we're now discussing. I think it's possible to work out a good cover for this operation and make it stick. We managed Chile, we can manage New York City."

Marks's statement was so unusually forthright that Cosgrove was startled, and the President was visibly relieved. Marks went on in this vein, quickly becoming more specific.

The President began nodding. "That works," he said. "It's not really lying, but it's a good cover . . ."

"Right," Marks said. "Say we launch the operation in the morning. Tomorrow night you can go on television and explain that you have saved New York."

The President nodded. "Dear God in Heaven, this is . . . I think your suggestion is valid. But I still don't know whether I could ever bring myself to do this." His voice trailed off.

Cosgrove had listened to Marks with growing impatience. He was impressed with Marks's gentle approach in dealing with the President—the avoidance of head-on arguments, the skillfully-timed interruptions of the President's already distracted train of thought. But Cosgrove also felt that delicate persuasion was too time-consuming. In a week or two Marks might be able to convince the President. By then it would be too late. "No, Mr. Marks. With all due respect, I must disagree. I think that the President must immediately alter his present public stance. Mr. President, you can't afford to promise to save something that cannot possibly be saved, or even to claim after the fact that you have saved the city. Instead, sir, you have to lay the groundwork in the public mind for the drastic decision that lies ahead.

"I would recommend that you go on television right away and emphasize the containment of the plague," Cosgrove went on. "Then you can start talking about the outcome of the last two pandemics, when most of the world was destroyed, when civilization was practically wiped out. And you can then suggest—and I understand, deeply, how painful this is to you, and to all of us, Mr. President—and you can then suggest that we may have to consider priorities of survival."

"Do you actually think that approach is best?" Marks asked. "Don't you think that an announcement like that would trigger a new panic, that the population now trapped on Manhattan and kept quiescent by your promises of rescue would make another furious attempt at escape? If only one or two plague cases brought down the city of New York, how many escapees from Manhattan would it take to destroy the United States? No, it has to be kept absolutely covert until the operation has been completed. Then we have clear-cut explanations we can set into motion. In fact, the need to explain anything may never arise. Of course, the Soviets and the Chinese should know *exactly* what we did—I can't imagine a better bolster to our credibility, a better deterrent than our demonstrated willingness to go to such lengths in order to save our country. But it is quite possible that the questions that worry us most right now may never be asked. The Warren Report was never questioned until long after the fact. We can count on mass sentimentality and emotional outpourings to obscure the crucial events."

Cosgrove stood up and paced back and forth. Dozens of sensations were assaulting him, all quite uncomfortable. This man Marks was amazing. But what the hell was he ultimately up to? "Mr. President, let me urge you to do the following. I agree with Mr. Marks that your statement before the operation should not be of a nature to incite panic in Manhattan. But you should be frank, sir, about the fact that this is the greatest trauma in global history and that every possible effort is being made to effect a resolution. If you like, you can say that I, General Cosgrove, have come up with a workable plan and that it's being put into motion immediately. As soon as the operation has been accomplished, you can go on TV again with the explanation. I could even appear with you. After you apprise the public of the enormity of the catastrophe that your wise decision has just averted, you'll be acclaimed by the entire nation. By the world. You would say, in effect, sir, 'I made a good decision and I stand by it.' If you cover it up, it's bound to come out sooner or later and the public will not remember how grave the threat of plague actually was. The public will only remember what you did."

The President rubbed his face with his palms, smearing the pancake makeup that had concealed the hollows of his sagging cheeks. "No human being should ever be put in the position I'm in at this moment." He seemed to shudder or to sob behind his hands. "I'm not God, I'm only a man."

Cosgrove immediately wondered whether the entire conversation was being taped. It was impossible to tell —the President often spoke as though hoping his words would be permanently engraved on the tablets of history.

60

"SO THERE'S an astronauts' convention," Katz said, leading Hart and Rodriguez to the Mayor's headquarters, a big open-sided tent in the middle of the Great Lawn. "The American astronauts stand up and say, 'We're going to the moon!' and everybody cheers. Then the Russian astronauts get up and say, 'We're going to Mars!' and everybody cheers. And finally the Polish astronauts get up and say, 'We're going to the sun!' And everybody says, 'But you'll burn up—it's very, very hot on the sun!' But the Poles just smile. 'Oh, no that won't happen,' they say. 'Because we're going to go at *night.*' "

"Jesus, Alan, we've been talking for over an hour and that's the first joke you've told," Hart said. "Are you sure you're okay?"

They made their way past hundreds of tents, lean-tos, mattresses, blankets, and hammocks where every imaginable category of humanity slept, bathed, and prepared food. There were nuns feeding several dozen toddlers; three rabbis with long beards and *payess* immersed in an argument in Yiddish; Puerto Ricans roasting a pig over cherry-red embers in an open pit; two wraithlike hippies with waist-length hair crying "Wacky Weed, temple hash, Mexican brown, best rates"; a muscular half-naked black man standing on his head in the yogic pose of the full lotus; a man with a goose on a leash; a fierce-eyed man playing jazz saxophone; some well-tailored middle-aged women handing out leaflets (Hart accepted one but could not read it in the flickering light; it was signed by The 94th Street Block Association); two skinny, feral-looking, carefully groomed blonde women wearing a great deal of jewelry who sat, their arms crossed, on a Vuitton trunk with several dozen other pieces of luggage stacked around them ("Those I call the Killer Debs," Katz said. "Andrews and I think that they come down from an alien planet at night and turn eligible young men into Vuitton luggage. Night of the Living Debs!"); a photographer with three cameras dangling from his neck and a tripod in his hand; a band of Chinese carrying a red flag; a Greek orthodox bishop with a long gray beard and voluminous black robes; and, over all, the constant wail of babies, the chatter of several languages, the sound of congas, bongos, shreds of rock 'n' roll, fragments of a string quartet, and a car horn that kept repeating the first several notes of "Never on Sunday."

Katz explained the way in which the encampment had been organized, shouting from time to time to make himself heard. When the remaining Health Department staff had arrived in the park on Friday and found the Army epidemiological units, several hundred people had already taken up residence in the open spaces around the Lake and the Reservoir because their homes had been burned or the plumbing had failed. Immediately, the work of organization had begun: Calabrese and Andrews supervised the digging of latrines and the burial of the dead in slit trenches in scattered areas well away from the water; Katz sprayed for fleas; makeshift hospitals were established in tents, and gasoline generators were brought in from the abandoned hospitals to provide electricity. Savage Shadows patrolled the area beyond the hospital zone and made armed forays out of the park for food.

"How about water?" Hart asked.

"On the way uptown, we saw people who looked like they might have dysentery," Rodriguez said.

"Yeah—same here. Sam and some of the others from the environmental division and the Army guys rigged up a system to filter the mud out of the reservoir water. First we were just mixing Clorox into the drinking water. We started rationing, but this morning the Army airlifted in an amazing machine called an Erdalater that converts the filthy sludge in the lake into potable water." Katz beamed. "People have been working hard. They bitch and complain. But I think there's a lot of pride that we've managed to pull things together here."

Hart said nothing. He, too, had been moved when he had looked out over the camp from the hillside with Katz. The panorama of people working together and surviving had been an antidote to the terrible scenes he had witnessed downtown. But his mind kept returning to the same question he had carried with him the entire day: Where were the feds? Surely peo-

ple in the park did not expect to go on playing Boy
Scout indefinitely.

"Why hasn't somebody tried to get the water pumps
for the city working again?" Hart asked.

"Interesting you should ask," Katz said. "The May-
or's disasterologist, Kaprow, says that when the electricity failed and the pumping stations stopped, the
water pressure probably dropped so fast in the tunnels
that they might have collapsed in places—they're very
old—and sewage has probably also backed into the
system."

"But what about City Tunnel Number Three?" Hart
asked. "The new one that they were building? How
much work would it take to get water pumping through
it?"

Katz shrugged. "Good question. We should talk to
the Mayor about that."

"Dave! Dave!"

Hart looked across the crowd and saw Andrews
moving toward him, limping and waving, escorted by
Kingbop. Hart pushed his way through the crowds toward Andrews and they closed in on each other. When
they met, they stopped—they didn't know what to do.
Finally Hart extended his hands.

Andrews squeezed them so hard it hurt. "As I live
and breathe! I knew you'd make it! The only thing
kills a jaded New Yorker like you is fresh air." He
gave Rodriguez a hug. "Ah tell you, I was scared to
face Dolores here," he told Hart. "I promised her I
was going to look after you up at Met, and after I
climbed all those stairs and found your bed empty, I
said, 'Uh-oh, that Po'ta Rican honey is gonna skin me
alive!' "

"You bet I would have, too, man," Dolores said,
slipping her arm around Hart's waist.

"Anyway, if you were well enough to be moved today we were going to try to get you to the Park. I sure
am glad you moved yourself."

"How's it going?" Hart asked Andrews.

"Oh, terrific." Andrews grinned and tugged at his beard. "We got a text-book emergency health station going. I told the CDC guys to go fuck themselves, and you might say the Mayor has made me an honorary citizen of New York."

They resumed walking toward the Mayor's tent. "What I want to know," Andrews continued, "is this, and maybe you have the answer, Dave. Why did we live? Why did you get the plague and not die? Gayle died. Why were we spared when so many others—? It's a thing that I keep trying to understand. You believe we should have handled this mess differently? Would that have helped?"

Hart looked at Andrews. At the moment, he did not look or sound like someone capable of the feats of organization Katz had just described. He had the manner of an angry boy whose father has been absent too long. Hart wondered whether Andrews had been riding high on the crisis and then, upon seeing Hart, his official superior, had suddenly caved in.

"I don't know about any of this, Sam," Hart said. "I don't know what we could have done differently. It just happened—we didn't cause it. I'm glad I'm alive; I'm glad you're alive. I'm glad you took care of everything so well while I was out of it."

Andrews looked at him eagerly.

"You're doing very well." Hart touched Andrews on the shoulder. "Keep it up. Don't stop just because I'm here."

Under the khaki-colored canvas roof of the open-sided tent, women were busily setting rows of tables covered with butcher paper. Light bulbs concealed in colored Japanese paper lanterns bobbed in the breeze. The serious bustle and good cheer of the women and the smells of cooking gave the general impression of a church supper. The Mayor's wife was in command, and she looked uncannily serene. She had been a committeewoman for the Democratic party and now she was in charge of mayoral dining.

At the head table, the Mayor and Calabrese sat sipping wine from tall goblets. "So I tell Dan Rather, 'Dan, we're going to rebuild from scratch,'" the Mayor was saying. "'With the President's Disaster Relief Fund, which we are going to . . .'"

Calabrese watched Hart approaching, but did not recognize him until they were shaking hands. The older man was wearing a sweatshirt and blue jeans instead of an Italian silk suit, and his face was gaunt and creased. "My God, Dave, I didn't think you had a chance!" He rose and cupped his hands around Hart's cheeks. "You owe Dolores quite a thank-you, you know. She insisted on going up to Met even when everyone tried to stop her. She was in a lot of danger on your account. She's a very determined young lady."

She looked away and shrugged. "He doesn't owe me anything," she said.

Calabrese reintroduced Hart to the Mayor, who did not remember him. "Good to have you aboard, Dr. Hart. We're in the midst of New York's gravest crisis. We need the help of all good New Yorkers, and—I'm afraid to say it—the help of the federal government as well. But I'm confident we'll pull through this one as we did other crises in the past. I appreciate your work. I don't think anything else could have been done under the circumstances, which just grew too big and too fast and which caused this horrible, horrible tragedy. But now we have to go to work putting our house in order again."

Hart suddenly felt very weak. His leg muscles let go all at once and he sank down on a folding chair.

"Are you all right?" Rodriguez asked.

"All that beer on an empty stomach," Hart said. "I just need some food." He caught Katz's eye and the two men exchanged a look of understanding. No wonder Katz had wanted him to see the Mayor.

61

HART STARED at the shiny black dab of caviar and the thin crescent of lemon arranged on the paper plate before him.

"I could kill for some sour cream," he heard the Mayor's wife say.

"So whaddya want for a nickel, lady?" Katz replied. "I think my boys did very well just to get this."

"It's pretty impressive," Hart said, wondering if his stomach would be able to accept the hors d'oeuvre.

"Well, I had to train my men," Katz said. "First they raided the supermarkets and came back with half-thawed frankfurters and muscatel. So I told them to try Zabar's delicatessen. But that place must have been cleaned out even before Tiffany's. I shudder to think what the last stand there was like."

"Probably like a normal Sunday afternoon, only with better weapons," Hart said.

"Yup. Well, Manuel figured out what kind of people would stock up at Zabar's, and he just picked out luxury buildings, broke in, and raided the refrigerators. Your better class of greaser, Manuel is."

The second course was a steaming mound of linguine with a sauce made of Italian sweet sausage.

"This meal is a politician's dream," Hart remarked to Calabrese. "Is the next course Peking duck?"

"We've done very well under the circumstances," Calabrese said. "Did Sam tell you about the health station?"

"A little, yes."

"He really organized the whole thing. He established a triage system, assigned the nurses and doctors to shifts, set up the hospital equipment. We raided Roosevelt and Mount Sinai for a lot of supplies. We had doctors pouring in from all over before the military stopped the civilian helicopters from landing. And a lot of internes and residents who probably could have gotten out stayed in the city, and a few surgeons, thank God. We have a lot of trauma—broken bones, burns, gunshots. We converted a city bus into an operating room and it's a madhouse—they work around the clock over there. But the worst are the plague victims. We have them isolated and I think we've managed to save a lot of them. The pathetic ones are the hallucinating screamers."

Hart nodded. "I know. And the zombies."

Calabrese surveyed the hundred or so diners in the tent. "The people have been good. They eat in shifts. Block-association ladies have organized everyone into groups, each with different assignments: food and water details, housing construction, medical, burial." He paused, closing his eyes. "So many people have died. We've had to bury them fast. Tried to get their identification before we put them in the trenches, but lots of them didn't have any. The Army epidemiologists have some system for identifying the dead in case we have to dig them up when this thing is all over with. We buried the plague victims separately in a deeper trench, using lime on top. We won't dig up that grave, and the Parks Department will have to cement the area over when we get the city back into shape next week."

"Next week?" Hart exclaimed.

"Yes." Calabrese smiled. "By next week everything will be back to normal. I've spoken with the Surgeon General, and Sid has talked to the President. The whole world is watching, you know. Everyone wants to help New York. We've gotten offers of help from Israel, Kuwait, Sweden . . . This thing will all be over by next week!"

Hart stopped eating, his fork poised in midair, and looked closely at Calabrese. "What's going to happen to solve everything in one week?"

"The feds! They've really changed, Dave. They're going to do everything they can. They've already dropped us a million dollars' worth of medicine and supplies."

"That's all well and good, but what I meant was a real, direct, immediate, sensible solution—like a lot of troops coming in to treat the sick and bury the dead. There are corpses all over the city and thousands of sick people wandering around in midtown. Shit, they should be in here establishing order and starting up the vital services and getting the whole thing going again."

"Dave, I'm disappointed in you." Calabrese put his hand on Hart's. "You've been very sick, though. You don't understand—the feds are not the way they were. They'll come through! Plague has changed everything! The President told the Mayor that there will be at least twenty billion dollars to restore the city."

"When?"

"As soon as a method can be organized. The feds are taking care of everything."

Hart said nothing. He resumed eating. He felt extremely tired and angry. Rodriguez placed her hand on his knee and smiled up at him.

After dinner the Mayor produced a Bible. "Now, I never read the New Testament . . . " he began.

There was laughter around the table.

"But I think it's important. Earlier today the Reverend Billy Graham called me up on the radio-telephone and suggested I read the last book in the New Testament, which is the Book of Revelation. As a Jew I would like to say there are parts of it which I didn't understand, but on the other hand I would have to say that there were other parts which I thought would be nice to share at this time when we are about to begin the work of rebuilding New York City."

Again Katz caught Hart's eye and nodded almost imperceptibly.

The Mayor began to read. " 'And there came unto me one of the seven angels which had the seven vials full of the seven last plagues, and talked with me, saying, Come hither, I will shew thee the bride, the Lamb's wife. And he carried me away in the spirit to a great and high mountain, and shewed me that great city, the holy Jerusalem, descending out of heaven from God. . . . ' "

Hart looked at the men and women seated at the Mayor's table. Many were bureaucrats; he recognized Irving Kaprow from the disaster-planning task force, and Strohman from the Health and Hospitals Corporation. They had a look of contentment, like children after a long day and a filling meal, though marks of crisis remained—unshaven chins, bruises, and staring eyes.

That was it. The eyes!

" '. . . and the building of the wall of it was of jasper: and the city was pure gold, like unto clear glass. And the foundations of the wall of the city were garnished with all manner of precious stones. The first foundation was jasper; the second, sapphire; the third. . . . ' "

"Be right back," Hart whispered to Rodriguez. He stepped outside the tent.

The Mayor's voice carried through the cool night air.

" '. . . And the twelve gates were twelve pearls; every several gate was of one pearl; and the street of the city was pure gold. . . .' "

Hart sighed deeply. The faces of the people in the tent . . . His senses, having been shut up for three days of illness and then assaulted relentlessly throughout the day, had sharpened to a new level of acuity. He was sure of his observations in the tent, and they disturbed him. With the exception of Dolores and Alan, everyone at dinner had appeared to be asleep. Their eyes had been open, but dreams had flitted across their faces like rapid eye movements during real sleep.

Weinstein's voice grew richer. Those words obviously moved him. " 'And the nations of them which are saved shall walk in the light of it: and the kings of the earth do bring their glory and honor into it. And the gates of it shall not be shut at all by day: for there shall be no night there. . . .' "

"All that talk about a lamb makes me hungry." Katz materialized next to Hart and lit a cigarette.

"That's a Jew for you," Hart said. "I've heard more of the Bible today than in my entire life."

"Yeah, there's a lot of that going around," Katz said.

"I guess the Mayor is getting ready to build the New Jerusalem, then?"

"It sounds to me more like the Polish expedition to the sun," Katz said. "He's been through as much as anybody in the past few days."

"What do you think of Calabrese?"

"Same. They're kind of like little kids, you know. They're lost, and they hope Big Daddy is going to come and take care of them, and they're pathetically grateful for the encouraging words and Ace bandages the feds toss our way. They should know better, but they're in shock, and so they buy everything Washington tells them. Little do they know that the federal government has been run for years by the Albanians."

"The Albanians?" Hart laughed.

"Well, that's what I call them. Some weird bunch of aliens who aren't particularly interested in reality. They're for sure not interested in the people of New York City. That's what worries me about these dreamers around here. That's what I wanted you to see—the way they think everything's going to be okay. That is definitely not the message I'm getting."

"From what I saw today going through the city, I'd have to agree with you," Hart said. "But the thing I keep going back to is the incredible amount of money being lost as long as New York is like this. That fact has got to be bothering plenty of people. There must be a lot of pressure to open up New York. And there must be some humanity left somewhere in Washington."

"Well, I gather that the Surgeon General has been trying. At any rate, she's always talking to Calabrese. But the plague scares people worse than earthquakes, or hurricanes, or volcanoes. That could be what's kept most of the disaster relief away."

"I can understand that," Hart said. "And the media is probably playing up all the historical stuff—the hundred million who died in the Plague of Justinian—"

"Aaaah, million, schmillion, they'd all be dead by now anyway," Katz said. He sounded impatient, as though he had heard that statistic too often. "I suppose that's about what's happening, though." He scratched his chest. "On the other hand, it just seems that a hell of a lot more could have been done, no matter how scared they are—a hell of a lot more *would* have been done, except that something else is going on. I've listened to Calabrese on the radio to Washington, and it's like they're thinking in Albanian. They're coming at this thing from a completely different point of view. There's something they're not saying."

They stood together in the dark. After a while, Hart said, "How has Sam been?"

"He goes in and out of it. Most of the time he handles everything very intelligently, but then all of a sudden you'll see him grasp what's happened and he just gives out for a little bit. People have a tough time handling the fact that there's nothing they can take for granted anymore. It freaks them. I'm lucky. I was head of Pest Control and Animal Affairs, and I still got pests to control and the animals are still having affairs."

62

ONE OF the oil paintings, *Gettysburg,* was crooked. Cosgrove paused to straighten it before sitting at his desk. The President was coming around; or at least he was beginning to grasp that he could not make any contrary decision. But the histrionics! Of course it was a horrible business, but tears did not help. Heroism was what was needed. The decision had been hard for Cosgrove, too. The whole night before, he had paced, he had reconsidered, he had reviewed the chain of events from other angles. But he always returned to the primary plan.

It helped to think of New York as a foreign city—and, insofar as so many of its residents were dark-skinned, spoke foreign languages, entertained oddball political notions, and were cut off from the mainland of the United States—it was.

He thought of Eisenhower's anguish at having to drop paratroopers behind German lines knowing that the majority would be killed. Dresden, Hiroshima, Nagasaki—those decisions could not have been as hard to make. The United States was at war, and those bombings hastened its end. He recalled Bill Colby's silent acceptance of the burden of ordering the deaths of 20,000 Viet Cong in Operation Phoenix—again, it was war. And then there was the President's own favorite example, Churchill's decision to let Coventry be bombed rather than give the alarm and reveal to the Germans that the Allies had cracked their radio code.

He asked himself if, deep inside, he felt badly about the New York decision. At that moment the sensation of splitting recurred, very briefly, and he realized that while he wished that he could feel bad, he did not. He knew that he was acting for the best of all concerned. But if it ever came out in the open that the decision had its roots in Operation Visitation—then he would feel very bad indeed.

Gazing at the row of military paintings, he saw, too, that his theory of history was again demonstrated. Ever since the day he had entered the Point he had been preparing for this moment. Waves set into motion thirty years earlier were now coming together and he stood in their midst. He looked at the framed portrait of his mother, who was now a heap of bones in an Arlington nursing home. When he had told her he was now National Security Advisor, she had turned her face to the wall and murmured, "Why couldn't you have been a doctor?" Perhaps he should have carried out her wishes. If he had been a doctor, he would never have had a decision of such historical magnitude thrust upon him. He made a mental note to set down this series of thoughts for his memoirs.

63

AROUND THE stage where Shakespeare's plays were performed during the summer months, an audience of several thousand watched a fat, disheveled stand-up comic go through his shtick. ". . . So the wife says to me, 'Here, take these garlics and wear them around your neck, they'll protect you from the plague.' And I says to her, 'You crazy or somethin'? You want me to be eaten alive by Sicilians?' "

Hart, who stood at the edge of the audience with Rodriguez and Katz, was surprised at the great delight of the crowd; the laughter went on much longer than he would have thought appropriate. "Get the hook!" someone cried. The comic hung his head. "I don't get no respect!"

"Last night we had Woody Allen and Bob Dylan," Katz said. "And Bobby Short. I don't know what went wrong tonight."

Hart looked over the rows and rows of heads. Belvedere Castle was a black finger against a backdrop of orange flames coming from apartment buildings on the East Side. He recalled nights when he had walked along Fifth Avenue and Central Park West and tried to peer up into the windows of the buildings: chandeliers, hanging plants, mobiles, sculpture, toy sailboats in the first-floor corner windows of the Dakota, dinner parties, a naked woman brushing her teeth, an old woman leaning out over the sill of a high window—all the fragments of complete, complicated dramas which, joined together in the unconscious night, had made up the story of the city.

He joined Rodriguez and Katz on a narrow path that had been worn in the grass over the past few days by tens of thousands of feet. On either side of the path were tents, small campfires, groups of people talking. From time to time, Hart would catch bits of conversation: ". . . and I tell her, forget the fucking diamonds and give me the banana!" . . . "You're being reductionistic about this: it's the dialectic in action, no question about it . . ." "As soon as we're rescued . . ." ". . . You start with the cunt, see . . ." ". . . Is that *Jackie?*" . . . *"No, no vale la pena . . ."* ". . . I put everything into Triple-A municipals. If I'd put it into T-notes I'd be sitting pretty today. I'd give my right arm to talk to my broker." ". . . That's no contract, I said—that's a lawsuit!" ". . . I put it all into the Cuisinart for five minutes, and then drink it." ". . . I said, yes, I love you, don't drop the stereo or I'll kill you." ". . . Yea, though I walk through the valley . . ." "Such a *shmuckele* he had!" ". . . Ten percent going in, ten going out, and five off the top— would I lie to ya?"

"There are eight million stories in the naked city," Katz muttered. "And I've heard 'em all."

"The Mayor's wife told me a good one about a boy," Rodriguez said. "He kept coming to see the Mayor in the tent. He was about fifteen or so, with big thick glasses, and he had these Star Trek patches sewn on his clothing, and he had a suitcase, and he kept telling the Mayor that he was a 'mathematical genius' and that the Mayor had to get a helicopter to pick him up to take him to Boston. He was supposed to give a lecture or something. Each time he would come to see the Mayor, he'd open his suitcase and show him all these papers covered with numbers and stuff. And the Mayor kept explaining that he couldn't get the helicopters to land and that the boy would just have to wait. So finally this morning the kid started crying and he said no one was being logical, and he was getting out if he had to walk. He just came back to the Mayor's tent and he was still mad. He said he walked all the way to Queens and hitched a ride to La Guardia, but no planes were being allowed to take off, so he turned around and came back."

"How did he walk to Queens?" Hart asked. "How did he get past the vigilantes?"

"Oh, he went through some tunnel. Or maybe it was the subway. I don't remember."

"It must have been the water tunnel," Katz said. "All the subway exits in Queens are sealed." He stopped. "Well, see you tomorrow. You need some sleep—you can use my tent. Manuel brought it from Abercrombie and Fitch."

"What about you, Alan?"

"Me, I got a date with Kingbop's little sister over at the Boat Pond."

64

THE PRESIDENT sat with his back to Cosgrove and Marks.

Cosgrove's stomach was jumping; he had never been so exhausted in his life. It took a great deal of effort for him to preserve outward composure. He pressed his hand to his cheek to still a tic under his eye.

"Every minute you delay takes us closer to the edge of all-out catastrophe," Cosgrove told the President.

"Yes, but we might be getting closer to a better solution. The Surgeon General called me a few minutes before you came. She's been talking to one of the health officials up there in New York who had what she and the CDC people agree is a fairly sensible plan. The Army sends in a few thousand troops—all volunteers, all of whom have been given protective doses of strepto, strepta—"

"Streptomycin."

"Right. Dan, I'm so tired, I can't get my words to come out properly. Anyway, she wants to send in the protected troops to Central Park, where it's safe. The troops help the mobile health units to treat the sick. This fellow up there says they can treat twenty to thirty thousand people a day if they get some federal help. They would set up checkpoints at each entrance to the park and code incoming people with an ultra-violet marker, treat them for five days, and then, if they don't show any signs of the plague after that, transfer them by helicopter to Fort Dix to be processed. In a few days, large numbers of people could be certified plague-free. It's a minimum-risk, minimum-commitment deal."

"That would take months," Cosgrove said. "And when the so-called plague-free New Yorkers are lifted out, who guarantees that not one single infected flea goes with them? Let me repeat, sir, that I'll be happy to go on television with you—both beforehand, for a nonspecific preliminary set-up speech, and then after-ward, for the explanation. I'll take the responsibility for everything if you like."

"That never works out," the President said. " 'The buck stops here.' "

"In any case, we have deniability," Cosgrove said. "We have documentation worked out. Sheffield and I have taken care of the c.y.a. aspects of this. Every day—every minute—that you procrastinate, sir, the country goes closer to ruin. The danger of the epidemic increases tenfold. The economy—"

Cosgrove paused. Marks had come into the Oval Office, taken a chair and pulled it into the space between Cosgrove and the President's desk.

"In purely practical terms," Cosgrove went on, "you have to weigh the constituency of the population of one city, which will probably never regain its former power, against the constituency of the other two hundred and nine million Americans."

"I have new intelligence." Marks actually looked rested. His voice was steady.

"Look," the President said. "I don't care what you have. I'm not going to go along with this scheme. I've thought about it and thought about it, and I'm not going to do it." His voice was ragged.

"What?" Cosgrove stood up and started toward the President.

"Very well, then," Marks said. He remained quite still, his hands folded on his lap.

Cosgrove stopped. He wondered whether Marks were on some psychotropic drug, something cooked up at Detrick to tranquilize without slowing down the mind. It was possible.

"We'll leave, then," Marks said, getting to his feet.

"But I think we should discuss this further," Cosgrove began.

"With all due respect, General, I disagree," Marks said, going to the door. "I only thought I should mention that on November 2, 1963, a Mafia yacht dropped off two Cuban exiles on the Cuban coast near Havana. They were working for Executive Action, part of the AM/LASH CIA base in Florida, and they each carried two specially designed bulbs filled with the organism Y*ersinia pestis,* or plague. They were to be picked up the following night, but they never reappeared. None of our assets in Havana ever learned what happened to them. The venture was known as Operation Visitation, and until tonight I had only heard stories about it—the records were supposedly destroyed. But now I am in a position to confirm that the action did take place and that those responsible are still highly placed in the government."

65

HART LAY down on the neatly made-up mattress in the tent. He listened to the rustling sounds of Rodriguez removing her clothing in the dark. He could sense his muscles relaxing, his heartbeat working in harmony with his breathing. His mind was full of voices and images of everything he had seen that day, and through this hectic conglomeration three thoughts kept repeating themselves: I have survived, I have found Dolores, and this city is doomed.

It was indeed incredible to him that he had survived, and yet he already took it for granted: had there ever been any doubt that he would live? It was incredible to him that he had found Dolores, that she was well, that she cared for him, and had in fact risked her life to save his; but he did not believe he should have anyone as good as she was, as miraculous, so close to him. And it was incredible to him after all the destruction and carnage he had witnessed, that somehow a center or order had been created and that he had found it; and yet he felt a premonition of dread. The childish, traumatized behavior of the leaders in the park, the continual military frenzy overhead, just out of reach, and the extravagant promises of the federal government gave him a bitter taste which he recognized all too well. He had felt it the morning his wife had found the lump, and when the Medical Examiner had given him the autopsy reports on the prostitute and the pimp. His unconscious mind was shot through with millions of linkages that he could not make voluntarily; it could warn him only by giving him a bitter taste in his mouth.

"Are you all right?" Dolores asked, her hands traveling over his chest and thighs. "Maybe you're tired tonight?"

"I'm not," he lied. "I just dozed for a second. I'm sorry—"

"Ah, yeah, now I know you're okay—you're apologizing, just like normal." She teased him with her fingernails.

He rose up and pulled her to him, shaken by a sudden powerful rush of desire.

"You go into the park at night, you get what's coming to you," she said, wrapping her arms and legs around him.

66

HART OPENED his eyes and brushed a fine strand of Rodriguez's hair away from his face. He watched the rise and fall of her bare breasts and the slight movement of her eyes under closed lids. Her cheeks were flushed and shiny, her mouth was slightly open and he could see the pink tip of her tongue. She was so beautiful. The morning sun on the canvas roof filled the tent with a brownish-orange light, and a soft wind made the walls billow and slacken, billow and slacken. He heard the steady pulse of a generator and the chirping of birds. For a few seconds, he had no idea where he was.

A faint tune wound its way into his hearing; at first it was so remote that it might have come from inside his head, but soon it grew louder. A group of strolling musicians came closer and closer until they passed the tent, their shadows moving across the canvas wall. As they walked they played pipes and long-necked stringed instruments and tambourines, and a clear, vibrating tenor sang an old song:

> O, my luve is like a red, red rose
> That's newly sprung in June ...

Rodriguez stirred and nestled against him.

The timbre of the receding voice gave him a brief, rich vision of his life. What was he? Why did he live? He was a collection of tissues and systems that moved energy around for 25,000 days and nights and then stopped. Was it energy that he served? He was a breathing history of billions of impressions of taste, touch, sight, smell, sound, motion, able to distinguish ten billion different colors and textures, one hundred trillion subtleties of light, one trillion sounds, and countless other sensations. Maybe he was just a membrane between two universes—the outer and the inner. Or perhaps he did not live at all—perhaps he was lived by something else, dreamed by something else. And if all the "lived" and "dreamed" parts were shed, what would remain? An awareness of a fading song, the amber light, the smooth skin of a woman?

Hart was gently kissing Rodriguez's eyelids when he heard his name being called. He pulled on his pants and stepped outside. The brightness made him blink. The sky had cleared except for a hazy rose band over the treetops. Most of the camp still slept.

"Dave, Dave," the shouts came again. It was Katz, running toward him faster than he had ever seen the stocky man move. "Come with me, quick!" he called when he saw Hart. He turned and ran uphill toward the terrace overlook next to Belvedere Castle, and Hart followed.

On the terrace, encircled by Savage Shadows, lay Kingbop. He was gasping and drooling.

"Out of the way!" Katz yelled, and the Shadows drew back.

Hart knelt beside Kingbop and examined him. His arm was slack and his pulse was very slow but regular. His pupils were contracted to pinpoints, and tears streamed from his eyes.

Hart examined the boy's arms for needlemarks. "Has he been shooting up?" he asked.

"Don't think so," Katz said. "He's a Rastafarian—they don't do drugs."

"Get a medical bag over here immediately!" Hart said. Manuel raced away and Hart began external cardiac massage, pressing his crossed hands down on Kingbop's sternum. Katz began to give him mouth-to-mouth resuscitation.

"He has no temp, his pulse is slow," Hart said. "This probably isn't plague." He continued pushing Kingbop's chest. "Chino, was he complaining about anything before this happened?"

"No, sir, he was fine, he just started breathing funny a few minutes ago!" The boy was very frightened.

"Did he say anything about chest pain?"

"Nothing. He just say he felt weak, and he sit down and can't catch his breath."

"You're sure he didn't take any drugs? No shooting up, or pills? This looks like a heroin or morphine overdose."

"No, man, he's clean!" Chino cried. "I swear it."

They contined working on Kingbop, but finally he gave one gasp and ceased to move.

Katz and Hart stared at the limp dark form on the concrete. His gold medallions and rings and bangles gleamed in the sunlight. His face was shiny with tears and saliva, his braids were soaked with perspiration.

Chino crossed himself, took off his black denim jacket, and covered Kingbop's face with it.

"This isn't plague," Hart said again to Katz. "What was Kingbop doing before he got sick?" he asked Chino.

"He just carryin' this estrange thing we find uptown, we bringin' it up the steps to show Gato." He pointed to a white object lying near Kingbop's body. It was about two feet long and tapered on one edge like the blade of a sword.

"He was holding it like this, see? And then he put his finger in here." Chino picked up the object, hooking his thumb into a hole at the wide, rounded end.

"DROP THAT!" Hart roared.

Chino froze for a moment and then let the blade go. It clattered on the concrete.

Rodriguez ran up the steps, followed by Manuel carrying a medical bag.

"Oh, Kingbop." Manuel squatted down beside the body.

Katz and Hart bent over the object. It resembled part of a propeller blade molded out of hard plastic, and it had a small aileron at the tip. The broad end was rounded and in the center was an opening containing a fan.

Dolores stared at Chino. Tears were streaming from his eyes and his face and neck were beaded with sweat. A spreading, wet stain appeared on his trouser leg.

"Hey—what you pissin' in yo' pants fo', Chino!" someone exclaimed.

"He's sick," Dolores said. She went up to him and felt his forehead. He made a choking noise.

"I can't breathe!"

Hart looked into the boy's face. His pupils were rapidly shrinking to tiny black points. "Alan, come here—it looks like organophosphate poisoning. Dolores—quick—get a syringe with one c.c. of atropine!"

Katz and Hart helped the boy lie down, and Hart checked his pulse. "Slow," he told Katz. "But regular."

"His pupils—it's like Parathion poisoning," Katz said. "It's okay, Chino, we're gonna fix you up fast."

Rodriguez hurriedly prepared a syringe from the medical kit, and Hart inserted the needle into a vein in the boy's inner wrist.

Within ten seconds Chino's pupils stopped contracting and began to dilate. His breathing cleared. He shook his head. "I feel better," he said weakly.

My God, it worked, Hart thought.

"Don't anybody touch that fucking thing!" Katz yelled. The Shadows backed away from the object.

Dolores began washing Chino's hands with alcohol. "Parathion is strong, Dave, but not enough to get a reaction like this." Katz lit a cigarette and handed it to Chino. "Relax, kid, you're gonna be fine."

"You don't think it's Malathion or Parathion?" Hart asked.

"It *could* be. They could conceivably use it to take out fleas," Katz replied. "But they wouldn't have to —DDT would do the job just as well, and it's safer."

"Dolores, would you keep an eye on Chino?" Hart said. "Give him a shot of atropine every half hour, and keep checking his pulse rate. If it drops below sixty, give him an additional half-c.c." He found some rubber gloves in the medical bag, put them on, and then picked up the blade.

Stenciled on one side were the words VECTOR CONTROL US ARMY and a symbol composed of red interlocking crescents—the international biohazard warning. It was identical to the sticker Sam Andrews had pasted on the shipment of plague specimens bound for the Center for Disease Control.

"I don't know," Hart said. His palate went bitter.

"Me neither," Katz said.

"There were a bunch of them lying around uptown," Chino said.

"Did you see anyone else picking them up?"

"No. We didn't see anybody alive up there at all. Kingbop was gonna report to you about that. See, he got friends at UCLA." He was referring to a store in Harlem at 125th and Lenox that sold herbs and books and was called the University on the Corner of Lenox Avenue, the Palace of Proper Propaganda with All the Books with All the Knowledge You Need to Know but Don't Know that You Already Know. "His friends, they got a special plague-protection medicine, and Kingbop, he wanted to get some more of it. But when we get there, nobody movin'! Everybody dead. Kingbop's friends, they fine yesterday, dead on the floor now. And Kingbop was so sad, man, and then we seen these estrange things lying around."

"Gimme the gloves," Katz said. He unsheathed his

hunting knife and used it to pry apart the molding along a seam. At last the case broke apart. "Look. This is some jobbie. A compressor, a little remote control radio unit—see where it says '72 millihertz'? And here's a tank and a spray nozzle."

"It's a monocopter," Andrews said, looking at the viscera of the device scattered across Katz's card table. "I saw a demonstration of one at the CDC just before I moved to New York. The Army uses them for adulticiding."

"This has been killing more than adult mosquitoes," Katz said. "I wonder why I never heard about it at Pest Control."

"It probably hasn't been declassified yet," Andrews said. "The Army demonstration I saw was supposedly secret."

"That's no ordinary pesticide inside," Katz said. "It's concentrated enough to kill a human in a couple of seconds."

"Nerve gas," Hart said. "It can't be anything else."

"Nerve gas!" Rodriguez exclaimed.

"That's pretty incredible," Andrews said.

"Well, the Army keeps stuff like that around," Hart said. "The idea is to assault the nervous system—to overstimulate acetylcholine release. When it happens, the creature that owns it goes very fast."

"Organophosphate pesticides are just dilute nerve gas," Katz told Rodriguez.

"But how come here?" she asked.

Everyone was silent.

"What else do we know about this?" Hart asked himself aloud. "We know that Chino and Kingbop saw several of these monocopters up in Harlem, that everybody's dead on 125th—including people who were alive yesterday."

"We know that a lot of people believe the plague started in Harlem and that blacks and Puerto Ricans spread it," Rodriguez said.

"Right," Hart said. "And we know that Manhattan is cut off and under heavy military surveillance, martial law, and military censorship. And we know that the people just across the East River, the Harlem River, and the Hudson River are scared enough of the plague to shoot anyone leaving Manhattan. What would you do if you were President? You'd figure that the only way to stop the epidemic and get the city working again would be to kill every flea, rat, and human in Harlem."

"How do we know it's just Harlem they're sending these monocopters to?" Katz asked.

"I don't see how anyone could be that mean," Rodriguez said. "Spraying nerve gas everywhere? That's too evil."

"Nobody ever thinks that what they do is evil," Katz said. "Even the Shadows. They never think, 'I'm going to do something really evil now.' They think, 'I gotta defend my turf,' or 'I gotta take revenge for what they did to my brother.' "

"That's true," Hart said. "These things just start happening. The Army would think they were acting on the noblest impulses you can have. And the President must be thinking how important it is to protect the rest of the country from plague."

"But what about tetracycline and streptomycin?" Rodriguez asked. "The real way to protect yourself?"

"Dolores," Hart said, "you know better than anyone else that no one believes it could be that simple. They hear 'plague,' and they panic. Or rather, they hear 'plague,' believe that modern medicine can work miracles, and then, if it doesn't seem to do magic, they panic. And then any means are justified if the end is to save lives."

"This news is going to break the Mayor's heart," Katz said. "Those streets of gold will have to wait."

67

HART, KATZ, and Andrews stood in a small room on the second floor of Belvedere Castle. The walls were covered with soot, and the only light came from two gas lanterns suspended from the ceiling. The Mayor, Calabrese, and a man in Army fatigues sat around a large transcontinental radio on a rickety table.

"Dave, let's face it. You've been very sick." Calabrese spoke soothingly. "You've been through a lot. You've got to rest quietly for a few days and calm down. Then you'll see things in quite a different perspective. The Surgeon General just called me back. She asked General Charles at the Pentagon about the monocopter and he explained that they were simply testing a new pesticide to kill the rats and fleas simultaneously."

"And everyone in Harlem as well," Katz said.

"Alan, I don't mean to disparage your boys, your gang, but they could be exaggerating. And are they qualified to tell whether deaths have resulted from plague or from nerve gas?"

"No, they aren't," Katz said. "But we watched one of them die from touching the monocopter."

"Alan, the Mayor and I have been in constant touch with the Washington people. They are very receptive, very anxious to help."

"The kind of help we're getting we don't need," Katz muttered.

The Mayor watched the men conversing for a few

minutes. "Vincent, I think I'll let you handle this—I have some important business to take care of." He picked up a paperback cartoon book from the table. "I'm sure all of you know how dangerous it would be to start spreading around rumors about nerve gas and strange flying objects."

He went up a short flight of stairs leading to the turret.

"The federal government, the Army—God knows who—is trying to kill off all carriers and potential carriers of the plague!" Hart said. "Why else would they have released these monocopters full of nerve gas in Harlem, where everyone believes the epidemic started? Why wasn't the Surgeon General told about that?" Hart realized he was shouting.

"Why don't you take a Valium?" Calabrese reached into his pocket and pulled out a yellow pill. "Remember that the Surgeon General promised another big airlift late this afternoon; the President has promised us a workable plan for getting the city back on its feet. What you're talking about is—is unthinkable! We're United States citizens—"

"No—to the rest of the country, you're a wop and I'm a Polack kike, and everybody else is a nigger, and we're *all* on welfare," Katz said. "Do you know what the three greatest lies of the twentieth century are? One: It's a standard deal; Two: The check is in the mail; and Three: I won't come in your—"

His words were drowned out by the crackle and whine of the public address system. "Good morning, New Yorkers," boomed the Mayor's voice.

A rolling cheer went up all across the Great Lawn. "In today's installment of *Peanuts,* Charlie Brown is talking to Snoopy, and Snoopy has a heckuva sad look on his mug . . ."

68

"WHY DO you keep bringing up that old AM/LASH operation?" the President asked Marks.

"I suppose I underestimated General Cosgrove's modesty," Marks said. "General Sheffield tells me that Dan was in charge of Operation Visitation and has managed to keep his role in it concealed for nearly two decades."

The worst had happened. Cosgrove froze. A thousand denials erupted in his head, but he could not make his voice work. He realized that he had been anticipating this moment almost constantly for years and years, that it had preoccupied him more than his yearning for the moment of his grand leap to power. He wanted to vomit, to weep—any release from the horrible collision of sensations and thoughts inside. For once he was unable to plot a new move and immediately organize his mind to carry it out. He was afraid, as deeply afraid as he had ever been in his life.

"My point, Mr. President, is that the epidemic in Manhattan may have originated years ago in the Army lab at Fort Detrick," Marks said. He was still utterly calm, pale; his hands lay in his lap as though they were not his own. "And that General Cosgrove knows a great deal more than he has wished to say."

"Well," the President said, smiling, "if this is Castro's germ-warfare attack on the United States, and we can prove it, we'll retaliate and the world will cheer."

Cosgrove felt a great deal of relief. But he watched Marks.

"Of course," Marks said. "I guess I should be more direct. You're receiving counsel from General Cosgrove who is the best person in the United States to turn to in regard to a solution to the New York problem, and I bring up Operation Visitation only to make you understand how imperative it is that you follow the plan we have presented."

Cosgrove could not believe what he was hearing. He had never been afraid that he would be found culpable for the New York epidemic. If the plague bacilli had been captured by the Cubans, he could scarcely be blamed for what they chose to do in retaliation. In the back of his mind, almost eclipsed, was the awareness that there was strong evidence that the epidemic had originated naturally on the West Coast. But those facts did not fit the structure he had built. It was the failure of the operation, and the subsequent rationalizations, and Sheffield's betrayal that gnawed at him. Castro had something on him, and now Marks did too. He had always been terrified of being exposed as a failure, punished for violating the first-use germ-warfare clause of the Geneva Convention, and forced out of the permanent government. Operation Visitation was his only vulnerable spot, and Marks had found it.

He kept his eyes on the floor. He did not trust his control over his expression. At the same time, he was astonished that he was now surviving the moment he had dreaded for so long; he was now faced with the fact that, except for Marks, his role in Operation Visitation was of absolutely no interest to anyone.

69

"SHELTER," HART said to Katz. "What if we move everybody into basements?"

"Nope," Katz said. "Nerve gas is very heavy. It sinks. The most dangerous places are the lowest."

"We get everybody into the top floors and penthouses, then."

"Well, I was talking to Bo Korski, the guy in uniform in the tower, while you were going round three with the Mayor and Calabrese," Katz said. "He was one of the survivors from the Army epidemiological units, a sharp guy. He's very pessimistic. He thinks those monocopters up in Harlem were trial runs. He says if the Army decides to hit Manhattan, they'll do it very fast. They'll send in thousands of monocopters to disperse the gas between buildings. Those things have sensors, like guided missiles, and they're easy to target. And they'll probably use regular helicopters with spray canisters, too. The top floors won't be safe either."

"So we don't have an effective shelter against this—"

"Wait—what about Kaprow, that little ferret who does disaster planning for the mayor?" Katz ordered the nearest Shadow to fetch Kaprow on the double. "He's all fucked up, but maybe he has a decent idea or two."

"I'll feel a lot better when Manuel gets back from the armory," Hart said. Katz had already sent forty or fifty Shadows and members of their brother gangs out in search of atropine, the only antidote to nerve gas. Hospitals usually carried supplies of it, and he was hoping that the armories would also have it, along with the spring-loaded surettes necessary for injecting it. He was also hoping that atropine would work for everyone in the park as well as it had for Chino. If the concentration of the nerve gas was high enough, atropine would be useless. There *had* to be an alternative.

"You were smart to give up on convincing the Mayor and Calabrese," Katz said.

"The more I talked, the crazier they thought I was. It was just like the day of the first plague case and no one would believe me. But I had evidence that time, and Calabrese was with me."

"Don't worry about it," Katz said, lighting a cigarette. "Believe me, if we're dead wrong about this, I'll be the happiest person in the world."

"True," Hart said. "Anyway, it gives us something interesting to do instead of sitting around waiting for rescue."

Kaprow appeared. He looked faintly miffed at being escorted to Katz's card table on the terrace by a fourteen-year-old Savage Shadow in high-heeled pimp shoes.

"What do you know about shelters from nerve gas in Manhattan?" Hart asked him.

Kaprow blinked, trying to register the question. "There aren't any." The mention of nerve gas failed to stir him. He had a faraway look in his eye, as though he were actually in a much more interesting place thousands of miles away.

"How about the sewers?"

"They aren't very deep under the ground."

"Plus you got rats in them," Katz said. "Of course! That's why the heavy gas—to get the rats in the sewers."

"I don't know what you're talking about," Kaprow said, with the intonations of a robot.

"We're just imagining what would happen if Manhattan were sprayed with nerve gas," Hart explained.

"That would never happen," Kaprow said. "It's against the Geneva Convention."

"Oh," Katz said. "What about other tunnels?"

"You want to know about tunnels? On an ordinary day, the Holland and Lincoln tunnels have traffic in excess of twenty-two million vehicles per year. In addition, there are eight subway tunnels under the East River—"

"Wait, stop, hold it," Katz said. "How about using the subway tunnels as shelter?"

"It would take a long time to clear away the bodies and the wreckage," Hart said. "From what I saw myself and from what I've been hearing about since I came to the park, people jammed into the tunnels right away, and anyway they were sealed off in the other boroughs. Any more tunnels, Kaprow? Deeper ones?"

"There's City Tunnel Number Three," Kaprow intoned. "It goes through Central Park and extends nine miles into Queens, terminating at Ridgewood Reservoir. It's twenty feet in diameter and five hundred to six hundred feet down. It has elevators in the tunnel shafts at Seventy-eighth Street in the park and at 102nd and Columbus. It has railroad tracks and ore cars to convey the debris from blasting through the bedrock. Construction on it has been halted—"

"City Tunnel Number Three—I'll bet that's the one that Star Trek mathematical-genius kid escaped through," Hart said. "And then came back. Alan— maybe instead of looking for shelter, we could just get out. Kaprow, could a person walk out of Manhattan through the tunnel? To Queens?"

Kaprow blinked again. "But who would want to do that?"

70

"THE FACT is, Mr. President, you have no choice whatsoever," Marks said. "You have no decision to make. The decision was made in New York ten days ago when the first victim was infected. Your command to General Charles is merely a technicality. And quite frankly, if you don't agree, we would be compelled to recommend to the Alternate Executive Committee immediate implementation of the Presidential Pre-emption option contained in Classified Executive Order 1127 of April, 1957, which you, like all of your predecessors, ratified the day you took office."

The face of the President crumpled. "There has been no nuclear attack, and I have not been incapacitated," he said, half pleading, half protesting.

"If I might remind you, sir, the order refers to 'any ultimate and immediate threat to the very existence of the United States by nuclear assault or other total warfare means' and it leaves the matter of judging incapacity to the Committee. I feel certain that a telephone call will produce unanimous concurrence in our judgment that your incapacity to act upon this clear threat to our nation is 'sufficient presumptive evidence' to trigger the removal machinery."

The President swung around in his swivel chair and presented his back to Marks and Cosgrove

"If I may say so, Mr. President," Marks continued, his voice softening, "it was for the very reason we now feel obliged to raise the Order in this discussion that it was first conceived by General—President—Eisenhower. The realization that in the final minutes before annihilation, a single man might shrink from—as you put it, sir—playing God, led him to provide for some means for him to share the terrible decision, and, if necessary, to let others bear the weight of it. I think it was a wise and compassionate piece of foresight."

There was a long silence.

Marks pitched his voice even lower. "It may seem irrelevant to you gentlemen, but I have a story to tell you. Howard Hughes told it to me the day Robert Kennedy was shot. Hughes was very interested in American Indians. He had an almost religious appreciation of their customs. He liked to tell about a pueblo of Christian Indians in New Mexico. Usually the priests who are assigned to the pueblo are Irishmen from Boston who know nothing of Indian customs and believe they are being sent to a parish no different from one in Detroit. They think they will be showing the Indians how to live better, more pious lives. The Indians have another viewpoint, though. They don't mind having a priest around—they think it's a good idea to have all the bases covered, so they continue worshipping the old gods and are happy to throw in the Holy Family as well. Well, whenever a new priest arrives at the pueblo, the first thing he sees is that the church is all painted up inside with symbols of the corn god and the rain god and so on. The Indians explain their customs to the priest very graciously as they take him around the church. Just when the priest is about to tell them how all that has to go, that it's a Catholic church, not a pagan temple, the governor of the pueblo leads the priest up behind the altar and shows him a row of skulls on a shelf. The Indian politely explains that these are the remains of former priests who did not understand the local customs. At that point the priest either packs up and goes back to Boston or he goes along with what the Indians want." Marks smiled.

Cosgrove was stunned by Marks's artistry. In the

space of an hour he had managed to orchestrate terror, gratitude, and submission not only in the President but in Cosgrove as well. Was it his voice? His perpetual calm? Cosgrove did not know. His head pounded.

The President swiveled around again and faced them. His eye sockets were black, from smeared television makeup and fatigue, and his powdered forehead was spectral. He seemed to have aged forty years in a few minutes. He punched the intercom button on his desk. "Lisa, get me General Charles on the scrambler phone. He's in the War Room at the Pentagon."

71

"YOU WERE RIGHT!" Calabrese ran up the terrace steps to Hart and Katz, his face flushed. "It's the most horrible thing I've ever heard. But if Cronkite will buck the military censorship and break this story, we've gained some time . . ." He looked entirely different. His cheeks were no longer slack, his eyes had lost their languor. "I began to get upset when I heard what Lieutenant Korski was telling Alan. I talked to him myself, and then I talked to the Surgeon General again, and she admitted she's extremely worried. The tone of her voice scared the shit out of me. She mentioned a General Sheffield at Fort Detrick. That scared me more. I know that guy. He's the one—I told you about this—who secretly gassed the New York subway system in a CIA experiment. So when I heard his name, something clicked. I asked the Surgeon General, and finally she told me she's found out that there's a massive air operation being prepared at Fort Bragg and Maguire Air Force Base. She's been trying to learn more, but nobody's talking." Calabrese stopped and then forced himself on. "Frankly, I think they're planning to wipe us out."

It shocked Hart to hear what he had already suspected being stated so starkly by a man he knew to be cautious. "Have you told the Mayor?" he asked Calabrese.

"I told him. He doesn't want to believe it, but he's scared. It's quite a strain on a strained man. He's waiting for the President to call him. They've been having daily chats at one. It's almost two and Sid can't get through and no one is calling him. But I did call Cronkite and he was flabbergasted. He may not have believed me, but he said he would check with the White House and call back."

"We're going to check out a tunnel shaft," Katz said. "Care to come along?"

"What do you have in mind?" Calabrese asked.

"It might be a very good way to avoid heavy tolls," Katz said.

72

HART STOOD on the turret of Belvedere Castle and took the microphone in his hand. Simply by clearing his throat he was able to capture the attention of well over a hundred thousand people. Throughout the camp, they stopped whatever they were doing to listen.

He paused. He would have to be very careful about

his words and his tone of voice. The people were used to being reassured and lulled by this PA system, and what he was about to tell them would be so upsetting they might stop listening if he was not careful.

"All of you have been through a terrible disaster. All of you are survivors. You were smart enough to stay alive when everyone else was dying. I've been in midtown and downtown. There are a lot of victims, passive people who don't care what happens to them. But you do care—otherwise, you wouldn't be here in the park, you wouldn't be trying to make the best of it and to help one another. Now there's a new threat, but it's one we can get around if we behave intelligently and carefully.

"Sometime in the next few hours or days—we don't know when—the Army is going to spray the area with a dangerous pesticide to get rid of the rats and fleas. It is extremely dangerous to humans. I repeat, it is extremely dangerous to humans. We cannot remain in the city. I repeat, we *cannot* remain here.

"We have worked out a plan for saving ourselves. But first I want to tell you about my walk through the city." He told them about the piles of corpses around the subway-station entrances, about the dead people in stalled automobiles, about the victims of the vigilantes patrolling the other side of the East River. And then he told them about the monocopter, and how it killed.

At first the people were spellbound. And then a noise arose from the crowd. Thousands of complaining voices swept up to Hart like a wind before a storm. The people did not want to hear about death. They wanted to hear the Mayor read the funnies.

"You too will die," Hart said firmly, "if you don't follow instructions. Most of those people in midtown died simply because of panic. There is no need for *us* to panic. There *is* a way out of Manhattan," he said, lifting his voice, "but we must be careful. There is a tunnel to Queens. It's an unfinished water tunnel that goes to Ridgewood Reservoir. There's no water in it because it hasn't been lined yet. But it has electricity that works—it comes in from the Bronx—so there will be lights. And there are railroad tracks and cars.

"There are two entrances near here. One is at 102nd and Columbus. The other is on the hill in the park near the Seventy-ninth Street transverse. At each entrance there are shafts leading down five hundred feet, and there are elevators. We have to use both entrances, so that we can get all of you down there faster. Both entrances get you to Queens. The tunnel is about twenty feet wide. And we all can get out through it. The first to go will be children and old people, and they'll be accompanied by armed guards. Anyone who can't walk will be carried there, and will ride through the tunnel in the railroad cars.

"The spraying may start before we are all safely into the tunnel. But we can protect ourselves. You probably noticed throughout the day that my assistant, Sam Andrews, and the nurse epidemiologists from the Bureau of Preventable Diseases have been going through the camp with surettes of atropine and demonstrating how to use them. The atropine will give you full protection—but it won't last long. So you must not use it until we give the signal over the PA system. We will be watching for the approach of aircraft with canisters on their undersides to spray the chemical. If we spot any, we will give the signal for you to inject the atropine.

"To insure that we do not spread the plague into Queens, armed guards will be set up at the exit shaft to keep everyone in the immediate area. At that end of the tunnel we'll set up a health station and administer antiplague medication to everyone who comes out. The guards will protect us from any vigilantes who might turn up, and will make sure nobody leaves the area until they've been examined for plague.

"We *can* save ourselves—we have the knowledge and the means."

The crowd murmured an assent and then fell silent as Hart introduced the volunteer marshals who would be in charge of each section of the camp. Then he gave them simple instructions on where to gather.

The Mayor took the microphone. "We can do it," he said. "Let's try to be decent to one another and to be as helpful as we can. Let's make up for what we didn't do last time around. And then let's come back when it's safe and get this great city going again."

"I've had it with New York. I'm here all my life, but this is it. I lived through the *hurricane,* the big *blizzard,* the *blackout,* the *transit* strike, the *garbage* strikes, the *building* strikes, the *plague.* But this is *it.* I mean, a person can only take so *much,* right? And now this with the poison spray—who *needs* it?" The woman was part of an immense, irregular procession that began between the Obelisk and Belvedere Lake and extended southeast across the East Drive toward Fifth Avenue and the Seventy-ninth Street entrance to City Tunnel Number Three. "I'm moving to Westchester. Jersey, maybe. I don't know. I'm getting out. I could use some fresh air. I still got my health." The woman was blond, with a tan, and she wore a black pantsuit, gold eye shadow, and a gold chain around her waist. She carried a toy poodle. "When they reopen Bloomingdale's—well, maybe I'll come back just to visit. But I'm telling you, I've *had* it. Oh, there's the *Mayor* up on top of the castle. And that *doll,* that Doctor What's-his-name! Mmmmmmmmmm!" She blew the two men a kiss.

Hart waved back and looked out across the Great Lawn. It was five in the afternoon, and the light was growing muted. Another procession pushed north on the bridle path past the Reservoir in the direction of Columbus and 102nd Street, where the second tunnel shaft was. Smoke from extinguished campfires on the Great Lawn made his eyes smart. People were still hurriedly collecting suitcases, babies, pets, and anything

341

else they were able to carry away with them. Figures in black denim jackets carrying billy-clubs, rifles, and small machine guns moved through the crowd. As soon as a Savage Shadow began to bellow at a cluster of people who were still packing, they quickly pulled together their bags and bundles and joined the moving ranks. Near the reservoir, in the hospital tents, doctors and nurses were busy loading patients onto stretchers.

Hart studied the overall motion of the crowd: it was a single, variegated being, moving with intelligence and speed. He looked into face after face after face— dour old men, tall models, little girls carrying stuffed animals, Japanese businessmen . . . mostly he saw thousands of ordinary-looking human beings. It was an amazing phenomenon, something he never would have imagined after years of watching the manic rush of midtown Manhattan, and after witnessing the aftermath of the panic. The only explanation he could think of for the beast's change of heart was the fact that almost everyone who wanted to panic or to hurt himself had been winnowed out. Every person he saw below was a survivor, a human being who valued life and would act sensibly to sustain it. Some were undoubtedly psychopaths, felons, brawlers, hustlers—the worst, the pits, the scum—but they were all determined to live.

On the rooftops of the buildings along Central Park West, he could see two or three hundred figures. They were gang members, street fighters: Hell's Angels from the Lower East Side; Les Baron Samedi Haitiens from the Upper West Side; the Ghost Shadows from Chinatown; the Savage Skulls, the Savage Shadows, the Savage Souls, the Savage Nomads, the Savage Sisters, and other Savages from Harlem. They had armed themselves with a staggering arsenal from the National Guard armories nearest to the park and were preparing for the biggest gang war in the history of New York. Manuel had let it be known that this time their turf was threatened by the United States Army.

When Hart heard about the rocket launchers, the fragmentation grenades, the mortars, and the Claymore mines, he had begged Katz to use his influence to stop them. But Katz had shrugged. "I couldn't do anything if I tried. They want to help—they want to slow down the spray attack if it comes. Obviously they're gonna lose. But if this hadn't happened, most of them would be dead from ODs and gunshot wounds by the time they were twenty-five. The way they see it, what's to lose?"

As Hart was checking his cellophane packet of atropine and its accompanying surette, Rodriguez and Andrews appeared.

"Ah just wanted to say goodbye and good luck," Andrews said, talking Southern for the occasion.

"You're heading for the tunnel now?" Hart asked.

"Yeah, Ah'm going over with Sid. Ah'm an honorary New York Citizen now, you know. The Mayor promised me the Fox Lock to the city when this is all over. Anyway, I gotta make sure my Queens health station looks real pretty when the CDC boys show up to take credit for everything."

"Listen!" Hart said. "The sky has suddenly gotten very quiet."

"Where's all the aircraft gone?" Andrews said. "I've been so busy I didn't even notice."

They looked up at the empty sky.

"The wind's come up a little, too," Hart said. "It seems to be blowing out of the north." He went to the stairs that led down to the radio room. "Alan? Better tell your boys to speed it up."

Katz was using a citizen's-band transmitter to speak to the marshals who were in charge of the evacuation and who carried back-pack radios from the Guard Armories. He set down his microphone. "You've spotted something?"

"No, but all the aircraft have disappeared."

"Gotcha. Now it gets interesting."

On the other side of the turret area, the Mayor and

Calabrese had been conversing and waving to the processions. Now Hart called to them. "I think something's about to happen. You'd better head for the tunnel."

"I think I should stay on my ship," the Mayor said.

"Ship!" Andrews exclaimed. "Ship!"

"We'll really need you in Queens to keep everyone together, Your Honor," Hart said. "Besides, someone has got to explain to the residents there why their population has suddenly increased by some hundred thousand or so. Anyway, all of New York City is your ship. Even Queens."

"Ship!" Andrews could not contain his excitement. "Excuse me, but I just have to ask—is it the *Titanic*, Dave?"

"Yes," Hart said. "Congratulations. You've just solved a very tough epidemiological puzzle. And it took you only a few days longer than Dolores to figure it out."

Weinstein shook Hart's hand. "Mostly this was a totally unnecessary tragedy which I am determined to get to the bottom of."

"There are going to be hearings and investigations until the cows come home," Katz said. "Not that anything will come of them."

Hart and Rodriguez remained on top of the tower. He watched the faces of the departing New Yorkers. Thousands must already be emerging in Queens, but thousands and thousands more still shuffled toward the tunnel entrances. It was as if he were seeing their faces for the first time, every one of them different and astonishing, every possible physiognomy, skin hue, garb, and expression. And yet every face seemed familiar. He saw great beauty wherever he looked; he even heard it in the catcalls and threats and shrieks of the marshals and their charges as they pushed toward the tunnel shafts. He was glad he had lived long enough to find such a moment. And he hadn't even been searching. A door could be closed for a hundred years and then suddenly open.

"Dave! Look!" Katz was pointing to the northwest. On the horizon was a long black dotted line—helicopters. Their drone sounded like the buzzing of flies.

A flock of gulls rose from the reservoir, shattering its rippled surface. A wind shook the boughs of the trees. The noise of the helicopters filled the sky now, filled everything. Traveling below the line of helicopters were uneven rows of white, whirling blades that began to drop down among the buildings. The noise vibrated in his chest. "Take the atropine NOW!" Hart announced over the PA. The chant was picked up and carried outside the park to the people in the line for the northern tunnel entrance.

He handed Rodriguez an atropine packet and gave himself an injection of it. Red flares launched by the gangs on the rooftops burst around the bellies of the helicopters. Grenades exploded in midair over the West Side; mortars streaked through the line of helicopters, and one of them began to burn. It fell behind the Dakota like a moth on fire.

Rodriguez grabbed his hand and they ran down the tower stairs and toward the tunnel entrance. The atropine was taking effect. His vision grew blurry, as though sheets of rain were falling, and he could sense the blood surging up through his arteries; his heart seemed to expand. They moved in a slow, leaping run, and he had a giddy, playful sensation: if they were to die, this was as good a time as any.

73

WHEN MARKS and Cosgrove left the Oval Office, Cosgrove thought momentarily that he might faint. He felt enormous relief that the decision had at last been implemented.

The press secretary hurried up to them. He was very haggard. "Cronkite is on the phone," he said. "He's quite concerned about a report from a very credible source, a man who says he's the Health Commissioner in New York. Apparently the man got in touch with Cronkite and begged him to go on TV and announce that the Army is using deadly nerve gas in Manhattan and that people have already died from it. He said there's some kind of flying gadget . . . ?"

"Tell him the man is crazy," Cosgrove said. "I'll tell him myself if I have to."

"No," Marks said. "Tell him nothing. And remind him that the press caused the panic in the first place. And nothing else. We've had ten times as much work to do isolating and eliminating the plague, thanks to the media. Tomorrow, however, you will have to have a statement ready.

"There is going to be a massive decontamination effort in New York. Now, obviously we can't conceal some of the facts about it. But we *can* explain our actions in such a way as to mitigate the popular response to the outcome. For one thing, septicemic plague, which occurs when an infected flea bites a human on a vein, results in death within a day. The bacilli instantly poison the bloodstream and, without any outward symptoms, the victim suddenly drops—just as though he had been administered nerve gas. Decontamination crews coming into the city after the operation—three days afterward, the gas will have dissipated—will find thousands dead of pneumonic plague with the attendant symptoms of hemorrhage, thousands dead of bubonic plague with buboes on the corpses, and thousands more dead without a mark. Now some of those in the last category will probably have died of septicemic plague. And some from the side-effects of a powerful pesticide. Now, what will you tell the media and the public? That New York, the most powerful city—except for Washington, of course—in the world, has been cleansed, and that the President, the administration, and the Armed Forces are working night and day to restore the city. Working, in fact, to make it a better, cleaner, safer place to live. The clean-up crews will inevitably find people who have survived the pesticide. Those survivors can be easily rounded up, quarantined, and medicated. They will be much more grateful and tractable than the present population of the city. The troops responsible for preparing the gas canisters for the operation have been told that the gas is pesticide. That happens to be true—pesticides generally *are* nerve gases.

"For the next several weeks, we will have to put forth an intense media campaign emphasizing how we saved the lives of millions of Americans by rapid neutralization of the plague."

The press secretary was stunned. He looked at Cosgrove, who said nothing. Finally the man started to speak.

"That's all," Marks told him. "You can leave now."

The man hurried away.

Cosgrove understood that the power had shifted. He knew that he would remain, and that Marks would remain. Marks was now also part of the permanent government. But he would now have to take Marks into consideration at every turn. "Bryce, I just want to say that I respect the way you've handled this." He shook Marks's hand and was surprised to notice for the first time how short the Director was.

Marks smiled briefly. "Thank you. Don't you think you should rest, Dan? You look very tired, and we have a great deal of work to do."

"In what regard?" Cosgrove waited for the blow.

"There were a lot of loose ends that never got tied up with Cuba. If you and I combine our expertise, I think we can take advantage of this opportune moment. There are a dozen covert operations we should begin right away. See you tomorrow."

74

THE ENTRANCE to City Tunnel Number Three was near the Metropolitan Museum in an area of the park known as Dog Hill. It was enclosed by a high plywood fence painted over with bright graffiti. In the enclosure were several corrugated iron sheds, spools of cable, pieces of digging and blasting equipment, trucks, a yellow tower with enormous spools at the top to take up the tons of cable needed for lowering and raising the elevators the fifty stories into the bedrock, and a house trailer where the watchman lived. He had a small vegetable garden nearby, which was quickly trampled as the marshals summoned the people at the head of the procession to go to the elevators, fifty at a time.

Other marshals continued shouting orders over the din of the helicopters and mortar fire, making certain that everyone had gotten atropine. Hart and Rodriguez joined them, moving among the crowd, giving injections when needed, and reassuring those who seemed anxious.

From time to time she returned to his side to touch his shoulder and look at him intensely, her eyes dilated by the atropine. He realized that she was afraid he would not leave with the others, that he would stay in the park. "I'm coming out with you," he told her, but he could not even hear his own voice. She broke into a big smile—she had understood.

There was a part of him that wanted to stay, the part that had yearned for death on a hundred dismal nights alone. But he was through with it. He pulled her to him and pressed his mouth to her ear so that he could be certain she heard him. "I love you!" he said. At that moment he felt as though he had just drawn his first breath and begun to live.

The people kept coming. Hart wondered if they would ever stop. But elevator-load after elevator-load had dropped into the deep shaft, and in fact, many thousands were already waiting around the Ridgewood Reservoir in Queens, policed and protected by Shadows.

The gas was invisible and odorless. From time to time someone who had refused atropine would suddenly fall over like cut wheat. Stray dogs dropped to the ground, and squirrels and birds fell from the trees. Gulls plummeted from the sky. The monocopters moved back and forth in descending arcs, they zigzagged down Fifth Avenue, they whizzed over the heads of the people like whirling swords. He marveled at these engines of destruction, which the Puerto Ricans were already calling "Angeles del Muerte." They behaved as though they were sentient. When he recalled that in fact each monocopter was operated by a human seated overhead in a helicopter, he wondered what was human and what was machine.

He could smell extreme fear in the crowd. The deadly threat was now all around them, and even within them, since the gas had seeped throughout their systems. They froze when monocopters suddenly rushed at them. They covered their ears when the thunder of chattering helicopters made their cranial bones rattle. But they did not panic.

And this, to Hart, was a miracle.

75

SKOURAS KARAMESSINES drove his taxi along the Interborough Parkway, ensconced in a bower of plastic carnations, dangling rosaries, and pictures of children and saints. The sun was just rising and burning away the fog. Deep rose rays struck the thousands of headstones, crosses, and vaults of the vast patchwork of cemeteries that lay on the border between Queens and Brooklyn and surrounded Ridgewood Reservoir. The misty light also illuminated the skyline of Manhattan, which Karamessines loved so much that he brought it into his apartment, painted in red on black velvet. He had come from Smyrna at the age of twelve as a cabin boy on a freighter, and he had never forgotten the first morning that he had awakened in America and stood on a pier in New Jersey admiring the sight of Manhattan. He had thrown his arms wide to embrace it. "What city is like this great city?" he would cry, after a few glasses of retsina. His wife, who was American, born and bred in Queens, could not have cared less.

Now it was almost time to go off duty. Business was very bad, since half of Queens was occupied by troops and everyone was staying indoors. He was very tired, and he had developed a cough during the night. He was not getting any younger; he had to start taking better care of his health.

Then he saw the vision. He slammed on the brakes and crossed himself. He pulled the cab off the highway and stared. Moving down the slope from Ridgewood Reservoir and among the tombstones of Salem Field Cemetery were thousands of spirits in the vanishing pink fog. Thousands, tens of thousands. They perched on the sepulchers, they picked their way among the crosses, they called out to one another.

He knelt by the road, smelling the hot, oily breath of his cab, and asked God to grant him absolution for his sins. Then he drove home and went to bed. He did not tell his wife what he had seen. He closed his eyes and dreamed of seas of glass mingled with fire and of crystal rivers and of a tree bearing twelve kinds of fruit.

By noon he had a terrible fever, and his wife drove him in his taxi to an emergency clinic that had been set up in the gym of a nearby high school. He was examined and medicated and placed on a cot near the bleachers. His wife sat beside him on the cot and alternated between sobbing and calling him a stupid old fool.

He had worked hard all his life. He had been a cabin boy, a cook, a steward, a first mate, a gunner, a smuggler, a dishwasher, a peddler, a part-owner in a restaurant, and, finally, a cabdriver. He could close his eyes and visualize the streets of every port city in the Mediterranean. He could speak eight languages and sing in twelve. He liked to dance to bouzouki and loud music, and also to Frank Sinatra. He had four children who grew up Americans and moved away to places like Iowa City and Phoenix. He did not like these cities of the interior of America, and he rarely visited his children and grandchildren. To him, they were not even real cities. They had no skyline, they had no savor, they had no promise at sunrise, no mystery at sunset. Who would own a velvet painting of Phoenix? Who would weep over the beauty of Iowa City? He often asked these questions of his customers as they rode through the night streets of New York.

Skouras Karamessines died of the plague at midnight, twelve days after Sarah Dobbs had brought it to New York City. His death was duly recorded by the Nassau County Acting Coroner, and a report of it was sent by Margie Pindere, nurse epidemiologist with the Queens Station of the Bureau of Preventable Diseases for the City of New York, to the Center for Disease Control in Atlanta. He had had an estimated sixty-two contacts during the contagious stage.

It was not known for several weeks that his death was officially the last to be caused by the plague. The epidemic was over. Army clean-up squads entered the city and were dumbfounded by the numbers of corpses. Estimates of the total mortality wavered between three hundred and five hundred thousand. The President announced his deep regret that so many had perished and asked the nation to turn away from grief. A grave crisis threatened to erupt in regard to Cuba, and he now begged the nation to give him its undivided support.

A great many men believed, for one reason or another, that their particular actions had halted a great pandemic and saved millions of lives. The medical community gave thanks to its expertise and to antibiotics; the media, to their efforts to keep the public informed; the churches, to the grace of God; the federal government, to the military and its thorough campaign to eliminate all carriers of the disease. Many New Yorkers, especially those who had escaped from Manhattan through the water tunnel, thanked no one.

But nothing men could do would ever end the plague. There was no reason why the organism stopped with Skouras Karamessines. If it had chosen to continue, nothing could have halted it in its course. It vanished as suddenly as it had come. And nothing could prevent its return.